THE SHADOW COLLECTOR

Kate Ellis

piatkus

PIATKUS

First published in Great Britain in 2013 by Piatkus
This paperback edition published in 2013 by Piatkus

Copyright © 2013 by Kate Ellis

The moral right of the author has been asserted.

A CIP catalogue record for this book
is available from the British Library.

ISBN 978-0-7499-5800-8

Typeset in Baskerville by M Rules
Printed and bound in Great Britain by
Clays Ltd, St Ives plc

Papers used by Piatkus are from well-managed forests
and other responsible sources.

MIX
Paper from
responsible sources
FSC
www.fsc.org FSC® C104740

Piatkus
An imprint of
Little, Brown Book Group
100 Victoria Embankment
London EC4Y 0DY

An Hachette UK Company
www.hachette.co.uk

www.piatkus.co.uk

For Olly and Sam (not forgetting Fin)

Chapter 1

April 1994

She had no face. She rocked to and fro in the chair like a waxen doll come to life. And she hummed. A low hum like the buzz of distant flies.

Lilith sat at the kitchen table and watched her. Perhaps this was all her fault. Perhaps this was the price she had to pay for what she'd done.

The woman with no face began to rock faster. Creak, creak, creak on the worn linoleum floor. Lilith turned away and picked up the soft toy on the table. It was a small bear, a silly love token he'd given her in those first rapturous days when the world had been a bright place full of hope and passion. But now the thing was worn and stained with tears. Love had died. Everything had died.

She picked up the jewelled dagger, thrust it into the

animal's belly and watched as the white stuffing spilled out like pale entrails onto the table.

The cow lowing mournfully in a distant field sounded like a soul in torment. And there was grunting too, an unearthly, primitive sound. Then Gabby remembered that the women kept pigs round the back of the house. She could smell the scent of their excrement on the night air and she wrinkled her nose in disgust. She was beginning to wish she hadn't come. But Joanne had promised entertainment – and Joanne could be very persuasive.

Joanne grasped her arm and dragged her through a gap in the ramshackle chicken wire fence that marked the boundary of the cottage garden. She pointed to an uncurtained window, lit up like a stage. 'There she is. She's holding something. It's a wax doll. She's sticking pins in it. I told you, didn't I? I said she was a witch.' Joanne tightened her grip on the sleeve of Gabby's denim jacket and began to pull her towards the house.

Gabby knew her companion wasn't going to give up. An owl fluttered somewhere in the nearby trees and suddenly she wanted to go. She'd had enough. And she knew that if she didn't put a stop to this soon, she'd be stuck there for hours with the stench of the pigs and mud seeping through her trainers. 'This is boring,' she whispered. This, she knew, was the ultimate put down. Joanne hated boring.

But Joanne carried on as though she hadn't heard, pulling her forward. Gabby was tempted to break away. But it was a dark, lonely way home through shadowy fields and glowering trees. Besides, she'd promised her mother they'd stick together.

As they crept closer to the house Gabby could see the kitchen clearly through the open curtains. In the pale yellow light of a single overhead bulb she could make out the old-fashioned cupboards painted a sickly green.

One of the women was sitting in a rocking chair in the corner. Her face was covered with a white handkerchief, draped like a shroud. She rocked to and fro like an animated corpse in a grisly tableau, her wispy grey hair protruding from the edges of the cloth.

The other woman was much younger with wavy black hair to her shoulders and a strong face with high cheekbones and dark eyes. She was quite unlike the witches of Gabby's childhood imagination but, with the wisdom of her sixteen years, she knew that appearances often deceive.

The younger woman sat at the kitchen table, absorbed in her own thoughts, ignoring the faceless creature in the rocking chair. She was holding something but Gabby couldn't make out what it was. Joanne's guess of a wax doll was a possibility . . . or it could be wildly off the mark.

The pigs were grunting louder now, as though they were warning of intruders. Suddenly a dark shape appeared on the windowsill, outlined against the light.

'It's a cat. It's their familiar.' Joanne said the final word in a gloating hiss.

'I'm fed up with this. I'm going.' Gabby hoped the threat would bring Joanne to her senses.

'All on your own in the dark.' There was mockery in Joanne's voice. 'Don't you want to see what they do? John said they dance naked when it's a full moon. Can you imagine them with nothing on? I've got to take a picture – I've brought my camera.'

'Why?'

'For a laugh. Don't you want to see John's face when we show him the pictures?'

'He's not interested in you any more. Why don't you leave him alone?'

The sound of a bolt being drawn back echoed like a gunshot through the darkness. Gabby took a step back but she felt Joanne's fingers pulling at her jacket again, clutching like the talons of a bird of prey. 'Stay where you are.'

She let go of Gabby's sleeve and edged forward, creeping across the cobbled path towards the house.

Then Gabby saw the door open and the younger woman loomed against the rectangle of light like a predator scanning the horizon for its next meal. 'Run. Now,' she hissed.

Joanne started to giggle, a wild sound, on the edge of hysteria. But after a few seconds she began to move off and when Gabby tried to follow, terror slowed her feet.

She knew the way out was within reach but she felt herself slipping on the damp cobbles. She hit the ground with a heavy thud and lay for a second, too shocked to move. Then as she raised her head, she saw Joanne standing a few feet away, her slender clawing fingers threaded through the chicken wire, rattling at the fence like a trapped beast.

October 2012

The woman in the red coat stood on the hill looking down at the farm buildings nestling in the lower ground. She had waited a long time to catch sight of her quarry. It was her job to make sure every deception came at a price. Maximum payment. Maximum grief. Maximum sales.

She edged away from the grazing sheep. She'd never been close to sheep before and they seemed so much bigger than she'd imagined. A city dweller, born and bred, she felt uncomfortable in the relentless countryside with its high hedges and rolling fields fringed with brooding trees. And her high-heeled patent leather boots were beginning to let in water.

She thrust her hands into her coat pockets, her attention divided between the house below and the sheep who seemed closer every time she looked round, slowly encroaching on her space in an ovine game of grand-mother's footsteps.

After a while her patience was rewarded when she saw a man leave the farmhouse carrying a bucket. This wasn't the big story but it'd do for now. Until she could engineer a meeting. Until she could find out the truth for sure.

She was about to raise her phone to take a photo when she heard a sound behind her. She turned her head and saw a dark figure climbing over the rusty farm gate set into the hedgerow.

The newcomer jumped down into the field and made straight for her. And she knew she had a problem. Or was it an opportunity?

'Hi. I'm glad you're here. I've been wanting to talk to you,' she said, confident she could turn this to her advantage.

But there was no reply as the newcomer approached. She stepped back instinctively, further and further until the spiky hedgerow was digging into her back. Then, before she could put up her arms to defend herself, she felt a sudden sharp pain. And when she looked down she saw blood soaking through her red coat, forming a wet shadow.

She fell to her knees and the green world turned black.

Chapter 2

Statement of Elizabeth Hadness, October 1st 1643

Alison Hadness is a witch. A woman of darkness. A collector of shadows. You cannot imagine her wickedness, the dreadful spells she hath wrought upon our neighbours and my father, her husband.

She has confessed to me that she loves Satan and that he has been privy to her secret places. She has confessed that he has had carnal knowledge of her on divers occasions, sometimes in the form of a cat, sometimes in the form of a goat and oft times in the guise of a young dark man.

I state that all the accusations laid against her are true.

'Shouldn't Uniform deal with this?'

DI Wesley Peterson studied the sheet of paper he'd just been handed. A routine report – a break-in at a smallholding outside the village of West Fretham. But from the look on DS Rachel Tracey's face he knew something was bothering her.

For a few moments she said nothing. He could see dark rings beneath her eyes as though she hadn't slept well and her fair hair, tied back in a businesslike pony tail, seemed more untidy than usual. He wondered whether her forthcoming wedding was causing her sleepless nights. She was the daughter of a well-respected farmer, marrying into another local farming dynasty, so it was bound to be a big and stressful affair.

'It's Devil's Tree Cottage.' Her words were loaded with a meaning Wesley couldn't quite grasp.

He gave her an enquiring look.

'Don't you remember? Dorothy and Lilith Benley. They murdered two teenage girls eighteen years ago and fed the bodies to their pigs.'

Wesley's brain, lulled into a stupor by the crime statistics he'd been compiling, eventually trawled some half-remembered facts of the case from the depths of his memory. Eighteen years ago he had just started studying Archaeology at Exeter University and the papers back then had been filled with every sad and sordid detail of the Devil's Tree Cottage case. But, being a student at the time, he'd had other things on his mind.

However, he did remember that it was the kind of case the tabloids pounced on like starving lions on the bleeding corpse of a wildebeest. A titillating combination of witchcraft, grisly death and nubile teenage girls. And around the same time the papers had also been full of the abductions of young girls in various parts of the country by a van driver who had changed his name by deed poll to Satan Death. It had been a murderous time. A season of the dead.

Rachel leaned towards him. 'The boss was a DS at the

time and he worked on the case,' she said softly. 'The Benley women were convicted of the murders of Gabrielle Soames and Joanne Trelisip. It was one of those cases everyone dreads. I don't think anybody comes away untouched from something like that.'

Wesley understood. He'd worked on cases like that himself and he knew now why Gerry had never mentioned it. There are some things you don't like to dwell on.

'So what's this about a break-in? Who lives in Devil's Tree Cottage now?'

'That's just it,' said Rachel. 'She's back.'

'Who?'

'Lilith Benley. She's been released on licence and she's gone back to Devil's Tree Cottage. She claims she's had a break-in and she insists on seeing the DCI.'

'He's in a meeting with the Chief Super. Do you want to tell him when he gets back or shall I?'

She gave him an enigmatic smile and began to walk away so he knew he'd been landed with the job of breaking the news. And he wasn't sure how Gerry was going to react to having this particular part of his past dug up again like a rotting cadaver.

He didn't have to wait long to find out. Gerry returned to the CID office a few minutes later, marching purposefully towards his glass-fronted lair. He was a large man with grizzled hair and blue eyes that usually held a spark of humour. But today he looked deadly serious. Wesley followed him and as soon as he sat down on the visitor's chair, Gerry started to complain loudly about the gruelling encounter he'd just had with Chief Superintendent Nutter about the overtime budget.

Wesley interrupted before he warmed to his theme.

8

'There's been a break-in at Devil's Tree Cottage. Lilith Benley's been released on licence . . . and she's asking to see you.'

Gerry froze and sat staring ahead as though he'd just had a vision of hell. 'I suppose I'd better go and see what she wants,' he said after a few moments.

'I'll come with you if you like.'

Gerry shot him a grateful look and muttered something about being glad of the company.

'I'm surprised they've let her out so soon,' Gerry said as they were driving up the hill past the Naval College. Wesley could just see his own house through the trees on the left. His wife Pam would be at work and the children at school so it would be empty and peaceful apart from a prowling cat.

'She served eighteen years.'

'Hardly justice for what she did.'

'It's a long time ago and I can't remember all the details. How were the girls killed?'

'The mother said they'd stabbed them. Sacrificed, she called it. Mind you, she was mad as a cartload of electrified frogs.'

'And she was believed?'

'All the evidence confirmed it but we didn't get there till a week after they vanished so there was nothing left of the bodies.' He wrinkled his nose in disgust.

'Rachel said the mother died in custody.'

'Dorothy Benley was sent to a secure psychiatric hospital and died two years later. The daughter, Lilith, served her time in Holloway. Model prisoner apparently. She always protested her innocence. Not that it cut any ice. She was guilty. No question about that.'

'So what was all this witchcraft business?'

'The two women had a reputation locally for being witches. The mother had been heavily into it for years, apparently. Although Lilith always swore she was just a white witch. Wicca I think it's called. She made a big thing at the trial about never having anything to do with Satanism.'

'Any evidence that she did?'

'There was stuff in the outbuilding where the girls' clothes were found; wax dolls, black candles, things nicked from churches. There were rumours about kids dabbling in black magic around that time but nothing was ever proved so if there was any sort of organisation, it was a pretty shadowy one. One of the local vicars said he'd heard of things going on in more isolated churches, not that any of his colleagues had experienced it themselves, of course. It always seemed to have a smell of the urban myth to me – or should it be rural myth round these parts?' He looked out of the car window. 'It was always something someone's second cousin or neighbour's friend's dog had heard of, if you know what I mean.'

Wesley knew only too well how stories of the dangerous or exotic could gain a life of their own. He drove on, turning right at the top of the hill onto the road that ran along the coast. The rain of the past few days had vanished and it was a bright October day without a cloud in the sky. The sea sparkled to their left and it was only the half-bare trees fringing the rolling fields to their right that betrayed the season.

'Were the women suspects from the start?'

'No. At first we worked on the theory that the girls had been abducted by that Satan Death. Remember?'

10

'I remember.'

'Not that anyone knew his identity back then, of course. A girl had gone missing in Cornwall a week before so it seemed likely he'd struck again. He was a delivery man and this part of Devon was part of his patch.'

'They never found any of his victims' bodies, did they?'

'He'd never say what he'd done with them. In the end he was caught trying to abduct a girl in Weymouth when a dog walker heard her screams. He was convicted through blood traces in his van and the records the delivery company kept of his whereabouts – always coinciding with when the lasses went missing. In the end he confessed to all the abductions . . . except for Joanne and Gabby's.'

'But he could have been lying. He could have been playing games with the police?'

'That was always a possibility. He was certainly in the South West at the relevant time. He killed himself in prison soon after his conviction so we can't ask him, I'm afraid.'

'So what put the police onto the Benleys?'

'We had an anonymous phone call a week after the girls disappeared. The caller said that if we wanted to know what had happened to them we should go to Devil's Tree Cottage and when we got there we found enough evidence to convict the Benley women – the girls' bloodstained clothing and traces of blood around the pig sty. The mother made a full confession . . . although it was confused and contradictory.'

They drove on in silence for a while. After what Gerry had told him Wesley felt a little apprehensive about coming face to face with Lilith Benley. He had met many murderers in the course of his career but her crime seemed particularly callous. To slaughter two young girls and feed

11

them to pigs seemed to deserve more than eighteen years' imprisonment. But he knew it wasn't his place to question the vagaries of the criminal justice system.

They'd just passed through West Fretham, an unremarkable but pretty village boasting the requisite pub and church, when Gerry twisted round in the passenger seat. 'Did you see that?'

Wesley slowed the car to a crawl. There was a farm entrance to their left and at the end of the driveway stood a collection of farm buildings – a stone farmhouse and several large barns filled with farm machinery and silage wrapped in glossy black plastic. There were cars parked there too; a couple of SUVs, a BMW and a small blue sports car. But, more unusually, there was a large van in front of the farmhouse with Poputainment TV written in bold white letters on the side. Heavy cables ran from the vehicle to the house like monstrous umbilical cords.

'Looks like they're filming something,' said Wesley, pressing his foot gently on the accelerator.

'*Celebrity Farm*, it's called,' said Gerry triumphantly. 'Our Sam was talking about it the other day. They put some has-been celebrities together on a farm and film them looking after the animals. Then they're voted off one by one by a panel of so-called experts. Our Sam says it's the animals he feels sorry for.'

Gerry's son was a local vet so Wesley supposed his concern was only to be expected.

'It'd be a brave farmer who'd risk his livestock like that,' he said. He'd been born and bred in London but after living so long in Devon he felt he was developing a tenuous affinity with the rural way of life. Working so closely with Rachel Tracey for so long he supposed it was inevitable.

'Don't believe everything you see on telly, Wes. I bet the farmer's always on hand to do the real work. It's just down here. Next left.'

Wesley turned the car down a narrow lane where the hedges rose like walls on either side, hiding the fields beyond. Weeds sprouted from the road surface, suggesting that this was a route rarely travelled. But it was the way to Devil's Tree Cottage.

'If I was Lilith Benley I'd have changed the name of the house,' said Wesley.

'Perhaps it doesn't bother her.'

'The notoriety or the link with the devil?'

'Both. It's not far now . . . just on the left.'

'Well remembered.'

'It's not something you forget in a hurry, Wes. I had nightmares about it for months afterwards.'

Wesley glanced at him and saw a haunted look in his eyes. Glimpses of Gerry's softer side were rare. In fact few people in CID knew it existed.

He spotted a pair of stone gateposts, one leaning at a drunken angle. There was no sign bearing a house name. Maybe there had been once but it had been taken down when the place had become synonymous with evil. Wesley steered the car carefully into the entrance. The track leading to the house was darkened by overhanging trees and rhododendron bushes. The surface was rough and pitted with potholes filled with muddy water from the recent rain and Wesley was glad he was driving a pool car and not his own. New exhausts cost money.

'Isolated place.'

'Too right. You could get up to all sorts here and nobody would ever know,' said Gerry quietly.

Wesley was impatient to see the house, unsure whether this was out of morbid curiosity or a simple desire to get the whole business out of the way. As the car emerged from the tunnel of rhododendrons Devil's Tree Cottage came into view.

Somehow he had expected some sinister Gothic edifice, all dark stone and gables, and the reality surprised him. Devil's Tree Cottage was a low cob building, typical of rural Devon, its pale pink walls flaking and discoloured with the dirt of decades. The cottage was in sore need of a coat of exterior paint and the roof was slate rather than traditional thatch but the impression was quaint rather than sinister. The surrounding land had long since returned to nature and weeds sprouted between the cobblestones leading to the front door. Here and there the rusted chicken-wire fence, that had once separated the small front garden from the rest of the land, lay battered to the ground, a few supporting wooden stakes still protruding from the overgrown earth like grave markers.

According to Gerry, the place had been empty for eighteen years so the dereliction was only to be expected. He was surprised it wasn't a lot worse.

The front door was studded oak, weathered silver-grey from years of neglect. Gerry sat quite still in the passenger seat, gazing at it, breath held, as though he expected to see something terrible emerge. Then, as Wesley cut the engine, he saw the door open slowly.

'Do you want me to deal with this?'

'No. She asked for me.' Gerry was staring at the woman who'd just appeared in the doorway. 'Bloody hell, she's changed.'

The DCI's movements seemed unusually clumsy as he

wrestled with his seat belt and clambered out of the car. Wesley put it down to his reluctance to face the woman who was waiting for them, arms folded, a hint of challenge in her eyes.

Wesley climbed out of the driver's seat and shut the door, flicking the lock absentmindedly even though he knew this particular security precaution was unnecessary in that isolated spot. He saw the woman look him up and down with undisguised curiosity: perhaps when she'd last lived in Devon a policeman of West Indian origin was a rarity. His parents had raised him to believe that it was rude to stare but he couldn't resist the temptation to study Lilith Benley in return. She was tall, around five feet ten, and although her frame was big she looked slim and muscular, as though she'd spent time working out. Her thick black hair was peppered with grey and cropped short, emphasising her strong features, and she wore a long black skirt and tight black T-shirt. She was what Wesley's mother would have described as a striking woman – only on the verge of beautiful but impossible to ignore.

He felt Gerry's arm nudge his and they began to walk towards the house, Gerry sticking close to him as though he needed support.

'Sergeant Heffernan, thank you for coming,' she said formally as they approached. Her voice was quite high-pitched, more feminine than Wesley had expected.

'It's Detective Chief Inspector Heffernan now.'

'Congratulations.' She looked at Wesley. 'Aren't you going to introduce us?'

'This is DI Peterson.'

'Pleased to meet you, Detective Inspector Peterson,' she said with a hint of irony. She looked at Gerry, a smirk on her pale lips. 'I should have known you'd bring a friend. Policemen always go round in pairs, don't they ... like the old music hall comedians.' The smirk turned into a smile that lit up her face, but her eyes were watchful, hard.

'You'd better come in,' she said after a few moments. She turned her back on them and disappeared into the house and when Gerry followed, Wesley fell in behind.

As he entered the indoor gloom of Devil's Tree Cottage he took in his surroundings. The place clearly hadn't been touched since the time of the murders. There were cobwebs everywhere, like some fairy-tale castle frozen in time. Traces of grey fingerprint powder could still be seen on the woodwork, as though someone had made an effort to clean it off but hadn't made a very good job of it. The heavy brown furniture in the shabby parlour was shrouded in a layer of dust and grimy curtains hung in limp tatters at the windows. An empty rocking chair stood near the fireplace, its cushion torn and tattered, stuffing bursting from its innards like the guts of some dead, mauled creature.

'I apologise for the state of the place. I only got back a few days ago and I haven't had a chance to do much. I'm only relieved that it wasn't vandalised when I was ... away. But I expect it was protected by the superstition of the locals,' she added with a hint of bitterness.

'I believe you reported a break-in.' Gerry sounded businesslike, erecting a barrier of reserve between himself and the murderess.

'Somebody broke in yesterday evening while I was out.'
'What was taken?'
'A book.'
'What kind of book?'
She paused, as though she was considering her answer

16

carefully. Whatever this book was, Wesley knew it wasn't just the latest bestseller. This book had significance.

'It's called Book of Shadows. I ... I used to be what's sometimes called a white witch, a follower of Wicca. The book contained spells and details of my personal spiritual journey. It was on the shelves up there.' She pointed to a battered bookcase full of faded paperbacks and dusty china. 'I'd been for a walk and when I came back I found a pane of glass smashed in the back door.'

'Is that all they took, this Book of Shadows?'

'As far as I can tell at the moment.' She gave a bitter smile. 'I thought a reputation like mine would guarantee that I was left in peace.'

The words were defiant. And unrepentant. Whatever this woman had done in the past, Wesley suspected that she had few regrets. Or if she did she was doing her best to hide them.

'You say you used to be a white witch. Given it up, have you?' Wesley could hear the scepticism in Gerry's voice.

Lilith looked away. 'Prison changes people, Chief Inspector. Not always for the better.'

'I'll get our crime scene people out here to see if your intruder left any fingerprints,' said Gerry. He was shuffling towards the door as though he was anxious to be gone. 'If that's all ... '

'No it isn't all. I'd like some protection. Let's put it this way, the local community has hardly been welcoming. And I feel vulnerable here on my own.'

'Vulnerable like those two lasses you killed?'

She flinched as though Gerry had struck her. 'I had nothing to do with their deaths. I was innocent.'

'Your mother confessed.'

17

'The state she was in, she would have confessed to anything.' She almost spat the words.

'We haven't got the manpower to mount a round-the-clock guard,' said Wesley. 'Anyway, your intruder was probably an opportunist who thought the place was empty. As far as I can see there's no evidence you're in any danger ... unless you've received any threats you haven't told us about ... '

She shot a glance at Wesley, as though she was unsure how he'd react to what she was about to say. 'I want the case reopened. I need to clear my name.'

'Have you got new evidence?' Gerry sounded distant, as though he was reluctant to get involved.

'Not yet but ... ' She looked Gerry in the eye. 'You were more sympathetic than the rest of them back then. They decided right from the start that Mother and I were guilty but you kept an open mind. You asked questions.'

'I always keep an open mind ... so does Inspector Peterson here. But it didn't do much good in your case, did it? You killed those two lasses. The forensic evidence proved it.'

'That evidence was planted. We had nothing to do with those girls' deaths.'

Wesley noticed that her hands were clenched in frustration.

'A jury thought otherwise so unless new evidence comes to light I can't help you. We'd better be off.' Gerry made for the door and Wesley followed. But when he reached the threshold he turned. 'Why did you come back?'

'I've got permission,' she said. 'Apparently my so-called victims' families have moved away and I'm not considered a danger any more.'

'Are you planning to stay?'

'It's my home. Any reason why I shouldn't?'

Gerry didn't answer. He marched quickly out of the cottage and made straight for the car.

'Well?' Wesley said as they were driving away.

'I just wish she'd stayed away.'

'Any chance she was innocent?'

'No chance.'

He didn't say another word until they arrived back at the police station.

As soon as the meeting with the conservation officer was over, Neil Watson of the County Archaeological Unit took his mobile phone from his pocket. But before he could key in the number he wanted, he heard a voice calling his name.

'Dr Watson. Are you there?'

'Yes, I'm here.' He was standing in the long-disused east wing of Mercy Hall, in a spacious, oak-panelled room that would become a study once the renovations were finished. He stood by the open trapdoor, gazing down at the top four steps of what seemed to be a buried staircase. If Neil's suspicions were right, the stairs had once led down to some sort of cellar, long since filled in with soil and building rubble.

Evan and Harriet Mumford had purchased the historic house on the hill overlooking Tradmouth eighteen months ago and, as it was grade two star-listed, they were having to jump through any number of hoops to undertake its restoration. Two thirds of the house had already been restored to what estate agents call a high standard. But the builders had only just begun work on the semi-derelict east wing where, in the room called the small chamber on the plans, they'd discovered the filled-in cellar. The conservation officer had insisted on calling in the County Archaeological Unit, which would add to the cost but money didn't seem to be a problem for the Mumfords. All right for some, Neil thought.

Evan Mumford owned an import company – although Neil wasn't sure exactly what he imported. He was a big man with a florid face, an ill-tempered mouth and a liking for expensive suits, but fortunately he was too busy making money to interfere much. His wife, Harriet, however, was a sweetie, a sculptress by occupation who displayed a sporadic enthusiasm for the history of the house, like a child who picked up a toy for a while then soon became bored once something more interesting came along. She was in her thirties, around ten years her husband's junior, with straight blonde hair that framed elfin features. She was the sort of woman who was aware of her own sexual allure and the skin-tight jeans and white T-shirt she was wearing that day showed off her slender figure to best advantage.

'How's it going?' she asked, picking her way across the debris towards him.

'I've put a probe down and I reckon the cellar's about seven feet deep. It's just a question of digging it out to see what's down there. I'll need some help, of course . . . '

'More archaeologists?' She sounded as though the prospect pleased her. Perhaps, Neil thought, she'd always harboured ambitions to follow the profession: many people seemed to – until they learned of the need to work in a muddy trench in all weathers and the paltry financial rewards.

'My team are still working on Princes Bower – the Civil

War fortifications up by the castle – so I can't really spare anyone at the moment. But it's important that we don't miss anything of significance down there so if some of your builders are willing to work under my supervision . . . '

'I'll ask them.' She sounded a little unsure of herself, as though she suspected their reaction might not be altogether positive.

'The Conservation Officer wants the panelling in this room removed and stored somewhere safe while the building work's going on.' He pointed at the dusty oak panelling; classic Tudor linenfold, well preserved considering the state of the room. It was an original feature of the house and it was in danger of being damaged. 'It'll look great polished up and replaced once the work's finished. But it needs to be handled very carefully.'

'I'll tell Lee.'

There had been a succession of tradesmen traipsing in and out of the house but Lee seemed to be a regular fixture. Lee was small with blotchy skin and a midriff that bulged over his jeans – and he didn't look the sort who'd take much interest in archaeology.

Harriet hovered there, as though there was something else she wanted to say and Neil waited for her to continue. She and her husband were paying for his time and expertise so he was happy to work at the pace she wanted.

'There's something I'd like to show you when you've got a moment,' she said.

'No time like the present,' said Neil, brushing the dirt off his hands.

'It's outside.' She looked grateful that he was taking her seriously – perhaps her husband didn't.

He let her lead the way out past the half-demolished

skeleton of a lath and plaster wall in the passage and when they reached the back door they stepped out into the cobbled kitchen yard where a rusty water pump still stood in the corner above its crumbling stone trough.

'It's out here,' she said, glancing back to make sure he was following. 'The stonemason found it and he thought I'd be interested. I promised to show you.' Neil was walking beside her now and when she linked her arm through his, he hoped that the filthy sweatshirt he wore for digging in the cooler months wouldn't soil the pristine white of her top. But she didn't seem to care so why should he?

She stopped and pushed back the evergreen foliage that grew over a low wall. 'There it is.' She pointed to a stone, larger and smoother than its fellows. There was something carved on it; letters below a rough, almost childlike, picture.

'It looks like a gallows,' she said. 'And the writing underneath looks like AH October 2nd 1643.'

Neil considered all the possibilities for a few moments. 'The initials above your front door are MH and the date's 1594 so this could be a relative of the original builder. I looked into Tradmouth Library yesterday when I'd finished at the dig and I found out that this house was built by a Matthew Hadness around that date.'

She gave him a sideways look, a secretive half-smile on her painted lips. 'You've been doing your homework.'

'I like to know what I'm dealing with.' He stared at the stone. At first he thought he might be mistaken about the gallows . . . but he wasn't. They were plain to see, as was the little stick figure dangling from the rope, like a completed game of hangman. Only the figure wore a long skirt. A woman.

She tilted her head to one side. 'Does it mean that some-one connected with this house was hanged in 1643?'

'That was the year Tradmouth was besieged by the Royalist army during the Civil War.'

She touched his arm, her fingers with their short, unvar-nished nails resting for a while on his sleeve. 'I never paid much attention to history at school but you bring it to life. Maybe I could go down to the library myself. You could give me a few hints about what books to look for.'

For a few moments Neil didn't answer, trying to ignore the look in her eyes; rapt attention and something else. It was something he hadn't seen in the eyes of a woman for quite a long time – too long maybe. The flirtatious glint of sexual interest. But her husband looked the sort you didn't cross.

'There's also that interesting motto over your drawing room fireplace,' he said, trying to steer the conversation away from the personal. 'Mors vincit omnia.'

'What does that mean?'

'Death conquers all.'

The production team of *Celebrity Farm* referred to the place as a set. But to Rupert Raybourn, Jessop's Farm was all too real; smells, muck and all.

When he'd wrestled with the milking machine first thing that morning, watched with quiet amusement by the farmer, Joe Jessop, Rupert had experienced another of those pangs of regret that had become so familiar in recent weeks. His agent had persuaded him to take part in the show to revive his flagging career. But Rupert suspected it had been a mistake to agree. The whole thing seemed to him to be a terrible ordeal by humiliation.

He'd told himself to think positive: they were all in it together; has-beens trying to earn a crust and resuscitate moribund careers. He'd managed to make the final two, the others having been voted off one by one by the panel of experts and more popular celebrities. However, he couldn't shake off the suspicion that they'd retained him and Zac James for their entertainment value rather than their agricultural skills. But money was money and, as his agent kept telling him, all publicity is good publicity.

Apart from the strain of having to keep up the banter his public were used to from his glory days as a comedian and quiz-show host, he was forced to share the house and the attention with Zac James. Zac was in his mid-thirties and fourteen years ago he'd topped the charts as the lead singer of Ladbeat, a boy band that split up as soon as it had started a rapid downhill slide from the pinnacle of fame. Recently Zac's face had featured regularly in the more lurid tabloids and his struggle with drink and drugs had been tediously well documented. Zac's PR people reckoned appearing on *Celebrity Farm* would help him launch a solo career, but Rupert wasn't convinced. Once they were alone and the cameras had stopped rolling, Zac always seemed fragile and edgy as though he found the place and the situation deeply troubling. And his brooding jumpiness was taking its toll on Rupert's nerves.

Originally there had been six contestants. The first two to be voted off were a middle-aged soap actress whose roles had dried up since her character had met an untimely end beneath the wheels of a tram, and an aging female former TV presenter whose brushes with the cosmetic surgery industry had kept the tabloids happy until a better story came along.

Then there'd been Jackie Piper who'd left ten days ago, an androgynous singer/songwriter and arrogant little shit who'd thought the programme would raise his elevated profile even higher. He'd attracted a horde of screaming teenage girls who'd been a terrible irritation. But when their hero had departed, so had they.

Rupert had got on quite well with the man who'd been voted off the previous week; a disgraced former Member of Parliament called Charles Cloaker who, having lost his seat following the expenses scandal, was now pursuing a career in the media with dogged determination. Cloaker had been amiable company but Rupert suspected he was using *Celebrity Farm* and those around him for his own ends. But weren't they all?

Now he was stuck with Zac. Two final competitors and a film crew on the edge of a village in the middle of nowhere. Rupert knew how isolated West Fretham was: the village hadn't changed in that way since 1994 when he'd done that summer season at the Morbay Hippodrome just after he'd hit the big time.

There were few modern amenities at Jessop's Farm. No central heating and certainly no luxuries. The TV company had chosen the place to present the six products of spoilt, urban existence with a challenge that would amuse the viewers. It was a small cable channel so everything was done on a shoestring. No gourmet catering vans and the crew were billeted in a rented cottage in the village nearby. He just hoped the farmer, Joe Jessop, was being well paid for the disruption.

Rupert had just finished washing up after the home-made soup he'd made with the slug-infested cabbage provided: it had tasted foul, as expected, but there would have been no entertainment in success. He dried his hands on the damp tea towel, thinking that he needed to get out for a while. Away from the shabby farmhouse, the ubiquitous cameras and the man who was destined to share his life for the next week until the final fateful decision was made and the victor of *Celebrity Farm* crowned. At least, unlike in some reality shows, the contestants had the run of the farm when they weren't actually filming, and the crew were taking a break in the back parlour, playing cards as they always did, so if he went out now the cameras weren't likely to follow him up to the far field. Even though he was wary of the sheep, it was worth the risk of being mobbed by an unpredictable woolly audience for a slice of precious privacy.

He walked into the kitchen, heading for the back door, and found Zac James sitting at the scrubbed pine table. He looked gaunt, almost ill, with his pallid skin and his bleached blond hair, and the posing wanker was wearing his dark glasses indoors as usual. Zac was so engrossed in his iPhone that he didn't look up. He wasn't supposed to have the phone and Rupert wondered how he'd managed to get hold of it, but he wasn't in the mood to ask questions. Besides, Zac looked edgy and beads of sweat were forming on his forehead. Rupert assumed his coke habit was responsible. But that was really none of his business.

Fearing there might be a hidden camera left running somewhere, he fixed a wide grin to his face. 'Hi, Zac, I'm just nipping out to see a man about a sheepdog.' When Zac ignored his feeble quip he hurried into the hallway, pulled on a pair of green wellingtons and stepped outside.

He passed the barn where he'd been filmed earlier throwing feed to a trio of bored-looking hens and opened the metal gate to freedom before tramping across a muddy field, his feet squelching into earth softened by days of relentless drizzle. Then another gate, and another, until he was climbing the grassy hillside dotted with grazing sheep. From this higher ground he could look down on the house and the outbuildings and if the grass beneath his feet hadn't been wet, he would have sat down and spent a leisurely half hour watching the comings and goings of the crew and the people who lived in the elegant Georgian house next door – the house that had once been the village Rectory but was now home to some author he'd never heard of. But instead of enjoying the view, Rupert began to wander up towards the top of the field. The hedge was too tall to see over but there was an old metal gate in a gap further along, secured with a rusted padlock which clearly hadn't been used for decades. When he reached the gate he stopped and peered over at the sloping land on the other side. The grass was tall and there was a dark copse of trees halfway down the hill. Around three hundred yards away, just before the land started to rise again, he could see the pink cottage tucked into the hollow, half hidden by trees and vegetation.

He knew what the place was. He could hardly forget because he'd been in West Fretham at the time the girls vanished. He saw a wisp of smoke rising from the cottage chimney. He'd heard Lilith Benley was due for release on licence and he'd wondered whether she'd have the gall to return to her old home. Now it looked as though she had.

He stood staring at the cottage for a while but when he turned his head he glimpsed a flash of red on the ground further up the field. The woman he'd seen earlier walking down the lane had been wearing a red coat. He'd noticed her because she'd looked so out of place, as if she should have been in a fashionable London street rather than walking in the Devon countryside.

Now here she was in the field with him; blonde, stick thin ... and lying perfectly still on the lush grass next to the hedgerow.

After a few moments of hesitation, he shouted to her, earning himself reproachful stares from the assembled sheep.

'Are you all right?'

When she didn't respond he began to approach her slowly. Perhaps she'd fainted or had some sort of accident. The sheep were glaring at him malevolently. Perhaps they'd attacked her and knocked her unconscious. He wasn't quite sure what sheep were capable of.

But as he drew closer he saw that her brown eyes were wide open, gazing in astonishment at the sky. And he saw a dark patch of drying blood in the middle of her red coat, dotted with buzzing flies.

He backed away, heart pounding, and then he started to run as fast as he could, his feet skidding on the damp grass. And when he reached the bottom of the field he stopped and vomited onto the ground, watched by sheep who looked bored, as though they'd seen it all before.

Chapter 3

Journal of Thomas Whitcombe, Captain in the King's army, September 6th 1643

Exeter has fallen and is now for the King so Plymouth must be seized from the grasping hands of Parliament.

I myself was present this day when our commander, Prince Maurice, sent orders to Sir Edmund Fortescue and Edward Seymour Esquire, that the port of Tradmouth was to be brought under the King's control. I heard one of the officers say that Tradmouth is the most disloyal of towns, reluctant as it has been to pay the King's taxes. The town is the place of my mother's birth and I hold it in some affection so I held my tongue.

There is one there I know from visits to my mother's kindred, a young woman who bewitched me five years ago with her dark eyes and modest looks. I yearned for adventure in those days and the life of a soldier.

Yet I think often upon Alison. That bewitcher of men.

*

Even though Neil was impatient to return to the dig he knew this was a job that had to be done. Besides, Harriet Mumford had provided him with a sandwich for lunch – smoked salmon no less – so it would have been rude to dash off.

'How's it going?' he heard her ask in a little-girl voice he found slightly irritating.

'Slowly. Have you asked Lee and the others if they'd give me a hand?'

'I don't think it'll be a problem.' He thought he saw her wink but that could have been his imagination. 'I want to know what's down there as much as you do.'

Neil put his spade down and scratched his head. He'd decided to make a start on the cellar but it needed digging out properly and a solitary archaeologist wasn't making much impact. 'I don't think Lee likes me.'

Harriet raised her eyebrows. 'If I say he's got to help you, he will.'

Neil shrugged. When he'd attempted to speak to the builder he'd definitely sensed hostility. But perhaps it was nothing personal. Perhaps all it needed was Harriet's feminine powers of persuasion.

He climbed out of the cellar up the four visible steps. At present it was only three feet deep and the question of when it had been filled in, and why, kept nagging at him.

'When that panelling's removed I think I should be here. It needs to be done very carefully.'

She smiled. 'Sure.'

Neil looked at his watch. 'I'd better go and check how they're getting on up at Princes Bower but I'll be back tomorrow. The Conservation Officer's paying another visit so he'll want to talk to me.'

'Evan says he should move in with us – save him the journey,' said Harriet, rolling her eyes.

'The perils of doing up a grade two star-listed building. You've got to put up with a lot of intrusion.'

Harriet's small, clean hand brushed his, dislodging a little caked soil which drifted to the ground. 'Some intrusions I don't mind.' The touch was quite unexpected and he pulled his hand away as though he'd had an electric shock, immediately regretting his over-reaction.

But she carried on talking as though she hadn't noticed. 'Before I nipped over to the studio I went on the Internet and found a site about the history of Tradmouth. I printed some of it out.' She took a folded sheet of paper from the pocket of her jeans and offered it to Neil but he shook his head. 'I'll look at it later when I've cleaned myself up.'

Harriet unfolded the paper and carried on talking. 'It says here that Mercy Hall was owned by a Thomas Hadness who had Parliamentarian sympathies. That's the Roundheads, isn't it?' She didn't wait for a reply. 'His wife Alison was accused of witchcraft and hanged in 1643 just before the besieging Royalists took control of the town.'

'That's the Cavaliers,' said Neil, trying to be helpful. 'What is it they used to say? Cavaliers were wrong but romantic and Roundheads were right but repulsive.'

Harriet's eyes glazed over as if he was going into too much historical detail for her liking.

'This fits in with your carving of the hanged woman in the garden,' he said. 'AH. Alison Hadness. And the date's right.'

'So she was a witch?'

'Not necessarily. From what I recall if you didn't like

someone back then you could accuse them of witchcraft and sit back and watch while they were tried . . . and maybe even hanged.'

'So you don't think she cast spells and cavorted with Satan?' Harriet pouted in mock disappointment.

'She probably just got on the wrong side of the woman next door.'

She put the sheet of paper down on a packing case and took a step closer. 'I've always wanted to be an archaeologist,' she said. 'It must be terribly exciting.'

'There's not much money in it but it has its moments.' He kept the tone light. He felt a frisson of attraction, the sort of frisson he knew was unwise to act upon, in spite of the invitation in her eyes. 'Anyway, you're a sculptor, aren't you? That must be much more exciting.'

She tilted her head to one side. 'It's mostly tourist stuff. Hares are very popular at the moment. They're an ancient symbol of femininity. Some believe they're messengers of the Great Goddess, moving by moonlight between the human world and the realm of the gods.'

'I'll take your word for it,' he said. 'I'd better get cleaned up and go or I'll be late for my meeting.'

As soon as he'd said the words he heard a man's voice calling Harriet's name. He saw her flinch. Evan was home. Neil had met him on several occasions and thought he looked as if he'd be useful in a fight. The sort of man who'd always made him feel a little awkward.

'I'll be late tomorrow. I've got to visit the dig at Princes Bower first thing. I'm site director so it's expected.'

'I'll be at my studio in the morning but I'll be back later. See you tomorrow then,' Harriet said, her mouth forming a silent kiss, before she hurried out to meet her husband.

As Neil gathered up his equipment he had a sneaking feeling that he was about to step into a dangerous situation.

'So someone nicked Lilith Benley's book of spells. Very public spirited of them if you ask me.'

Gerry put his feet up on his desk and began to flick through the file on his lap.

'Probably means someone knows she's back in circulation,' Wesley said. 'I thought her release was supposed to be kept quiet.' He'd made himself comfortable on the visitor's chair and was nursing a mug of hot tea in his hands. Gerry had brought in his own kettle and tea bags because he considered that not having to suffer tea from the vending machine in the corridor outside to be one of the privileges of rank.

'There was a lot of bad feeling about those Benley women so I'm surprised the good villagers of West Fretham haven't been storming the place with pitchforks and burning torches.'

Wesley grinned. 'Isn't West Fretham mostly holiday lets and retired London lawyers these days?'

'That'll be why then.'

'I trust the victims' families have been told she's out. They've a right to know if anyone has.'

'No doubt someone will have let them know. As far as I'm aware, Joanne Trelisip's mother dropped off the radar a while ago. She was a single mother. I think her husband was some sort of entertainer but he'd walked out when Joanne was young.'

'What about the other girl?'

'Gabby Soames. Her folks moved away. Went to live in the North East as far away as possible. They were a nice family … until Gabby's murder destroyed them.' He paused, a distant look in his eyes as if he was reliving unhappy memories. 'I've sent the crime scene people over to the Benley place to see if the burglar left any fingerprints but I'm not inclined to push the boat out.'

'I suppose she's served her time.' Wesley's feelings on the matter were mixed.

Gerry snorted. 'Those girls' families have had to serve a life sentence so why shouldn't she? She'd never admit it, you know. I reckon that makes it worse. She refused to acknowledge what she'd done.'

Wesley hesitated. 'It's strange that only something linked to witchcraft was taken. Do you think one of the victims' relatives might be responsible for the break-in?'

'Anything's possible.'

'Who was in charge of the Benley case?'

'DCI Hough. I was his DS.'

'I don't think I've heard of him.'

'He was nearing retirement and it was his last major inquiry. Poor bloke keeled over with a heart attack soon after the Benleys were convicted.' He patted his ample stomach. 'Let that be a lesson to us all.' He hauled himself upright in his chair and craned his neck to see into the outer office. 'What's going on?'

Wesley looked round and saw that a uniformed constable was chatting to DC Trish Walton, whose eyes were shining as if she was in receipt of some juicy gossip. Gerry stood up and strolled out of his office, hands in pockets, trying hard to look casual. As he approached Trish's desk the constable straightened his back and began to edge towards the door.

'Anything new?' Wesley heard Gerry ask as he bestowed a gap-toothed smile on his underlings.

'Nothing much, sir. Just another complaint,' the constable said. He was young and he sounded wary, as though he feared Gerry was about to live up to his reputation and come out with some witty put-down that would send him back, red-faced, to his own department.

'What about?'

'They're filming some reality show at a farm out at West Fretham. *Celebrity Farm*, it's called.'

'So I've heard. What about it?'

'One of the neighbours put in a complaint about the noise and the traffic. Says he came to the country for some peace and quiet. It's the same bloke who complained about the fans who were on his land.'

Wesley emerged from the shelter of Gerry's office. 'Fans?'

'One of the participants was Jackie Piper.'

'Never heard of her,' said Gerry.

'He's a him. And he got voted off a while ago. Zac James is still there though – he used to be in Ladbeat but he's a bit past his sell-by date now so I don't think he attracts the same following. Fans are fickle,' said the expert in popular culture.

'I don't understand why you're telling CID. It's a job for uniform,' said Gerry. 'We deal with real crime here.'

'The farm where the programme's being filmed is next door to Devil's Tree Cottage land,' Trish said meaningfully.

'I still don't see ... '

'If any young girls decide to hang around in the hope of seeing any of the celebrities ... '

'Come on, Trish. Lilith Benley's hardly likely to be a danger now,' said Wesley.

This silenced the speculation that was bubbling round

the office and everyone returned to their paperwork, looking a little sheepish. Wesley followed Gerry back into his office and they sat down again.

'Why did that Benley woman decide to come back to my patch?' Gerry rolled his eyes to heaven as if his patience was being sorely tried.

'Maybe it's all she's ever known ... apart from prison,' said Wesley.

'Oh no. She'd lived in London for years before she came here with her mother. Bought that smallholding in search of the good life. Only it went bad. Before she came here she used to be some sort of civil servant, if I remember right. She's a bright woman so don't underestimate her, Wes. And now she's out I think we should keep an eye on her. If she steps out of line I want to know about it.'

Wesley saw an unexpected glint of budding obsession in Gerry's eyes. Having known the DCI so long, it surprised him.

The phone on Gerry's desk rang and he answered it. Wesley watched as his grip tightened on the receiver. From his expression, Wesley could tell the news was bad. He waited patiently for the call to end.

'A body's been found near the Benley Place.'

'Lilith Benley?'

Gerry didn't answer.

Wesley called home and left a message. 'Suspicious death. No idea what time I'll be in. Sorry.' Pam could probably recite those particular words in her sleep. He'd used them so often during the course of their marriage.

It was four-thirty when they arrived at Jessop's Farm and parked next to the large TV van they'd spotted earlier, the only obvious sign that the place was being used for the filming of *Celebrity Farm*. A constable stood on guard at the door and as Wesley and Gerry approached he made a valiant effort to look alert and on top of the situation.

'What have we got?' Wesley asked him.

The young man – the sort people are thinking of when they say the police are getting younger – cleared his throat. As far as Wesley could recall he hadn't met him before but the constable clearly knew who he was dealing with. Being one of the few ethnic minority officers in the local force, Wesley was known to most by reputation.

'They're filming here, sir. *Celebrity Farm*, it's called.'

'So we've heard,' said Gerry. 'It's not one of the celebrities, is it? That'd be too much to hope,' he added, muttering the words under his breath.

'No, sir. But one of them found the body. He's called Rupert Raybourn – used to be some sort of comedian I think. He went out for a walk during a break in filming and found it in the top field. There were sheep in there but the farmer's cleared them out.'

'So this farmer's been trampling all over the crime scene?' said Gerry, impatient.

'Well, the sheep needed moving so we had no choice. The farmer's name's Joe Jessop and he's staying in one of the farm cottages while the filming's going on. He's already given a statement. And I've organised for statements to be taken from everyone in the house; the film crew and the other celebrity. It's Zac James from Ladbeat. That was a boy band. They used to be big about ten years back.'

Everything seemed under control and Wesley told the constable he'd done well. He thought the lad deserved a bit of praise.

'Has Dr Bowman arrived yet?'

'It's not Dr Bowman, it's Dr Partridge.'

A forlorn expression appeared on Gerry's face. 'What's happened to Dr Bowman?'

Gerry and Colin Bowman were old friends but Wesley knew there was something more behind the anguished question than a yearning for the familiar.

'He's on a cruise, sir,' said the constable helpfully. 'Treasures of the Adriatic, someone said.'

Wesley had come across the formidable Dr Partridge before and knew her to be a woman of ample proportions and a bluntness to match Gerry's own. She and Gerry hadn't got on. He imagined they were too alike to hit it off.

Wesley had had the foresight to put on the wellingtons he kept in the car boot as soon as he'd arrived but Gerry's shoes were getting ruined as he skirted the house and traipsed across the muddy pasture. The land rose sharply behind the house and Wesley, who was used to a steep walk to and from work each day, was soon striding ahead.

Eventually they reached a large field on the crest of a rolling hill, Gerry puffing and panting behind. The crime scene tent set up to protect the body looked out of place amongst the lush grass and sheep droppings, and as Wesley slipped on his crime-scene suit, he could see the activity through the open flap. The photographer, the officer taking video footage, the forensic people negotiating the metal plates they'd placed on the ground to protect any footprints the killer might have left. And at the centre of it all, like a queen bee at the heart of a hive, he saw the statuesque form of Dr Partridge squatting next to the corpse. Wesley could see that the dead woman was wearing a bright red coat which looked smart and fashionable – not the sort of thing most people would choose for a walk in the country-side.

'Oh, it's you,' the doctor said as soon as she spotted Gerry. Her dark-rimmed glasses were perched on a hooked nose and Wesley guessed that she was in her fifties but he'd heard rumours that she was younger than she appeared. He'd also heard that she was married but nobody he knew had ever seen her husband. Gerry had once joked that she'd probably eaten him after their wedding night.

'Nice to see you too, Jane.' Wesley saw that his boss wasn't smiling. 'What have we got?'

Dr Partridge straightened herself up. 'Single stab wound to the abdomen. It's my guess – and this is only a guess – that her killer stood in front of her and thrust a knife into her stomach.' She mimed the action with some enthusiasm.

'So he would have been covered in her blood?' Wesley asked.

Jane Partridge stared at him for a few moments. It was hard to know what she was thinking. He found himself wishing that the affable Colin Bowman hadn't decided to take his holiday just at that time. Colin was only too happy to give chapter and verse on the cause of death but getting information out of Jane wasn't always easy.

'Not necessarily. Most of the blood would have been absorbed by the thick woollen coat she's wearing.

He forced himself to look down at the corpse. 'Any ID?'

She shook her head. 'Not that I can see. No handbag.'

'What kind of weapon?'

'A knife. A sharp one thrust in with some force. I'll be able to tell you more when I've got her on the slab.'

'Time of death?'

'She's not been dead that long. Two to four hours at a guess. But I can't be more specific,' she said in a voice that brooked no argument. 'I blame all these silly detective series for raising expectations.' She began to pack her equipment away. 'Postmortem tomorrow. Two o'clock sharp.' She looked directly at Gerry. 'Don't be late.'

'We won't,' said Wesley. 'Anything else you can tell us? Has the body been moved?'

'If it had been, I would have mentioned it,' she said sharply before marching away, off down the field towards the farmhouse without a backward glance. Wesley could see the vehicles lined up in front of the building next to the film van, looking like toys from a distance: three patrol cars, Jane's four-by-four, two unmarked police cars, including their own, and the black mortuary van waiting to convey the victim to a refrigerated drawer at the hospital.

Gerry stared at the dead woman as though he was willing her to get up and tell him who had done this terrible thing to her. She was probably in her twenties, and she had been attractive in a waiflike sort of way. And she looked totally out of place in that field with her short red coat and her shiny high-heeled boots.

'Doesn't look like one of nature's walkers, does she?' Gerry said.

'There've been reports of fans hanging around the filming making a nuisance of themselves.'

'That was a couple of weeks ago. That pop star's been voted off,' said Gerry.

'There's still Zac James. Maybe she was one of his fans. Or perhaps she was meeting someone.'

'Well we won't find out unless we ask.'

'Funny, we were near here this morning visiting Lilith

Benley. Her place must only be about a quarter of a mile from here.'

Gerry looked at him. 'Mmm. You can even see it if you stand at that gate over there. Bit too close for my liking.'

'You can't think ...'

'I don't know what to think yet, Wes.'

Wesley left the tent with Gerry trailing behind, as though he was reluctant to leave the dead woman alone. He nodded to the uniformed sergeant who had assumed the role of crime scene manager, and once he'd been ticked off on the clipboard that recorded the comings and goings, Wesley made his way back down the field, treading carefully over the uneven ground.

He waited for Gerry who seemed to be having some difficulty negotiating the terrain, and when they found themselves back at the farmhouse the PC they'd spoken to before was waiting for them at the door, looking alert.

'Anyone see any unusual vehicles earlier today? Or notice anyone strange hanging around?'

'Nobody's mentioned it in their statements and the TV people have been around all afternoon. No one saw anything until Rupert Raybourn went for his walk. Raybourn likes to get away on his own as soon as filming stops apparently, which doesn't go down well with the producer.'

'I would have thought he'd be the life and soul of the party type,' said Gerry.

The constable didn't answer. Wesley had vague memories of Rupert Raybourn on the TV in his early youth. One of those self-satisfied comedians who graduated to hosting TV quiz shows and upstaging the hapless contestants. He tried to recall his catchphrase but couldn't quite manage it.

'According to the pathologist the woman probably died between one o'clock and three,' said Gerry.

'The production team can vouch for each other all afternoon. Rupert Raybourn was feeding the animals till just before three then he went for his walk at half past four. Zac James was filmed cleaning the milking shed then he went up in his room at two-thirty or thereabouts and came down shortly before Raybourn went out for his walk. He's given a statement – says he didn't see or hear anything unusual but he seems very jumpy. He's gone to his room if you want a word. Raybourn's in the kitchen giving a statement.'

Wesley caught Gerry's eye. 'Want to speak to them now?'

'We might as well while memories are still fresh.' Gerry pushed the front door open. 'Joyce isn't going to believe I've been mixing with the rich and famous.' He looked at Wesley and grinned. 'I'll be able to shatter all her illusions.'

Wesley smiled. Gerry's lady friend, Joyce, who worked at Morbay register office, seemed to have become a permanent fixture in his life. Wesley was glad: Gerry's late wife, Kathy, had died some years ago and Gerry wasn't suited to a life of solitude.

The hallway was lined with laden coat hooks, walking sticks bristled from a large basket in the corner and lines of muddy wellingtons formed a guard of honour against both walls. They turned left into a large kitchen with a scrubbed pine table in the centre and a range at one end. A classic farmhouse kitchen. No doubt the house had been chosen by the TV company for its traditional features.

Wesley recognised Rupert Raybourn's face at once. Strange, he thought, how people who were on the TV screen regularly in your youth can seem like old acquaintances. The comedian was looking appropriately serious as he gave a written statement to DC Paul Johnson. If he had nipped upstairs to put on a black tie, Wesley wouldn't have been surprised. The man was still conscious of the effect he was having on his public – it was probably a habit that was hard to break.

Paul looked up at Wesley and nodded. 'We're just finishing here, sir. Everyone's given their statements now.'

Raybourn stood as Paul made the introductions and solemnly shook hands with the two newcomers. He was in his early fifties but his toned body, permanent tan and expensively cut hair – brown with a hint of distinguished grey at the temples – did wonders for him.

'It must have been a shock, discovering the dead woman like that,' said Wesley.

Raybourn nodded and bowed his head respectfully.

'What were you doing in the top field?' Gerry asked.

Raybourn answered quietly, not what Wesley had expected at all. 'There are a lot of breaks in filming so I seize every opportunity I can to get away. There's a stifling atmosphere down here in the house, you see. You're aware you're always on show and it drives you mad after a while. Especially now it's just me and . . . '

'Zac James?'

'I've had my fill of pop stars. When Jackie Piper was thrown off it came as a great relief. At least when that MP, Charles Cloaker, was here you got some intelligent conversation. He mostly talked about himself, mind, but . . . '

'Are you in the habit of going up to that particular field?'

'There's a spectacular view over the countryside from up there . . . '

'And across to the adjoining properties,' said Gerry. 'You can see Devil's Tree Cottage from up there, can't you?'

Wesley saw a flicker of panic in his eyes. 'Where?'

'The smallholding to the east of the farm. You'll have heard about the murders there eighteen years ago.'

Raybourn looked flustered. 'I seem to recall something about it but . . . ' He looked away. He wasn't a good liar.

'I believe there have been a lot of girls hanging round.'

'They were Jackie Piper's fans and they went as soon as he was voted off.'

'Doesn't Zac James have fans? Maybe ones who are a bit older?'

'Contrary to the way Zac talks, I think being followed by hordes of adoring fans is a thing of the past. I certainly haven't seen any.'

'I believe Jackie Piper's fans caused a bit of a nuisance,' said Wesley.

Raybourn shrugged. 'They used to stand in the lane screaming and they kept trying to slip into the farm but, by and large, the crew kept them away.'

'Had you ever seen the dead woman before?'

He hesitated. 'I think I've seen her hanging about in the lane but . . . '

'When?'

'Over the past couple of days. I can't remember when exactly. I didn't keep a record.'

'You didn't speak to her?'

'No. I only saw her from a distance. I'm not even sure it was her. I just saw a woman in a red coat. Sorry but I've told you everything I know.'

Wesley smiled reassuringly. 'Thank you, Mr Raybourn. We may need to speak to you again.'

Raybourn stood up, slightly unsteady on his feet, and left the room.

Once Wesley and Gerry were satisfied he was out of earshot, they sat down opposite Paul. Gerry leaned forward. 'Any chance of a cup of tea? I'm spitting feathers here.'

Paul stood up and walked over to the sink, opened the cupboard underneath and took out an electric kettle. 'They use a kettle on the range for the TV show. The producer says it's more authentic. But Mr Raybourn told me this was here.' He filled the kettle and clicked it on before collecting together some clean mugs and taking a milk carton from the old-fashioned fridge in the corner of the room.

'Right, Paul, what have we got?' Gerry asked once they had the tea in front of them.

'Everyone says more or less the same thing. People have seen her about over the past couple of days but nobody knows who she is. We've taken statements from the producer and the film crew but they all say they saw nothing out of the ordinary. The farmer, Joe Jessop, was at the market in Tradmouth all afternoon until someone phoned him to ask him to come back and deal with the sheep. If he's telling the truth it looks like he's out of the frame.'

'We've seen Rupert Raybourn. What about our other celebrity?'

'Zac James claims he went to his room around two-thirty after he'd been filmed cleaning out the milking parlour. Says he stayed there for over an hour then he came downstairs. The crew were taking a break. The next scheduled filming was of the two contestants making the evening meal with things they'd gathered earlier. That was due to start around five. James swears he never left the house but, according to the crew he could have slipped out any time

45

without anyone noticing.' He lowered his voice. 'Mind you, I think he might be telling the truth.'

'Why's that?' Wesley asked.

'He was very agitated when we showed up. Like he was high on something. And as soon as we arrived I heard the loo flushing a few times.' He raised his eyebrows significantly. 'I've heard his cocaine habit is legendary. And he's edgy, fidgety. Either something's really troubling him or he's high as a kite.'

'I'll take your word for it, since you're obviously more in touch with these things than I am,' said Gerry, a little surprised that the sober and sporty Paul was so au fait with the drug habits of has-been singers. 'Being high on coke doesn't mean he couldn't have killed that woman. And if he could have left the house any time without anyone noticing he goes to the top of our list. What do you make of Raybourn?'

'He seems genuinely shocked and I don't think he's putting it on. And he's telling the truth when he says he goes up to that top field regularly. According to the crew, he's been doing it since filming began. Probably to get away from the others. Can't say I blame him.'

'Any nearer getting an ID for the dead woman?'

'Not yet. But a couple of the crew thought she might have been a fan of Zac James.'

'I need to speak to this James character,' said Gerry. 'Go and get him, will you?'

Paul stood up. He was over six feet tall and lanky so he towered over them, temporarily blocking out the light trickling in through the dusty glass of the kitchen window.

Once Paul had left the room, Wesley walked over to the window to watch the activity outside. The body of the dead

46

woman was being loaded into the mortuary van and he had a sudden, uncomfortable feeling that he was intruding on an intimate moment so he turned away.

'What do you think, Wes?' said Gerry. 'Are we going to be able to make an early arrest and go home?'

But before Wesley could answer Paul burst into the room. And Wesley could tell from his forlorn expression that he was the bearer of bad news.

Zac James had gone. And so had his car.

Chapter 4

Written by Alison Hadness, September 8th 1643

I learned my letters as a young maid copying from the books of my brothers against my father's will, and so I write this for I fear that we are about to be overtaken by terrible events and I wish to set them down. My husband says I should look to my household duties so I will write this journal in a cipher of my own invention while he is about his work. I pray he does not learn of my defiance.

They say Exeter has been taken and now the townsfolk of Tradmouth set up barricades at each entrance to the town in fear of the King's army. My husband, William, hath much resentment of the King's taxes levied upon us and every port in the land. He fears his ships might be attacked by the forces of our avaricious Sovereign Lord and he says he will do all in his power to defend us against the enemies of Parliament.

The churches are made forts with guns set upon the towers to attack any who dare encroach upon our town, and the blacksmith, Master Penny, hath supplied much iron work to our fortifications.

Today my stepdaughter, Elizabeth, would not answer when I addressed her on the matter. I think she bears me much ill will. When I am about my work with my herbs she disturbs me not and I thank God for it for I cannot bear her hatred and her evil looks.

William came to my bed last night and I was forced to endure his advances. How I wish it would end.

Gerry kept asking how the hell it could have happened. The response from the officers meant to be keeping an eye on things was an embarrassed silence. Everyone had assumed Zac James had permission to leave the scene. It was a misunderstanding, that was all. Gerry fumed and issued vague threats but in the end they came to nothing.

Now all patrols were on the lookout for Zac James's blue sports car and Jessop's Farm was being searched for a weapon or any bloodstained clothing. However, all the search turned up was a trace of white powder on the polished surface of the dressing table in Zac James's room … white powder that turned out to be cocaine.

The farmer, Joe Jessop, had been told to stay put in the run-down farm cottage nearby that had become his temporary home during the filming. Rupert Raybourn had checked into a hotel in Tradmouth, while the crew had returned to their rented cottage in the village so they'd be available for further questioning if needed. Gerry had promised that filming could resume in a day or so. But if one of the participants in *Celebrity Farm* turned out to be a murderer, the show certainly wouldn't go on.

Once they'd calmed egos and sorted everything out at the farm, there was someone else Wesley and Gerry wanted to see. According to Dorothy Benley's statement eighteen years ago, Gabby Soames and Joanne Trelisip had been stabbed in the stomach, exactly like the woman who'd just died. In view of the similarity, they had to speak to Lilith Benley again as soon as possible.

Gerry sat quietly in the passenger seat as Wesley drove to Devil's Tree Cottage for the second time that day. Wesley knew he was thinking, turning over the possibilities in his mind. Had Lilith killed again? Perhaps she couldn't help herself. Some killers – the dangerous ones – couldn't.

When Lilith answered the door she was holding a wet dishcloth and the faded apron she wore looked as if it might once have belonged to her mother. She said nothing as she led them through into the kitchen where Wesley saw evidence that she'd been cleaning the cupboards. The place had been neglected for eighteen years, she explained. It was time she made a start.

'You've heard about what happened next door?'

It was difficult to read her expression as she put down the cloth and sank into a seat by the kitchen table. 'A couple of policemen came round earlier to ask me if I'd seen or heard anything suspicious. I hadn't.'

'Have you seen a young woman hanging around nearby? Blonde; late twenties. Red coat.'

'I've already said I haven't seen anyone. Don't you people communicate?'

'The woman was stabbed in the stomach. That was how you killed your victims.' Gerry's words were almost brutal and Wesley saw Lilith flinch. 'According to your mother you used a ceremonial knife – an athame, wasn't it?'

'That was taken off for examination at the time – I don't have it now. Look, I didn't kill those girls and I certainly didn't kill this woman you're talking about.' She spoke calmly, patiently, as though she was explaining something to a rather dim child.

'So was your mother lying about the girls' murders?' said Wesley.

She turned her head away, fingering the thin fabric of her apron. 'My mother was confused. She couldn't tell fact from her delusions.'

'There was the forensic evidence,' Wesley continued. 'And the girls' bloodstained clothes were found in your out-house.'

Lilith was staring ahead, her hands resting stiffly in her lap. Outwardly calm but Wesley could sense the turmoil inside. 'You don't seriously think I killed this woman, do you?'

'That's what we're trying to find out.'

'Why would I kill her? I didn't even know her. Anyway, I'm out on licence so if I put a foot wrong I'm back inside and that's the last thing I want. You're welcome to search this house if it helps to convince you.'

From the challenge in her voice Wesley knew that any search would prove fruitless. But the cottage was small so it didn't take long to go through the motions. They found nothing unusual or incriminating ... not even evidence of a recent fire where evidence could have been destroyed.

When they returned to the kitchen Lilith was still sitting motionless at the table, as though she hadn't moved in their absence.

'Find anything?' she asked.

Gerry didn't answer the question.

'By the way, something else is missing after the break-in ... apart from my Book of Shadows.'

'What's that?'

'A ceremonial cloak. Black satin. It used to be worn for Wiccan ceremonies. I've been clearing things out and I noticed it's gone.'

'You think your burglar took it?'

She shrugged as if she wasn't sure ... and didn't really care.

'Do you really think she's got something to do with it?' Wesley asked as he followed Gerry out.

The DCI stopped when they reached the car. 'She comes back here and then someone's stabbed in a field next door to her land. I don't believe in coincidences.'

Somehow Wesley didn't share his boss's certainty.

Gerry told Wesley to go home. All patrols were looking for Zac James and Wesley found himself hoping that the singer would go to ground till morning and then be spotted and detained at some civilised hour.

It was almost ten by the time he reached his house and the children were still up. Amelia had refused to go to bed until her dad's return and Pam, after a day's teaching, hadn't had the strength to argue. Michael too was in his dressing gown, lolling on the sofa watching a parade of vacuous celebrities on the TV screen, ignoring his little sister who was dancing around the room to the beat of the music. At least, Pam said, he'd finished his homework. It was a job getting him to do anything since he'd started in year six. All that early good behaviour and industrious learning seemed to be vanishing in the looming shadow of adolescence. He was a bright boy, always top of his class and, after much discussion, his parents had agreed that he should go to the nearest grammar school. But now Pam worried that he wasn't working hard enough to pass the entrance exam.

'I'll have a fatherly word when I've got a minute,' Wesley said. 'I'm sure it's just a phase.'

'Maybe.' Pam didn't look convinced.

They escaped to the kitchen and Pam sat down at the round table. She pushed her shoulder length dark hair back behind her ears and gave him a weak smile. She'd changed out of the clothes she'd worn all day at school and had put on tight jeans and a white T-shirt that flattered her slim figure. She looked good. But she looked tired. More than tired, despondent. The cat, Moriarty, jumped onto her lap and she put the animal back down on the floor again, ignoring its importunate meows. This was more than just tiredness after spending a day in the classroom and then trying to coax an obdurate child to do his homework. Something was wrong.

'What's the matter?'

She stood up, pushing her chair back so that it scraped loudly on the floor, setting Wesley's teeth on edge. She walked over to the worktop where he could see the half-full bottle of red wine they'd abandoned the evening before. She took two glasses from the cupboard and filled them to the brim. Then she returned to the table with the glasses and slumped back in her seat.

'I had a call from my mother.'

Wesley had never cared to use that old cliché 'the mother-in-law from hell' to describe Della but he had to admit she came pretty close: thoughtless, disruptive, selfish, occasionally drunk, a teacher at a further education college nearing retirement who seemed to regard her more imma-ture students as role models. Earlier that year one of her wild enthusiasms had almost resulted in Pam's death and that was something neither of them had been able to forget … or forgive. Pam reasoned that she didn't want Della, that most irresponsible of grandmothers, to influence their children's lives and Wesley tended to agree. On the other hand, Pam was her only daughter so he knew the estrangement was painful. He found himself torn between an unspoken, nagging sympathy for the woman's pathetic attempts to retain her fading youth, and his instinctive desire to protect his children.

'What did she say?'

Pam took a long sip of wine. 'She's come up with some story about one of her colleagues being in deep shit and wanting your advice. But it's only an excuse if you ask me. Have you had anything to eat?'

'I had a takeaway with Gerry in the office.' He reached over and touched her hand. 'Do you want me to speak to Della?'

Deep trouble could mean anything … especially when it was the gospel according to Della who always tended to over-dramatise. On the other hand, he hated loose ends and he couldn't help feeling curious.

Pam put her glass on the table. 'I put the phone down on her and I feel a bit bad about it now. She sounded genuinely worried. She said this bloke was in serious trouble so maybe you should … '

'No problem,' Wesley lied. In his experience anything connected with Della was likely to become a problem sooner or later. With a woman dead and Zac James still on the run, trouble was the last thing he wanted.

But family was family, even family of the estranged and feckless kind. He took out his mobile phone and found Della's number.

When she answered she sounded grateful that he'd taken

the trouble to call. This seemed like a new Della, chastened and repentant. But he was reserving judgement for the moment.

'You told Pam somebody's in trouble. Not you is it?'

'How can you think that, Wesley?' A few months ago, before Pam had come face to face with death, she would have countered with an insult but now she sounded hurt. 'It's a man called Simon Frith. He teaches History at my college and he's been suspended because someone's made an accusation against him.'

'What sort of accusation?'

'Sexual assault of a fifteen-year-old girl. All nonsense of course.'

'Is it?' Della was a gullible woman and he knew from his years in the police service that sexual predators can be remarkably plausible.

'Yes. He's a nice man. He's got a lovely wife and three kids.'

'That doesn't make him innocent.' She was beginning to irritate him and he knew he was in danger of abandoning his long-held policy of keeping an open mind until he'd collected all the facts.

'They picked him up at home a couple of nights ago and took him to Neston police station for questioning – locked him in a cell. Can you find out what evidence they've got?'

'I'm sure they're doing a thorough investigation. Is he still being held?'

'He's been released on bail. The trouble is, he doesn't even know why this girl's accusing him. Can you find out? Please. His wife's going out of her mind. It's the worst thing that can happen . . . to be accused unjustly like that.'

'Hang on, Della, all the students where you teach are over sixteen, aren't they?'

'He's been doing some private tutoring and it's one of those kids who's made the accusation. The police just kept on and on at him, asking all these questions. What happened when he was alone with her? Did he fancy young girls? They even took his computer away. Please, Wesley. I promised him you'd help.'

'You shouldn't have done that. I can't interfere in someone else's case. They'll have taken his computer to look for evidence ... e-mails, websites he's visited, whether he's into porn featuring young girls ...'

'I know that, Wesley. I'm not stupid. What I want to know is what you're going to do about it. We need to act now to avoid a terrible miscarriage of justice.' This was Della at her most unstoppable – her most pompous – and he felt a fresh stab of irritation. He had a killer to catch ... a killer who'd thrust a knife into a young woman's stomach and watched her die like a sacrificial animal in a cold field. He hadn't time to take part in one of Della's crusades for justice, especially if it involved coming to the defence of a child molester.

'There's nothing much I can do. Like I said, there'll be a thorough investigation and if there's no evidence against him ...'

'But this little minx who's accusing him will be believed,' she whined. 'They always are.'

'Not necessarily,' he said, uncomfortably aware that she might have a point. It's hard to prove a negative if your accuser appears to be a paragon of blameless innocence. 'I'm in the middle of a murder enquiry at the moment but if I have a moment I'll try to have a word with someone at

Neston ... just to find out what's going on. No promises, mind.'

'Thanks, Wesley. It'll mean a lot to Simon to know someone from the police is on his side.'

Wesley winced. She'd obviously misunderstood. But that was typical. 'I didn't say I'd do anything to influence the case. I couldn't even if I wanted to.'

His words didn't seem to register. 'Can I speak to my daughter?' she said, sounding positively cheerful.

He passed the phone to Pam and she took it reluctantly, as though she feared it was contaminated. Judging by the noises coming from the living room, it was time to play the stern pater familias and get the children to bed. He only hoped there wouldn't be a call from work to ruin the effect.

Rupert Raybourn had come to hate his famous catch-phrases. 'How ya doing?' and 'Rupert's rarely wrong.' At one time they'd been shouted at him in the street whenever he ventured out. And the people who quoted them always seemed to think they'd come up with something witty and original, which made it worse somehow. He'd been obliged to acknowledge them with a friendly smile even though he was cringing inside.

But these days this universal recognition wasn't automatic and he no longer had to resort to the disguise of wig and dark glasses to achieve anonymity. At times he found this liberating but at others he longed for the old days when he was someone; when his existence made a difference. Maybe that's why he'd agreed to take part in *Celebrity Farm*. Or perhaps there was another reason, one he hardly liked to acknowledge even to himself.

He'd been assured that filming would resume as soon as

possible but, on the suggestion of the police, he had moved temporarily to the Marina Hotel by the waterfront in Tradmouth, which was a vast improvement on the accommodation at the farm. The director and crew were still holed up in their rented cottage in West Fretham so, in Zac James's absence, he now had some much-needed privacy, which suited him fine. And, to top it all, the film company were paying for the hotel. Which was a good job because after his last divorce settlement he was skint.

The police would still be up at Jessop's Farm but he imagined their presence would have dwindled to a couple of constables by now, stationed there to keep the press and sightseers away.

They wouldn't see him if he drove up to Devil's Tree Cottage.

He still imagined Lilith Benley as she had been in 1989 when he'd first met her in Morbay.

He'd been top of the bill in the Pavilion Gardens back then and she'd come backstage, dumbstruck at meeting a celebrity as so many are. When he'd invited her out for a drink, as much for company as a prospective sexual encounter, she'd said she had to see her mother back to her hotel first. Lilith had been attractive in an unconventional sort of way and even the mention of a mother hadn't put him off. But then his plans had been thwarted and everything had changed.

Rupert's career had really taken off soon after. And Lilith Benley had become even more famous in her own way. But her kind of fame comes at a high price.

The knocking on the door had been loud and insistent. But Lilith had sat quite still, out of sight of the window, waiting for the visitor to go away. She'd heard more police cars going up and down the nearby lanes, wailing like banshees, and she knew they'd probably come for her again sooner or later. Give a dog – or a bitch – a bad name ... Her reputation as the brutal murderer of two young girls had kept trouble away in prison – but that same reputation was bound to attract problems on the outside.

In fact it had already started. She'd received a package just that morning and ever since then she'd been going over the possibilities in her head. Was it a message or was it a warning? Either way, it was something else she needed to hide from the police. And she'd hidden it well in a place they'd never find.

As soon as darkness had fallen she'd shut the tattered curtains, trying to make sure there were no gaps for any ill-wishers bold enough to approach the house to peep through. Then she'd lit the stove. It was October and even though the days were unseasonably warm and damp, the nights were bitterly cold. Once the logs she'd brought in earlier from the store outside were well alight, she'd switched on the lamp and picked up the book she was reading. Maybe she would buy a television. She needed to keep in touch. She needed to know what they were saying about her.

She had boarded up the pane of glass the intruder had smashed in the back door, nailing the square of hardboard in place, doing her best to make the place secure. She had called a glazier in Tradmouth who'd said he'd do the job later that day. He'd sounded friendly and helpful ... until she'd told him her name and address and his attitude suddenly changed. But she still needed a new pane of glass in that door so she'd meekly agreed to his terms – a week's time and twice the usual price.

Perhaps it would always be like this from now on. Perhaps she'd have to learn to do these things for herself so she wouldn't be at the mercy of gossiping tradesmen. She needed to be self-sufficient just as she had been in prison. When you're self-sufficient, nobody can hurt you.

When she peeped out of the window into the darkness she saw the tail lights of a car vanish down the drive. Whoever had pounded on her front door had given up and gone away. And she was thankful.

There were distant lights in the field beyond her far hedgerow, on Joe Jessop's land, and she stood at the window watching for a while. She couldn't see what was going on behind the wall of tangled foliage but she knew those lights meant bad news. They had brought in lights like that eighteen years ago when they'd conducted their detailed forensic search of Devil's Tree Cottage. They had frightened the pigs and the hens had stopped laying with all the disturbance. Lilith had hated those bright, relentless lights because they had shone into her darkest and most intimate secrets.

The next morning Wesley left Pam dozing, waiting for the alarm clock to signal the start of another day. The children were too old now to burst into the room at six-thirty and demand attention. There were times when Wesley missed this innocent disruption to his sleep. But you can't turn back time.

When he arrived in the CID office at seven o'clock members of the team were drifting in, depositing damp coats on the rack by the door then heading for their desks to check whether anything new had come in overnight. Gerry bustled in at five past, struggling out of his coat and moaning

60

loudly about the weather outside. Yesterday's half-hearted sun had vanished, to be replaced by grey drizzle floating in horizontal sheets over the choppy river. The outside temperature had plummeted at least five degrees but the office seemed stuffy.

At seven-fifteen an unsmiling Gerry emerged from his office. Photographs of the crime scene were already pinned up on the huge white board that filled the far wall. The image of the unnamed woman in the red coat was at the centre surrounded by pictures of Zac James, Rupert Raybourn, the four members of the film crew and Joe Jessop, the farmer who owned the field. Wesley found himself wondering whether Lilith Benley's picture would end up there.

Gerry called for attention and stood in front of the board like a teacher preparing to address a class. Wesley sat down beside Rachel who caught his eye and smiled. She looked more relaxed today. Perhaps whatever had been bothering her had been resolved.

'Anything come in from Traffic about Zac James's car?'

When the response was a negative murmur, Gerry pointed to DC Paul Johnson. 'Contact them, will you, Paul? Get them to examine all their cameras. Sometimes that lot need a bomb up their backsides. A man who flees the scene of a murder has to be top of our suspect list so we need to find Zac James fast. And we have another problem,' Gerry continued, looking round the attentive faces. 'We don't know who the murdered woman is yet. The search teams have been looking for a handbag or phone but nothing's turned up so far. We need to get a likeness that won't frighten the horses and circulate it quick in the hope someone recognises her.' He looked at DC Trish Walton who was sitting to attention near the window. 'Trish. Check that nobody matching her description has been reported missing.'

'Already done, sir. No luck.'

'Then check out all the hotels and B and Bs.'

Gerry distributed the other tasks but there were a couple he was reserving for himself and Wesley. Joe Jessop's neighbour – the one who'd complained about the filming at the farm – had been out when the door-to-door team had called the previous day and he wanted to pay him a visit. He also wanted a further word with Jessop himself. The body had been found on his land after all.

The complaining neighbour was called Shane Gulliver. Wesley was familiar with the name because Gulliver was often interviewed on chat shows and breakfast TV. Wesley hadn't read any of his books because the author's brand of maudlin fiction, inspired by his own tragic childhood, wasn't to his taste. But Pam, an avid devourer of books, had read a couple. They were well written she'd said, if a little self-indulgent.

Shane Gulliver's eighteenth-century rectory stood in an acre of land, separated from Jessop's Farm by a high hedgerow and a narrow footpath. When Gulliver had complained initially to the police he'd stated that he was a tolerant man who'd put up with the smells, inconveniences and unfamiliar sounds of the countryside. However, the constant traffic generated by the filming and the screeching girls who'd trespassed into his garden while Jackie Piper was in residence had tried his patience to the limit. He'd settled in the Devon countryside so he could write undisturbed. He needed peace and solitude ... not the three-ring circus Jessop's Farm had become of late.

Wesley had read the details of his complaint and rather

liked the bit about the three-ring circus. From what he'd seen of *Celebrity Farm* that summed up the situation nicely. He parked the car on Gulliver's gravel driveway and when he knocked on the glossy black front door, Gerry hung back a little as he often did when he decided that Wesley was more likely to strike up a rapport with the individual they planned to interview. The door was opened by a slender woman with short dark hair, a snub nose and large blue eyes. From the photographs on his dust jackets, Wesley knew that Gulliver was well into middle age, probably in his fifties, so if this was his wife, she was considerably younger than he was, maybe by twenty years.

'Mrs Gulliver?'

'I'm Gwen Gulliver, yes.' She made a show of examining their warrant cards and told them to step inside. She sounded slightly exasperated as though she was finding the whole business tedious, and Wesley couldn't help feeling like an estate worker who'd found himself on the wrong side of the lady of the manor. For a man who made so much of his humble roots, it appeared that Shane Gulliver had found himself a partner in life from a different world altogether – but it was a world Gulliver would probably have grasped eagerly the moment his first novel made the bestseller charts. According to Pam, although ninety-eight percent of writers struggle to earn a crust, a tiny handful right at the top could make serious money. Her own excuse for not embarking on the Great British Novel, apart from her children and her teaching career, was that she was extremely unlikely to find herself in the top two percent. She'd never been optimistic by nature.

Gwen Gulliver ushered them into a spacious drawing room, tastefully decorated in cream and gold; a tasteful, feminine room and an unlikely setting for a man who sold himself on his gritty credentials.

'I'll get my husband,' she said and turned to go.

'Actually we'd like to talk to you as well,' said Wesley. 'No doubt you've heard about the body that was found next door at Jessop's Farm yesterday afternoon?'

She turned back to face him and frowned. 'Body? No . . . I . . .'

'A woman was found dead in one of the fields. Did you see or hear anything suspicious?'

'No. Nothing. When I got home I heard a lot of sirens and police vehicles careering down the lane at high speed but that's all I know. Apart from that I didn't see anything out of the ordinary, I'm afraid. Do you know who she is? How did she die? Is it associated with the filming?'

'I'm afraid we're treating the death as suspicious. And we're still trying to identify the victim,' said Wesley gently. He saw Gwen raise her hand to her mouth. She looked shocked. But shock was natural in the circumstances.

'You didn't answer the door yesterday evening when my officers called round,' said Gerry.

'I must have been out picking Shane up from Morbay station.'

'Where were you yesterday afternoon?'

'I was in Plymouth . . . shopping. I got back around five-thirty.'

'Have you seen a woman hanging around recently . . . youngish, blonde hair, red coat?' Gerry asked.

Gwen shook her head. 'It doesn't ring a bell. But there have been a lot of strangers about because of the filming. We had to complain about teenage girls trespassing on our property.'

'This woman was probably in her late twenties.'

'The ones I saw were teenagers and it was over a week ago.'

'Have you ever had any dealings with a woman called Lilith Benley?' Wesley asked. 'She lives on the other side of Jessop's Farm land ... place called Devil's Tree Cottage?'

Gwen Gulliver shook her head again. 'The name's familiar because there was a TV documentary about her a couple of years ago ... and from time to time the papers do a feature on horrific crimes when they've nothing better to write about. She's in prison, surely.'

'Not any more,' said Gerry. 'She's out and she's come back. I wondered if you'd met her.'

Gwen's eyes widened and a look of affronted horror appeared on her face. 'Why on earth would I have anything to do with someone like that?' She shuddered. 'I'm sorry, I'd like to help you but ... '

'In that case we'd better speak to your husband,' said Gerry.

'I'll check whether he's free to see you.'

This was too much for Gerry. 'This is a murder enquiry, love. He'll either see us here or down at the station.'

Wesley liked Gerry's use of the traditional northern endearment and he resisted the temptation to smile at the startled look on the woman's face.

'Nice place,' he said after she'd hurried from the room, leaving them alone.

Before Gerry could reply the door opened to reveal a middle-aged man. His jet-black hair fell in curls around his shoulders and his body was tanned and athletic. Only the lines on his neck betrayed the fact that he wasn't in the first flush of youth. He looked a good deal younger than the photograph on his dust jacket. Wesley suspected that he had undergone surgery at some point and his hair was almost certainly dyed.

He held out his hand. 'Shane Gulliver. I suppose this is about that business at the farm next door. The wife's just told me . . . '

'We're hoping you can help us.'

'I don't see how. But go ahead – ask anything you want.' He tilted his head to one side and assumed a co-operative expression. Wesley had seen similar expressions before, usually on the innocent . . . but sometimes on the guilty.

'You were out yesterday when my officers called.'

'I was up in London all day – doing research for my new novel. Didn't get back till the evening. Gwen, the missus, picked me up from the station.'

'You've made several complaints about the filming at the farm next door.'

'There was some pop star there and his fans reckoned they had the right to come in our garden and get through the hedge. The TV company had people guarding the gate while he was here, you see, so they tried to get in another way. They made a bloody racket . . . screaming this bloke's name. Jack something.'

'Jackie Piper,' said Gerry. 'He was voted off about ten days ago.'

'Well, there's still all the bloody traffic and the disturbance. I need peace and quiet while I'm working. No distractions.'

Gerry stopped him before he warmed to his theme. 'So apart from the goings-on next door, have you seen or heard anything unusual over the past few days?'

Gulliver looked at Gerry as though he was being particularly dense. 'If I had I would have mentioned it.'

'The dead woman was blonde, late twenties, wearing a red coat. Have you seen her around at all?'

Gulliver shook his head, his eyes lowered.

'Your wife wasn't here yesterday afternoon?'

'She was shopping in Plymouth.'

'So she said. Was anybody else here, a cleaner or a gardener maybe? Have you any children?'

'We've got a son ... or rather Gwen has from a previous relationship. He usually gets a lift home from school with a friend – gets in around half four. I'm sure he wouldn't have seen anything. He's only fifteen and ...'

'I suppose he took an interest in Jackie Piper?' said Wesley.

'Alex is a Goth – don't think Piper was his cup of tea. As I said, he'll be back around four-thirty so if you want to come back and speak to him then ...'

'We'll see,' said Gerry, leaving the threat hanging in the air.

Wesley asked Gulliver about Lilith Benley and got the same reply his wife had given. Surprise that she'd been released and horror that she was living in such close proximity. Standard stuff.

Gerry thanked Gulliver and made for the door. They weren't going to learn anything here. Mrs Gulliver had been in Plymouth, her son had been at school and Shane Gulliver had been in London. Nobody was aware of anything out of the ordinary over the past few days, apart from the filming at Jessop's Farm. Certainly not a knife-wielding murderer fleeing across their garden.

If the killer had made his escape through the front gate he would have been spotted by the film crew, all of whom had been interviewed and had seen nothing. And as the rectory route seemed unlikely, that left Devil's Tree Cottage land. If the murderer had parked a vehicle at the end of Lilith Benley's winding drive, it wouldn't have been visible from the cottage – and if he'd skirted round her fields, he could easily have gained access to the field where the body had been found by climbing the gate.

'Maybe once we've seen Joe Jessop, we should have another word with Lilith Benley,' said Gerry as they walked to the car.

'She's already told us she didn't see anything. Wouldn't that be construed as harassment?'

'If she didn't want the police to harass her, she shouldn't have murdered those two lasses,' said Gerry righteously.

Wesley said nothing.

The sun was peeping half-heartedly through the clouds as Neil watched his colleagues working in the trench. From the wooded spur of land that had been named Princes Bower during the Civil War – after King Charles I's nephew, Prince Maurice, who had laid siege to the town – there was a spectacular view of Tradmouth Castle and the wide expanse of sea beyond. But his mind was on the excavation as he walked around the edge of the trench examining the contents of the finds trays; a motley collection of musket balls, coins and clay pipes, mundane souvenirs of extraordinary times. The members of the public who had participated in the dig so enthusiastically all summer had long departed, back to their day jobs and colleges, leaving the professionals to tie up the loose ends before returning the site to nature and the occasional adventurous walker.

The fortifications at Princes Bower had been built by the Royalist army that had taken Tradmouth in 1643 after a month-long siege. Three years later they'd served as a refuge for around a thousand occupying Royalist soldiers who'd fled the town when Tradmouth was retaken by General Fairfax. Because of the site's inaccessibility and the fact that it was on protected National Trust land, it was a well-preserved reminder of the time England had torn itself apart. Brother against brother. Son against father.

With few exceptions, the citizens of Tradmouth back then had supported Parliament's cause against King Charles I who had demanded exorbitant fines and taxes from the port to support his unpopular regime. Nobody likes the taxman. Some things never change.

The carving in the garden at Mercy Hall, the image of the hanging woman and the date 1643, had aroused Neil's curiosity so he'd done some research of his own. In 1643 Mercy Hall had been a notable house overlooking the town, elevated above the bustle of the quayside and the narrow, stinking streets. It had been home to the Hadness family who has prospered from Tradmouth's burgeoning trade with Newfoundland. He'd also found an account of Alison Hadness's trial for witchcraft. When he visited the Hall again, he'd tell Harriet Mumford all about it. But in the meantime he had a job to do.

Yielding to temptation, he took his trowel from his pocket and grabbed a kneeling mat before climbing into Dave's trench where his colleague greeted him with a nod and a grin.

He worked for an hour or so, scraping away the earth, and he had just uncovered a trio of musket balls when he heard a female voice calling his name. He looked up and saw Harriet Mumford standing a few feet away on the edge of the trench, wrapped up warm against the cool breeze blowing in from the English Channel with a red woolly hat hiding her long, silky hair.

Neil straightened himself up, suddenly aware of his unkempt appearance ... and hoping she wasn't there to bring him bad news.

A strand of hair escaped from her hat and she pushed it back with an ungloved hand. 'I thought I'd better come and tell you. The builders have been removing that panelling and ...'

'I thought they were going to wait till I was there.' They'd disobeyed his instructions and he felt a pang of irritation.

'The Conservation Officer came and said it was OK,' she said. She looked anxious. Maybe there'd been an accident and that ancient panelling was damaged beyond repair. He waited for her to continue.

'They found something in the space between the panelling and the wall.'

'What was it?' Neil felt relieved ... and suddenly hopeful that his routine job as local conservation officer might yield something out of the ordinary.

Harriet lowered her voice. 'It's a coffin,' she said. 'They've found a tiny little coffin.'

Chapter 5

Journal of Thomas Whitcombe, Captain in the King's army, September 10th 1643

Our commander offered most generous terms for Tradmouth's surrender but the people have erected barricades at each road and track into the town, strengthened the forts and fortified the churches. Such gross defiance caused Prince Maurice to lay siege to the town and we have made our headquarters at Hilton Farm, not half a mile from the church of St Leonard on the hill overlooking the town and the river.

At the farm I share my quarters with six other officers while Prince Maurice and his servants have the best chamber. The men shift for themselves in tents and outbuildings but I fear the ground has become a mire as rain pours incessantly from the grey sky. Such weather does not bode well for our campaign and I fear that the men will grow restless if our victory is not swift.

As I already have knowledge of the town, I will find a way through the barricades and spy upon the townsfolk.

The prospect of a meeting with Alison tempts me greatly. But I know not if she still resides in Tradmouth . . . or even whether she still lives.

Lilith Benley had told them nothing the previous day. All she wanted, she'd said, was to be left in peace. But her very presence there bothered Gerry. And it was starting to bother Wesley too.

As they drove the short distance to Jessop's Farm, Wesley asked Gerry if he thought Lilith had been telling the truth. Gerry had known her all those years ago. He'd seen her being interviewed and he knew how she reacted. And whether or not she was a convincing liar.

'We won't know if there's a connection with Benley until we know who the dead woman is,' Gerry replied.

To Wesley the answer seemed disappointingly noncommittal. He parked the car near the gate and they walked in amicable silence towards Jessop's Farm. The TV company's vehicles had gone and, according to the constables on duty, Joe Jessop had been complaining about the interruption to his new and valuable source of revenue. Times were hard for farmers, he said, and he was still having to put up with unwanted intrusion while the crime scene team continued their search. Jessop's animals had had to be moved so the police could do their job unhindered by a woolly audience. Only Fin, Jessop's enthusiastic young border collie, seemed to be relishing the extra work.

Wesley and Gerry found Jessop hosing down the cow shed, a martyred expression on his face. The farmer was in his forties but his weather-beaten face and greying hair made him look a lot older. As soon as he spotted the two detectives he turned off the hose.

'You in charge?' he asked Gerry accusingly.

'Sorry for the disruption, Mr Jessop. And thanks for letting us use your house. Your co-operation's much appreciated,' Wesley said, calming the waters.

Jessop gave a curt nod of acknowledgement.

'We need a word,' said Gerry.

'I've already made a statement. I never saw that dead woman before and I've no idea who she was or what she was doing on my land.'

'We've met before.'

The farmer's defiant expression vanished and he suddenly looked wary, as though Gerry's words had resurrected bad memories. 'Aye. Years ago.'

'Wasn't your dad running the farm back then?'

'He died two years back.'

'Sorry to hear that. This is DI Peterson, by the way.'

The farmer nodded to Wesley who gave him a businesslike smile in return.

'You gave evidence at the Benley women's trial,' Gerry said.

Jessop didn't answer.

'How do you feel about Lilith coming back?'

'She's done her time.'

'Have you seen her since she came back?' Wesley asked.

'No. But I need to ask her if she wants to sell some of her land. She's got a couple of fields I wouldn't mind getting my hands on. And with her being on her own, I reckon she won't be needing them.'

'At the trial you said you saw the two girls hanging round,' said Gerry. 'You said they'd been tormenting the Benley women.'

'I told the court what I knew. Those girls hung around

73

the Benley place, giggling and chanting. Calling them witches. You can only push people so far.'

'Did the girls give you any trouble?' Wesley asked.

He didn't answer for a few moments. 'I think they left a gate open once and some of the sheep got out . . . not that I could prove anything.'

'I believe they lived in the village.'

'That's right.'

'So you knew them?'

'Not really. They were just a pair of silly kids.'

There was another question Wesley had particularly wanted to ask. 'Is it normal for pigs to eat dead bodies?'

'Pigs'll eat anything that's put in front of them.' The farmer grinned showing a row of uneven grey teeth. 'Even a ham sandwich.'

'Even bones?'

'They've got strong jaws.'

'Let's talk about the woman who was murdered yesterday,' Wesley said, trying to banish the lurid vision of the girls' gruesome fate from his mind. 'You sure you didn't see her hanging around? She was wearing a bright red coat.'

'If someone's up in that top field I can't see them from down here.'

'But you saw those girls eighteen years ago?'

'It was lambing time,' he said as though this explained everything. 'I was seeing to the ewes at all hours of the day and night and I was there when they were walking up to the Benley place. I told the police all this at the time.'

'Could the woman in the red coat have gained access to your field via Lilith Benley's land?' Wesley glanced at Gerry and saw that he was listening intently.

'It'd be easy enough. There's an old gate set in the

hedgerow. It's been rusted shut for years but anyone could climb it. And the TV people were coming and going round the drive and the house so she can't have got in that way without being seen.'

'What about your other neighbours? The author and his wife?'

'Never had nothing to do with 'em. They don't bother me and I don't bother them.'

Wesley heard someone calling Gerry's name. A uniformed constable was hurrying towards him, bursting with untold news. They walked to meet him, leaving Jessop to his work.

'What's up?' Gerry asked as soon as he was within earshot.

'The search team's found a handbag stuffed into a hedge not far from where the body was found . . . on the Benleys' side it was. It's been taken to the farmhouse if you want a look.'

'Well let's have a shufti,' said Gerry, rubbing his hands together with anticipation. He began to march towards the house and Wesley followed. If their luck was in they might soon have a name for the victim.

Wesley glanced at his watch with a nagging feeling of dread. The woman's postmortem was in two hours. And there wouldn't even be Colin's customary tea and biscuits to sugar the pill.

As soon as they reached the farmhouse door it began to drizzle again. Rain wasn't good for crime scenes and the CSIs would be cursing. They were using Jessop's house as a temporary base during the search – somewhere they could co-ordinate everything and make the essential cups of tea that oiled the wheels of any investigation. Although Wesley had told Joe Jessop that his co-operation was appreciated, he hadn't mentioned that he was a suspect. Joe had been around eighteen years ago helping his father run the farm. And he was still there. Living alone with only his dog for company.

They made for the kitchen where three officers were sipping tea and chatting. As soon as Gerry and Wesley entered the room mugs were drained and the underlings tried their best to look busy.

DC Nick Tarnaby was standing by the window and Wesley asked him how far they'd got with the house-to-house enquiries in the nearby village.

Tarnaby dragged his hand through his thinning red hair and said he thought they'd finished and the reports would be back at the station.

'I want to set up an incident room in West Fretham,' Gerry announced. 'Nick, you seem to be standing there doing nothing so can you set the ball rolling? See if you can get the church hall. It'll be easier than trailing to and fro from Tradmouth all the time.'

Gerry was right. Things would be much easier with a dedicated incident room, somewhere the locals could visit easily if they had anything to report. Wesley saw a flash of panic in Tarnaby's eyes, as though he feared he was out of his depth. The man wasn't the brightest star in the Constabulary's firmament and Gerry had often contemplated returning him to Uniform. But Wesley knew that the DCI was softer than he liked his colleagues to believe and, so far, he had always given the man another chance. One day, however, Nick's chances were bound to run out.

Wesley caught Nick's eye. 'If you have any problems, see DS Tracey,' he said quietly.

Tarnaby didn't react, not even a grateful look. Sometimes Wesley wondered if it was the colour of his skin that made the man so stand-offish. But anything like that would be hard to prove, any hint of racism being the ultimate taboo in the modern police service.

'Where's this handbag then?' said Gerry, looking around.

A young female PC stepped forward, bolder than the rest who were edging sheepishly towards the door. 'It's bagged up in the parlour ready to be taken back to the station by the Exhibits Officer.'

'Let's have a look.' Gerry sounded impatient.

The woman hurried away and returned a few moments later with a plastic evidence bag containing a soft tan leather shoulder bag, undoubtedly expensive. Wesley put on his crime scene gloves before taking it out of its protective cocoon and placing it on the table by the window. The room had emptied now. Only Nick Tarnaby and the PC remained, staring at the bag as though they expected it, like Pandora's Box, to release all the evils of the world.

Wesley poured the contents out. A hairbrush with fine fair hair caught up in its bristles; a pack of tissues; a purse containing thirty pounds in notes and some loose change; a pen; a nail file. No diary, no credit cards, no mobile phone and no address book.

'Somebody's been through it and removed anything that could identify her,' he said.

'Which means that if we knew who she was, we'd be halfway to identifying the killer,' said Gerry. 'He's done a thorough job of searching the bag which means he didn't panic. And nobody saw him so he's either been lucky or clever.'

'Joe Jessop has every reason to be round and about the

farm. He could have killed her before he went off to the market. Rupert Raybourn's been in the habit of going up to the top field to get away from the others. And Zac James said he was holed up in his room all afternoon but he could easily have sneaked out. We need to go through all the TV company's footage to see if there's anything to place Raybourn and James at the appropriate time. And we mustn't forget the crew, although they're all vouching for each other.'

'Zac James has buggered off and there's still no sign of him. That's hardly the behaviour of a man with nothing to hide.'

'He has got something to hide. The drugs.'

'Doesn't mean he's not a killer, Wes.'

Wesley looked at his watch. If they grabbed some lunch now there would be plenty of time to get to the hospital for the postmortem at two.

'Fancy a sandwich?'

Gerry sighed. 'As long as it's not ham.'

Neil held the little coffin in his hands with horrified care like a bereaved parent carrying the body of a child. Constructed from roughly hewn wood, it was barely two feet in length.

'Where exactly was it found?'

'They removed the section of panelling nearest the fire-place and found it resting on the floor behind.'

'Where are the builders now?'

Neil looked at Harriet. He was sure she blushed but it might have been his imagination.

'A couple of them went off in the van to fetch some materials but Lee's around somewhere. They're all pretty spooked.'

'Have you looked inside?' Neil hoped the answer would be yes. He'd never thought of himself as superstitious but he didn't fancy being the first to break the seal of centuries. Some atavistic voice deep inside warned of ancient curses. But he told himself not to be so childish and placed the box on the old table in the corner of the room where it lay, a grim reminder of mortality.

'Do you think it's a child?' Harriet asked as he stood staring at it.

This was what Neil feared most; opening the box and finding a tiny skeleton lying there inside. That would involve the police and the coroner and he didn't feel up to facing all that just now. Besides, the thought of the small person, discarded and lying cold and forgotten behind the panelling, uncared for in death as in life, disturbed him more than he'd expected.

The wood had been fixed down firmly but time had corroded the nails and when he touched it he knew that the top would lift off easily. The scientist inside him noted that the wood was in a good state of preservation because of the dry conditions.

He lifted one small plank away with tender care. Then another. Then he leaned over to look inside the void and he could sense Harriet behind him, smell the perfume she always wore.

'What is it?' she whispered. He felt her warm breath on his ear.

As he removed the final plank he could see that this was no new-born child, disposed of without ceremony to avoid disgrace. This was a thing with waxy skin bristling with rusty pins.

It had a grinning face ... and teeth. It took Neil a few

seconds to realise that these weren't real but chips of painted wood. There was evil in the thing's smile . . . even Neil with his scientist's scepticism could see that. The very sight of it lying there in the rough wood coffin made his flesh crawl. It wore a long black gown, roughly made, and its hands resembled the talons of a bird. The eyes were gouged out hollows and one eye was pierced by a pin, protruding from that dreadful waxen face like an arrow. The other pins had been stuck in the body, in the belly, the breasts and between the legs. As Neil gazed at it he could almost feel the hatred that had brought about its creation.

'God, it's horrible.' Harriet stepped forward and reached down to touch it, something Neil hadn't cared to do.

'Be careful of the pins.'

She withdrew her hand quickly as though she'd been stung. 'I made one at school once,' she whispered.

'What?'

'I made a doll out of candle wax and I stuck pins in it. It was supposed to be a girl who was giving me a hard time. I even got hold of some hair from her comb and stuck it on the doll's head.'

Neil looked round. 'Did it work?'

'She broke her leg so I'd say that was a result.' There was a hint of satisfaction in her voice. 'What shall we do with it?'

'I'll need to show it to an expert.'

He walked away from the table and stood by the trapdoor looking down into the cellar. The builders had been working down there, digging out the section nearest the steps and he could now count thirteen stone steps leading down to the newly uncovered flagstone floor. The space was about seven feet deep now but there was little more he could do until more earth had been dug out. He wanted to find out how big the cellar was . . . and discover what was down there.

'I want to find out when this basement was filled in,' he said, suddenly businesslike. The sight of that doll had shaken him but he was trying his best to hide it.

'You think there's a connection with that thing behind the panelling?'

'Well if there was witchcraft going on here maybe something happened in the cellar. Maybe it was connected to Alison Hadness and her family filled it in after she was hanged.'

'So that doll thing might have belonged to her?'

'It's unlikely there was more than one witch in the house.'

'I don't know. What about the Pendle witches up in Lancashire? A lot of them were related, weren't they?'

Neil didn't really feel like speculating until he had more information. 'Have you got a clean box I can put that thing in? I'll take it to Exeter and show it to someone at the museum.'

Harriet left the room and once Neil was alone with the doll in the coffin he experienced a feeling he'd heard described by more imaginative souls as 'someone walking over your grave'. It seemed to be smirking at him as if it knew some evil secret, and he looked away, avoiding its mocking gaze.

He heard Harriet returning with a cardboard box. He couldn't help fancying her and he suspected that the feeling was reciprocated. But his survival instinct, honed over the years, told him that acting on that primitive physical attraction would be a grave mistake. Besides, he'd seen how she flirted with the builders. She was probably the sort of woman who liked to have power over men. A tease.

She placed the box on the floor and began to rummage inside, spilling snowy polystyrene packing beads on the floorboards.

Neil watched as she thrust her hand inside the box, feeling around amongst the soft white spheres. Then she suddenly frowned, as if she'd made an unpleasant discovery.

'I thought it was empty,' she said. 'Evan must have left this inside by mistake.'

She brought her hand out slowly and he saw that she was holding something that glinted in the light from the window, withdrawing it from the box and holding it aloft like the Lady of the Lake wielding Excalibur. It was a knife, shining and sharp. And the blade looked lethal.

Although his parents and sister were all members of the medical profession, Wesley had always found the business of postmortems unsettling. Colin Bowman's habit of providing appetising refreshments afterwards and a pleasant social chat usually made the situation bearable. But today Colin wasn't there and, from the impatient look on her face, Jane Partridge wasn't going to make allowances for a squeamish detective inspector who really should have developed a harder shell by this stage in his career.

He was glad that Morbay Hospital's white-tiled mortuary was state of the art, so he and Gerry could stand behind a glass partition with speakers and microphones instead of at the heart of the action near the smells and sounds of death.

For a while Jane Partridge stood staring at the woman on

the table. Then she began to work, swiftly and efficiently with the minimum of chat, unlike Colin who always kept up a running commentary of his observations. Wesley found he missed it.

She examined the dead woman's abdomen and as she delved into the single wound, measuring its depth and angle before studying the edges with a magnifying glass, she began to speak. 'I'm sticking to my initial conclusion that the weapon was a long flat blade, sharpened on both edges so not a carving knife. Possibly something like a hunting knife. Or even a short sword. The wound is clean and deep so the blade was quite sharp. But even so it would have taken her a couple of minutes to die.'

Wesley found her words chilling. The woman must have been aware that she was dying there in that cold, damp field, away from all possibility of help with only her murderer for company. She must have lain there knowing that the life was seeping out of her.

'Anything else you can tell us?' Gerry asked.

'Only to be patient,' she said sharply.

Gerry bowed his head like a scolded schoolboy and she carried on working in silence, cutting into the body, withdrawing and weighing the internal organs. The stomach contents were emptied into a bowl and Wesley saw her examine them, sniffing then wrinkling her nose.

'She'd eaten a hearty meal an hour or two before death. This might not be entirely accurate but I think she had steak and all the trimmings. Then some kind of sponge pudding . . . sticky toffee pudding perhaps.' Wesley saw her lips turn upwards in a grim smile. 'My favourite. I'll get the stomach contents analysed, of course, but it's my guess she ate in some pub or restaurant. This isn't the kind of food you usually bother preparing for a solitary lunch, is it? And I know all about solitary lunches, believe me.'

Wesley noticed that a shadow of sadness passed across her face, there for a second then gone and replaced by her usual severe mask. Eventually she finished her work and as her assistant began to sew up the incisions she'd made in the dead flesh, Wesley's phone rang. As he answered it he could see Jane scowling at him.

It was Paul Johnson. And he sounded excited. 'Sir, the lab's just been on. That handbag we sent over ... they've found something trapped in the lining. It's a business card. Someone called Dan Sericold – describes himself as a free-lance press photographer. There's a phone number.'

He glanced at Gerry who was watching him expectantly. 'Can you read it out?' he asked, taking his notebook from his jacket pocket. With no luck so far from Missing Persons and the team's round of the local hotels, he'd begun to despair of identifying the dead woman quickly. But Dan Sericold might be the answer to his prayers.

Paul recited the number and as soon as Wesley had made a note of it, he ended the call, relayed the news to Gerry and keyed in Sericold's number, switching on the speaker-phone so Gerry could hear. After a few moments he heard a voice on the other end of the line. A growling male voice, the sort that told of a lifetime's dedication to cigarettes and whisky.

'This is Detective Inspector Wesley Peterson, Devon and Cornwall police. Is that Dan Sericold?'

There was a long silence before the man replied. 'Yeah. What can I do for you, Inspector?' Sericold sounded cautious, but, in Wesley's experience, an encounter with a police officer affected a lot of people that way.

Wesley explained. As the man was a press photographer, there was probably no need to dress it up in tactful words. On the other hand, he didn't want to say too much and give Dan Sericold a premature scoop.

'This is in connection with a murder enquiry. The victim had your business card on her when she died.'

Another silence, shocked this time. 'I must have given my card to hundreds of people in my time and I won't remember most of them. What did this victim look like?'

Wesley gave a description of the dead woman, half expecting to draw a blank. But when he heard a note of recognition in Sericold's voice he knew he was in luck.

'It could be Boo Flecker. She called last week and said she was going to Devon to try and get something on some celebrity taking part in one of those reality TV shows. She'd got a sniff of a scandal and she wanted to arrange an interview . . . an exclusive. She specialises – specialised – in investigative stuff.'

The news that the dead woman was a journalist surprised Wesley. She had looked small, vulnerable and fragile, not really his idea of an investigative reporter. But he supposed they came in all shapes and sizes and he, of all people, knew the perils of believing in stereotypes.

'She was freelance but we often worked together. She was good, always on the lookout for a new angle.' His voice sounded a little unsteady now, as if the full horror of Wesley's news had begun to dawn.

'Did she tell you the name of the celebrity?'

'Only that he was down to the last two in this show, whatever it was. Something to do with farming, I think. I don't watch things like that myself,' he added with a hint of distain.

Wesley felt a glow of satisfaction. Maybe this would be easier than he'd imagined.

'Do you know where we can find her next of kin? We need a proper identification.'

'No idea. Sorry. But I think she came from Yorkshire, judging by her accent. It wasn't something we ever discussed.'

'Was she married?'

'No. And before you ask, I don't know if there's a boyfriend on the scene just now … although she was no nun. Boo was a woman with a healthy appetite.' Something in Sericold's voice suggested that he might once have been on the receiving end of Ms Flecker's carnal largesse.

'Is Boo Flecker her real name?'

'As far as I know. I asked her once what Boo was short for and she said it was Boudicca. Apparently her father was some kind of historian.'

'Can you remember anything else about her or the story she was working on down here?' he said. 'Anything at all.' Through the glass screen he could see the mortuary assistant wheeling the body away to lie in refrigerated peace until someone came to claim her.

Sericold didn't answer for a few moments, as though he was trying to dredge something from the depths of his memory. 'Actually she did leave a message on my voicemail a couple of days ago but it was a bit vague. I was to stand by. She might need me to get down there. She said she thought she could be onto something new.'

'About the celebrity?'

'That's what I assumed. She said she'd let me know when she knew for definite. I've been waiting for her to get in touch but she hasn't. That's all I can tell you, I'm afraid.'

'Have you got an address for her?'

He heard a shuffling sound, as if Sericold was looking through a diary or address book. After a while he recited an address in Southwark and when Wesley asked him whether Boo had lived alone, he said he didn't know.

'Have you got a photo of Boo Flecker by any chance?' he asked, hoping the answer would be yes. The sooner they had a positive ID, the better.

'I can arrange to e-mail you the photo she uses for her column. Would that be all right?'

'That'd be fantastic.'

Once Wesley had recited his e-mail address he ended the call. And a few minutes later the image came through on his iPhone.

There was no doubt about it now. The dead woman was Boo Flecker, daughter of the historian who'd named her after the vengeful queen of the Iceni. And that meant they had to find out exactly what she was up to in Devon as soon as possible.

It was all too likely that Boo Flecker's investigation had been about to uncover a secret that somebody was determined to keep hidden. And men had killed for less.

Chapter 6

Written by Alison Hadness, September 11th 1643

I hear that the army is led by Prince Maurice who is nephew to the King himself. I have heard say that his brother, Prince Rupert is most handsome but I have heard little of Maurice. I wonder if I shall see him.

They are camped at Hilton Farm, having claimed the place for their headquarters. It is not far from Mercy Hall and I fear they may come at night, bent on conquest of our town. William says I am foolish to have such fears as his musket is ever beside him and he will fight to the death to defend our household.

The weather is foul, all rain, wind and mist. It is to be hoped the King's soldiers will yield to this sign of God's displeasure.

Yesterday I went into the town with my maidservant, Dorcas. The people there no longer smile, rather their faces are stern and determined, like the puritans many of them are.

It is said that soon there will be scant food in the market if the farmers cannot bring it from the countryside around. Each road into the

town is guarded by Prince Maurice's men and the King's ships block-
ade the harbour. I fear what will become of us.

My husband came to my bed again last night. He complains that
there is still no sign that I am with child. It may be that Elizabeth has
put a curse upon me but William will hear no bad word against her.

Alexander Gulliver wished his mother hadn't insisted on
him taking his stepfather's name when she married. When
they'd studied Jonathan Swift at school he had been the
butt of his classmates' brand of cutting wit. Going on your
travels, Gulliver? Where are you off to now ... Lilliput?
Bloody hilarious.

His mother had married Shane four years ago and, after
almost three years in London, Shane had made the unilat-
eral decision to move to the Devon countryside. Gwen had
resisted strongly but Shane insisted that he was finding it
increasingly hard to write in the chaos and noise of the
metropolis, so he presented his wife with a fait accompli.
He'd found the perfect house, and the payment he received
when his first book was made into a major Hollywood
film – the action transferred from the East End of London
to a trailer park in Alabama – would fund the move.

Alex, however, saw nothing perfect about the house
Shane had chosen. For a start it was in the middle of
nowhere, stuck on the very edge of a very dead village
halfway between Tradmouth and Dukesbridge with a
twice-daily apology for a bus service. Shane was a pain in
the neck with his insistence on silence in the house when he
was working and his intermittent draconian discipline. And
he never let anyone forget what a miserable upbringing
he'd had. He'd made a fortune from it with those dreary
books of his. Not that Alex had ever read one. He was

forced to live with the man. He didn't want him inside his head too.

He'd asked his friend Ben's dad to drop him off at the end of the lane because he wanted to see what was happening at Jessop's Farm. Things had started to look up when the TV people arrived and Jackie Piper's nubile female fans had begun wandering through the Rectory garden to avoid the security that had been put on the farm gate while the singer was in residence. Alex had summoned the courage to talk to a couple of the girls; he'd even asked one out for a drink, although he knew no pub in the vicinity would be likely to serve him. But once again Shane had put paid to his fun by calling the bloody police. Sometimes he wanted to kill the man. He'd become a Goth to show Shane that he was different, that he didn't belong in his world. But Shane had said nothing. He probably didn't even care.

At least the murder next door had livened things up a bit. He'd heard the victim was a young woman and he wondered if it was the one he'd seen a couple of days ago. He remembered her because she'd looked so out of place with her smart red coat and her shiny boots. At the time he assumed she was something to do with the TV people but now it seemed she'd had a different agenda. Perhaps he should have told the police about her. At least it would be something to talk about at school. It wasn't everyone who became involved in a murder enquiry.

As soon as he'd mumbled goodbye to Ben's dad, he dawdled down the lane, aiming occasional kicks at the tufts of grass that grew down the centre of the rough tarmac, the bit untouched by the tyres of passing cars and farm vehicles. He kept his eyes on the ground. There was no point looking around because all you could see here were high hedges growing like walls either side of the road. Alex couldn't imagine why people from cities raved about the countryside. Maybe it was because they didn't have to live there and they didn't know how boring it was. A bit like death.

When a police car roared past he flattened himself against the hedge and the twisted branches grabbed at his coat. He brushed them off and carried on walking, his footsteps slowing as he neared the Rectory gate.

If he let himself in quietly he could get his metal detector from his room without his mum and Shane knowing. He'd do a bit of detecting in one of the fields on the other side of the lane before the light went, anything rather than go home and face Shane's unpredictable temper. And he'd heard of people finding hoards worth millions so there was the chance that he might find some treasure that would earn him a fortune so he could get a place of his own. With Shane around, that couldn't come a moment too soon.

He opened the front door and crept upstairs on tiptoe to dump his school bag in his bedroom and retrieve his metal detector, along with the small trowel he'd pinched from the garden shed. He carried them downstairs and shut the front door carefully behind him. Once outside he ran down the drive and when he glanced back, he half expected to see an angry face watching him from the window. But it seemed his arrival and swift departure had gone unnoticed so he carried on past the gate and walked towards Jessop's Farm.

He didn't know the farmer – his mum and Shane had never had anything to do with him – but he'd seen him on his tractor with his sheepdog sitting up beside him, a brown and white border collie with keen eyes and an intelligent face. Alex would have loved a dog of his own, a creature to keep him company and greet him with a wagging tail and an unconditional love he felt he'd never known. But Shane hated animals.

He was almost at the farm gate now and he could see a bored-looking constable standing there on guard. He ignored him and hurried on, taking a left turn down a narrow lane. When he'd gone a few yards he saw a pair of gateposts on his left, one leaning at a precarious angle. Beyond the gateway was a dark tunnel of bushes and trees, bending over the drive, blocking out the light as if it was a place of permanent night. Alex knew this was the witch's house. They'd been talking about it at school. People had gone in there and never come out.

He stood for a few moments, staring in horrified fascination. But he knew this wasn't somewhere you hung about if you were alone.

He went a little further down the lane and when he spotted a metal farm gate to his right he stopped and leaned on it, gazing into the field beyond. This was somewhere he hadn't detected before; virgin territory potentially full of precious things: coins, golden torques and Viking silver hoards. There were grazing cows in there, black and white and vaguely menacing. When he climbed onto the first rung of the gate the cows continued chewing like a gang of bored youngsters hanging around the village bus shelter. Alex knew how they felt.

He lowered the detector down carefully onto the grass on the field side of the gate before clambering over, keeping a wary eye on the cows who seemed to be edging nearer ... or maybe that was his imagination. He switched on the machine and for a while he was disappointed when the low whine didn't change pitch as he swept it over the ground. But in the detecting game patience was everything.

There was a patch of bare soil to the right of the gate, which looked as if it had been disturbed by something, wild animals maybe. Alex's idle curiosity got the better of him and when he passed the detector over the area, it began to scream. He crouched down to investigate with his trowel and when he'd dug down a couple of inches, he saw a glint of shiny metal so he carried on, heart beating, hands trembling with anticipation.

When he'd finished digging he pulled the object out and placed it on the grass. It was a knife, sharp and lethal. And the smooth surface of the blade was crusted with something that looked like rust.

The little wooden coffin lay in a cardboard box cushioned with polystyrene packing beads supplied by Harriet Mumford. She had a lot of packaging around the house, she said – something to do with Evan's import business. Neil hadn't taken that sinister wax doll from its resting place. Instead he had replaced the top carefully and left it lying in situ like a tiny corpse. He thought it best if the experts who were used to handling old and fragile artefacts, dealt with it. Besides, he didn't really fancy touching the hideous thing.

He'd put the box on the back seat of the Mini and, even though he'd always prided himself on rejecting superstition of any kind, knowing it was there made him uncomfortable.

Making a great effort to concentrate on the road, he tried not to think about his strange back-seat passenger. Instead he went through his plans in his head. He'd take the doll to Exeter for conservation and then visit a couple of colleagues at the University who were reputed to know about such things.

He had just reached the difficult right turn onto the Neston road by the petrol station when he put his foot on the brake pedal, ready to bring the car to a halt. But nothing happened. He pumped the brake again, jamming his foot to the floor, but the car kept on going, out of control. Foot pumping. Adrenaline pumping. Time suspended.

Then came a bang like deafening thunder and the impact jolted his body sideways. For a few seconds he sat, numb with shock, before daring to look round. Another car, a small grey hatchback, had collided with him, crumpling the Mini's front end into an unrecognisable tangle.

He felt an agonising pain in his ribs and when he looked down he saw he was bleeding and that his legs were trapped beneath the steering wheel. If he hadn't been wearing a seat belt he knew he would have been dead.

The woman driving the hatchback emerged slowly from the driver's seat. He could see that her car had sustained minimal damage, just a broken headlight and a mildly crumpled bonnet. But the Mini – his faithful Mini that had served him so well over the years – was a write-off.

The woman was opening his door. She was elderly with a hairdresser-fresh grey coiffeur and the tears trickling down her face made dark tracks in her thick foundation. 'Are you all right?'

He didn't reply because he didn't know the answer.

'You just shot out in front of me. I couldn't stop in time,' she said, full of breathless apology.

He was confused, unsure what to do, what to say. The

woman looked as stunned as he felt. Thank God it wasn't some bloke full of testosterone and road rage.

'I think my brakes failed,' he gasped.

'Keep still. Don't move. I'm calling an ambulance.' She took a tiny mobile phone from her shiny leather handbag and punched out 999. Neil could see her hands were shaking.

He put his hand down to his abdomen and felt round tentatively. He was hurting like hell now and when he lifted his hand away he saw that it was covered in blood. As he listened to the woman making the urgent call he felt light-headed, as if he'd had too much to drink, and he tried very hard to focus on his surroundings because he knew that if he didn't stay conscious, he'd be finished.

He turned his head painfully and caught sight of a small pale figure lying next to the gear stick, grinning up at him, malevolent and triumphant.

Then he lost his fight and felt himself drifting into oblivion.

As soon as he'd left Morbay Hospital, Wesley called a former colleague at the Met. He needed somebody to visit Boo Flecker's address in Southwark. Then her next of kin had to be found. Dan Sericold said he was coming down to Devon and would get in touch as soon as he arrived. Everything was in hand but Wesley felt impatient for a result. He wanted to know more about Boo and what, if anything, she had discovered while she'd been in Devon.

Jane Partridge hadn't hazarded any opinion about the killer's nature or state of mind. Unlike Colin Bowman who was always happy to share his theories, she'd only given them the bare facts so it had been up to Gerry and Wesley to speculate, using each other as a sounding board for each possibility, wild or mundane.

They were making for the car park when Wesley's phone rang and, for once, it was good news. Zac James had just been picked up speeding on the M4, heading for London. He was being brought back to Tradmouth and would be at the police station by six. Another late night. Another take-away in the office.

'Chinese, Indian or fish and chips?' Gerry asked, as if he'd read Wesley's mind.

'We had Chinese last night,' he replied absentmindedly, just as his phone began to ring again.

After a brief conversation, he ended the call. Gerry had begun to walk ahead and Wesley quickened his pace to catch up.

'That was Traffic. There's been a crash on the Neston road. It's Neil ...'

Gerry's features rearranged themselves into a worried frown. 'Is he OK?'

'They've taken him to Tradmouth Hospital and he's asking for me.' He looked at his watch.

'If you want to go ...'

Wesley hesitated. 'He's got no family nearby so ... I'd ask Pam to go but she'll have the kids.'

'You go, Wes. But don't be too long. Zac James'll be in Tradmouth in an hour or two.'

Wesley felt dazed as he drove back to Tradmouth with Gerry sitting silently beside him in the passenger seat. He steered automatically down the familiar roads, hardly aware of his surroundings, the news about Neil dominating his thoughts. He dropped Gerry off at the police station and continued on to the hospital, dreading what he might find. Neil had been a constant in his life since his student days. Always the same, mildly unworldly and slightly anarchic with an almost religious dedication to the world of archaeology. Friends like Neil seem indestructible. But fate can play unpleasant tricks.

Dark possibilities hurtled through his mind as he reached the hospital entrance. What if Neil was seriously injured? What if he was paralysed? What if he didn't make it? These vague feelings of dread caused an almost physical pain which was hard to shake off.

He showed his warrant card to the woman on the reception desk and asked where Neil was being treated. If he hadn't had his ID he knew that getting information, let alone access to the patient, would have been a problem, but as it was he soon found himself standing by the nurses' station on the ward, talking to a staff nurse. She told him that Neil had been drifting in and out of consciousness but in his lucid moments he'd been asking for Wesley. He seemed anxious, she said. And she got the impression he had something important to say.

The way the nurse spoke about Neil, in that cautious way that professionals have when they're trying not to alarm worried friends or relatives, only fuelled Wesley's fears. He wondered whether to call Pam but he didn't want to alarm her before he knew the true situation.

Eventually the nurse gave him permission to enter the side ward where Neil was lying, sprouting drips and monitors. A machine was bleeping in the corner and Neil lay quite still on the narrow bed with his eyes closed and his long hair spread out on the crisp white pillow like a halo. For a brief, horrible moment Wesley thought his friend was dead. Until he realised the monitors were bleeping just as they should be.

'Don't tire him out,' the nurse ordered. 'The doctor'll be here to see him in a minute. He wants to do more tests. And we might have to operate.'

At the sound of her voice, Neil's eyes flickered open and Wesley moved forward into his line of sight. He suddenly felt nervous and unsure which words to choose that wouldn't sound like a police interrogation. If Neil had been involved in a road traffic accident, the questions would come all too soon.

'What happened, mate? What have you been up to?' Wesley was finding it difficult to sound cheerful. But he felt he had to lift Neil's spirits somehow and strengthen his will to recover.

'I couldn't stop. The other driver was OK but I came off worst. Or rather the Mini did.' He took a deep breath and winced with pain.

'What does the doctor say?'

'They've been poking and prodding but they won't tell my anything. But every breath I take hurts like hell.'

Wesley could see the fear in his friend's eyes; the fear of death … or of a life spent dependent on others; of a life without getting his hands dirty delving into the past. 'Can you do something for me?'

'What's that?'

'There's something in the car,' he said in an urgent, breathless whisper.

'What?'

'A coffin.'

'A coffin?' Neil had always been unpredictable but this was something new.

'A little one with a wax doll inside. It's a horrible thing stuck with pins. I was taking it to Exeter to be examined.

When you've got time can you pick it up for me ... make sure it's safe?'

Wesley nodded. 'OK. I'll find out where they've taken the car and rescue it.'

'Odd, isn't it?'

'What?'

'That the crash happened when it did.' He winced with pain. 'I tried to stop at the junction but I just kept on going. I think my brakes failed. But why then? Why did it happen when I had that thing with me. I think it might have belonged to a witch.'

This was something Wesley had never encountered before. A superstitious Neil imagining curses and evil dolls. 'A few days ago you would have said all this business about wax dolls and witches was a load of nonsense,' he said lightly.

Neil turned his head away. 'Ignore me. It must be the drugs they keep pumping into me.'

This sounded more like the old Neil. Wesley touched the motionless hand lying on the bedspread. 'I'll sort everything out.'

The nurse entered the room and looked at Wesley mean-ingfully. It was time to go. 'I'd better be off. Do you want me to tell anyone what's happened?'

'Better let my folks know. My mobile's in my jacket. And the Unit. Dave'll have to stand in for me at the Princes Bower dig. And the Mumfords should be told. I was super-vising their builders to make sure they didn't destroy anything important. That's where the coffin and the doll came from. Tell Dave he'll have to take over there too, will you?'

Wesley found Neil's jacket hanging in a wardrobe near

the window and took the phone from the pocket. 'Pam and I'll see to it between us.'

'And the Mini . . . ?'

'No problem.'

He felt reluctant to leave but there were things to do. And the strange cargo to retrieve from the wreckage of the car.

Alex wasn't quite sure why he'd wrapped the knife in a sheet of lined A4 paper he'd found in his pocket and taken it home. Perhaps it was a desire to have a secret that could shock the world. His own private bombshell.

He took it up to his room hidden under his coat and placed it on the chest of drawers. The woman in the red coat had been murdered. And he knew the woman who lived on the other side of Jessop's Farm was a witch who'd killed some girls. His mum and Shane had never mentioned it in his hearing but somebody at school had said she'd just got out of prison. He'd hardly imagined anything so exciting could happen in that godforsaken place.

The knife wasn't that big, only nine inches or so, with a plain silver handle and a sharp, tapering blade. It lay on the unfolded paper and the crusted red-black substance on the blade had a smell about it that wasn't nice – soil and something else. Something metallic and meaty like he'd smelled once in a butcher's shop. Blood. Probably the blood of the woman in the red coat.

Suddenly he didn't want it there in his room any more. It was out of place in his sanctuary plastered with posters of his favourite bands and if he kept it and someone found it, it would look bad. It might even make him look guilty. He had to get rid of it.

After wrapping it in clean paper torn from the pad on his desk, he packed it up in his rucksack and crept downstairs just as his mother was emerging from the room she referred to as the drawing room – the room his friends called the lounge or living room.

'Where are you going?' She was using that voice again ... casual yet forced, as if it didn't matter when it obviously did.

'Out.'

'Haven't you got homework?' Her voice had become heavier, more authoritative.

'I'll do it when I get back.'

Before she could object he was out of the front door, heading down the gravel drive. Once in the lane, he made for Jessop's Farm. The policeman was still there at the gate. This was his chance to look good. To look innocent.

The policeman was pacing up and down, looking as if he was playing a private game of I Spy. When he saw Alex approaching he stood to attention, suddenly alert. There was no backing out now.

'Er ... I've found something,' Alex said.

'What's that, son?' The policeman asked, positively delighted that someone had come to relieve his tedium.

Alex flinched at the use of the word. He wasn't the man's son. His real father was the only man who had the right to call him that and he didn't even know what he looked like. According to his mother, he'd disappeared abroad when he was just a baby. He was now in some unspecified foreign country while Shane replaced him in his mother's bed like some incubus, exerting a malevolent power over her.

He took the package from his rucksack and handed it to

the policeman who held it very carefully, as though it was some precious and delicate treasure.

'I was out with my metal detector and I found it in a field over there on the other side of the lane.' He waved his arm in the vague direction of the field. 'I thought I'd better hand it in in case ...'

As the paper fell open, the policeman swore. And then he began to talk on his radio. Result.

Wesley called Pam to tell her about Neil's accident. Then he made the other call to Dave who promised to assume the mantle of Site Director at Princes Bower until Neil recovered. Dave sounded shocked and worried, as though he wasn't looking forward to the unexpected opportunity to emerge from Neil's shadow.

It turned out that Neil's wrecked car had been taken to the police garage at Neston, and Wesley called to tell them he'd be down at some point to pick up an archaeological artefact that had been left inside. However, he was busy with a murder enquiry so he wasn't sure when it'd be. The officer he spoke to didn't quibble. He told him the car hadn't yet been touched and he was welcome to come and pick up the artefact any time. He pronounced the word 'artefact' as though it was something slightly rude.

After the calls were made Wesley sat at his desk, head in hands, and when Gerry came up behind him and placed his hand on his shoulder he jumped.

'What's the latest on Neil?'

'They're doing tests and they might have to operate, but he's conscious.' Wesley didn't want to voice his fears. Until he knew for sure, he felt he ought to keep up a show of optimism. 'He thinks his brakes failed.'

'Well that car of his is a relic in itself. I always thought he must have dug it up at one of his excavations.'

Wesley knew Gerry was right. Neil's distinctive yellow Mini was old. A friendly garage in Exeter had serviced it annually and coaxed it through its MOT but things can deteriorate fast between one check and the next.

His thoughts were interrupted by Trish Walton who was hurrying towards him. She held a piece of paper in her hand and the look of triumph on her face told him she had important news.

'Durham police have visited Gabby Soames's family but none of them have been near Devon in years. It's been checked out.' Her eyes shone, as if she was saving the best till last. 'I've also had a call from Jessop's Farm. A young lad's handed in a knife he found in a nearby field. Looks like it could be the murder weapon.'

Wesley saw Gerry roll his eyes. 'Don't know what our search team do with themselves all day. Dozy lot. We'd better get over there and have a word with this lad. The sooner we get that incident room at the village hall up and running the better.'

He watched Gerry grab his anorak from the coat stand – a new model which, owing to Joyce's benign influence, was a vast improvement on the disreputable garment he used to wear.

'Don't forget Zac James is due here any moment,' said Wesley as Gerry made for the door.

'The wait'll do him good,' was Gerry's reply. Wesley was inclined to agree with him. Zac James had kept them waiting and they were only returning the favour. And a wait in the Spartan interview room would focus his mind wonderfully.

The traffic was heavy on the main A road out of Tradmouth, but as they turned off onto the coast road they almost had it to themselves. They drove on until they saw the sign informing them that West Fretham welcomed careful drivers. Gerry was right about the incident room. It would save time if they were nearer the heart of things, able to pick up on local knowledge. They needed gossip about Lilith Benley's return. And whispers about what Boo Flecker had been up to.

A young uniformed constable greeted them at Jessop's Farm, eager as a border collie in a field full of rebellious sheep. He proudly showed them the knife which had been placed in an evidence bag and neatly labelled. It certainly matched Jane Partridge's description of the murder weapon and, after placing it carefully on the back seat of the car, Wesley drove the short distance to the Rectory. As he passed through the open wrought-iron gate into the drive he saw Gerry twist round in his seat to look at the knife and wrinkle his nose in disgust.

Gwen Gulliver answered the door. Her aloof manner had vanished and she stood aside to let them in, head bowed. 'Alex told me what he found. He's a bit shaken.'

'We'll be gentle with him,' said Gerry.

Gwen's eyes widened as though she didn't believe a word, but she led them through to the kitchen. Alex was sitting at the long pine table in the centre of the room, a half-empty dish of pasta in front of him. He had jet-black hair and clothes to match and his corpse-pale skin was pierced by several pieces of interesting metalware. They'd already learned from Shane Gulliver that Alex was a Goth. But even though Goths weren't known for their cheerful, outgoing natures, they were, by and large, a harmless bunch and often deceptively amiable. Alex gave them a wary look and carried on shovelling food into his mouth. His discovery hadn't ruined his appetite.

'After you found the knife how long did it take you to show it to the constable next door?' Gerry asked.

Alex's mouth was full so Gwen answered for him. 'He told me he found it with his metal detector and took it up to his room for half an hour or so but as soon as he realised what it was he took it next door to the farm and handed it in. Isn't that right, Alex?'

Alex nodded.

'I suppose you'll have to take Alex's fingerprints . . .'

'If he touched it. Just for elimination,' said Gerry. 'And yours and your husband's if you handled it.'

Gwen shook her head. 'I didn't touch it. I never even saw it and neither did Shane.'

Alex's dish was almost empty and he was studiously retrieving the last morsel. He didn't look particularly upset . . . not like his mother who was wringing her hands as if all the evils of the world had been released into her tasteful home.

'We'd like to ask you a few questions, Alex,' Wesley said gently. 'Nothing to worry about. Can you tell us exactly what happened?'

The boy's mother sat down beside him and placed a protective hand on his shoulder. But Alex didn't look as though he was in need of maternal comfort. On the contrary, Wesley suspected he was enjoying the drama of the situation. The boy's black T-shirt bore the grey outline of a pentagram behind a superimposed skull. Death and the occult.

'I just found it,' the boy said.

'Where?'

'Just past Jessop's Farm in a field on the other side of the lane. I climbed over the gate with my metal detector. There were cows in the field but cows don't bother me,' he added with casual bravado. 'I saw a patch of soil that looked as though it had been disturbed so I swept the machine over it and it gave a strong signal – really loud. I started to dig and there it was an inch or so down.'

'Why did you bring it home?' Wesley asked.

'I collect things. I thought it might be old.'

'What made you take it to the police?'

Alex glanced at his mother. 'When I had a proper look at it I realised it wasn't rust on the blade. I thought it might be blood and I'd heard about the murder next door so I ...'

'You did the right thing.' Wesley smiled to reassure him, although what he saw on the boy's face wasn't apprehension, it was disappointment. Perhaps he'd been hoping for a valuable addition to his collection of treasures and murder had got in the way.

'What else have you found with your metal detector? I studied archaeology at university so I'm interested in that sort of thing.'

Alex looked at him curiously, as though he didn't quite believe that this policeman could be telling the truth. 'I've found coins ... and a funny bottle with nails inside.'

'Can I see them?'

Alex hesitated for a moment before standing up. 'They're in my room. You can come up if you like.'

Gwen Gulliver looked as though she was about to object but Wesley gave her a hopeful smile. 'Is that OK, Mrs Gulliver?'

'Inspector Peterson loves anything old. He'd turn our

police station into a museum if he had his way,' Gerry said with an avuncular twinkle in his eye.

Gwen gave her consent. In view of the detectives' joint charm offensive it would have seemed churlish to object.

Wesley followed Alex upstairs and, once in his room, the boy opened a large built-in cupboard to the side of a Victorian cast-iron fireplace. He took out a pair of large cardboard boxes and placed them on the desk beneath the window, pushing his laptop to one side to make room.

He drew the items out one by one and placed them on the desk. Wesley made a show of examining them. A spur, probably from the Civil War period; a variety of coins, mostly Victorian but a couple from the eighteenth century and the earliest from the time of the first Queen Elizabeth; an assortment of parts from ancient farming equipment and a rather pretty gold ring, probably the treasure of the collection. Then he pulled something else from the box – a bottle made of cloudy green glass. He shook it and it rattled.

'It's got nails inside,' Alex said. 'I couldn't get them out because there's a stopper.'

Wesley examined it. 'It's a witch bottle,' he said. 'People used to hide them in buildings as protection against witches.'

'It was buried near a hedge in a field on the other side of the lane,' he said as though he suspected Wesley didn't know what he was talking about.

'They were sometimes placed on boundaries to protect farmers' animals and crops from the evil eye. It's an interesting find. Any ambitions to be an archaeologist?'

He could sense Alex relaxing. Perhaps it was his mother's absence. Or perhaps it was the fact that somebody in authority was treating him as an adult.

'If you did archaeology at Uni, why are you a policeman?'

'Long story.' Wesley smiled. 'My grandfather was a Chief Superintendent of police in Trinidad and they do say that inside every archaeologist there's a detective trying to get out. Can you show me exactly where you found the knife?'

'Sure.' The boy put his collection of treasures away carefully, picking up the witch bottle with exaggerated care.

'It must be exciting to have all this going on next door. First the TV people and now the police.'

'Mum and Shane freaked out when Jackie Piper's fans started coming into our garden but it was cool. This place is usually like the morgue so ... I was sorry when he got voted off. Some of the girls at school are crazy about him and a few of them came down here.'

'Was it you who told them they could get through to the farm from your garden?'

Alex grinned. 'Might have been.'

'Do you watch *Celebrity Farm*?'

'Yeah.'

'Zac James is still in it.'

'He was before my time,' he said solemnly. 'And I can't stand that wanker of a comedian. He gives me the creeps'

'I get the impression you don't like Shane much either.'

'He's a dickhead. A pain in the arse.'

'Why's that?'

Alex was busy returning the boxes to the cupboard and it was a few moments before he answered. 'He's a fraud. A loser.' He turned and looked directly at Wesley. 'I saw her, you know. That woman in the red coat. She was hanging around. Watching.'

'Watching where?'

Alex hesitated, almost as though he was afraid that he'd already said too much. 'In the lane near the farm.'

'Why didn't you tell us this before?'

'I was out when the police came so I haven't had a chance.' He paused, as though he was making a decision. 'Shane saw her too. He was giving me a lift home from school a couple of days ago and she was hanging round. He was having a go at me but as soon as he saw her he shut up. Didn't say anything till we got in.'

'Did you ask him if he knew her?'

'You don't ask Shane questions. And if you do, he won't answer them. But he might if *you* ask him. You can't play games with the cops,' he added sagely. And the smug expression on his face made Wesley wonder whether this particular story had been made up or exaggerated to cause trouble for his stepfather.

Alex led him downstairs and they went outside, leaving the front door on the latch. The light was fading now but Wesley had a torch in his pocket. They walked together out onto the lane past Jessop's Farm to the turning that would take them to Devil's Tree Cottage. There he saw a metal farm gate filling a gap in the hedgerow. Alex was about to climb it but Wesley stopped him. 'Better not touch it. There might be prints. Just point out where you found the knife.'

Alex obliged, looking pleased with himself. Wesley flashed his torch at the spot before making a call to Forensic to get someone over to examine the scene, although he wasn't holding out much hope. It had rained a lot since Boo Flecker's murder and the gate had probably been well used by farm workers, smudging any prints the killer may have left.

They returned to the Rectory in amicable silence and,

once inside, Wesley made for the kitchen, Alex trailing beside him like his new best friend.

Gerry was still sitting at the kitchen table draining a brightly coloured mug, a satisfied look on his face. Gwen was hovering nervously by the large Belfast sink. She asked Wesley if he would like a drink but he declined.

'Mrs Gulliver, is your husband home? I'd like a word with him.'

'He's had to go to London again. He's got a meeting with some TV people who are thinking of dramatising one of his books and he won't be back till late tomorrow.' The words were casual but Wesley sensed a tension behind them.

'Perhaps you could ask him to give me a call.' Wesley handed over his card and Gwen took it, a doubtful look on her face, as though she knew her husband would be reluctant to co-operate.

Wesley smiled at Alex. 'Thanks, Alex, you've been a great help. And if you ever want any advice about archaeology, your mum's got my number.'

When Alex gave him a coy nod, Gerry stood up. It was time to go.

Gwen saw them off the premises like a good hostess. Or maybe, Wesley thought, she was making sure that they actually went.

'Doing a bit of bonding?' Gerry said as they fastened their seat belts.

'Something like that. Alex reckoned his stepfather recognised Boo Flecker when they drove past her in the lane. Only I don't know whether he's telling the truth. I picked up a lot of resentment there.'

'It's worth following up though. The station called while

you were upstairs with Son of Dracula. Zac James has arrived in Tradmouth and he's demanding his solicitor . . . the expensive of the species all the way from London. I told them to let James know that if his brief doesn't arrive in the next hour or so we'll put him up in our luxury accommodation overnight . . . nice single cell with en suite facilities. How much do you bet that when we get there we'll find he's opted for the duty solicitor like everyone else?' Gerry added with a wicked grin.

He turned in the passenger seat, picked up the bag containing the knife from the back seat and sat examining it through the plastic.

'Vicious looking thing,' he said absentmindedly. 'Underneath all that soil and blood the blade seems shiny . . . like chrome. It looks a bit . . . ' He searched for the word. 'Ceremonial.'

'Maybe it is.'

'I think there's some sort of label on the blade underneath the dried blood. Forensic should be able to tell us if anything's written on it.'

Wesley thought for a moment. 'Didn't Lilith Benley and her mother murder those girls with a ceremonial dagger – an athame?'

He'd been about to start the car but instead he took his iPhone from his pocket and brought up images of athames used in Wiccan rites. The murder weapon certainly resembled the pictures on the tiny screen. He handed it to Gerry.

'Let's go and show it to her, Wes,' he said. 'See what she has to say for herself.'

'My thoughts exactly.'

Instead of heading straight back to Tradmouth, Wesley drove past Jessop's Farm and then turned down the narrow lane leading to Devil's Tree Cottage. He sat in silence, the thought of another meeting with Lilith Benley having driven all words from his mind.

Her crime had been unspeakable but when he'd met her she'd looked quite ordinary and he'd had to keep reminding himself of what she'd done. Perhaps the banality of evil was the most disturbing thing of all.

He parked in front of the cottage. It was dusk now and Wesley could see Lilith in the light streaming from the open doorway. She was sorting through a pile of wood that hadn't been there when they'd last visited. She stopped and watched them get out of the car, like a nervous animal contemplating flight. He could see she had a clawed hammer in her right hand, poised as if to defend herself.

'I'm building a chicken run,' she said, almost defensively, as though she was trying to explain away her possession of a potentially offensive weapon. 'It's about time I got this place back on its feet.'

'Very commendable.' As soon as the words left Wesley's lips he knew they sounded patronising. 'Can we go inside?'

She put the hammer down and led the way into the house. As soon as they were in the parlour Gerry held out the bag containing the knife. 'We think this is the weapon that killed that woman at Jessop's Farm. Recognise it?'

Lilith took the bag and squinted at the weapon inside. 'I've never seen it before in my life.'

Wesley saw her eyes flicker away and he knew she was lying.

'But it is a ceremonial knife . . . an athame. Like the one you used to have.'

She held the weapon up in the air and stared at it for a few seconds. 'Where was it found?'

112

'In a field on the other side of your lane. We're going to get it tested for fingerprints,' said Gerry. 'Sure there's nothing you want to tell us?'

She sighed and handed back the bag. 'How many more times do I have to spell it out? I never saw the woman who was killed and I had nothing to do with her death.' Her voice was calm, almost resigned. As if she was just going through the motions of protesting her innocence but didn't expect to be believed.

'So you don't want to add anything to your original statement?' said Gerry.

'No. Now if you don't mind I'd like to get on with my work before it's too dark to see what I'm doing.'

Wesley knew she was holding something back. But he also knew she wasn't going to talk. Not then ... maybe not ever, unless they managed to find some evidence against her.

They needed some luck.

As they neared Tradmouth they found themselves stuck behind a tourist coach; late season visitors in search of non-existent Devon sunshine heading back to their hotel for the evening after a day's sightseeing. As Wesley turned towards the police station the coach headed off in the opposite direction to the waterfront, probably making for the Marina Hotel to enjoy a three-course dinner and a comfortable bedroom with a spectacular view over the river. An autumn break in beautiful South Devon.

As soon as they reached the CID office they were greeted by Trish Walton who told them that Zac James had decided to make do with the duty solicitor until his expensive brief arrived. He'd said the sooner he could get out of there, the better.

Gerry passed the dagger over to Paul Johnson to be sent off to Forensic and Wesley watched Trish's face as he left the office. Until fairly recently Trish and Paul had been going out together. Then the murder of Paul's cousin had changed everything. The shock of the loss had made Paul serious, morose even, and Trish had found solace with somebody else. For a while there had been an awkward atmosphere in the office until Gerry had lost patience and bawled at them, telling them not to bring their personal problems into work. The boss's outburst had seemed to have worked, although sometimes Wesley still sensed a well-concealed tension between them.

Wesley was asking Rachel whether anything new had come in, when Gerry interrupted. Zac James was waiting for them in Interview Room one.

The man they found sitting on a metal chair fixed to the floor in case of violent outburst, didn't look much like a celebrity. Leaning on the table, crushing an empty plastic cup with restless fingers, Zac James had the bland, almost childlike good looks of a teenage heart throb. Until you looked closer and saw that the flesh beneath his bloodshot eyes was sagging and his skin was blotchy and pale as though he rarely saw the sun. Zac James was past his prime and trying his best to hide it.

As they sat down opposite he raised his head. He looked twitchy. Probably in need of some of the white powder they'd found in his room at Jessop's Farm. The duty solicitor, in contrast, was a small thin man in a crumpled suit who seemed bored by the proceedings.

'I hear you were on your way to London when the patrol car pulled you over,' said Gerry after they'd made the introductions and switched on the tape recorder.

'I wanted to get back.'

'What for?'

'Things I needed.'

'What things?' Wesley asked.

No reply.

'You disappeared sharpish yesterday after that woman was found dead,' said Gerry.

Zac's fingers began to drum on the table. 'It freaked me out.'

Wesley asked the next question. 'Where did you stay last night?'

'Morbay. The Riviera Towers.' He gave a nervous grin. 'The best in town.'

'Rupert Raybourn checked into the Marina Hotel in Tradmouth.'

'I know. But I fancied the Riviera.'

'Why's that?' Gerry leaned forward, invading the man's personal space.

Zac sat back in his seat, a momentary flash of panic in his eyes. 'I'd heard it was good.'

'Your home address is in Essex, I believe,' said Wesley.

'That's right.'

'Funny. I could have sworn I could hear a hint of Devon in your accent.'

Zac shrugged. 'I pick up the local accent wherever I go.' He began to examine his fingernails.

'You must have known we'd need to talk to everyone at Jessop's Farm,' said Wesley. 'Surely you realise that disappearing like that looks suspicious.'

Zac James shrugged again. 'I didn't see anything or hear anything. I don't even know who that woman was.'

'She was a journalist and she was down here

investigating one of the contestants on *Celebrity Farm*,' said Gerry. 'She'd had a sniff of scandal.'

'Wasn't me. Must have been Rupert,' Zac said quickly as though he was desperate to shift the blame.

'Could she have been looking for some dirt on you? Your cocaine habit, for instance? Is that why you were off to London? Supplies running out?'

He straightened his back, suddenly alert, and Wesley knew Gerry had hit on the truth. 'So? It's no big deal. And I'd hardly kill someone to keep it out of the papers 'cause it's already common knowledge. And I only use – I don't deal.'

'You still fled the scene of a murder,' said Wesley.

'The killer might have been after me. That woman might have got killed by mistake. You attract nutters when you're a celebrity. Never heard of stalkers?' he added in a self-righteous whine.

Wesley watched him. He was clearly feeling sorry for himself, believing his own publicity.

'So you've had trouble with stalkers, have you?' Gerry asked.

'Yeah.' He suddenly seemed unsure of himself. 'Some of them think you're in love with them. When it dawns on them you're not, things can get nasty.'

'So you think you might have been the target?' Wesley could hear the sarcasm in Gerry's voice. 'Surely even a very short-sighted murderer wouldn't mistake the victim for you in broad daylight. Wrong sex for a start.'

The duty solicitor sighed and began to play with his pen. His unwilling client was doing himself no favours.

'The victim's name was Boo Flecker. Ever heard of her?' Zac shook his head.

'Ever heard of Lilith Benley?'

He focused his eyes on the table top. 'No. Who is she?'

'Her and her mother murdered two girls eighteen years back. She was released from jail a couple of weeks ago and she came home to West Fretham. Her land butts onto the top field where the body was found.'

'So?'

'Just saying.' Gerry stood up. 'That's all for now, Mr James. I'll send someone to take your statement. Don't leave the area again without telling us, will you? We may need to talk to you again.'

As they were about to leave the room, Zac James spoke. 'Look, I had no reason to kill this bird I'd never heard of ... but maybe Rupert did.'

As they walked down the corridor, Wesley thought Zac James might have a point. He wanted to speak to Raybourn again. And he wanted the truth this time.

As soon as the phone rang Pam knew it would be Wesley apologising for being late again. She had become used to it long ago ... giving the children their dinner alone and then watching TV and marking books with a solitary glass of wine. When you marry a policeman it comes with the 'for richer or poorer, in sickness and in health' bit.

But today she wished more than ever that he was there. She'd rung the hospital earlier and been told Neil was 'stable'. She'd known him since university – she'd even gone out with him for a short time before she met Wesley. Although she knew they would have been a disaster as a couple, Neil being even more obsessed by archaeology than Wesley was with his police work, he was part of her life. And she couldn't stand the thought of him lying in that hospital bed without company.

Fortunately both children were booked to have tea with friends after school so as soon as she escaped work, avoiding the head teacher who was prowling the corridors in search of members of staff to harass, she drove straight to Tradmouth Hospital. She found Neil surrounded by his colleagues from the dig at Princes Bower. They were talking shop and Neil lay propped up on his pillows, smiling weakly while a bearded man talked about a visit to a house to check out a cellar. She was reminded of a seventeenth-century painting she'd seen once of a deathbed scene. The man about to meet his Maker bidding farewell to his devoted family.

When Neil saw her he raised a weak hand in greeting while the colleagues shifted round to make room for her.

'How are you feeling?' she asked, aware that he'd probably been asked the same question a thousand times already. But she wasn't in the mood to be original.

'Lots of cuts and bruises and they reckon I had concussion.' He gave a tentative nod towards his colleagues. 'I was just telling this lot they operated on my leg this morning and it went okay. They've done more scans and x-rays but they haven't told me much apart from the fact that I've got a couple of fractures and three broken ribs.'

'He's indestructible,' said the bearded man. 'Remember that time up on Dartmoor when that trench collapsed and you climbed out looking like the creature from the black lagoon?' The assembled archaeologists chuckled dutifully. They were doing their best to keep Neil's spirits up. But he looked so bad that Pam felt like screaming at them to get real.

'Has Wes arranged to get that thing from my car yet?'

'I don't know. What is it?'

'That's the million dollar question.'

The archaeologists made noises of agreement. Whatever the mysterious object was, it was causing some interest.

'Will you remind him when you see him?'

'I don't know what time that'll be. He's working on a murder case and he'll be late.' She stood up. Her fears that Neil was lying there alone and in pain had turned out to be unfounded and she had things to do. 'I'd better leave you to it.'

'You'll come again, won't you?'

Pam smiled. 'Try and stop me.' She knew she was doing the same as his colleagues; masking her worry with forced jollity.

She had never seen Neil look so ill and frail. It was as though all the certainties of life and friendship had been shaken up and broken into shattered shards. If Wesley had been there he would have known how she felt. But he wasn't.

She drove home, picking up the children from their respective friends' houses on the way. She'd decided not to tell them about Neil's misfortune just yet. She'd wait until she knew more.

Michael was quiet, as if he was nursing some precious but uncomfortable secret, but Amelia was chatty as usual. She was the type of child who never shut up but at least you could always tell what she was thinking, unlike her elder brother.

Once back home she put on her stern teacher act, the one she'd been putting on all day for her class, and ordered homework. Amelia settled down at the dining room table but Michael just sat staring at the TV.

'Haven't got any homework,' he said, twisting his head to see round her as she stood in front of the screen.

'Of course you have. Get on with it.' She switched the TV off and looked at the boy with his olive-brown skin and his black wavy hair. Up until a few weeks ago he'd been such a studious child and she felt worried about this change in her son. She had sometimes seen it in children she taught and had always been ready with advice for their concerned parents. But this was her own child and she was floundering. When Wesley had some free time she'd ask him to intervene. Michael might take more notice of his father. A mother's nagging words can become so familiar that they float over a child's head.

She watched as Michael dragged his rucksack along the floor into the dining room to join his sister, a picture of reluctance. He took out some books and placed them in front of him, regarding them with distaste for a while before he picked up a pen. Then she watched in horror as he began to doodle absentmindedly on the blank page of an exercise book.

'What are you doing? Where's your homework?'

'Told you. Haven't got any.'

'You must have some. What about your exam?'

He turned to face her, his brown eyes defiant. 'I haven't.'

'Then have a look at one of the work books I bought you.'

As a teacher's child Michael had always been well supplied with the means to exercise his developing brain. Educational toys; music lessons; work books. Now he was due to face the entrance exam for the local grammar school, Pam's efforts had intensified. It was vital, she thought, that her children had the best start in life, especially as there were so few other mixed-race children in the school. In an ideal world it shouldn't matter but she feared

120

that it did. She wanted Michael and Amelia to achieve the best ... and mix with the best of company.

She found the work book and when she placed it in front of him she saw him roll his eyes. But before she could say anything, the phone began to ring.

She'd hoped it was Wesley and her heart sank when she heard her mother's voice. 'I need to speak to Wesley.'

'He's at work. Murder enquiry. Don't you read the papers?'

'Never. Nothing but bad news, darling. Has he spoken to anyone at Neston about Simon yet?'

It took Pam a few seconds to realise what she was talking about. Then she remembered. Simon Frith was the teacher who'd been accused of that most heinous of crimes, the sexual abuse of a child. The very nature of the allegations made Pam reluctant to co-operate. There was no smoke without fire ... was there? 'He hasn't mentioned it, but that's not surprising because he's been so busy.'

'They've taken Simon in for questioning again. Can you ask Wesley to call me as soon as possible?'

'Even if he wasn't tied up with this murder enquiry, he can't interfere in someone else's case, surely you can see that.'

'But it's destroying Simon and his family. He's an innocent man. Get Wesley to call me as soon as he can.'

Pam sighed. She'd run out of things to say. With Wesley's absence and Neil's accident, it was all too much. And when she heard Amelia calling through from the dining room to complain that Michael was teasing her, she put the phone down.

Rupert Raybourn had been relieved when Zac James decided to do a runner. Not only did it take the pressure off him as far as the police were concerned, it meant that he didn't have to put up with the obnoxious little shit in the congenial surroundings of the Marina Hotel. Working with Zac had been like sharing a room with a chimpanzee from the zoo.

The Marina Hotel was comfortable and, while the TV company was paying, the arrangement suited him fine. But he knew he had to return to West Fretham. There was a visit he had to make. Something he'd put off long enough.

At ten o'clock he slipped out of the hotel, walking casually past Reception and out into the car park. To his left the river glinted, reflecting the lights from the restaurant. He could hear the lazy lapping of the oil-black water and he could smell the salty tang of seaweed in the air. A little further downstream the car ferry was still chugging its way backwards and forwards, brilliantly lit like a spacecraft landed on the river from some distant planet.

Rupert got into his BMW, started the engine and steered out of the car park. He drove past the picturesque white-washed pub on the corner, changing into second gear to negotiate the steep road out of town, and continued on the coast road until he reached West Fretham.

He parked at the end of a cul-de-sac of small retirement bungalows not far from the medieval church and sat in the car for a few minutes, gathering his thoughts, before walking to the white-painted bungalow at the end, the one with an aging but immaculate little Toyota parked outside. There was a light on behind the frosted glass door but he waited for a few seconds, knowing that the door wouldn't be answered at that late hour without some reassurances. He took his mobile phone from the inside pocket of his leather coat and, after a brief conversation, he saw a dark shape in the hall, outlined against the light.

The door opened to reveal a tall elderly woman who was hugging a purple quilted dressing gown around her thin body.

But before he could say anything she stepped forward and put her face close to his. He could smell peppermint on her breath. Toothpaste. 'That Benley woman's out of prison,' she said in a low whisper. 'She's back at the cottage.'

'I know.'

'And she's gone and killed someone else so maybe this time they'll put her away for good.'

As the woman stood aside to let him in, he saw a look of bitter hatred on her face.

Chapter 7

Journal of Thomas Whitcombe, Captain in the King's army, September 15th 1643

I went in daylight clad in the garb of a humble farmer, the better to sneak unnoticed past the road blocks. Although I did not sneak, I pulled my homespun cloak around me against the rain and with cheery 'good morrows' I walked unchallenged through the streets.

I am a well-set young man with an open face and I am accustomed to being trusted by all I meet. And, being familiar with the local speech, I was able to unlock the doors of their suspicion and convince all that I was a farmer from Bovey Tracey come to sell my wool to one of the merchants who reside in the town and that I planned to bring in my wares by stealth to defy the besieging soldiers. I feigned amazement at the fortifications and told how I slipped past the King's men by concealing myself behind a hedgerow. I cheerfully cursed King Charles and his taxes and such was my confidence that no one I met harboured one moment's suspicion that I was a spy in their midst, although that was indeed my role.

I went to Baynard's Quay and stood for a while watching, the stench of newly landed fish in my nostrils. I have heard it said that Alison's father and mother are dead and that she no longer resides there. If she lives I must get word to her.

Written by Alison Hadness, September 15th 1643

Elizabeth is a sullen girl of fifteen summers, thin with lank hair the colour of rope and marks upon her face from the smallpox she suffered as a child. She is ever resentful of me. Her mother died in childbed some three years since and William asked for my hand in marriage but a year later. I imagined she would welcome me into the household for any mother is better than none. But I am close to her in age so she regards me as a rival. I know the truth of it now.

The thought of William's flesh joined with mine sickens me and I think often of Thomas and how, in the folly of my youth, I bought the love philtre from the old woman in the village of Stoke Beeching. It may be that I should obtain another so that William will quicken my heart and yet I fear the strongest magic will not avail against my indifference. I am an incorrigible sinner but I dare not beg God's forgiveness for I know my sin will persist until death.

It may be that there is some herb that will put all right.

'Keeping you up, Wes?' Gerry said as Wesley stifled a yawn.

Wesley smiled dutifully. Gerry could usually come up with something better than that, even at seven-thirty in the morning.

'How's Neil?'

'Comfortable, according to the hospital.'

'Good.'

'I hear the incident room at West Fretham's going to be ready later today.'

'About time too,' Gerry muttered before bellowing out an order for attention. The chatting and sorting through paperwork stopped as everyone turned to face the notice board while Gerry went over the latest developments, assigning jobs and making observations.

The statements they'd taken from the TV crew and the footage they'd shot had to be gone through to make sure nothing had been missed. Everyone in West Fretham had been interviewed but nobody had admitted to seeing anything out of the ordinary. It appeared that Boo Flecker's killer had vanished into the landscape, leaving no trace behind. And the easiest escape route from that field, Gerry observed, was towards Devil's Tree Cottage. Lilith Benley was high on their suspect list.

They needed to discover everything they could about the victim and find out exactly what she'd been doing while she was in Devon. It was likely she'd been trying to dig up dirt on Zac James or Rupert Raybourn. But Dan Sericold had also said she might have been onto something new. Every possibility had to be checked out.

After Zac had been released the night before, with strict orders not to leave the area, they'd tried to contact Rupert Raybourn at the Marina Hotel but he hadn't been there. The man might have gone for a walk or a quiet drink at one of Tradmouth's many pubs but Wesley had felt uneasy about his absence. However, when one of the DCs had called at the hotel first thing that morning, she'd been told that Raybourn had returned just before midnight.

Gerry had a theory that Boo had set out to investigate Raybourn or James but had diverted her attention to Lilith Benley when she'd learned of her release. The case had been notorious and Lilith's new life would have made a

126

good story. Wesley couldn't argue with his reasoning. But he still had some niggling doubts.

There was still no sign of Boo's phone. Gerry had asked someone to contact service providers so her calls could be traced but it was taking time. They were still waiting for news.

'Do we know where Boo Flecker was staying yet?' Wesley asked once the briefing was over.

'The team's drawn a blank at all the local hotels and B and Bs. But I'm not giving up hope.' Gerry sounded remarkably cheerful, considering the investigation hadn't progressed very far. 'What did you make of the lad who found the murder weapon? Alex? He's got a chip on his shoulder if you ask me.'

'He doesn't like his stepfather.'

'Probably an age thing,' said Gerry.

Alex's attitude might have been a case of teenage angst or it might have been something deeper. But Wesley couldn't see Alex Gulliver stabbing a woman in cold blood. If he was going to kill anyone his stepfather would surely have been a more likely candidate.

'Alex said he thought Shane Gulliver recognised the victim.'

'Might want to get him into hot water,' said Gerry. 'Gulliver won't be back till tonight. If he doesn't call us we'll pay him a visit.'

The phone in Gerry's office began to ring and he hurried away just as a mousy-haired young woman from Forensic arrived at Wesley's desk. He recognised her as somebody who'd brought them good news in previous cases. He hoped she wouldn't disappoint now.

She was holding a file in her left hand which she opened and studied with a satisfied smile on her face.

'That knife you sent us has been examined and the blood definitely matches the victim's. And we found something interesting. There were two small sticky labels stuck to the blade, the sort you'd usually remove before use. They were badly stained but we managed to read what was underneath. One refers to the manufacturer in the Far East and the other appears to be the name of the company that distributes the things in this country. It's a local firm, head office registered in Tradmouth. Just thought you'd like to know.'

She took a sheet of paper from the file she was holding and placed it on the desk in front of him.

'Thanks.' He gave her a smile of humble gratitude. It was always wise to keep well in with Forensic. In these days of budget cuts and delays, favours were becoming more precious than ever.

Wesley needed to get this new information checked out. But everybody seemed to be engrossed in their own tasks so he picked up the phone. Delegation's all very well but sometimes it's quicker to do things yourself.

As soon as he'd finished his brief conversation Rachel entered the CID office, her arms filled with old box files. She was making for her desk but when Wesley called her name, she stopped.

'I've got an address for the company that supplied the murder weapon,' he said.

'And you want me to pay them a visit and get a list of their customers?'

She'd always been able to read his mind.

'I'll come with you. I'd like to see the setup for myself and talk to the person in charge.'

'If you think it's necessary.' Rachel sounded as if she

suspected Wesley of wasting precious resources. She let the files drop on his desk and a musty smell wafted towards him. 'These are the files on the Benley murders. I'm going through them to see if any familiar names came up back then.'

'Surely that's already been done.'

'The main players, yes. I'm looking at the peripheral people who were around at the time but didn't give evidence at the trial. The boss wants to see if there's any link between the girls' murders and this latest one.'

Before Wesley could say anything, he heard Gerry's voice. 'It's time we had another word with Rupert Raybourn. Find out if he has any nasty little secrets he'd kill to keep hidden.'

Wesley gave Rachel an apologetic look and said he'd see her later. He was impatient to see what the importer of the murder weapon had to say for him or herself but at that moment Rupert Raybourn took priority. Dan Sericold had told them that Boo Flecker was looking for dirt on one of the *Celebrity Farm* contestants. And if it wasn't Zac James, that only left one possibility.

They walked the short distance to the Marina Hotel and found Raybourn in the lounge. He was dressed casually today in chinos and a polo shirt with a pastel blue cashmere sweater draped around his neck. He looked calm and untroubled but it could have been an act. Like his performances in days gone by.

'I don't suppose you've heard when they can resume the filming?' he asked as soon as they sat down. 'I did wonder whether it would be in bad taste in view of what happened but ...'

'The show must go on, eh,' said Gerry. 'The producer's

been moaning to our Chief Super that this business is costing the TV company a fortune. You're happy to carry on?'

'Money's money, Chief Inspector. How can I help you?'

'The victim, Boo Flecker, was a freelance journalist. We think she might have been investigating you.'

The mask of co-operative concern slipped for a split second. 'What makes you think that?'

'She didn't approach you?' asked Wesley.

'No.'

'We only have your word for that, sir.'

'How do you prove a negative? If she wanted an interview surely she would have contacted me?'

'Maybe she did. Maybe she arranged to meet you in the top field and you killed her there to keep whatever she'd turned up about you quiet.'

Wesley saw Raybourn's eyes widen in panic. 'That's not what happened. I found her, that's all. I didn't kill her.'

'She told a colleague that she was investigating one of the finalists on *Celebrity Farm*. We've spoken to Zac James and he denies there's any dirt to find on him that isn't already public knowledge. That leaves you.'

Raybourn looked affronted, the picture of injured innocence. 'She'll have been on a fishing expedition ... trying to dig up non-existent muck. I know what these people are like.'

'You mean they've had dirt on you before?'

'You're twisting my words.' He sounded irritated now, as though Wesley was starting to break down his defences. 'She couldn't have found any dirt because there is none to find. And if she'd been stupid enough to publish false allegations, I would have sued her and whatever paper was stupid enough to print her poison for libel. Even if she did intend to write some scurrilous article about me, I had no reason to kill her. On the contrary, I could have made a fortune out of her.' His lips twitched upwards in a nervous smile. 'My attitude has always been "publish and be damned" – and she would have been.'

'So there's nothing in your private life you'd want to keep under wraps?' Wesley asked.

'My life's an open book,' he said with brittle confidence. 'Now if that's all ... '

He stood up and extended his hand. 'Always happy to co-operate with the police. Sorry I can't be more help.'

'Believe him?' Gerry asked as they left the hotel.

'No. But we haven't any reason to arrest him.'

'Except for crimes against humour,' Gerry said with a grin.

The drizzle turned to rain as they walked back to the police station. In the middle of the raindrop-mottled river a Royal Navy frigate lay at anchor, its grey hull matching the colour of the water.

Mist lay over the hills behind the town, almost hiding the rocky outcrop guarding the river mouth, the site of Neil's excavation. The thought of Neil brought the worry back like a physical blow.

'You going to see Neil later?' Gerry asked, as though he had read his thoughts.

'If I have a chance.'

'Makes you realise how fragile life is, doesn't it?'

Wesley didn't answer. He couldn't have put it better himself. Neil's accident had given him a new feeling of vague dread, like a mild stomach ache that takes you by surprise every so often. Perhaps it was all part of growing older, the gradual but relentless shedding of your youthful invulnerability.

His phone began to ring. It was one of the detective constables who'd been given the job of finding out where Boo Flecker ate her final meal. The landlord of the Ploughman's Rest in West Fretham had reported an abandoned car in his car park. It turned out to be a hire car and, on further investigation, the DC found it had been hired by Boo Flecker in Exeter on the Thursday before her death. He surmised that she must have left it at the pub and walked the half mile or so to Jessop's Farm. Best way, he reckoned, if she'd wanted to stay inconspicuous.

He'd also discovered that Boo had eaten at the pub that had recently rebranded itself as a gastro pub for the discerning diner. The manager remembered Boo and her bright red coat because she'd sent her steak back twice, complaining that it wasn't done exactly to her liking. He remembered her companion too.

When Wesley relayed the information Gerry's eyes lit up. 'That place used to be a dive but I've heard it serves a decent pint these days.'

'Don't forget I want to visit the firm that supplied the murder weapon.'

'You and Rach can do that later.'

They picked up the car at the police station and drove straight to the Ploughman's Rest. The rain was stopping as Wesley steered into the car park, as though it had made a great effort but no longer had the energy to carry on. The newly painted pub in the centre of the village looked inviting and picture-postcard pretty with its hanging baskets filled with flowers and its leaded windows lit by a golden, cosy glow, and soon Gerry was marching towards the entrance like a thirsty man making for a mirage in the desert. Wesley followed, knowing that, as he was on duty and driving, nothing more interesting than orange juice awaited him inside.

It was the manager himself who greeted them at the bar, a man too young and smartly dressed to be the classic mine host – more like an off-duty city banker playing the part.

'You told our officer that you saw the murdered woman on Tuesday lunchtime,' said Wesley.

'That's right. They're saying that's around the time she was murdered, is that right?' he said with a worried frown.

'We think so, yes. What can you tell us?'

'I noticed a grey Ford had been in the car park since Tuesday so I reported it. The officer who came made some enquiries and found out that it had been hired by that poor woman.'

'Can you describe her?'

'Slim, blonde hair, red coat, shiny boots, sharp features. Most of our lunchtime customers are holiday makers but we also get quite a few business people from Dukesbridge. If it hadn't been for the man she was with, I'd certainly have put her in that category but ... '

'Who was she with?'

'He was elderly. Could have been her father, I suppose. But she didn't behave as if he was her father. She kept complaining about the steak for a start. Sent it back twice. And the body language was wrong. As if they were strangers rather than relatives. You get to notice things like that in this job.' He leaned on the bar and smiled. 'I've always been a people watcher. Interested in what makes the punters tick.'

'Ever thought of joining the police?' said Wesley.

'I did as a matter of fact ... once. I suppose you want a description of this old chap. He was tall, around five eleven.

And he had grey hair, quite a lot of it. No male pattern baldness. He wore a tweed jacket with patches on the elbows – very old fashioned – and twill trousers, beige. I'd have put him in his early seventies. He had a long face. And glasses.'

'Did you notice if he arrived in a car?'

'Sorry. We were busy. They both ordered steaks but he ate his without moaning – cleared his plate so he must have enjoyed it. She paid which I thought was a bit unusual. They didn't seem to belong together, if you see what I mean. I couldn't quite work out the relationship between them.' For a man who prided himself of being an observer of his fellow men, the manager now sounded unsure of himself.

'Actually we know she was a freelance journalist so it was possible she was interviewing this man about a story she was working on.' Wesley thought it would do no harm to pass on this snippet of information.

The manager gave a solemn nod. 'That would certainly fit.'

'I don't suppose you happened to overhear what they were saying?' Gerry asked, eyeing the hand pumps greedily.

'Well, I did hear her mention a name.' He paused, like a game show host about to announce a winning contestant. 'Lilith Benley. That murderer. I couldn't make out anything else she said but when I went over to ask if everything was all right I definitely heard her mention Lilith Benley. They've just let her out of prison, haven't they? There's been a lot of talk about it in the village. Bad feeling.'

Wesley and Gerry exchanged looks.

'Would you know this man if you saw him again?' Wesley asked.

'I think so.'

'I notice you've got CCTV cameras outside. Are they working?'

'They certainly are. I check them myself regularly.'

Wesley glanced at his watch. 'I'll send someone round to check out the footage for the relevant time if that's okay.'

'No problem,' said the manager, all co-operation.

Wesley looked round and saw a grin of satisfaction spread across Gerry's chubby face, creasing the flesh around his eyes. 'Good thinking, Wes. But it'd be rude to go without sampling the beer.' He surveyed the array of hand pumps, smacking his lips. 'I'll have a half of Doom Bar. My round.'

Dave Saunders was a field archaeologist, a man of the soil. And he knew that he looked the part with his beard, wide-brimmed hat and real ale gut.

He had been taking an all too active part in excavations for fifteen years now and the excitement of discovery, the unveiling of history and the camaraderie of the dig, still set the adrenaline coursing through his body. However, he'd always left Neil Watson to do the talking. Over the years Neil had become adept at scolding greedy developers, fighting the Archaeological Unit's corner at meetings with ignorant officials and liaising with the public and heritage organisations. Neil shone at the things he tended to avoid and Dave had felt no secret satisfaction when he'd heard of Neil's accident, no ambitious relish at being promoted from second in command. On the contrary, he'd found himself dreading the new and unlooked-for challenge.

Taking over temporarily as site director at the Princes Bower dig wasn't a problem because all that remained was to complete the excavation, fill in the trenches, process the finds and write up the reports, all tasks well within Dave's self-imposed capabilities. But the small additional job Neil had taken on at Mercy Hall was another matter.

At the request of the local Conservation Officer, Neil had been calling at the house regularly to see what progress was being made as the builders cleared the soil from the newly discovered cellar, giving advice and assessing anything of a historical nature that turned up down there. Dave knew Neil hadn't particularly got on with the builders, describing one of them as a little runt of a man called Lee who had bad skin and breath to match. According to Neil they'd treated him with suspicion and smirked at each suggestion he made. But their attitude changed when they found the thing behind the panelling.

Before the crash Neil had called Dave to tell him about the little coffin. It was an important discovery, he'd said; a valuable piece of social history from a superstitious age. He'd been taking it to Exeter for conservation when he'd had the accident that had thrust Dave into his unfamiliar new role.

Now Dave himself was visiting Mercy Hall, having put on a fresh pair of jeans and tried, without much success, to prise the dirt from his fingernails for the occasion. He was greeted by the owner of the house, who introduced herself as Harriet Mumford. Dave was used to women in soil-caked digging clothes who'd join him for a pint after the dig in the evenings – women who weren't afraid to get their hands dirty – but this one looked as though she'd use rubber gloves to pick up a pair of dirty pants. Neil had said she made sculptures but somehow Dave found it hard to imagine those elegant hands covered in clay.

Faced with Harriet Mumford he felt like some clumsy medieval peasant intruding on a high born lady. But she smiled and shook his rough hand limply, saying how shocked she was by the news of Neil's brush with death, before leading him through to show him how work was progressing on the cellar.

When they reached the room Dave saw three builders standing by the window drinking tea from stained mugs. They nodded a greeting with slight smirks on their lips. Dave nodded back, feeling awkward.

'You another archaeologist then?' one of them said. He was stripped to the waist, his tanned and hirsute torso bulging with muscles. When he put his mug down he folded his tattooed arms and waited for an answer.

'My colleague had a car accident so I'm standing in till he's on the mend.'

'But he's going to be okay is he ... your mate?' said a younger man who fitted Neil's description of Lee, the one he'd described as the Runt. He sounded genuinely worried, which surprised Dave a little. Perhaps Neil had misjudged him.

'The doctors aren't sure yet,' said Dave. 'How are you getting on with the cellar?'

The third man answered. 'We've dug out the section by the steps but I reckon it carries on under the whole length of this room. Someone went to a lot of trouble to fill it in. Don't know why 'cause it looks like a good dry cellar.'

They all looked at Dave as though expecting him to provide an explanation. But Dave hadn't a clue why someone in the past should have filled in a perfectly serviceable cellar so he said nothing.

'What about the panelling?'

'We stopped taking it down when we found that thing,' said Lee.

'The conservation officer wants the rest of it removed to see what's behind it. Then it's got to be put back when the work on the room's finished.'

For a moment Dave feared the men were going to object but they said nothing.

'What have you found in the cellar?'

Lee scurried out of the room and returned a minute later with an old garden trug filled with objects. As Dave took it he felt his confidence flooding back. He picked up the pieces one by one and examined them. A trio of clay pipes, early seventeenth century. A fragment from a Bellarmine jug. More pottery, late Tudor early seventeenth century. A James I coin dating from shortly after the gunpowder plot and another of Charles I dated 1642. Nothing later.

Dave looked up and saw the men watching him, as if they were waiting for his verdict. He didn't like to disappoint them. 'From these finds I'd guess that the basement was filled in around the mid-seventeenth century. But I can't be absolutely sure.' He saw the men glance at each other. Just another boring archaeologist harping on about the past.

'We'd better get on,' Lee said wearily.

'If the conservation officer wants the rest of the panelling removed maybe you should do that first. But be careful not to damage it.'

Without another word they began to prise the panelling away from the wall, surprisingly gently, exchanging the odd comment about last night's football. Dave hovered at a distance, unsure whether to lend them a hand. But they seemed to know what they were doing as they removed a small section of the old panelling with great care and leaned it against the wall. Then he heard Lee swear loudly and all three men scrambled away from the wall at lightning speed, almost colliding with him as they rushed past.

'What's the matter?' he called after them.

Lee turned and Dave saw that the blood had drained from his face. 'Have a look for yourself.'

Dave made his way across the room and leaned over the half-removed section of panelling. Then he saw it lying on the flagstones like something in a medieval image of Judgement Day.

Another tiny, rough-hewn coffin.

The new incident room was up and running in West Fretham village hall. A single storey, whitewashed building near the church used by everyone from playgroups to the WI, from Scouts and Guides to the local amateur thespians. But now it was Gerry Heffernan's temporary kingdom, a cavernous space with open rafters and brick walls painted in dirty cream gloss. There was a stage at one end with faded blue velvet curtains. When Gerry had first walked in, he'd been tempted to get up there and address his team with a few well-chosen words from Shakespeare's *Henry V*. But he reckoned that would be taking leadership a step too far.

The newly installed phones and computer equipment seemed to be working, which seemed to Gerry, who had never put too much faith in technology, like a miracle in itself. He stood by the white board beneath the stage and looked around at the officers hard at work. Wesley had gone off with Rachel to interview the suppliers of the murder weapon, surprisingly located at the address where Neil had been working, and now he had an important job to assign to somebody. Important but deathly boring. And after a few moments he spotted the lucky winner.

Nick Tarnaby was sorting through witness statements with a faraway look in his eye. Gerry knew when someone was pretending to look busy as the boss prowled about. He'd done it himself in his younger days.

'Nick. The manager of the Ploughman's Rest's got some CCTV footage for us. Go and get it and then go through it, will you? We need to find the victim in the car park with an elderly man.'

'You want me to go now, sir?'

'That's the general idea. The manager promised to find it for us by three and it's half past now. No sampling his wares, mind.'

Nick stood up, uncharacteristically enthusiastic. Perhaps it was the mention of licensed premises that had put a spring in his step, although Gerry had never had him down as a great drinker.

As Nick was struggling into his coat Gerry's phone rang. It was Dan Sericold. He'd arrived in Devon and he had some business to attend to that afternoon but he'd meet them the next morning at the pub where he was staying. Anything he could do to find the bastard who killed Boo. Gerry put the phone down, hoping that Sericold would give them something new. They needed all the help they could get.

Harriet Mumford looked rather distracted when Wesley and Rachel arrived at Mercy Hall. And when Wesley asked her whether something was wrong she explained that half an hour before their arrival her builders had made an

140

unpleasant discovery. She didn't elaborate further and, even though he was intrigued, he really didn't have time to ask.

He held out the bag containing the bloodstained knife while Rachel watched silently.

'Do you recognise this, Mrs Mumford?'

Harriet Mumford wrinkled her nose with distaste. She had taken them into a half-finished dining room with bare floorboards and roughly plastered walls. There were new electric sockets and new wooden windows, exact copies of the originals. No expense had been spared.

'We've traced the label on the handle to an import company registered at this address.'

'My husband's in London and he won't be back till tomorrow.'

'Then perhaps you can help us,' said Wesley. He wasn't falling for the little woman who knows nothing act.

Harriet bowed her head as though she realised she'd been found out. 'It's an athame. A ceremonial dagger used in Wiccan rites. My husband supplies various outlets throughout the country.'

'Any locally?'

'Several shops in Glastonbury, but more locally there are two shops in Neston. I'll print out the details in the office if you want to come with me.'

Wesley glanced at Rachel. He had known her long enough to sense that she had taken a dislike to Harriet Mumford. No doubt she'd explain the reason to him in due course.

Harriet led them out into the passageway and pushed open the door of the room opposite. Wesley was surprised to see that it was a well-appointed modern office, furnished with a couple of pale wood desks, complete with computers and the latest printing equipment. A pile of cardboard boxes stood against the far wall bearing the same Chinese supplier's label as had been found on the murder weapon.

'Do you supply these things directly to customers?'

'Yes. We sell them via the Internet and mail order.'

'Sold any to anyone local?'

For a moment she looked uncertain, as though she was deciding whether to tell the truth. 'I think so.'

'I'll need names and addresses.'

Without another word she typed something into one of the computers and the printer whirred into life.

When it had finished she handed a sheet of paper to Wesley. He examined it and handed it to Rachel. There was one name in particular that had caught his eye. A few days ago Lilith Benley had purchased three athames by mail order and they'd been delivered to Devil's Tree Cottage shortly before Boo Flecker's death.

Chapter 8

Written by Alison Hadness, September 16th 1643

Dorcas has been quiet of late and when I asked her why she told me that she was afraid. I thought that her fear was of the army camped out at Hilton Farm but she said it was a matter concerning my husband's daughter.

She had discovered certain strange items in Elizabeth's chamber, hidden at the bottom of her linen press. Before I speak of it to Elizabeth I must ascertain the truth of it.

While Elizabeth was sewing in the parlour Dorcas showed me what she had found. My heart leapt when I saw the thing she held within her hand. I imagined at first that it was merely a doll, something Elizabeth had fashioned out of candle wax for play, but when I looked closely I saw it was dressed in a makeshift gown that resembled my own and the black hair upon its head was also my own, filched, perhaps from my comb. The doll's belly had been pierced with a nail, as had its head. I have of late suffered cramps in my belly and sick headaches and I have no doubt that this is the cause.

I told Dorcas I would speak with my stepdaughter and she went away mumbling prayers.

There is much talk in the town that grain is scarce and we will want for bread.

Rachel drove back to West Fretham with Wesley in the passenger seat. He hadn't said a word and she guessed his mind was on the horrible thing the builders had discovered behind the panelling, the little box she'd assumed belonged to a new-born baby, hidden there to avoid bringing social shame upon its mother in a time less permissive than her own. When Wesley told her about Neil's discovery, the coffin with the wax doll inside, it had seemed more sinister to her than a set of sad little bones.

'So we're going to see Lilith Benley?' Rachel asked when they arrived in West Fretham.

'We need to ask her about these knives she ordered,' Wesley answered.

'Released back into the community and this is what happens. Almost makes you wish they'd bring back hanging.' She saw Wesley give her a shocked look.

'You really think so?'

She hesitated. 'Not really. It's just when I think about those poor girls ...'

'You're sure she killed Boo Flecker then?'

'Aren't you?'

Wesley didn't reply. It annoyed her when he went silent like that and she didn't know what he was thinking. She glanced in his direction, taking her eyes off the road for a second. From the moment she'd met him she'd found him attractive with his dark skin, delicate features and warm, watchful brown eyes. But he was married and, unlike many men she'd come across, he showed no signs of straying. She wasn't sure whether this disappointed her. She wasn't sure of anything any more ... except that her wedding was approaching like an advancing juggernaut, crushing everything in its path.

As they passed Jessop's Farm Wesley spoke. 'Surely it'd be in Benley's interests to keep her nose clean. She's out on licence so the first hint of trouble she'll be back inside. She'd have to be stupid to draw attention to herself by killing so close to home. I've spoken to her and she seems like an intelligent woman.'

Rachel snorted. 'Maybe that's how she reacts to anything she perceives as a threat. Maybe Boo discovered something about her that'd put her away for good. No hope of parole. Perhaps it's an unsolved case that nobody's linked to her before.'

'It's the next turning,' said Wesley.

'I know.'

Rachel steered the car up the rutted driveway and Devil's Tree Cottage came into view. She'd been thirteen at the time of the murders, not much younger than the two victims, but she'd devoured every morsel of information from the TV news and the local paper her parents had taken at the farm. First there'd been the girl Satan Death had abducted in Cornwall which had been far too close to home for her parents' comfort. She'd bridled against being accompanied everywhere by her parents or one of her brothers but now she understood the reason for their caution. When the Benley case had come to light it had seemed like a bad fairy tale – Hansel and Gretel in the Devon countryside. The tale of two innocents falling into the hands of witches. She'd always identified with those two girls and the powerful narrative had stayed in her head, preying on her imagination. And now she was here where they'd died, at the dilapidated cottage with green moss staining the flaking pink walls. A place of evil. A place where bad things happened.

She turned off the engine, suddenly reluctant to leave the shelter of the car. Wesley was already out and making for the front door, as if he was embarking on a routine visit. But Wesley hadn't been in the area eighteen years ago – Wesley hadn't believed in those two devil women squatting in their lair like fat spiders in a web awaiting the arrival of the next blameless fly. With a great effort of will she forced herself to get out of the car and follow him to the front door.

'She's not answering,' he said after he'd knocked and waited a while. 'I'll look round the back.'

'Be careful.'

He gave her a sceptical look, as though he thought she was over-dramatising the situation. She'd always prided herself on her level-headedness so she felt a sudden stab of resentment. 'Do you believe she was burgled or did she stage it herself for some reason?' she asked.

'I don't know. But we need to find out whether that murder weapon belongs to her.'

'It must do. She sent for those knives. She lied to us.'

'Actually she didn't lie. We didn't know she'd sent for them when we spoke to her so we never asked. And if we didn't ask the question, there's no reason she should have mentioned it.'

Rachel followed his logic but she wasn't convinced. 'Even if she was a white witch, why would she need to buy three lethal knives?'

'Maybe they need more than one for their ceremonies. I don't know much about it. Perhaps I'll ask my sister's husband.'

'Is a vicar likely to know the ins and outs of devil worship?'

'It's Wicca, not Satanism. They're quite different.'

'Even in Lilith Benley's case?' She regretted the words as soon as they left her mouth. She was showing her prejudice. Even, horror of horrors, being unprofessional.

She waited by the front door while Wesley walked round to the back of the cottage, unwilling to follow him because she knew that was where Lilith and her mad mother had fed the girls' bodies to the pigs. Being a farmer's daughter, Rachel had always been fond of pigs and the thought of what had happened somehow tainted the funny, intelligent creatures. As if an old and well-loved family friend had turned out to be a serial killer.

Wesley returned after a few minutes. 'No sign of her. And the glass in the back door hasn't been mended yet. Looks a bit unsafe if you ask me.'

'Maybe she couldn't get any local workmen to come out.' Wesley didn't reply.

Her phone rang and she took it from her jacket pocket. She saw Wesley watching her expectantly, as though he was hoping that it was something that would lead to a breakthrough.

'I asked for a routine check on all the names that have come up so far,' she said when she ended the call. 'Harriet Mumford leases some studio premises in West Fretham. Apparently she's a sculptor ... probably a hobby,' she added dismissively.

Wesley raised his eyebrows. 'It might be worth having

147

another word with her to see whether she was in the village when Boo died.'

'And there's something else.'

'What?' He sounded slightly impatient.

'Rupert Raybourn's real name is Eric Bourne. Rupert's his stage name.'

'So?'

'A woman called Vera Bourne was interviewed during our routine house to house visits in West Fretham after Boo Flecker's murder ... and eighteen years ago a Vera Bourne at the same address gave a statement when the girls were killed. She saw them early on the evening they disappeared. They were hanging around the bus stop, making a racket, and Vera went out and complained. She got a mouthful for her trouble. Vera had a nephew called Eric and he was visiting from London at the time. He was there at his aunt's house that night.'

'You sure it's the same Eric Bourne?'

'When she was interviewed at the time Vera made a great thing of her nephew being on the TV – very proud of it, she was.'

'So why didn't Raybourn mention this?'

'That's what I want to know,' said Rachel.

'Lilith Benley wasn't answering her door,' said Wesley.

Gerry looked up. 'Maybe she's avoiding us. How did you get on with the company who supplied the murder weapon?'

'Lilith Benley bought three identical knives. Sent for them by mail order and they should have arrived on the day of Boo Flecker's murder. She sent a letter with cash enclosed.'

'Unusual.'

'That's what I thought. But apparently it sometimes happens in the New Age community.'

'Have they kept the letter?'

'Afraid not. Once details of the purchase were put onto the computer, the original letter was destroyed.'

'Lilith never mentioned it. But if she'd killed Boo Flecker she wouldn't, would she?' Gerry stretched himself out in his chair, his shirt parting a little to give a glimpse of white vest beneath, and gave a loud yawn which rather took Wesley by surprise. 'Any other familiar names come up as customers of this outfit?'

Wesley shook his head.

'We need to speak to Lilith Benley. Top priority,' Gerry said.

'Rachel reckons she did it.'

'Bit stupid of her to piss in her own back yard but she has to be top of our list. No fingerprints on the murder weapon, by the way.'

'Pity.' Wesley sighed. A nice set of clear prints would have been too much to hope for. 'The knife was supplied by a company belonging to an Evan Mumford — and his wife, Harriet, has a sculpture studio in West Fretham. I've sent someone over to ask if she was there at the time of the murder. She might have been missed by the house-to-house team.'

'Think she's in the frame? She had access to the murder weapon.'

'We'll have to see whether she can come up with an alibi,' said Wesley. 'You've heard about Rupert Raybourn's link with the original case?'

'Yes, but I don't know how relevant it is.'

149

'He was around eighteen years ago at the exact time the girls were murdered and he was here when Boo Flecker died.'

'So was Joe Jessop. And a fair chunk of the local population. But you're right, Wes, we should have another word with our Mr Raybourn to ask him why he didn't mention his aunty. I don't like it when people keep things from us.'

Wesley thought for a moment. 'If the girls' bodies were never found how can we be absolutely sure that they died in the same way as our latest victim?'

'Dorothy Benley's statement described how she and Lilith went after the girls. She said Lilith stabbed them both in the stomach.'

'Dorothy Benley was deranged.'

'Doesn't mean she wasn't telling the truth.'

Before Wesley could say any more they were interrupted. 'Excuse me, sir. I've just had a call from Uniform.'

Wesley turned his head and saw Paul Johnson standing there with a solemn look on his face. 'Rupert Raybourn's been arrested at the Marina Hotel. He went berserk and punched a photographer. The barman who called us said he thought he was going to kill him.'

Gerry assumed a martyred expression, as if Raybourn had done it just to try his patience and increase his workload.

'He's in the custody suite at Tradmouth. The photographer wants to press charges.'

'His name's not Dan Sericold is it?'

Paul looked surprised. 'Yes. How did you know?'

Wesley looked at Gerry and raised his eyebrows. 'Presumably this was the business he said he had to attend to,' said Gerry. 'Maybe this isn't the first time Raybourn's

150

lost control with a member of the press who's been asking too many questions.'

At eight o'clock precisely Wesley received a call from Shane Gulliver. He'd just arrived home from London to find his message waiting. Gulliver sounded positively eager to help the police with their enquiries. Somehow Wesley wouldn't have expected such enthusiasm from a man who liked to play up his criminal background at every opportunity. But people sometimes surprise you.

When Wesley asked him if he'd seen Boo Flecker, neglecting to mention Alex's accusation, Gulliver denied it. If she'd been there, he hadn't noticed. He'd been busy working on his next book and he'd been in London on the day of the murder so that was that.

Wesley thanked him and ended the call. He'd get Gulliver's alibi checked out, just in case. Alex hadn't exactly spoken fondly of his stepfather so maybe the prospect of causing trouble for him was more appealing than telling the truth to the police.

Gerry had decided that they wouldn't talk to Rupert Raybourn till the next morning because he wanted to give him a chance to cool down. He'd called Dan Sericold and been told that he wouldn't be available till the following morning either. But even with this small respite, Wesley didn't manage to leave the incident room before nine o'clock, too late for visiting time at the hospital. But he told himself that Dave would already have visited and told the invalid the exciting news about the second little coffin to take his mind off his afflictions.

The thought of Neil reminded him that he'd promised to visit the police garage at Neston to pick up the strange cargo his friend had been carrying when he'd had his accident. Pam wasn't expecting him back till late so he decided to make a detour on the way home and as he drove inland to Neston in the dark it began to rain heavily. He flicked his wipers onto double speed, concentrating hard on steering down the winding main road, squinting each time he was dazzled by oncoming headlights. In those conditions he suddenly regretted his decision and longed to get straight home. But he'd always believed in keeping his promises.

He swept into the car park at Neston police station at nine-thirty, having called ahead to make sure there'd be someone there. He was greeted by one of the mechanics who was working late, a big bald man in a blue overall who looked him up and down with curiosity.

'So your mate was in that Mini, was he? Nasty one. How is he?'

'The hospital say he's stable.'

'That can mean anything,' said the prophet of doom. 'I believe you've come for the devil doll. I'll be glad to get it out of the place, I can tell you.'

He led Wesley over to the wrecked Mini. Wesley had noticed it when he'd first entered the cavernous garage but he'd been reluctant to take a proper look. Now he could see that the bonnet was crushed, the driver's door had caved in and the front wheel was lying at a crazy angle. Neil had been lucky to get out alive.

'I didn't fancy touching the thing so it's still in there,' said the mechanic. 'I'd get it out through the passenger door if I were you.'

Clearly the man wasn't going to do the job for him so Wesley walked round the vehicle and opened the passenger door which had emerged from the collision virtually unscathed. He could see the doll lying by the handbrake, covered in broken glass from the windscreen. To his surprise it seemed undamaged. Some superstitious souls might have said that some dark force had protected it but Wesley tried to dismiss such thoughts as nonsense.

The wooden box lay behind it in the foot well in front of the back seat, having spilled out of the large cardboard box still wedged on the seat spewing white polystyrene balls like snowflakes. Wesley picked the doll up carefully, repelled by the cold waxy flesh which felt like a dead man's, and placed it on the ground before retrieving the coffin. The top had sprung off and he placed the doll inside on top of a bed of ancient yellowed paper, wincing as his hand brushed the rusty pins protruding from the roughly shaped body. He looked down at his hand and saw a dot of blood.

'What the hell is it?' the mechanic asked, peering at the doll, his nose wrinkled with distaste. 'Is it some kind of voodoo doll?'

'I've no idea,' said Wesley softly, lifting the box and cradling it in his arms.

'If I didn't know better I'd have said that horrible thing's cursed.'

'How do you mean, if you didn't know better?'

'Well I can't see a devil doll cutting someone's brake pipes, can you?'

Wesley stared at the man, lost for words.

When Pam greeted Wesley at the front door she looked tired and her eyes were bloodshot as though she'd been crying. His first thought was that she'd heard bad news about Neil but when he asked her she said she'd visited the hospital on her way home from work and he'd seemed much better; on the mend.

He put his arms round her and kissed the top of her head. Her hair smelled of something fruity, probably the new shampoo she'd bought half price in their local Sainsbury's. She squeezed his hand as though she was seeking comfort and his instincts told him that something was wrong. And his news would make things worse. Someone had cut Neil's brake pipes. Their friend had been the victim of attempted murder. The thing the mechanic had referred to as 'the devil doll' still lay in the boot of his car, safely packed in the cardboard box protected by snowy beads. Given Pam's mood he'd probably been wise not to bring it into the house.

Amelia was in her room getting ready for bed but Michael was still up, ostensibly finishing his homework but in reality listening to music on his iPod. When Wesley marched into the dining room the boy looked up and took his earphones out, a half-smile of greeting on his face. Then the sullen look returned, as though he'd suddenly remembered that displaying enthusiasm about the arrival of a parent wasn't the done thing.

'How's it going?'

Michael hung his head, avoiding his father's eyes. 'OK.'

'Something the matter?'

'No.'

'Homework bothering you?'

'No. It's easy,' was the indignant reply.

'Your teacher says you're very bright, you know. The best.' It was always wise, he thought, to start with a bit of flattery. 'That's why your mum and I want you to do this exam.'

'I don't want to go to that grammar school. It's rubbish.'

'Who's been telling you that?'

'My mates.' Michael began to write in his exercise book, a signal that, as far as he was concerned, the conversation was over.

Wesley put his hand on the boy's shoulder and was gratified when he felt him relax. 'You don't have to take any notice of them, you know. They're probably jealous.'

Michael said nothing for a while. And when he spoke, the words came out in a whisper as though he didn't want to be overheard. 'Nathaniel's doing the exam and they've started picking on him.'

Wesley knew Nathaniel, a quiet boy with glasses who resembled a young Harry Potter. Nathaniel and Michael had been inseparable until Michael, desperate to belong, had begun to seek the approval of a cooler crowd. He leaned over and whispered in his son's ear. 'And you don't want them to do the same to you?'

The answer was a vigorous nod.

'You don't have to say anything about it at school. Nobody has to know.'

Michael shook his head vigorously. 'Mrs Hughes keeps on about it. She takes a group of us out of the class for extra work.'

'So it's not just you and Nathaniel?'

'There's six of us. Me and Nathaniel and some girls.'

Wesley resisted the temptation to smile. In a few years' time, Michael probably wouldn't be taking such a dismissive attitude towards the opposite sex. 'Want me or your mum to have a word with Mrs Hughes? I'm sure she'll understand.'

Michael jumped in his seat, alarmed. 'No. Don't say anything. Promise.'

'OK. But whatever you do, don't stop working. You can't pass up a once in a lifetime opportunity just because a few lads in your class don't think it's cool ... or whatever the word is nowadays.' He grinned. 'I'm so old that I've lost touch.' Wesley ruffled Michael's hair and the boy brushed his hand away. 'It's time you got some sleep.'

He saw Michael roll his eyes then slowly, reluctantly, he put his things away in his school rucksack and crept unwillingly out of the room. Wesley sat for a while, hoping his words had got through. He remembered exactly what it had been like to be young and different because of the colour of his skin, to be desperate to belong and to be tempted to follow the pack blindly. It was a temptation which, after some difficult times and family help, he had managed to resist. And he'd hoped attending the local grammar school would help his son to do the same.

As soon as he joined Pam in the living room she asked him if he'd eaten. When he told her he'd already had a takeaway curry with Gerry she looked relieved.

She reached for the wine bottle on the coffee table and refilled her glass.

'I've spoken to Michael and it seems these new so-called mates of his have been giving him and Nathaniel a hard time about trying for the grammar school. I think Mrs Hughes has been drawing attention to the group doing the exam and that's what's been causing the trouble. It might be worth having a word with her.'

Pam gave an absentminded nod and he could tell that something other than their son's educational future was troubling her. 'Something the matter?'

'My mother rang just before you arrived. She's on her way here. I told her it wasn't convenient but . . . You know what she's like.'

He could see the strain on his wife's face, the fine but deepening lines and the dark shadows beneath her eyes. In spite of everything that had happened and all Pam's efforts to distance herself, her mother still had the power to disturb the equilibrium of their existence.

The doorbell rang and he saw Pam flinch. She picked up her glass and took a large sip. Dutch courage.

Wesley hurried into the hall, hoping the noise hadn't disturbed Michael and his sister who were upstairs, probably looking for any excuse to delay bedtime. But when they didn't appear at the top of the stairs he took a deep breath and opened the front door. Della was standing there with a bright shawl draped around her shoulders and standing slightly behind her, looking nervous, was a man.

Wesley stood aside to let the visitors in and the man nodded to him gratefully, as though he'd expected to be turned away. He wore jeans and an open-necked striped shirt underneath his leather jacket. His light brown hair was peppered with grey and the flesh sagged a little around his jowls, but he was still a good-looking man, even though his eyes were bloodshot as though he hadn't slept – or he'd been crying.

'This is Simon Frith,' Della said breathlessly. 'Simon, this is my son-in-law. He's going to help us.'

Wesley's heart sank. This was the man who'd been in custody at Neston, accused of molesting a child. He saw it all now and felt like cursing Della for her thoughtlessness.

Wesley addressed Simon. 'I'm sorry if Della's misled you. I really can't interfere in someone else's case.'

'But you can have a look at the files,' Della interrupted, pleading. 'The policemen who arrested him automatically assumed the kid was telling the truth and Simon was lying. You can look at the evidence with fresh eyes and see if there are any loopholes. Simon's life is being ruined. He's got young children ... there's even talk of him not being allowed to live with them. Please.'

Wesley looked at Simon and saw a film of tears welling in his eyes. If Della was right and the accusations against him really were malicious, the man was in a truly dreadful situation. On the other hand, he knew molesters could be convincing and manipulative. And if anybody could be manipulated, it was Della who'd always been a sucker for any waif and stray that crossed her path. An inveterate believer in even the most far-fetched sob story, she always relished having a cause to fight for – some more worthy than others.

'What if someone made false allegations against you, Wesley?' she continued, warming to her theme. 'How would you feel if you were in danger of losing everything? Your family, your job and your good name? Just think about it.'

He looked round and saw Pam standing in the doorway, arms folded, eyes focused on the floor. 'Couldn't you just talk to the officer in charge of the case?' she said quietly. 'Sometimes people get on the wrong side of the wrong kid and ... These accusations against teachers are all too easy to make.' She shrugged, resigned, as though she was talking about some minor occupational hazard.

Wesley was aware that all eyes were on him now. 'OK. If I get a chance I'll have an informal word with the officer in charge of the case, just to see the lie of the land. I'm afraid it's the best I can offer.'

To his surprise Simon Frith grabbed his hand and began to shake it, like a parched man greeting a water carrier in a desert. 'Thank you so much, Wesley. You don't know what this means ...'

Wesley was doing his best to keep his distance, to keep reminding himself that this man might be guilty as charged. But, along with everyone else, he found himself being swept up in the wave of optimism. 'No problem,' he heard himself say. 'But I can't promise anything.'

'Why don't you tell Wesley your side of the story, Simon,' Della said like a pushy mother coaxing a child to speak in front of the grown-ups.

Wesley raised his hand. 'I'd rather you didn't. I need to keep an open mind when I talk to the officer in charge of the case.'

'It's a DS Geoff Gaulter at Neston.'

'I've heard the name. If I need to speak to you later I'll be in touch.'

To his relief Della looked at her watch. 'Let's get you home, Simon.'

Simon suddenly looked apprehensive, as though he was unsure of the reception he'd receive from his family. But he followed Della out, thanking Wesley profusely. Wesley stood at the door with Pam by his side, watching Della drive off.

'Do you think I've done the right thing?' he asked.

Pam put her hand around his waist and squeezed. 'Like I said, it's so easy for a kid to make a false allegation if they've got a grudge against a member of staff and even if the story's proved to be a complete fabrication, there's very little come-back. I know any form of child abuse is a dreadful thing but Simon deserves a chance like every other suspect.'

Wesley didn't answer. Instead his mind had turned to Neil and the visit he'd made earlier.

'I went to the police garage at Neston and saw Neil's car.' He paused, unsure how she'd take the news. 'The mechanic there said his brake pipes had been cut.'

Pam's eyes widened with shock. 'Are you saying someone tried to kill him?'

'It looks that way.'

'But Neil doesn't have enemies. Who would . . . ?'

'God knows. But I intend to find out.' He hesitated. 'While I was there I picked up that thing he found at Mercy Hall. I'd better get it from the car.'

'Neil said it was some kind of doll.'

Wesley didn't answer. He went outside. The rain had stopped and the cloud cover had vanished to reveal a full, bright moon and a dark blue sky filled with stars. He stood there looking upwards for a few moments, awed by the vastness of the universe which made the problems he dealt with seem almost insignificant. But those problems were anything but trivial to those involved. He had seen the despair on Simon Frith's face. He had seen Neil lying injured in a hospital bed. He had seen Boo Flecker's body lying in that field like a broken toy abandoned by a vicious child.

He opened the car boot and removed the box containing the wooden coffin carefully. The top had been replaced so that the doll inside was hidden. But Wesley knew it was there. He could almost feel its presence.

And when he showed it to Pam a few minutes later, she insisted that he take it outside and put it in the garden shed. She didn't want the thing in her house. And Wesley couldn't blame her.

*

160

It was ten o'clock when Lilith Benley looked out of the window. She could see the moon was full, casting a silver light over the landscape. Full moon – once she'd believed it meant something. But prison had changed all that.

Earlier she'd heard the police at the door but she'd pressed her back against the damp wall by the window and stood, breath held, until they gave up and drove away.

It had been the black detective who'd come before with DCI Heffernan. An attractive man with kind eyes, polite and well spoken, unlike most of the policemen she'd encountered eighteen years ago. Most of them had been stupid and ignorant, prejudiced in the true meaning of the word. Gerry Heffernan had seemed different – but he hadn't been in charge back then so he'd had to do as he was told.

The black detective had called with a young woman; an efficient-looking blonde in a dark trouser suit who'd reminded her of one of the Assistant Governors at the prison where she'd spent so many wasted years. She'd reminded her a little of someone else too – of one of the girls who'd brought about her downfall. She'd been blonde too, with the sharp, merciless features of a cat. If the man had been alone she might have spoken to him but the woman wouldn't have understood the emotions that had led her to West Fretham. And she wouldn't have been able to comprehend the all-consuming urge to protect her weak, half-crazy mother either.

But that was in the past. Now she had her freedom. But when you've become used to the protection and routine of an institution, freedom is a hard beast to handle.

To take the edge off her hunger, she'd made herself beans on toast. It was her last tin of beans and the bread had been stale but it hadn't tasted too bad. Sooner or later she'd have to hire a taxi and venture into Tradmouth or Dukesbridge to stock up on supplies. But she knew she'd run the risk of being recognised. Her notoriety would mean stares of fear and disgust. Sins must be paid for.

She made herself a cup of tea and switched on the radio, Radio 4 just to add some life to the place, and gazed at the wood fire blazing behind the stove's grubby glass, wondering what other steps she'd have to take to ensure she'd no longer be dogged by the shadows she'd collected in her past. But she feared that, whatever she did, they'd always be with her.

She sat for a while with her hands cupped around the hot mug, comforting herself with the warmth. There was a problem she had to deal with. When the athames had arrived in a parcel on Tuesday morning she'd shoved them in the back of her wardrobe, out of sight. Then, after the murder, she knew she'd have to find a safer hiding place. There was a loose brick in the old pantry where she used to keep any spare money and treasures. She'd looked there as soon as she returned from prison and found her mother's engagement ring still there in the gap, undisturbed even after all the years the house had been empty. This secret place was impossible to detect unless you knew it was there, better than any safe, and even the painstaking police search of the cottage eighteen years ago hadn't found it. There had just been room for the knives in there but she needed to dispose of them permanently. She wanted them out of her house but she knew it would be wise to wait until the fuss had died down.

And there was something else she needed to do – a piece

of the past that had to be destroyed. She stood up and walked over to the chest of drawers. When she opened the bottom drawer she saw that the little bear was still there, threadbare and stained with grubby stuffing protruding from the belly where she'd thrust in the knife that night. She took it from its resting place, opened the stove door, threw it onto the flames and watched it burn. As the fire consumed it she experienced a feeling of release. She'd done it, just as she'd promised herself she would during her time in prison. That particular part of her life was over for ever.

She curled up in the old worn armchair and it seemed to mould to her shape, even after so many years of absence. The voice of an actor soothed from the radio speaker, a restful book at bedtime, and for the first time in over eighteen years she felt herself relaxing.

She looked at the empty rocking chair in the corner, imagining the old woman rocking to and fro, her face covered with the white handkerchief that made her look like a giant, faceless doll. Sometimes she still dreamed of that figure without a face ... that and those dead girls.

The clock on the wall was still ticking. It had been her mother's – a wedding present. One of the first things she'd done on her return was to wind it up and listen to its comforting tick tock in the cold silence. It kept good time, but then it was an antique and they knew how to make things properly back then ... that's what Mother had always said before she lost her mind.

Suddenly she heard hammering, a relentless thumping on the door. Something malevolent was outside trying to invade her new-found peace. Her body tensed as the noise stopped and then she heard something clatter to the floor in

163

the back hall. She pressed her body into the chair, breath held, heart pounding.

Then the back door creaked open and she heard soft footsteps walking slowly towards the parlour door. Getting nearer.

Chapter 9

Journal of Thomas Whitcombe, Captain in the King's army, September 17th 1643

Prince Maurice is restless. He pores over maps and charts all day, planning his attack while the men outside consume the ale we have procured. Some deserted yesterday, weary of the rain and mud. Was ever weather so unfavourable to our cause.

Our good prince supposes that siege is the only way to overcome the town for no man or woman can withstand starvation. One of our captains says the townsfolk are using witchcraft against us, conjuring this infernal rain and wind in their defence.

I will venture once more into Tradmouth tomorrow but Prince Maurice fears my constant presence will arouse many suspicions. Yet he knows not the true purpose of my endeavours.

Written by Alison Hadness, September 17th 1643

Sometimes Elizabeth watches me with the shadow of hatred burning in her pale eyes as if she can see into my very soul. She swears the dreadful manikin was none of her work. I do not believe her but I cannot tell her father of her lies and her evil actions for he will hear no word against his own blood. How shall this be remedied?

Dorcas says Elizabeth wishes me ill and she fears her as I do. If William will not come to my aid it may be that I should take measures to resolve my dilemma.

How I curse the King for taking Thomas from me but I pray for his safety. It may be that I shall never see him again in this life.

The nightmare had awoken Wesley at one-thirty that morning, leaving him shaking and sweating with terror. In his dream the wax doll in the little coffin had come to life. It had climbed in through his bedroom window and floated towards the bed, bristling with quivering blood-rusted pins, smiling its rictus smile. It had stabbed at Pam's throat with a shiny knife and he had struggled to defend her before it turned its deadly attentions on him. He'd known he was losing the fight for life as the thing leered above him and when he'd lifted his arms in self-defence, the cold wax hands had grabbed his wrists, leaving him helpless and paralysed by fear. He'd woken Pam when he'd lashed out in an attempt to fight the thing off. But, unlike him, she'd managed to get back to sleep again.

When morning came and the daylight trickled in through the curtains he showered, dressed quickly and made himself an early breakfast, taking Pam a cup of tea which she received with bleary-eyed gratitude.

As he sat at the kitchen table eating a slice of toast he looked out on the garden. Behind the foliage, turning to autumn yellows and browns, he could see the small wooden shed and he couldn't help picturing the thing inside it. He was tempted to retrieve the doll that had haunted his sleep and take it up to Exeter himself just to get it off the premises. But with things as they were, there wouldn't be time.

He was due at the incident room early so he left Pam half awake to deal with the kids and get ready for work. Once they had Boo Flecker's killer in custody he promised himself he'd make it up to her somehow.

He drove out to West Fretham with the radio on, catching up with the morning's news, relieved that there was no mention of Boo Flecker's murder. When he arrived at the incident room it was already buzzing as the night shift brought the incoming officers up to date with new developments before hurrying home to get some rest. Gerry was at his desk, looking as tired as Wesley felt.

'Anything new?' Wesley asked as he sat down opposite the DCI.

Gerry's face brightened. 'Rupert Raybourn's spent the night in the cells at Tradmouth. I said we'd be over as soon as I'd finished the morning briefing. And Nick Tarnaby's been going through the CCTV footage from the Ploughman's Rest half the night and he's found us a registration number for Boo Flecker's mystery companion. Boo was talking to a man in the car park who matched the description the manager had given. He got into a ten-year-old Ford Mondeo and drove off while she walked off down the main road in the direction of Jessop's Farm and never came back. Her hire car's been examined, by the way, but they didn't find anything useful. Only a sweet wrapper and a ticket for the car park in Neston. Still no news on where she was staying.'

'Any chance the Mondeo driver was our murderer? If he followed her . . .'

Gerry shook his head. 'Can't see it myself, Wes. But I could be wrong, of course. It has been known.' He gave a weary smile. 'The car's registered to a Laurence Roley. He's a retired teacher. Taught English at Dukesbridge Comprehensive for twenty-six years before he packed it in.' He paused, as though he was saving the best till last. 'He was interviewed as a matter of routine eighteen years ago when the girls went missing. He was their form teacher.'

Wesley raised his eyebrows. 'Wonder what Boo wanted with him.'

'We'll have to ask him. I sent someone round to Lilith Benley's first thing but there was still no answer.'

'She might have gone away.'

'More likely she's avoiding us. But we'll keep trying. I sent someone to have another word with that knife woman as well – Harriet Mumford . . . the sculptor.'

'And?'

'Turns out she was working in her studio in West Fretham on the afternoon of the murder but she claims she didn't see or hear anything suspicious.'

'But she was definitely there in the village?'

Gerry sighed. 'So were a few hundred other people.'

'But nobody who had ready access to the murder weapon,' said Wesley.

'What would this Harriet woman have against Boo Flecker?'

'We won't know until we've checked out her background. I'll get someone onto it.' He paused. Something else was on his mind and it was time he shared it with Gerry. 'I had some news of my own last night. Neil's brake pipes were cut.'

Gerry stared at him for a few moments. 'You're joking.'

'I spoke to one of the mechanics at Neston police garage. He's sure.'

'I know Neil can be a pain in the backside sometimes but why would anyone want to do something like that?'

'That's what I want to find out.' He wondered whether to mention the strange doll but decided against it. Last night in the darkness it had seemed relevant ... now it seemed fanciful and ridiculous.

'Has Neil any idea who might be responsible?'

'I haven't had a chance to ask him yet. He's still in hospital and I didn't want to upset him.'

'He'll have to know sooner or later.'

'I believe the Collision Investigation Unit at Neston's started to make enquiries. Maybe it's best to leave it to them.'

'Keep me posted, eh.' Gerry looked at his watch. 'We'll pay this Laurence Roley a visit – see what he has to say for himself. But first we'd better speak to Raybourn. A night in the cells should have softened him up nicely.'

'He was here visiting his aunt when those two girls were killed. Was there anything to connect him with the crime at the time?'

'No, but I agree, Wes. We need to ask him about it.'

'Of course he might have chosen to take part in *Celebrity Farm* because he had links with the area.'

'It's possible.' Gerry hesitated. 'And we mustn't forget we're seeing Dan Sericold later. Hopefully he might be able to shed some light on exactly what Boo was up to.'

Wesley picked up his car keys. It was just their luck that, now the incident room had moved to West Fretham, their first port of call was back at Tradmouth police station. As they drove down the steep road into the town, he wondered whether to ask for Gerry's thoughts on the Simon Frith case. Should he obey his first instinct and learn the facts before judging for himself whether Della had been right to leap to the man's defence? Or should he steer clear of the whole thing?

'Gerry, there's something I'd like your opinion on.' That was it. He'd said it and it was too late to change his mind now. He explained his dilemma, eyes fixed on the road ahead and the river at the foot of the hill, sparkling grey and dotted with boats at anchor. It had begun to drizzle again and he flicked his wipers to clear the windscreen.

When he'd finished Gerry said nothing for a few moments. He spoke as Wesley was steering right to drive along the esplanade.

'I know Geoff Gaulter,' said Gerry. 'He's a good bloke and I'm sure he won't mind giving you the bare facts. You won't be able to interfere, mind.'

'I know.'

'My Rosie told me about a teacher she works with who was accused of hitting a kid. It turned out it was all lies so I know things like that happen, particularly with stroppy adolescents who know their rights ... and their powers.'

Maybe if Gerry's daughter, Rosie, hadn't told him a similar tale, he might not have been so sympathetic. But as it was, Wesley now felt reassured that contacting Geoff Gaulter would do no harm. But he'd do it later, when he had a free moment.

When they arrived at the station Rupert Raybourn was awaiting them in Interview Room Three. The room had just been redecorated so it was the smartest of the three interview rooms and still smelled of fresh paint. Perhaps it had been allocated to Raybourn because of his celebrity status. Or perhaps Wesley was reading too much into it.

Gerry sat down opposite the comedian and his brief, who had just arrived from the capital and looked remarkably unconcerned, as though it was some routine meeting to be got through as quickly as possible.

'Well, Mr Raybourn, we meet again. I believe you've been indulging in fisticuffs with the Press. Never a good idea in my opinion.'

Raybourn gave Gerry a withering look. 'I never asked for your opinion, Chief Inspector. I admit I lost my temper and punched the man because he was in my face taking photographs and asking intrusive questions. OK?'

'I hear he wants to bring charges.'

'I was provoked.'

Wesley watched as Gerry put his face close to Raybourn's. 'Yesterday you told us you had nothing to hide. What exactly did this photographer say to make you lose that temper of yours, Mr Raybourn?'

When the man didn't reply, Gerry spoke again. 'We'll ask him so you might as well tell us. Get it off your chest.'

Raybourn took a deep breath. 'OK. I'll be straight with you. He said he'd heard a young man had come forward. As far as I know I've never met him but ... ' There was another long silence. 'Allegedly I took him to a party, which is a lie. However, I can't prove it because I was at home alone at the time he's claiming it happened. It turns out he's a rent boy and he wants to sell the story of how we spent the night together.'

'Is that all?'

Raybourn glanced awkwardly at Wesley. 'This man's also been claiming that I made a number of racist remarks about one of the other people at this party. Apart from the fact that I wasn't even there, I'm not a racist and these days any allegation like that can ruin a man's reputation and career in a second.'

'And you've been around far too long to get caught out like that,' said Wesley sweetly.

'I told you. It's all lies.'

'Has this man got witnesses?' Gerry asked.

'He can't have. I wasn't even at this damned party. As far as I know I've never even met him.'

The way he said it told Wesley he was probably lying.

'But you have used rent boys?'

Raybourn bit his lip. 'Once or twice. But I've always been discreet. I've had to be. I make my living as a family entertainer. No doubt this man's made the whole thing up and he's selling this fictional story to the highest bidder.'

'No doubt,' said Gerry. 'Any idea why someone would want to discredit you?'

'All successful people make enemies over the years.'

'And this young man's one of them?'

'I don't know. I honestly don't remember him. I've asked my agent to make enquiries about his background. This is a nightmare.' Wesley could hear a pleading note in his voice and for the first time he found himself unexpectedly feeling a twinge of pity for the man.

Gerry spoke next. 'I believe your real name's Eric Bourne.' His eyes were focused on Raybourn's face, awaiting a reaction. But he was disappointed when the man seemed to relax.

'A good stage name's important and there's nothing like a bit of alliteration. Let's face it, Chief Inspector, a lot of performers aren't blessed with a real name that rolls off the tongue.'

'It's just that an Eric Bourne was interviewed when two girls were murdered in West Fretham eighteen years ago.' Gerry was watching the man as a cat watches a mouse. 'He was visiting an aunt in the village at the time they disappeared. That you, was it?'

'I was down here doing a gig in Morbay and I visited my aunt when I had a free evening. Me and Aunty Vera have always been close.' He was doing his best to sound casual, as if it was of no consequence.

'You didn't stay with her?' Wesley asked.

'No. I stayed at the Riviera Towers. I was doing well back then. On the TV most weeks.'

'Yours must be a funny old life,' said Gerry. 'Up and down. You hit the top and then you're on the downward slope.'

'It's unpredictable. People go through bad patches and make comebacks all the time. Maybe that's why we carry on ... because you never know what's round the corner. I hoped *Celebrity Farm* would give my comeback a kick start. It's a matter of public perception, you see. I was hoping that those other prats would make me look good. I worked bloody hard on that farm, shovelled all the shit while the others posed and Zac was out of it half the time and high the other half. I took the part of the peacemaker, the one they all liked and trusted. That's why I made the final two. The last thing I need is for these allegations to ruin it all.'

'Sorry if this is getting in the way of your brilliant career,' said Gerry. Wesley heard the hint of sarcasm in his voice but it seemed Raybourn didn't.

He waved his hand in modest dismissal. 'The show's still going ahead. The producer assures me it's just a delay.'

'I still can't get the fact that you were in West Fretham

173

eighteen years ago out of my mind,' said Gerry. 'Then as soon as you're back, lo and behold, there's another murder. Was Boo Flecker onto you?'

'I don't know what you mean.'

'Dan Sericold, the photographer you attacked, was her colleague. He's been following in her footsteps, hasn't he? She got hold of the rent boy story first and confronted you. You lost your temper and killed her.'

'That's not true. She never approached me and that's God's honest truth. It wasn't me she was interested in.' Raybourn half rose from his seat.

'Then who was it?' Gerry said sharply.

'I've no idea. This has nothing to do with me.' Raybourn's cheeks had gone an alarming shade of red and Wesley put it down to high blood pressure.

'Have you seen your aunt while you've been down here?'

'I visited her a couple of days ago. She's in her eighties but her mind's still sharp.'

'Did she know the Benleys?' Wesley asked.

'They kept themselves to themselves but she sometimes used to see them in the village.'

Wesley caught Gerry's eye. 'Did she say anything about them?'

'Only that they were weird and people kept away from their place. There were all sorts of stories going round even before those girls got killed.'

'What stories?'

'People used to say they conjured demons and sacrificed animals.' He gave the knowing smirk of one far too sophisticated to give credence to such claptrap. 'I must admit I was surprised when it turned out they'd killed the girls. I hadn't believed the rumours but it looks like I was wrong.'

'Lilith Benley always insisted she was innocent.'

Raybourn looked up. 'I thought she confessed.'

Wesley shook his head. 'That was her mother. She had dementia and the doctors reckoned she didn't understand what she was saying.'

'Or she was too crazy to think up any clever lies.'

'Did anybody in the village actually witness any of these rituals the women were supposed to have taken part in?'

'Not as far as I know. But the truth never gets in the way of a good story, does it, and the tabloids have nothing on an isolated community.'

'What about the girls? Did your aunt know them?'

'I don't think she knew them well . . . although she sometimes mentioned a Mrs Trelisip. I think she lived nearby. She was very upset when the girls disappeared but that's only natural. Look, is this photographer going to press charges?'

'We'll have to wait and see,' said Gerry.

'I need to know where I stand because my agent wants to talk to me about something that's just come up . . . a show for a cable network. He says it's an exciting opportunity.' He gave a bitter smile. 'He must live in a constant state of excitement if his phone calls and e-mails are anything to go by. After a while you learn not to get your hopes up.'

Gerry considered the matter for a few moments. 'We'll keep you posted.'

'And you should be sorting out that lying bastard who's been making up these things about me. I could sue, you know.'

'Not our department,' said Gerry without much regret.

Raybourn bowed his head, newly humble as if he'd suddenly realised the potential damage to his precious reputation. A dark cocktail of seedy sexual shenanigans and alleged racism could put a stop to his agent's 'exciting opportunity' before you could say 'lucrative contract'.

As they stood up to leave, Raybourn spoke again. 'That Lilith woman . . . is she a suspect?'

Something in the way he said it struck Wesley as unusual. He sat down again. 'Why do you ask?'

Raybourn didn't answer.

'Have you met her at all while you've been down here?'

There was another long silence. Gerry was waiting by the door and Wesley caught his eye.

Eventually Raybourn spoke. 'I met her once briefly many years ago but I can't say I knew her.'

'When was this?'

Raybourn seemed flustered now. 'Back in the nineteen eighties, I think. Can't remember exactly.'

'How did you meet her?' Gerry growled.

'Er . . . she came to the theatre in Morbay. She was a fan – or it could have been her old mum, I can't remember.' He gave a nervous half-smile. 'I used to get lots of them in those days . . . wanting autographs and all that.'

'Is that all?'

'Yeah. That's all. She got my autograph and I hardly said two words to her.'

'But you remembered her?' said Wesley.

'I remembered the name. It's unusual. And she was a striking woman. Not easy to forget. That's it. End of story.'

Wesley glanced at Gerry who raised his eyebrows. There was another question he needed to put to Raybourn. More fishing in the hope of enlightenment.

'Have you ever come across a retired teacher called Laurence Roley?' he asked.

Raybourn made a great show of thinking. 'The name's not familiar. Can I go now?' He looked from one policeman to the other hopefully.

Gerry gave him a brisk nod and left the room. Raybourn was still up there on their suspect list but the clock was ticking and they both knew they couldn't keep him in custody much longer.

'Bit of a turn up him knowing Lilith Benley,' said Gerry as they walked off down the corridor.

'Think it's relevant?'

Gerry thought for a few moments. 'Probably not. He must have had loads of fans back in the day. It's time we talked to Dan Sericold. I want to get the full story. If Boo was onto Raybourn first . . . '

'You think he killed Boo Flecker to stop it coming out that he uses rent boys and he's a racist?'

'With the wholesome image he's always tried to create something like that could finish him.' He looked at Wesley. 'You must have developed a feeling for these things, Wes. Do you think he's a racist?'

'If he is, he wouldn't be stupid enough to let it show in front of us, would he?'

'What about the weapon . . . the athame? Is it likely he'd be carrying one around on the off-chance he might meet some journalist who might be writing an unfavourable story about him? Benley ordered three of the things so she's a much more likely candidate.'

'If Lilith's hiding the fact that those knives were pinched in that burglary at her place, the thief could have dropped one somewhere. Maybe Raybourn found it just before he met Boo so he had it with him.'

'Bit far-fetched.'

Wesley knew he was right. 'I was just thinking aloud. We need to see Lilith again and ask her about those knives.'

'I reckon she's our number one suspect. And Raybourn's coming up a close second.' He stopped so suddenly that Wesley almost collided into him. 'I forgot to tell you, Wes, someone left a message on my desk. They've spoken to Boo Flecker's mum – she's widowed and she lives up in Yorkshire. She's coming down tomorrow. Rachel said she'd pick her up at Morbay station.'

Wesley said nothing. A mental picture of the victim's mother identifying her dead daughter flashed into his head, causing a knot of tension to form in his stomach.

He was glad that they had two visits lined up – Dan Sericold the photographer and Laurence Roley, Boo's lunch companion. Anything to take his mind off the prospect of facing the bereaved mother.

As soon as they got into the car Wesley began to drive towards Neston. But on the way they stopped off at the pub in the village of Whitely where Sericold was staying.

They found him in the bar sipping coffee. He was in his forties and dressed in denim with a scarf draped around his neck. Wesley knew they'd found the right man because he had a black eye, badly bruised and still half-closed. Raybourn had packed a hefty punch.

'We meet at last, Mr Sericold,' said Gerry, shaking hands heartily. He introduced Wesley and they ordered more coffee. Wesley felt he needed something to stimulate his brain.

'Boo Flecker's death must have come as a shock,' Wesley began.

'Yeah. I'm gutted. I can't believe it.' Wesley didn't think he looked particularly grief stricken. But it's often hard to tell.

'You were friends?'

'More colleagues. Boo was good at her job. Single-minded. Always on the lookout for a new story or a fresh angle.'

'I take it you haven't come all the way down to Devon just to help us with our enquiries,' Wesley said. 'You could have done that over the phone.'

Sericold's lips turned upwards in a secretive smile and he tapped the side of his nose. 'Boo said she was onto something. I don't only take photographs. I sometimes work on stories of my own. It pays to diversify.'

'This story . . . it was about Rupert Raybourn?'

'I assumed it was about Raybourn. I know he's a bit of a has-been but he's still newsworthy. Lots of old ladies still think the sun shines out of his arse.'

'And Boo found out different?'

'As soon as I heard what had happened to her I started asking around. That's when I heard about the rent boy.'

'You think Raybourn killed Boo to stop that coming out?'

'If she hadn't got the story someone else would. He probably just lost his temper.' He pointed to his eye.

'But murder?'

'Like I said, the guy has a temper.'

'Did Boo ever mention Lilith Benley?' asked Gerry.

Sericold shook his head.

'Anything else you can tell us?'

Sericold hesitated. 'That voicemail message I mentioned when you first rang – I listened to it again. Her exact words were "one thing leads to another". I assumed it was about Raybourn but . . . '

Wesley leaned forward eagerly. 'But she could have been referring to someone else?'

Sericold shrugged and put his cup down. 'Could have

179

been. But the way Raybourn reacted it must have been about him, mustn't it?'

They talked to Sericold for a while, learning more about the dead woman, about her nature and her ambitions. He didn't tell them much but at least they now had a better idea of what Boo had been like. Tough. Determined. Not the sort of woman who'd have any scruples about raking up uncomfortable secrets.

When they took their leave they drove straight to Laurence Roley's address on the outskirts of Neston. It turned out that the retired teacher lived on the outer fringe of the town in a brick bungalow built in the nineteen-seventies, architecture's least inspiring days, and fronted by a pristine garden where late roses still bloomed. The blue Mondeo, familiar from the CCTV footage, stood polished and immaculate in the drive, telling them that they'd come to the right address.

Warrant cards at the ready, they rang the doorbell and stood there expectantly. After a while the door opened to reveal the man they recognised immediately from the CCTV footage as Boo Flecker's companion.

When they introduced themselves he looked surprised but he invited them inside and offered coffee. Wesley felt he needed another one to keep him alert after his restless night so he accepted gratefully, as did Gerry.

Roley disappeared into the kitchen and when he returned a few minutes later with the drinks he made a great show of putting down coasters so the cups wouldn't damage the polished surface of the coffee table. The room was as neat as the garden, not a thing out of place, and there were fresh flowers in a cut-glass vase on the sideboard.

Wesley had assumed that there must be an unseen wife

fussing somewhere in the background and he was a little surprised when another man, small and dapper with snowy hair and a tan suggesting a recent holiday in sunnier climes, entered the room. Roley introduced him as his partner, Ian, and both policemen stood up and shook hands with the newcomer, who sat down in the armchair opposite as though he was determined to stay.

'Mr Roley, I believe you met a woman called Boo Flecker for lunch at the Ploughman's Rest last Tuesday,' Wesley began. 'I don't know whether you've heard that the body of a woman matching her description was found in a field near the village of West Fretham later that day. Her name hasn't been released yet but . . . '

Roley's hand went to his mouth. Either he was an extremely accomplished actor or his shock was genuine. 'Oh my God . . . it wasn't her was it?'

Wesley saw Ian rise from his seat and perch himself on the arm of Roley's chair, placing a protective arm around his shoulders.

'I'm sorry if it's come as a shock, Mr Roley, but you'll understand why we need to speak to you.'

'Of course, Inspector. I'll help in any way I can.'

Laurence Roley assumed the half eager, half worried expression that Wesley had seen on the faces of so many concerned, law-abiding citizens, only too anxious to assist the police.

'How did you come to know her?' Gerry asked.

'She contacted me out of the blue that morning. Said she'd been looking into a murder case from many years ago and she'd tracked me down. I'm not sure how she traced me but I believe it's not difficult . . . the phone book, the electoral register and . . . '

'Yes, Mr Roley,' said Gerry before the man became side-tracked. 'Which murder was this?' They already knew Roley had been interviewed when the girls had vanished eighteen years ago but they wanted to hear it from the man himself.

'Two of my pupils – sorry, we have to call them students nowadays, don't we – were murdered.'

'Were these students Gabrielle Soames and Joanne Trelisip?' Wesley asked, his instincts telling him that this was important.

'That's right. They'd been in my form that year and Boo wanted to talk about them.'

Wesley caught Gerry's eye. According to Dan Sericold, Boo had been investigating Rupert Raybourn but one thing had led to another and, presumably, an even better story had come up – one she hadn't cared to share with her colleague at that point. The Benley case hadn't been mentioned but now it looked likely that the story she'd stumbled on might have been Lilith's return to the scene of her grisly crime. Cases like that always captured the public imagination.

'Did you know that Lilith Benley's been released from prison?' he asked.

'I had heard,' Roley said softly. 'It only happened eighteen years ago. In those women's case I would have thought life would mean life.'

'The mother died in a secure hospital. And now Lilith's moved back into her old home. Boo Flecker was found near there.'

Roley pressed his lips together in a determined line. 'That Benley woman's a danger to society. She should be put away for good.'

'What exactly did Boo Flecker ask you?'

'She wanted the dirt on those two poor girls. Somehow she'd heard that they weren't exactly angels but I didn't give her what she wanted.'

Ian gave his shoulder a comforting squeeze. 'Larry's not one for speaking ill of the dead, are you, Larry?'

Roley shook his head.

'Sometimes it's necessary to get at the truth,' said Wesley quietly.

Roley sat for a while in silence and as Wesley watched him he saw the emotions pass across his face; worry, grief and indecision.

'You're not doing the girls or Boo Flecker any favours by not giving us the whole picture,' said Gerry. Roley's bland statement eighteen years ago had read like a eulogy but the passage of time would, hopefully, have stripped sentiment away.

The blunt words seemed to jolt Roley out of his reverie. 'Very well. I'll be honest. I can't pretend that Joanne and Gabrielle were easy students. Well, Gabrielle had been a nice girl when I'd taught her English in the lower forms but I'm afraid she was rather easily led so when she came under the influence of a stronger personality . . . '

'Joanne called the shots?'

'I suppose you could put it like that. But whatever Joanne might have done those poor girls didn't deserve . . . ' He took out a spotless handkerchief and dabbed at his eyes while Ian hugged him, full of concern. 'Boo wanted to know about the girls . . . about their relationships and their love lives. I thought it best to plead ignorance because I guessed what kind of article she had in mind. Sensationalist tabloid rubbish.' He pursed his lips with disapproval and Ian nodded in agreement.

Eventually Roley spoke again. 'It was Joanne who attracted the boys. Gabrielle was ... ' He hesitated. 'What some unkind people would call the plain friend – although she wasn't plain, she was just quieter.'

'Did Joanne have a boyfriend?' Wesley asked.

'She used to chase after John Grimes; he was in the year above and he had a reputation for being the class Romeo.' A small smile appeared on his lips. 'John was one of my star pupils. I like to think I introduced him to the joys of poetry. In fact we became quite close.' He suddenly realised that his words might be misconstrued. 'I don't mean that anything untoward went on. It's just that when you get an extremely talented student who shares a passion for your subject, it's rather a wonderful thing.' He sighed. 'Such a shame he dropped out of school after the tragedy and gave up going to university to join some pop group. It was a terrible waste.'

Wesley knew he had to interrupt Roley's fond reminiscences and return to the subject of murder. 'So John and Joanne ... ?'

'They were caught together in the art stock room ... having sex. And her behaviour towards authority left a lot to be desired. She was defiant and she didn't see why she should be working for her exams, which was a pity because she was very bright. She was, I regret to say, one of those girls whose hormones get the better of them ... always had the shortest skirt and the biggest mouth, if you know what I mean. But she was only sixteen so who knows what she might have become once maturity set in. That's what's so dreadfully sad about the whole thing, Inspector. Most people have a chance to grow up but she never did.'

'And Gabrielle?'

'She hung on Joanne's every word, although I did hear rumours in the staff room a couple of weeks before the tragedy that John Grimes had tired of Joanne and turned his attentions to Gabrielle. I must confess I hoped this might eventually herald a parting of the ways. Joanne's influence on her must have been a terrible worry for Gabrielle's parents – they were decent people. I did hear they'd moved away but I suppose that's understandable.'

Wesley nodded. 'What can you tell me about Joanne's family?'

'She was an only child. Absent father who'd absconded with another woman when Joanne was about eight and an ineffectual mother who found it hard to cope. Joanne had had no boundaries set so it's hardly surprising she ended up as she did.'

So far they hadn't spoken to Joanne's mother who seemed to have vanished from the face of the earth. If she was traced Wesley didn't relish the prospect of facing her – but police work, by its nature, was full of sad encounters.

'If you want the sorry truth, Inspector, I didn't think Joanne Trelisip was a nice person,' Roley said, glancing at Ian for reassurance. 'In fact she made life very awkward for me a few weeks before she died. This isn't something I'd normally share, of course, but if you heard it from someone else you might think ...'

Wesley saw Gerry was sitting on the edge of the sofa, waiting for the revelation. It was a few moments before Roley continued, as if he'd been summoning the courage to speak.

'Joanne used to write nasty little notes which she'd leave in peoples' lockers spreading rumours about various members of staff. For a few weeks I was her victim. She made allegations about my ... about my sexuality. She said I'd been touching the younger boys, which was absolute rubbish, of course. I can only suppose that she'd picked up on the fact that I was gay and thought she'd use it to amuse herself – unfortunately people weren't so tolerant in those days. Bullies behave like that, don't you find? They find somebody different and torment them because of that difference. I imagine it's a primitive thing; the fear of the other. It's something civilisation is supposed to eradicate.'

'Only it doesn't always work that way,' Wesley said quietly. He glanced at Gerry and saw he was nodding in agreement. 'You're sure it was Joanne who wrote the notes?'

'Oh yes. She was suspended from school for three weeks, which didn't really bother her because she just regarded it as an extra holiday. Look, the death of a young person is always a tragedy and this case was no exception ... but it would be dishonest to pretend Joanne Trelisip was an angelic innocent.'

'Did you share any of this with Boo Flecker?'

'Certainly not. I didn't want to see the girls' names dragged through the mud in a tabloid newspaper.'

'We have CCTV footage of you and Boo in the car park of the Ploughman's Rest,' said Gerry. 'You parted on amicable terms?'

'That's right, we did. I didn't particularly like the woman but we didn't fall out.'

'She left her car there and walked off in the direction of Jessop's Farm where that reality show was being filmed,' said Wesley. 'She told a colleague she was investigating one of the participants – Rupert Raybourn, the comedian. Did she mention that at all?'

'She said she was working on a story about a well-known celebrity. But she also said she'd had a more interesting lead. Then she asked me what I knew about Lilith Benley and did I know exactly where the two girls had been murdered.'

'And you told her?'

'It's in the public domain so I didn't see the harm.'

'When she left did she say anything about visiting Lilith Benley?'

'Not exactly but it wouldn't have surprised me if she'd gone up there. I don't think Ms Flecker was one to consider the finer feelings of others.' He hesitated for a moment. 'And if she did visit the Benley woman, you realise it means she's probably killed again. Perhaps you'll lock her up for good this time.'

'We'll have to bring Lilith Benley in,' said Gerry. 'I think Boo came after Raybourn then she found out Benley had been released and returned to the scene of her crime. What's the betting Boo Flecker went there wanting an exclusive story and she got more than she bargained for.'

Wesley couldn't argue with his logic. In spite of Raybourn's violent outburst against Dan Sericold he found it hard to imagine him committing murder. But Lilith, if her mother's evidence at her trial all those years ago was to be believed, had once thought nothing of killing two young girls who'd made a nuisance of themselves. Lilith had ordered three knives from Evan Mumford's company – athames identical to the murder weapon – and as yet they hadn't been able to ask her whether she could account for them. If Boo had met her after leaving Laurence Roley that day, she might well have lost control and killed again.

'We'd better get up there and hope she answers the door this time,' said Wesley. 'But there's something I need to do first.' As they were already in Neston it made sense to visit the police station while he was there.

Gerry looked at his watch. 'The Nutter wants to see me – another ruddy meeting.' He rolled his eyes. Wesley knew it was years since Chief Superintendent Nutter had worked on the front line ... and sometimes his ill-timed interference sorely tried Gerry's patience. 'I'd better get a car to take me back to Tradmouth. Then as soon as I'm done we'll get up to Devil's Tree Cottage and bring her in for questioning. We'll keep her in custody on suspicion of murder if necessary.'

They drove the short distance to Neston police station in silence and while Gerry met the car which would take him back to Tradmouth, Wesley made for the police garage.

He looked for the man he'd met the night before but he was nowhere to be seen. However, when he saw a uniformed officer in the glass-fronted office at the side he walked over and introduced himself. There were several vehicles in the cavernous garage which smelled of oil and something else he couldn't quite put his finger on, some crashed, some intact and surrounded by police tape awaiting examination. He spotted Neil's wrecked Mini in the corner and the thought that someone had deliberately attempted to kill his friend made his stomach churn afresh. The officer was intent on his paperwork but he looked up when Wesley cleared his throat.

'I'm DI Peterson from Tradmouth. That yellow Mini belongs to a friend of mine. I believe the brake pipes were cut.'

The officer looked at Wesley curiously for a while then,

having made up his mind that he was probably who he said he was, he leaned back against the desk and folded his arms. 'Has your mate got any enemies?'

'He's an archaeologist not a Mafia boss.'

The man grinned. 'Rival archaeologist after the same buried treasure?'

Wesley shook his head. 'I was wondering if any prints had been found on the brake pipes.'

The officer shook his head. 'Nothing usable. Pity. How is your mate?'

'Still in hospital. He's had an operation on his leg and he's undergoing more tests. Do you happen to know if DS Gaulter's in his office?'

The answer was another shake of the head followed by an offer of the extension phone on the desk to ring through to CID. Wesley was in luck. Gaulter was in. And he was happy to have an informal word.

The CID office at Neston Police Station was smaller than the one at Tradmouth and the view wasn't so spectacular. At Tradmouth the large windows of the first floor office overlooked the river, the town of Queenswear on the opposite bank and the wooded hills beyond, a view the tourists paid good money for but the police had free of charge. However, here in Neston the unlovely view of the main road into town had to suffice. Almost a year ago a murder incident room had been set up here following a shooting in nearby Tradington and Wesley had felt rather claustrophobic working in the low-ceilinged, utilitarian room.

DS Gaulter was waiting for him. The two men had never met before but Wesley's first impression of Gaulter was favourable. His wispy fair hair was thinning on top and, with his round, amiable face, he looked like a rather worldly monk.

'What can I do for you?' he asked after inviting Wesley to sit and offering a cup of tea from the machine, an offer Wesley found easy to refuse.

'It's a bit delicate. A teacher has been accused of assaulting a minor and the consensus of opinion among his colleagues seems to be that he's innocent. Look, tell me to get lost if I'm treading on toes here but I promised someone who works with him I'd have a word.' He shrugged apologetically, half expecting Gaulter's welcoming manner to change.

'You're talking about the Simon Frith case, aren't you?' Gaulter began to search through the cardboard files neatly stacked on his desk. He found one and opened it, the frown of concentration on his face wrinkling his forehead.

'Do you mind talking about it?'

Gaulter didn't reply for a few seconds. Then he looked up. 'It seems pretty cut and dried. Jessica Gaunt is fifteen, and in spite of the fact she's one of those Goths, she seems a nice quiet girl from a caring family. Dad's a chartered accountant with offices in Morbay and mother's a part-time nurse and they answered an advert placed in a shop window by a teacher offering GCSE tuition. Frith teaches History at South Hams College of Further Education and came with excellent references. All was well at first then, after six months or so, the girl told her mother Frith had touched her inappropriately. Claimed he'd squeezed her breasts and made suggestive remarks ... something about Abelard and Heloise. They were a teacher and a pupil in medieval France who fell in love, I believe.'

'That's right. It does seem the sort of thing that might

spring to a History teacher's mind in those circumstances. The girl's stuck to her story?'

'Yes.'

'You've had a look at Frith's computer?'

'Yes. Nothing incriminating. No kiddie porn. Mind you, that might just mean he's been careful.'

'But something's bothering you?' Wesley knew the signs. He'd experienced that same feeling himself; a nebulous feeling that something wasn't quite right.

'The girl was very confident when she was interviewed. Maybe too confident, as if she'd rehearsed it all carefully.'

'Or cooked up the story with one of her mates?'

Gaulter thought for a few moments, turning the pen he was holding over and over in his fingers. 'There is a boyfriend; a lad from her class at school. Look, I've absolutely no proof that she's not telling the truth but I've seen how she behaves in front of her parents; all tears and shyness. I also caught her off-guard one day. I happened to call when she was alone with the boyfriend in the house and it was almost as if she had to remind herself to keep up the act. The female DC who was with me agreed. But it's hardly evidence, is it?'

'What about Simon Frith?'

'Nothing known against him. But there's always a first time.'

'This boyfriend, what's his name?'

'Alex something. Why?'

'What does he look like?'

'Average height, bit on the porky side. Dresses as a Goth with longish black hair and various bits of metal stuck through his face.'

Wesley hadn't been expecting a description of Alex

Gulliver but he'd got one. And the connection made his heart beat a little faster. Until he told himself that it was bound to be a coincidence. 'I'm working on the Boo Flecker case and a lad called Alex answering the same description found the murder weapon.'

Gaulter raised his eyebrows. 'You don't think there's a connection?'

'Probably not.'

'Unless the lad has a thing about the police ... like arsonists who set fire to things to watch the fire brigade arrive. Perhaps he likes the drama.'

'Anything's possible, Geoff. Look, thanks for seeing me.'

'We're still investigating Jessica's claims but I'll keep you posted.'

Wesley thanked him and as he left the police station he felt that at least he'd be able to tell Della that he'd tried. Hopefully that should keep her off his back for a while.

As he was getting into his car his mobile rang and when he answered it he heard Rachel's voice.

She told him to get back to the incident room. Gerry Heffernan had finished his meeting with the Chief Superintendent and he wanted to head up to Devil's Tree Cottage as soon as possible. Whatever was going on, Lilith Benley was at the heart of it.

When they arrived at Devil's Tree Cottage all the curtains were shut, exactly as they'd been when Wesley had called with Rachel the previous day. The place was silent and the possibility that it was the silence of death flashed into Wesley's head. Maybe Lilith Benley had committed suicide in a fit of remorse, he thought. With two – or perhaps three – terrible deaths on her conscience and a bleak future as a reviled outsider, it wouldn't have surprised him.

He knocked on the door but there was no answer.

'I reckon she's decided to scarper,' said Gerry, staring at the front door.

'Does she have a car?'

Gerry shook his head. 'Not as far as I know. She'll probably use taxis if she wants to go anywhere. I shouldn't think she has any friends willing to offer her lifts. I can't see her having any friends full stop.'

Wesley thought for a moment. 'She claimed she was a witch. Don't witches have covens?'

'You mean someone's given her a lift on their broomstick?'

'All I mean is that she might have contacts we don't know about.'

Gerry considered the matter for a few seconds. 'She says she doesn't practise any more but she bought those athames so it looks like she was lying. Unless she ordered them with murder in mind.'

'Is that likely?'

'Who knows, Wes. We'll contact all the local cab firms to see if anybody's picked her up. But before we do, I want to have a look around the back.'

Wesley followed reluctantly. A row of dilapidated redbrick pig sties stood behind the cottage. This was where, according to Dorothy Benley, the women had disposed of the girls' bodies. The thought made him feel slightly sick.

Gerry carried on walking in determined silence and when they arrived at the back door he stopped suddenly. 'Looks as if her burglar might have paid her another visit.'

The smashed pane of glass in the door had been

replaced by a piece of wood after the burglary, but now there was an unglazed hole where the wooden rectangle should have been. Wesley took a peek inside the kitchen and saw it lying on the floor. It had been held securely with nails and he could see them protruding from the wood. Somebody had smashed it in.

He took a pair of plastic gloves from his pocket; he was so used to being around crime scenes that the action was automatic.

'Go on, Wes,' Gerry said. 'Let's see if it's unlocked.'

Wesley put a gloved hand on the door handle and when he pushed it down the door swung open. He stared into the shadowy interior, wishing the curtains weren't drawn because it was hard to see much in the gloom. He had a strong feeling that something was wrong but he forced himself to cross the threshold.

Stepping into the kitchen he found the light switch. He flicked it down and in the sickly yellow light he could see a dirty plate and a pan encrusted with something orange and glutinous lying in the sink, half covered with greasy water. There was a blanket of toast crumbs on the chipped Formica table in the corner and a mug on the draining board contained the dregs of some brown drink. There was no sound in the room, not even birdsong from the fields round about. Just a heavy, ominous silence.

Gerry nodded towards the closed door leading to the small parlour and Wesley pushed it open. The curtains were drawn here too and he stopped in the doorway, reluctant to stagger in and tread on anything that might be evidence. Gerry, standing behind him, reached past the door frame and fumbled for the light switch. When he found it the room was suddenly bathed in the puny light from the bare sixty-watt bulb dangling in the centre of the ceiling.

Wesley had feared that he'd been about to blunder into a crime scene, splattered with dried blood and smelling like a slaughterhouse, and he was relieved to see that the room looked just as it had when he had last been there. Except for one thing.

On the floor lay a figure. It was smaller than a new-born baby and its roughly made black skirt was raised to its crotch. Its face was yellow-white wax with drawing pin eyes and a mouth of red thread. As Wesley moved forward he could see a tangled tuft of dusty black hair stuck to its scalp and a large nail protruding like a miniature javelin from its middle.

He heard Gerry's voice behind him, uncharacteristically hushed.

'I think it's meant to be Lilith Benley.'

Chapter 10

Written by Alison Hadness, September 19th 1643

When I married William he had no inkling of my deception. If he had he would not have begged my hand and I would not have had to endure this marriage my father arranged for me. I try my best not to think on Thomas Whitcombe. Such was his devotion to the King's cause that he had gone from Tradmouth before I could tell him that our sin had borne fruit. Maybe it was a blessing that the fruit withered and died within me and the bloody thing was pulled from my body and thrown upon the fire by Dorcas who has ever been a friend to me.

I went to gather herbs and ventured into the churchyard. There I did pray at the grave of my father, asking forgiveness for the ill will I bear him for arranging my marriage. I prayed also that I would find it in my heart to be a dutiful wife to William and a mother to Elizabeth and that I might learn to disregard her spite and hatred.

I could see the guns mounted atop the tower but I knew I was alone in the churchyard as I gathered the yellow flowers. I wished they smelled sweeter but they will suit my purpose. The infusion I made is stored now. If William ails again I shall use it.

Dorcas says the miller has rye flour for bread from a farmer in Derenham. The grain is not of the best but starving men cannot choose.

Dave was floundering, out of his depth. If Neil had been there, he'd have known what to say. But he wasn't so it was up to him to deal with the situation.

A phone call from Harriet Mumford had brought him rushing back to Mercy Hall, temporarily abandoning the dig up at Princes Bower.

As he drove his rickety Land Rover to the far edge of Tradmouth and parked it next to Evan Mumford's shiny new Mini Cooper, his mind was on the past. Mercy Hall would have been at the centre of things during the Civil War when Princes Bower had been manned by the Royalist army, and he knew Neil had intended to do some research into the Hall's history – until the accident put him in hospital.

Dave wasn't much good at comforting the sick but there was something he could do for Neil. He could discover all he could about the little coffins and the carving of the hanged woman he'd seen in the garden. People wrote things down in the seventeenth century so the truth must be there somewhere. It was just a case of finding it.

According to Harriet, when the builders had removed the rest of the panelling, they'd found a third wooden box containing a hideous wax doll – a man this time, dressed all in black like the others, the wax face leering above its small white puritan collar. This new find had seriously spooked them and now it looked as if it was up to Dave to be the voice of reason. The builders, Harriet said, were threatening to walk out and she wanted him to reassure them that there wasn't a curse on the place. Dave hadn't realised your average British workman was so superstitious

When he arrived he found four builders standing in the kitchen, sipping tea and looking mutinous.

Harriet stood beside the sink, wringing her hands, as though the latest discovery was the last straw.

'What do these things mean?' she asked him as soon as he walked in.

'I've got experts up at Exeter examining the one we found yesterday. Once I get their verdict . . . '

'The men say they're not working in there any more and the cellar's only half dug out. They say they're scared of what they'll find down there.'

'That's right,' said Lee who was standing in the centre of the group.

Dave cleared his throat. 'Look, there's no reason to think . . . '

A tattooed builder with a shaved head held up a band-aged hand, stepping forward and waving the soiled dressings in his face. 'Nothing's gone right since we found those things. You dropped a spade on your foot, didn't you, Lee?'

Lee nodded obediently.

'What's going on?'

Dave looked round and saw Evan Mumford scowling in the doorway. Harriet's expression suddenly changed and she took a step back.

'I've been looking for you,' he barked at his wife. 'Those invoices need sending out.'

Dave saw Harriet flinch as though he'd struck her. Then he saw a look pass between the builders, a look he couldn't quite read.

Evan spoke again, squaring up to the builders. 'And you lot can get back to work. That's what I'm paying you for.' He turned his hostile gaze on Dave. 'Have you finished?'

'I'm just off,' Dave said, only too aware that Neil wouldn't have backed off so easily. He'd have ensured that the new discovery was properly packed and safe before setting a foot outside. But Dave was made of weaker stuff.

Harriet followed her husband out of the room, and as she crossed the threshold she turned her head and gave Dave a pleading look.

But Dave knew he was no knight in shining armour. Just a middle-aged archaeologist in a muddy combat jacket. It was time to make a strategic withdrawal.

A search of the surrounding area failed to find any trace of Lilith Benley. She had gone. Either that or she was dead and her body would turn up in due course. There were a lot of places in the Devon countryside where a body could lie undiscovered for years: copses and ditches; isolated barns; shadowy woods and stagnant ponds.

Gerry seemed sure she was still alive, that she'd been sent the doll by an ill-wisher and she'd fled the cottage because it had scared her. Wesley however, wasn't so sure.

'Let's get out of here,' said Gerry, making for the door. 'I'll order a thorough search of this place – see if there's any sign of those knives she ordered.'

Wesley nodded. The thought of those knives made him uneasy. Wherever Lilith was she might have them with her . . . and that might mean she planned to use them.

'We should have taken her in when we had the chance,' Gerry said as they walked out into the fresh air. 'Kept her in the cells where we could keep an eye on her.'

'You really think she killed Boo Flecker?'

'If I was a betting man, Wes, I'd put money on it.'

Wesley said nothing until they were climbing into the car. 'I think we should speak to Joe Jessop. He'll have been out and about on his farm. He might have seen something.'

Gerry nodded in agreement and ten minutes later they were at the cottage where Joe Jessop had been staying since the filming began.

Jessop sat at his kitchen table, his sheep dog, Fin, on the floor by his side. Gerry leaned down and stroked the animal absentmindedly and when he stopped Fin nuzzled his hand, craving attention.

'Can't say I'm surprised the Benley woman's gone.'

'Why's that, Mr Jessop?' Wesley asked.

'A lot of people round here don't think she should have come back.'

'Have you seen anything suspicious? Anyone on the Benleys' land?'

'I told those policemen who came round earlier, I've seen nothing and heard nothing.' He gave an exasperated sigh. 'Those TV people said they'd come back as soon as the fuss died down. If this business scares 'em off it'll cost me a bloody fortune – and I wouldn't mind but it's nothing to do with me.'

'That's what you said when those lasses were killed eighteen years back,' said Gerry.

Jessop half rose from his seat, indignant, and Fin, aware that the strangers had upset his master, gave a token growl.

'It was true then and it's true now. The coppers who came wouldn't tell me what they'd found over at her cottage. You don't think she's done herself in, do you?'

'We haven't found a body,' said Wesley. 'You didn't hear anything suspicious last night?'

'Devil's Tree Cottage is a quarter of a mile away. The band of the Coldstream Guards could have been marching round up there for all I'd know.' He idly stroked Fin's head and the dog began to wag his tail as he gazed up at his master with unconditional adoration.

'You knew the dead girls, didn't you?'

Jessop looked at Wesley, suddenly wary. 'I only knew *of* them. They lived in the village.'

'We're having problems tracing Joanne Trelisip's family,' said Gerry.

'There was only the mum and she was a ewe short of a flock. No idea what happened to her. Her place is a weekend cottage now . . . so I've heard.'

'Rupert Raybourn.'

Jessop frowned. 'What about him?'

'His aunt lives in the village.'

'I've not heard that. What's her name?'

'Vera Bourne.'

'Doesn't ring a bell.'

They left Jessop to his work, promising they'd let him know as soon as permission was given for the filming to start again. The man's weather-beaten face didn't give much away as they took their leave. Wesley had the impression he was hiding something but he told himself that he might always have been like that, guarded and watchful. It probably came from living alone on an isolated farm which adjoined a notorious murder scene. Murder sends ripples out to stain everything and everyone around; neighbours, acquaintances, relatives, the innocent and those with a heavy conscience.

'I'll drop you off in the village,' Wesley said to Gerry as they were leaving. 'There's someone I want to see.'

'Who?'

'Shane Gulliver's son, Alex. He found the knife that killed Boo Flecker.'

'I'll come with you.'

This wasn't what Wesley wanted to hear. He'd wanted a private word with Alex. Off the record. Although Gerry was aware of the accusations against Simon Frith, making unauthorised enquiries on behalf of a suspect in someone else's case wasn't the done thing.

'It's just something I wanted to check,' he said, trying to sound casual.

Before he could elaborate his phone rang. It was Trish calling to tell him that they'd found the Bed and Breakfast place where Boo had been staying. It had taken a while – but then there were many such establishments in the area, not all of them on the official tourist trail.

He told Gerry the news. 'According to Trish, Boo left stuff in her room.'

Gerry's eyes lit up. 'Let's get over there then.'

Alex Gulliver would have to wait. Besides, Wesley felt he needed a little more time to plan what he was going to say. He wanted the boy to tell him the truth about Jessica and her dealings with Frith. And he wasn't sure that turning up in his policeman's role was the way to do it. His instincts told him the informal, archaeology and metal detecting route might be the best way to gain his trust.

Boo's B and B turned out to be a farmhouse in the middle of open countryside about a mile outside Neston. It was a working establishment and the scent of slurry hung in the air as they approached the front door. The paved farmyard was damp with a thin layer of brown mud and a sheepdog greeted them eagerly, tail wagging. It hardly seemed the sort of place an investigative journalist from London would choose to stay. Another mystery to add to their list.

The woman who opened the door introduced herself as Mary Broughton. She was well built with short brown hair and a grey tracksuit and she looked as if she'd have no problem wrestling a misbehaving sheep to the ground if the need arose. She led them into a utilitarian lounge with a busy patterned carpet, bare walls and a large flat screen TV in the corner, explaining that, in an effort to diversify and supplement the farm's dwindling income, she took in the occasional bed and breakfast visitor, advertising on the Internet. It was rare to get any takers out of season so she'd been glad to accept Boo Flecker's booking. Her guest had arrived on Thursday and most of the time she'd been out in her car. In the evenings she'd eaten out before returning to work in her room.

When Wesley asked her whether she'd heard about Boo's murder she looked horrified and shook her head in disbelief. She didn't listen to the news, she explained ... didn't have time. But she had wondered why Ms Flecker hadn't come back for her things.

'I thought she might have met some friends ... or possibly a man. She seemed that sort of girl,' she added with a hint of disapproval.

Wesley searched for a tactful way to phrase his next question. 'Did she say why she chose to stay here? It's not the height of the season so there'd be lots of vacancies in Tradmouth or Neston. I would have thought she'd want to be at the centre of things.'

Mrs Broughton fished in her pocket for a tissue to wipe her eyes of the tears that were on the verge of forming. 'She told me she was a journalist and she wanted somewhere she wouldn't be disturbed. She didn't talk about her work and I didn't ask. I mean, you can't be intrusive, can you? Then on Monday when she got in she seemed really excited. Not that she said anything to me, of course, but I could tell something had happened. She went to her room after that and then out for the evening so I didn't see her again until breakfast. She didn't say much then either. I don't think she was a morning person.'

They asked her if Boo had ever mentioned West Fretham or any of the names that had come up in the course of the investigation. But the answer was no every time.

'Did you get the impression that she was afraid of something or someone?'

She considered the question carefully. 'Now you come to mention it she did seem a bit nervy. She asked me if we got many visitors. How many people knew I did bed and breakfast, that sort of thing.' Her eyes widened. 'This story she was working on ... Do you think it had something to do with her murder?'

'We're not sure yet,' said Gerry. 'Are her things still in her room?'

'I didn't know when she was coming back so I haven't touched anything.'

'May we have a look?' said Wesley with a reassuring smile. Like most people leading a blameless, routine existence, murder wasn't something that normally touched Mary Broughton's life.

They followed her upstairs then along a narrow passage

with a bright pink carpet. When she reached the door at the end she stopped, as though she was reluctant to go any further. She took a deep breath before turning the handle and opening the door.

It was an old-fashioned room with flowery wallpaper, matching frilly curtains and fussy, lace-trimmed bedspread. The overall theme was pink and it was an overtly feminine room – as if Mrs Broughton had poured all her suppressed frivolity into this one chamber. There were clothes strewn on the bed; jeans, jogging bottoms and a couple of long-sleeved T-shirts. There was underwear too – probably worn – and a screwed-up pair of socks. Wesley peeped into the little en suite bathroom. The glass shelves over the sink were crammed with make-up and an array of half-used hair products stood around the edge of the bath. Boo Flecker hadn't been the tidiest of guests.

A suitcase lay on a low table next to the little TV. And beside the suitcase was what looked like a laptop case. Boo's mobile phone hadn't yet been found but there was a chance that her laptop might contain something important. Perhaps her decision to lie low in this unlikely setting had been the right one after all.

'I suppose you'll want to take her things.' Mrs Broughton's voice sounded a little unsteady.

'We'll have a good look round first, love,' he heard Gerry say. 'Sorry but there might be a few coppers with size twelve boots tramping all over your nice clean carpets for a day or so. Then it's all yours. Back to normal.'

Gerry gave her a big reassuring smile. But both of them knew nothing would be normal again. Not now that room had been tainted with violent death. Wesley put on his crime scene gloves and flipped open the suitcase. There were more clothes inside – Boo hadn't believed in travelling light. Gerry watched him as he pushed them to one side to reveal a blue cardboard file. His heart began to beat a little faster as he took it out and flicked through its contents.

Gerry turned to Mrs Broughton, beaming at her like a benevolent uncle. 'It's OK, love, we can manage now. We'll let you know when we've finished.' He spoke gently, as though he wanted to relieve her of the heavy burden.

She took the hint and left and once they were alone Gerry looked at Wesley expectantly. 'Well?'

'There's press cuttings in here about the Benley murders.' He began to read. 'Devil women sacrificed teenagers. Witchcraft led to double murder. Mother held girls while daughter stabbed them. Fed to pigs.' He replaced the cuttings in the file. 'No wonder Boo wanted a piece of the action. I'm surprised she appears to be the only one going after Lilith. Once she was released I would have thought she'd be fair game for anyone wanting a sensational story.'

'The Nutter told me her release was deliberately kept quiet, Wes. Apparently she was offered a change of identity but she refused. Said she was innocent so why should she hide. As soon as she turns up I'm pulling her in.'

Wesley couldn't argue with Gerry's logic but there was still a fragment of doubt in his mind, niggling away, ruining the neat solution.

'I'll call the crime scene people to get this room searched properly.' Wesley took his phone from his pocket. 'And I'll get Tom from Scientific Support to have a look at that laptop.'

'Still want to see Alex Gulliver?'

Wesley looked at his watch. 'He should be back from school by the time we get over there. Who knows, he might have seen something last night.'

Wesley felt that they were going round in circles. All this wasn't going to find Lilith Benley. And they needed to find her as soon as possible, dead or alive.

Ever since she'd watched her grandmother die, Harriet Mumford had always regarded hospitals as places of uncertainty where death was ever present, hovering around the curtained beds looking for fresh meat to devour. They were borderlands, shadowy barriers between one world and the next, and normally she avoided them at all costs. But in spite of this she'd been drawn to Neil Watson's bedside.

She'd told Evan she was going to her studio in West Fretham so no questions had been asked. She'd learned to tread carefully over the years.

The nurses, busy with their paperwork at the nurses' station, didn't glance up as she passed and she walked from one four-bedded room to another, peeping in nervously. Sometimes the patients in the beds would stare back at her as if they were half hoping for company, but most took no notice, ignoring her as if she was invisible.

She found Neil in a room by himself and she wondered whether this meant his condition was serious. He was lying perfectly still with his eyes shut and when she tapped nervously on the open door she saw his eyes flicker open.

'Hi.' His voice sounded weak, like an old man's.

'I thought I'd come to see how you're doing.' She sidled into the room, trying her best to sound cheerful, recalling her attempts to sound positive when her grandmother was dying – the stress and pain of keeping up the act. She'd been twelve years old then and the strain of supporting her mother through the crisis meant that she'd become adept at hiding her feelings and innermost secrets.

'It's good to see you.' Neil made a great effort to raise himself up on the pillows. His flesh was pale, the colour of parchment, and the blue-black circles beneath his eyes made him look as if he'd been punched. 'Always nice to be visited by beautiful women. Sorry I'm not at my best.'

'So you've had lot of beautiful women weeping at your bedside, have you?' She forced out a smile.

'Only the nurses and I've got to tell them they're beautiful or they stick needles in me,' he said weakly. 'My friend Pam's visited a few times.'

'And she's beautiful is she?' She regretted the question as soon as it had left her lips.

'I suppose she is now you come to mention it. Not that I think of her that way . . . '

'Why's that?'

'She's married to my best mate and I've known her for years.'

Harriet's nagging feeling of jealousy subsided just a little. But not much.

'How are you?'

'I've got a bad leg fracture which they've operated on, three broken ribs and I'm covered in cuts and bruises. I had concussion too. They did a brain scan and luckily they found I had one,' he said with a grin that looked more like a grimace of pain. 'They keep telling me I was lucky.' He tried to haul himself further up on his pillows but Harriet saw him wince. 'Dave's been keeping me up to date with what's been happening. He says they've found two more coffins.'

Harriet nodded. 'I wanted them out of the house so he's taken them to Exeter to show someone. You had one in your car when you crashed, didn't you? It makes you wonder . . .'

Neil said nothing. Perhaps the crash was something he didn't want to discuss and she wasn't surprised when he changed the subject. 'Have you found out anything more about Alison Hadness – your witch?'

'Sorry. I haven't had time.'

'Is something wrong?'

Harriet reached out and touched his hand. It felt rough and cold, not as she'd expected. 'I'm frightened, Neil. I'm really scared,' she whispered, the fear rising up inside her, vague and threatening.

'What about? What's up?'

'I've got to go,' she said before hurrying out of the room. The visit had been a mistake . . . possibly a big one.

Gerry's phone rang as they were driving back to West Fretham. After a short conversation he turned to Wesley. 'You'll have to deal with the Gulliver lad on your own. The Nutter's organised a press conference and I've drawn the short straw. Seems there's been a lot of interest from the press, the victim being one of their own. He wants yours truly to take part.' His eyes lit up. 'You don't fancy fifteen minutes of fame, do you, Wes?'

'I tried it once. Never again.'

A wicked grin spread across Gerry's face. 'I'll tell the Nutter you volunteered then.'

At first Wesley didn't know whether he was being serious. But he knew his boss's sense of humour of old so when he said no more he assumed that he was off the hook. With his no-nonsense attitude and his Liverpool accent Gerry came across well on TV – a real star, some said. A natural. There were even some who said he should have been doing Rupert Raybourn's job.

When they reached the Rectory Gerry mumbled something about Joyce saying he needed more exercise before asking Wesley to drop him off so he could walk back to the incident room. Wesley turned into the Gullivers' drive and parked next to a new black Range Rover.

Gwen Gulliver answered the door. As soon as she saw him she looked worried. But then everyone did when there was a murderer at large in the area and the police on the doorstep. She was wearing jeans and a sweatshirt today and there was a hint of pale root showing at the parting in her hair.

'We've already had more policemen round,' she said as she stood aside to let him in. 'They asked us if we'd seen that Benley woman from the smallholding on the other side of the farm. What's happened?'

'We just need to check she's safe, Mrs Gulliver,' he said as he stepped into the hall.

Gwen looked horrified. 'Check she's safe? Your lot seem more interested in protecting criminals than punishing them. If she killed that poor woman at the farm you should be locking her up again.' He could hear the panic rising in her voice now.

'We're keeping an open mind.' As he said the words he realised how unconvincing they sounded. He was hardly doing his bit to reassure the people who lived round about that they could sleep safely in their beds. 'Is Alex in?'

'Why?' There was a defensive note in the question. The mother protecting her young.

210

'I just wanted to ask him something. Nothing to worry about.'

'What's the matter?' The voice belonged to Shane Gulliver who'd just emerged from the drawing room. 'We've already had someone round,' he said as though Wesley was some door-to-door salesman. 'We haven't seen or heard anything out of the ordinary and I don't see how we can help you so I'd be grateful if you'd leave us in peace.'

'He wants to speak to Alex,' Gwen said meekly, as if she was afraid of upsetting her husband, or maybe of driving away the muse that paid the mortgage.

'I need to check something with him. Just routine. Nothing to worry about,' Wesley repeated, giving Gwen a reassuring smile.

'He's in his room.'

'OK if I go up? We had a nice chat about metal detecting last time I came.'

Gulliver raised no objection so Wesley climbed the wide oak staircase, aware that the author was watching him. He knocked on Alex's door and it opened almost at once, as if the boy had been listening in to the conversation downstairs.

'How's the metal detecting going?' Wesley asked cheerfully once he was in the room and Alex had shut the door firmly behind him.

'I haven't found any more murder weapons if that's what you mean.'

'Can I sit down?'

Alex made a vague gesture towards the seat by his computer. It was switched on and instead of the expected Facebook or computer game Wesley could see he was composing an essay. Perhaps his little pep talk had worked. He felt a faint glow of pride that he might have made a difference – perhaps teaching was more rewarding than Pam and her colleagues made out.

'I hear the murderer's on the run.' The boy's eyes were shining with enthusiasm. The subject of murder was clearly to his liking.

'I'm not here about the murder this time. Do you know a girl called Jessica Gaunt?'

A guarded look suddenly appeared in Alex's eyes. 'Why?'

'Is she your girlfriend?'

For several seconds he didn't reply to the question. Then he gave a casual shrug. 'Might be.'

'She reported her History tutor to the police. His name's Simon Frith.'

Wesley saw the boy clench his fists, as though he was preparing to throw a punch. 'The pervert groped her. She was dead upset.'

'Think she was telling the truth?'

''Course she was. They should lock the perv up and throw away the key.'

'Did she tell you what happened?'

'He groped her didn't he? Touched her tits.'

'He denies it.'

'Are you calling Jessica a liar?' The mask of righteous indignation had begun to slip.

'Mr Frith could lose his job so the police have to be absolutely sure.'

'He deserves all he gets.'

'Have you ever met him?'

'No. But my dad was going to ask him to come and help

me with my history. He got talking to Jessica's dad at a parents' evening and he recommended him.'

'Really? So how long did he teach Jessica before this, er . . . incident happened?'

'A while. Six months maybe.'

'And he'd never tried anything like that before?'

'There's always a first time, isn't there?' Alex said. 'I didn't know you were on that case. You never went round to see Jess.'

'No, that was another officer. Thanks for your help. Sorry to have bothered you.' He stood up and made for the door. 'By the way, did you see or hear anything suspicious last night? Strange cars on the lane or intruders in the garden?'

'Nah. It's all gone quiet since the TV people left. Like the bloody grave.' When Wesley was halfway out of the door Alex spoke again. 'Is it true she's a witch?'

Wesley didn't know the answer to that one.

None of the house to house reports Trish Walton had just finished collating had produced anything even vaguely helpful. Nobody in the nearby village had seen or heard anything suspicious or unusual on the day of Boo Flecker's murder. And nothing had come in on the whereabouts of Lilith Benley. Nobody had seen her on the night she vanished and no taxi firms had picked her up. Her disappearance was a mystery and all tests on the wax doll that had been found in her place had come up negative. No fingerprints. No DNA. No nothing.

Wesley, however, wondered whether the people of West Fretham would have confided in the police even if they'd seen someone killing Lilith in front of their eyes. Most of them were relieved she'd gone, expressing the hope that she'd never come back.

The routine checks he'd requested on Harriet Mumford hadn't revealed anything suspicious. As far as they could see she had no connection with Boo Flecker and no apparent reason to kill her. It seemed it was yet another dead end.

Gerry was in his office talking on the phone, a peeved expression on his face. No doubt Wesley would find out who he was speaking to in due course; Gerry wasn't a man who could keep things to himself. In the meantime he sat down at his desk, glad of a moment of calm. The information had been coming at him relentlessly over the past few days and he felt he needed time to think things through.

He'd already looked through the file of cuttings about the Devil's Tree Cottage murders they'd found in Boo Flecker's hotel room, but it would do no harm to look again. He was in search of inspiration, some hitherto ignored fact that would make everything fall into place so he opened the file and started to examine the photocopied sheets.

There were photographs of the girls, alone and together, and pictures the newspapers had obtained of the girls at school. One was a group photograph; several adolescents staring out at the camera, some smiling, some wearing a bored scowl. The two dead girls stood at the back, school ties unknotted in a small act of rebellion. Gabby was snuggled next to a boy who had his arm around her waist and Wesley focused on the boy's face, wondering if this could be the John Grimes who'd been mentioned: the boy who'd been going out with Joanne but had turned his attentions to Gabby a couple of weeks before the girls died. Finding Grimes was on his list of things to do, just in case he'd taken it into his head to wreak some sort of revenge on Lilith Benley for the girls' murders. But it had hardly seemed like a priority. Until now.

John Grimes hadn't changed very much in eighteen years. The hair was different and time and lifestyle had taken their toll. But that sulky, challenging expression was the same. John Grimes, the Devon teenager, had metamorphosed over the years, had escaped his chrysalis and had been transformed into the new creation that was Zac James.

Chapter 11

Journal of Thomas Whitcombe, Captain in the King's army, September 20th 1643

I will go again into Tradmouth in my guise of farmer. If I enquire of Alison it may fit well with my disguise for a spy does not speak of a lady he once knew, rather he is secretive and speaks to nobody except to ask about the town's defences.

So it was that I spoke with a man on the quayside, saying she was a distant kinswoman of mine. He told me she is still in the town and married to one William Hadness, a widower of Mercy Hall. I know the place. It is a handsome stone house not far from Hilton Farm where we are billeted. He made a ribald jest about an old ram not being able to satisfy a young ewe. I laughed as he expected, hiding my distaste at his words. The thought of sweet Alison in the bed of an old man, of him pawing her, his naked body joined with hers, made me angry enough to strike the teller and yet to learn that she is so near is the sweetest Providence.

I heard say that an old woman of the town has been conjuring demons, making her neighbours see visions of hell as they lie shaking at Satan's mercy. It is said she has been taken before the Magistrate and there are many who will testify against her. Without doubt she will hang as witches deserve.

Written by Alison Hadness, September 20th 1643

I learned the art of making physic from my mother who was skilled in such things. And yet there are many plants I do not grow in my garden. Instead I collect them in secret, sometimes at night. Even Dorcas does not know of this. If she did, she would say I was unwise. There are many prepared to cry 'witch' at one with my knowledge.

Elizabeth avoids me. She is a sly girl who keeps to her chamber and says little. Nobody is permitted to enter her chamber and her father indulges her whims. I observed her collecting candle wax in the shadows last night. I fear she plans to do me harm. I must think upon the matter for if I put it about she is using sorcery, she will be taken.

And yet I hesitate to denounce her for pity of her youth.

The palace of white stucco that was the Riviera Towers had dominated the sea front at Morbay since the resort's heyday in the nineteen-twenties. It was where the stars stayed, if they ever strayed in the direction of Morbay for summer season productions or Christmas panto. And it was where Zac James had chosen to stay, well away from Rupert Raybourn at the Marina Hotel in Tradmouth.

When Wesley and Gerry arrived they found Zac sitting in the bar swigging from a bottle of lager and wearing a pair of large and unnecessary dark glasses. As soon as he saw them he pushed the glasses back onto his head. His eyes were bloodshot.

'I've told you already, I don't know nothing about that reporter.'

'You've not heard then?' said Gerry.

'Heard what?'

'Lilith Benley's disappeared. It's been on the news.'

'Haven't seen the news today. The fucking TV company won't tell me what's going on.' He looked at Gerry accusingly. 'Do you know when the filming's starting again? I can't hang about here for ever, you know.'

'Did you hear what I said about Lilith Benley?' said Gerry, ignoring the question.

Zac took another swig of lager. 'If she's done a runner I guess it proves she killed that woman so the rest of us are off the hook. I heard about Rupert and that photographer, by the way.' He smirked. 'Never knew he had it in him.'

'Where were you yesterday?' Gerry asked. 'We think someone might have given Lilith Benley a lift.'

Zac snorted. 'Well it certainly wasn't me. I've got an alibi.' He emphasised the last word. 'I was here all day. Never left the hotel. And in the evening I was with someone. We ate at the Cheval de Mer on the sea front – two Michelin stars – and then she stayed the night in my room.'

'Where can we find her?'

'She works here on Reception,' Zac said, reciting her name with a confidence that convinced Wesley he was telling the truth. Interviewing the star-struck receptionist would probably be a formality.

Wesley had brought the picture he'd found in Boo Flecker's folder with him. He took it from his pocket, unfolded it and handed it to Zac.

'Is that you?'

Zac stared at it for a few moments but didn't answer.

'Why didn't you tell us you were at school with Joanne Trelisip and Gabby Soames?'

'You never asked.' He sounded like a petulant child, discovered doing something bad and trying to brazen it out.

'You told us you were from Essex,' Gerry said accusingly.

'I am ... now. I've lived there for years and so have my folks. Anyway, I didn't want to get involved. I'd had enough of your lot. Just because I had a bit of coke in my room ...'

'Your real name's John Grimes, am I right?'

'Yeah. But I changed it years ago.'

It was Wesley's turn to speak. 'We've been talking to an old teacher of yours. Laurence Roley.'

Zac's eyes brightened and he smiled, as if he was recalling fond memories. 'Old Larry Roley. He was amazing. My family went through a bad patch and I don't know what I would have done without him. Used to tell him all my troubles and he actually listened. He was gay, of course, but that didn't matter. Everyone knew I was one for the girls so no one got the wrong end of the stick. Larry was one of the good guys. Fantastic bloke.'

'You were friendly with Joanne Trelisip and Gabby Soames at the time they were murdered. In fact we've heard you were more than friendly.' Gerry put his face close to Zac's.

The glasses slipped down again. Wesley thought they must have made the world go dark. Or perhaps it was intentional. Perhaps he wanted to conceal his thoughts. Wesley suggested they find a quieter corner and, reluctantly, Zac trailed behind them, eyes still concealed and bottle in hand.

Zac slumped back in a plush seat, legs spread wide, trying to look unconcerned. 'I was in the year above Jo and Gabby but we were mates.'

'According to our records you were interviewed when they vanished,' said Wesley.

'So was everyone. I couldn't tell them anything. All I knew was that they were going to have a giggle with some witches. It was Jo's idea. She had a thing about them. That's all I can tell you, honest.'

'But you knew who they meant? Who the witches were?'

'Everyone knew but most people kept well away. They were supposed to have powers.'

'What sort of powers?'

'Search me. It was just something everyone said.'

'You didn't happen to follow the girls that night?'

'I was in Dukesbridge with some mates. Band practice. The police checked it out at the time. As soon as they disappeared they talked to all their mates.'

'Your parents were away at the time, I believe.'

'Yeah but I was with my mates.'

'How did you get to this band practice?'

'I drove. I'd just passed my test and my mum had let me borrow her car.'

'And you didn't see the girls that evening?'

'No. Like I said, I was at band practice all night.'

Wesley had already checked. John Grimes had an alibi for the evening the girls vanished, provided by his mates in the band. And it looked as if he had one now. They'd arrange for the receptionist to be interviewed but he wasn't holding out much hope. He'd known from Zac's confidence when he'd provided the alibi that he was telling the truth.

He had another question to ask. 'How did Gabby and Joanne get on?'

Zac stared at the bottle, avoiding his gaze. 'OK I suppose.'

'You don't seem too sure.'

'They fell out sometimes. Jo was ... I don't know ... reckless. That was probably why she got herself killed. I can just see her taunting those old bitches. She never knew when to stop.'

Wesley knew what Zac meant. He had met people who lacked control, often among the criminal fraternity. 'But Gabby was with her. She went along with her plan to torment the Benley women?'

'Jo was going whatever happened so I think Gabby went along to make sure she didn't get into trouble. She was like that. Jo told her it'd be a laugh.'

'Until she pushed things too far.'

'Or she was unlucky. They got caught and sacrificed ... '

Gerry had been listening intently but now he broke his silence. 'Come on, Zac, those women might have dabbled in white witchcraft and the mother might have been a bit doolally but human sacrifice?'

Wesley watched for Zac's reaction, unable to share his boss's scepticism. Who knows, he thought, what isolation from society does to a person. To be tormented by teenagers and shunned by your neighbours.

'They were just a couple of old witches ... ' Zac began to fidget, looking around as if he was anxious for the interview to be over.

'And outsiders have always been fair game,' said Wesley softly.

Gerry cleared his throat. 'I suppose you'll be catching up with some of your family and your old school mates while you're down here.'

'Like I said, my folks live in Essex – I bought them a nice new house. And most of my old mates have moved away.'

'We've been trying to trace Joanne's family. Do you know where we can find them?'

'There was only her mum. Her dad walked out when she was little. Someone I was at school with works here as a waiter and he told me her mum's still around. Says she's gone completely bananas. Jo always did reckon she was odd.'

'Where can we find this old mate of yours?' Gerry asked.

'Probably in the restaurant. And I'd hardly describe him as a mate. His name's Richard and he's a bit of a pillock.'

Wesley said they'd be in touch and when they left the bar he looked back over his shoulder and saw a look of relief on Zac's face.

'I want a word with Richard the Pillock,' said Gerry as he followed Wesley out into Reception, where they both stood for a few moments looking for a sign that would point them in the direction of the restaurant.

When they arrived at their destination they found the place half full of early diners, taking advantage of a special deal. Two steaks for the price of one and a complimentary glass of wine.

A waiter hurried up to them. He was round faced with slick hair and a waistline that poured over his tight black trousers. 'Table for two, gentlemen? Have you booked?'

'We're looking for Richard,' Wesley said.

'You've found him,' the man said, puzzled, as though he was racking his brains, trying to recall whether he'd met them before.

'John Grimes told us we'd find you here. We're police officers.'

Richard's small brown eyes widened in alarm, as though he feared imminent arrest.

'It's nothing to worry about. We just wondered if you knew where we could find Joanne Trelisip's mother. You told John she's still around.'

'That's right. And it's Zac now. Can't believe I know a celebrity,' he said, half awed, half proud, as if he'd encountered a heavenly being. 'My sister told me about Mrs Trelisip. She's a social worker, you see, and she only mentioned it 'cause she knew I'd been at school with Joanne and Gabby.' He was speaking fast now, trying to convince them that he had no association with the Trelisip woman, as though she was a creature of the shadows, tainted as an outcast.

'Do you know where we can find her?'

'She lives in a maisonette on the council estate just outside Tradmouth. I think she's got mental health issues. She calls herself Parry now. According to my sister it's her maiden name. Our Sarah says her place is in a right state. She's organising a home help for her. Look, you won't mention my sister, will you? She probably shouldn't have said anything.'

'Any idea of the address?' said Gerry with a hint of impatience.

'Off Garrow Road, our Sarah said.' He paused. 'I heard that woman's been let out of prison.' He looked at them accusingly. 'They say she's murdered someone else.'

'Not our decision,' said Gerry in a tone that didn't encourage argument.

Wesley went on to ask about Richard's relationship with Joanne and Gabby but the answers weren't much help. He hadn't had much to do with the girls because they used to laugh at him, especially Joanne. Gabby had been under her spell, easily led, but shortly before her murder she'd started going out with John Grimes who was in the year above and a conceited pillock. Funny, Wesley thought, that Zac had used exactly the same word to describe him. However, there seemed to be little animosity between the two old school-mates. They were just two men who'd once known each other in passing but who now inhabited different worlds now that one of them had been elevated to the glittering status of celebrity.

Wesley handed Richard his card with instructions to call him if he remembered anything else. Richard studied it for a few seconds then stuck it in his back pocket. As they took their leave the restaurant was filling up. It was a Friday night, the time when people went out enjoying themselves after the working week. Wesley watched the middle-aged women in black dresses, variations on a theme with added sparkle here and there, and their partners with their sagging jowls and smart casual jackets. They looked comfortable and slightly smug as Richard and his colleagues showed them to their tables.

'Think Joanne Trelisip's mum could have anything to do with Lilith Benley's disappearance?' Wesley asked when they arrived back at the incident room. The place was still buzzing with activity and everyone looked as tired as Wesley felt.

'The need for revenge never goes away, Wes. Best eaten cold, as they say. Maybe when she heard about Lilith's release and Boo's murder . . . '

'Somehow I can't see the mother making her way over to West Fretham and lying in wait for Lilith, can you? And even if she did, what's she done with the body? And what's the meaning of that wax doll?'

'Let's pay this Trelisip or Parry woman a visit,' Gerry said, looking at his watch.

Wesley shook his head. 'According to Richard she's vulnerable. I know it's not that late but it's dark and I don't think it would be a good idea for us to turn up unannounced. Might scare the life out of her. I vote we leave it till the morning.'

'I suppose you're right.'

'Mind if I go now, Gerry? There's someone I want to see.'

Gerry had started studying the paperwork that had piled up on his desk in his absence and he looked up sharply. 'Who's that then? I'm not letting you skive off to go and see your fancy woman.'

Wesley was too well acquainted with Gerry's brand of humour to take offence. He gave the boss an indulgent smile. 'My brother-in-law. I want some background on Lilith Benley's beliefs.'

Gerry raised his eyebrows. 'He's a vicar. Will he know much about witchcraft?'

'If he doesn't he might be able to put me in touch with someone who does.'

Gerry wished him luck and, after calling Mark to make sure he was home, Wesley put on the coat he'd just hung over the back of his chair and left the incident room. He felt mildly guilty about abandoning his post while the team were still hard at work but he wanted to learn more about Lilith and what might have driven her to her terrible crime. Besides, the doll left in her cottage bothered him. Someone had cursed her. Someone had used the occult against her. Fought her with her own weapons.

He switched his headlights to full beam as he drove down the narrow lanes leading to the main road. The rush hour was well over as he headed into Neston and the traffic lights seemed to be with him as he passed through the town and out towards the village of Belsham.

Belsham was a long, thin village on the main road from Neston to Morbay and the medieval church stood down a side street behind an extensive graveyard. The nineteenth-century vicarage next door to the church was, unusually, still home to the vicar, most similar houses having been sold off by the church authorities years ago, a high proportion to wealthy incomers. Perhaps it wasn't as architecturally appealing as many local vicarages and rectories. Or maybe the fact that it had once been the scene of a murder had made the church think twice about cashing in on this particular asset.

His sister, Maritia, opened the door to him, standing on tiptoe to kiss his cheek. He gave her a hug and asked how she was. She looked down at her swollen abdomen and patted it proudly. 'Twelve weeks to go.'

'Pam sends her love,' he said. He knew he'd be interrogated when he got home so he asked her how she was keeping. Luckily the news was all good. A textbook pregnancy. But then Maritia had always done things by the book from her trouble-free adolescent years to her academically distinguished medical training in Oxford to her marriage to the pleasingly inoffensive Rev. Mark Fitzgerald. She had never given their parents one moment of anxiety.

After refusing her offer of a drink, Wesley went in search of his brother-in-law and found him in the shabby study crammed with dark second-hand furniture and well-thumbed books. Mark was writing at a desk as cluttered as Gerry Heffernan's and when Wesley entered he looked pleased to see him, as though he was glad of the interruption.

'I always think less is more when it comes to sermons,' Mark said, pushing his notes to one side. 'Keep it short and to the point and you won't lose your audience.'

'Couldn't agree more. I need to pick your brains.' He sat down in the well-worn armchair on the other side of the desk.

'Fire away.'

'What do you know about witchcraft?'

'Are we talking about Wicca or Satanism?'

'Let's start with Wicca.'

'There's a lot of it about in Neston, but then the town's full of New Age stuff. It's supposedly a pagan, pre-Christian tradition. They worship a triple goddess and a horned god and have a lot of spells and rituals. One of their cardinal rules is that magic is only to be used for good. Harm none.'

'So a follower of Wicca wouldn't make human sacrifices or . . . ?'

Mark laughed. 'Oh no, it's not that sort of thing at all. It's more the "wise woman" scenario – healing and solving problems with magic. They believe in living in harmony with the natural world, which isn't a bad thing, I suppose.' His face clouded, as though he'd suddenly thought of something unpleasant. 'Mind you, Satanism's quite a different matter. I've heard there was a bit of trouble at a couple of local churches about twenty years ago.'

'Tell me about it.'

'I think it was the usual thing – church broken into; the cross off the altar pinched; pentagram chalked on the ground in the churchyard and burned-out black candles lying around. There was even talk of blood, hen's probably judging by the feathers found at the scene. I got all this second-hand from one of my churchwardens by the way, so the story might have been exaggerated in the telling.'

'This was twenty years ago?'

'Give or take a few years. Long before my time, anyway.'

'And there's been nothing like that since?'

'Thankfully not.'

'Tell me what you know about Satanism.'

Mark raised his eyebrows. 'It's conjuring demons to harness their power for your own purposes – conjuring the forces of hell to obtain earthly power. In the old witch trials of medieval times and later the accused was almost invariably alleged to have conjured demons, although I suspect most of them were just local wise women – or even ordinary women on the margins of society who'd got on the wrong side of their neighbours. To return to Satanism, there are certain ancient books that give detailed instructions on how to summon demons and the rest is made up by the nasty minds that are into that sort of thing. If you're looking for your human sacrifices and rapes, these are the guys you should be going after.'

'Would a follower of Wicca be involved in Satanism?'

'Highly unlikely. They're completely different philosophies. Not that I'm an expert.' The words sounded like a disclaimer at the end of an advert. 'Sorry I've not been much help.'

'On the contrary, you have.'

'I heard about Lilith Benley's disappearance on the news earlier. Saw your boss Gerry taking the press conference. I presume that's why you're asking these questions.'

For all his mild appearance, Mark had a sharp brain. 'That's right. From what you've told me, the witchcraft angle to the original crime doesn't make much sense.'

'Maybe the two women were outsiders. Maybe that's why those girls chose to torment them with tragic consequences. The women were merely driven beyond endurance and lost control. Nothing to do with magic at all.'

'Most women who were accused in the olden days were innocent,' Wesley said quietly.

'True. But those Benley women weren't, were they? Do you think Lilith Benley's killed again?'

'I don't know, Mark. I wish I did.'

He looked at his watch. It was time he got home.

Saturday morning dawned fine and Wesley lay in bed at six-thirty wide awake. Weekends were for other people. For him it was a working day like any other.

Pam was still fast asleep beside him, snoring gently. Normally she'd have been awake and alert by now but somehow her body knew it was a day of rest. He lay there watching her for a while. The previous night she'd greeted him, bursting with untold news. Her mother had been in touch again to tell her that Simon Frith still hadn't heard anything about his prosecution. The police were keeping him hanging on, she said, piling on the agony. She'd sounded, Pam reckoned, as if she was blaming Wesley personally.

She'd also told him that she'd been to visit Neil in hospital straight after work. He'd seemed a lot better and as she'd arrived at his room she'd passed a woman going out; a slim woman with long blonde hair, the type who looks like a teenager from the rear but whose face betrays her true age. The woman had made no effort to return Pam's inquisitive smile, instead she had shot her a hostile, resentful glance. Pam seemed to have taken an instant dislike to the woman who Neil had named as Harriet, the owner of the house where he'd been working before his accident. He still called it an accident even though he now knew the truth. Perhaps he couldn't deal with the thought that someone had wanted him dead. Wesley found it hard to deal with too.

He sat up and swung his feet down onto the sheepskin rug by the bed. He could see the book lying on Pam's bedside table; Shane Gulliver's latest. *Rejected*. Wesley often read Pam's literary purchases after she'd finished with them but when he'd scanned the blurb on the back cover somehow he didn't fancy this one. *Rejected* was a gut-wrenching story of a boy raised in poverty on a rough London estate by an uncaring mother who was an alcoholic prostitute. The blurb said that, like his four other gut-wrenching bestsellers, it was forged in a crucible of bitter experience. Shane Gulliver had risen above his semi-feral origins and used his background to tell it like it was.

Apart from a London accent, there were few signs now that the confident and urbane Gulliver, with his well-spoken and attractive wife and his large house on the fringe of a pretty Devon village, had come from such a humble background. If he'd started off as an abused kid on a sink estate, nicking cars and dealing drugs, he'd certainly travelled a long way. Four international bestsellers and a Hollywood film deal had probably helped ease the journey.

As he was heading for the shower, he heard Pam's voice. 'Neil said they might let him out of hospital on Monday. He's still in a lot of pain from his broken ribs. Do you think we should ask him to stay here?'

Wesley turned to face her. 'That's a good idea.'

'I'll go to see him this afternoon. I might leave the kids with your sister to give her some practice. Not that Michael will want to go. There was a time when he couldn't wait to visit Maritia and Mark.'

Wesley didn't reply, guilty that he was too busy with his investigation to do anything about his son's unwelcome change of attitude for the moment. He'd have to leave the problem, if there was one, to Pam.

The traffic was sparse as he drove to the incident room. But he was delayed when he found himself stuck behind a slow-moving tractor on a single-track road. He'd learned long ago that the only way to survive such bucolic irritations was patience and he switched on Classic FM, hoping for some calming music but getting the 'Ride of the Valkyries' instead. Music to drive fast to – hardly appropriate in the circumstances.

When he finally reached West Fretham village hall he found Gerry sitting at his desk, head in hands. He looked up when he heard Wesley's voice.

'I sent a team to make a thorough search of Lilith Benley's place first thing,' he said.

'Any sign of those knives she bought?'

Gerry shook his head. 'No. But the team found something interesting in one of the cupboards.' He stood up and walked over to a table in the corner where a number of items lay swathed in plastic evidence bags, waiting to be taken away for storage in the police station's exhibits store.

Gerry picked up a package and handed it to him. Through the plastic he could see that it was a book, beautifully bound in leather with an embossed gold pentagram set with red cabochon stones on the front cover.

'It's been dusted for fingerprints but there was nothing useful.'

Wesley extracted the book from the bag carefully and

opened it. Inside he saw jagged remnants of paper clinging to the spine as though the pages had been ripped out in fury. The destruction looked to him like a violent assault on something that had been precious to Lilith Benley.

'The cover fits the description she gave of her stolen Book of Shadows.'

'She could have done the damage herself – lied about it being pinched.'

'No, Gerry. I think this was done to scare her. I think whoever left the doll stole it and returned it like this.'

'We need some advice,' said Gerry, his mouth starting to form his familiar grin. 'We need to find a witch. There's never one around when you need one.'

'I'll get someone onto it.'

'Any news from Neston nick about Neil's accident?'

'Not yet.'

'Lazy buggers. Brake pipes cut – that's attempted murder. If I was in charge of the case . . . '

Wesley suddenly felt a pang of guilt. Gerry was right; even though Neil was recovering, the investigating officer at Neston should really be treating the matter with a lot more urgency. The best explanation offered once Neil had stated categorically that he had no enemies was 'kids messing about' but Wesley didn't buy that one. If he wasn't so busy he would have made a few discreet enquiries himself.

But other things took priority. All patrols were on the lookout for Lilith Benley, as was every force in the country. All ports and airports had been notified too. Even though, according to records, she didn't possess a valid passport there was always the chance she could have obtained a false ID, possibly from some useful contact she'd made in prison. Every line of enquiry had to be followed up.

In the meantime they needed to speak to Joanne Trelisip's mother. If the woman was in a fragile state it was as well to have somebody with him who was used to dealing with delicate situations. So he decided to take Rachel.

Nobody lives in complete privacy these days so it didn't take long for one of the DCs to find the address of the woman who was now calling herself Pauline Parry.

As Wesley was driving back to Tradmouth, Rachel was uncharacteristically silent so he asked if she'd set a date for the wedding, making conversation.

'Next June,' she answered, gazing out of the window.

'Hope me and Pam are invited.'

'I haven't thought about the guest list yet.' Her voice was quiet. Wesley remembered that when his sister had been planning her wedding she'd bubbled with excitement and enthusiasm.

'Everything OK?'

'Why shouldn't it be?' Her words discouraged further enquiry. There had been a time when Rachel had confided in him, told him her innermost thoughts. But it seemed that was over. And he wasn't sure how he felt about this loss of intimacy.

The houses of the Tradmouth Estate, perched on the hillside overlooking the town, were all coated with uniform cream pebbledash, armoured against the prevailing wind from the sea. Joanne Trelisip's mother lived in a maisonette in a small cul-de-sac, like the neighbouring semi-detached houses only with an additional storey on top and a concrete staircase protruding from the side of the building. Hers was the lower maisonette, the one with the drawn curtains stained with mildew. Rain had begun to fall, draining the scene of colour, and the concrete path leading to the front door glistened dark grey, reflecting the ominous sky above.

In the absence of a working doorbell, Wesley rapped on the front door and waited. Rachel stood a little behind him and when a slow-moving shadow appeared behind the frosted glass, she gave him a gentle nudge.

The door opened a fraction and Wesley, knowing that a lone woman often feels more at ease with someone of her own sex, left it to Rachel to make the introductions. The tactic worked because the door opened wider to reveal a small woman, almost as wide as she was tall. Her folds of fat were swathed in a shapeless grey garment which could have been a cardigan worn over a calf-length navy skirt. The clothes were stained and Wesley tried hard not to wrinkle his nose at the smell of unwashed flesh. The face above the cascade of chins seemed small, like a doll's, and her hair had been scraped back brutally into a steel-grey pony tail. She waddled slowly ahead of them into the front room and Wesley paused by the door. As his eyes adjusted to the gloom he could see piles of newspapers stacked up around the room like grey pillars reaching almost to the ceiling. There were a few lumpy shapes which may or may not have been furniture but he could make out the shape of a sofa near the window, masked by a cover of newsprint.

'You collect newspapers, Ms Parry,' he said. He was stating the obvious but he couldn't think up a more suitable opening line. 'It is Ms Parry, isn't it? Not Trelisip?'

She ignored the question. 'My Joanne's been in the papers. She's famous.'

Wesley caught Rachel's eye and saw pity there. He looked at the stacked papers and saw that tabloids were mixed with broadsheets; the *Sun*, the *Star*, the *Mail*, the *Express*, the *Telegraph*, *The Times* and *The Guardian* making

strange bedfellows. He thought the stacks didn't look particularly safe so he reached out a tentative hand towards
one of the pale grey pillars to check its stability. But as soon
as he did so the woman screamed at him not to touch and
he withdrew his hand rapidly as if he'd touched a burning
surface.

'Did you buy all these papers?' he asked.

She shook her head and perched precariously on the
edge of a side table littered with empty fizzy drinks cans
and fast-food wrappers. 'People leave them and I collect
them because my Joanne might be in them.' She folded her
arms proudly. 'She's famous is my Joanne ... been in all the
papers.'

Normally at this stage, he'd suggest they all sat down,
maybe with a cup of tea, but there was nowhere to sit so he
gave Rachel a small nod.

They'd worked together so often before that she understood the signal right away. 'We're sorry to disturb you, Ms
Parry, but we need to ask a few questions.'

The woman's small eyes lit up. 'My Joanne. You've found
her.'

'I'm afraid not. But the woman who was convicted of
her murder has disappeared and we're trying to find out
where she is.'

'I haven't seen her. I don't go out after dark. Bad things
happen if you go out after dark.' She recited the words like
a mantra; a spell to keep her from harm. Her fists were
clenched so tight that they must have hurt and the sight of
a trickle of water snaking down each cheek made Wesley
feel like a brute.

'Did you know Lilith Benley had been released from
prison?' Rachel asked.

She shook her head so vigorously that a small snowstorm of dandruff landed on her shoulders. The tears were streaming now and her nose was dripping mucus. She wiped it on her sleeve.

'Normally you'd have been notified but as you've changed your name . . .'

'They should have hung her,' she hissed. 'Put her on the gallows with a rope around her neck. She should have done the hangman's dance like the witch she is.' She stood up and shuffled towards them, flapping her arms as if she was shooing birds away. 'Get out. If you've not come to tell me my Joanne's coming back you can get out.'

'Coming back?' Wesley asked, taking a step towards the door.

'The dead walk, don't they? If you look hard enough you can find them.'

She sank painfully to the floor, her knees cracking, and began to sort through some of the papers that were strewn there. As she turned the pages, concentrating hard, Wesley knew they'd lost her.

Rachel didn't say much on the return journey, only that she hoped Social Services were on Joanne's mother's case. Wesley had assured her that they were . . . adding that her social worker's brother had been at school with Joanne and Gabby. Rather than looking impressed by his inside knowledge, Rachel had seemed preoccupied with her own thoughts.

Gerry greeted them on their return to the incident room, eager to find out how they'd got on. Wesley told him about Ms Parry and her collection of newspapers, adding that he didn't think she was capable of travelling to West Fretham, let alone evading the TV people and killing Boo Flecker or abducting Lilith Benley.

Gerry sighed and said that if she wasn't a suspect they'd have to forget about her and move on to more pressing matters. They had an imminent meeting with another bereaved mother. Boo Flecker's mother had caught the early train down to Morbay from her home in Yorkshire and she was due to arrive in half an hour.

Rachel went off to meet Mrs Flecker at Morbay Station and an hour later she called to say that she'd taken her to the Tradmouth Castle Hotel for lunch. Wesley was glad she'd used her initiative. A Spartan interview room at Tradmouth police station was hardly a suitable place for a grieving relative. He promised they'd join her as soon as they could.

At one o'clock Gerry suggested they kill two birds with one stone and grab a bar meal at the hotel. They drove to Tradmouth through a veil of rain, sitting in silence as they headed down the steep hill towards the river in third gear. The rain had stopped and the sun was peeping from behind the clouds, sending rays of light down onto the water. After parking by the police station they walked to the old hotel overlooking the boat float and found Rachel in the Schooner Bar sitting at a table for four by the window. Opposite her sat an elegantly dressed middle-aged woman who was sipping coffee from a small white cup.

Rachel made the introductions and Mrs Flecker shook their hands limply.

'I'm so sorry for your loss,' Wesley said.

Mrs Flecker nodded in acknowledgement. There was a serene quality about her with her immaculately made-up face and her sandy hair caught up in an elegant chignon.

'I'm only sorry if you've had problems contacting me. I've been away visiting a friend. I only got back yesterday and ... and found the local police have been trying to get hold of me.' She took out a small white handkerchief and dabbed at her eyes. 'I'm afraid it hasn't really sunk in yet. I didn't see that much of Boo because she had her own life in London – but we did speak on the phone quite often.'

'When did you last speak to her?' Wesley asked gently.

'Sunday night. She said she was staying at a B and B on a farm. I think she found the contrast to London amusing.' She broke off and bowed her head.

'What did she say when she called you?' Wesley asked.

She looked up, a businesslike expression on her face. But Wesley could see the film of half-formed tears in her eyes. 'She chatted about this and that like she usually did. And she seemed ... ' She searched for the word. 'Excited ... almost as if she was high on something. Not that she was ... I didn't mean to imply ... '

'Of course. Did she say what she was excited about?'

'What was Boo usually excited about?' She gave a fond smile. 'Work. It was always work with her. A new lead. An exclusive story. I always joked that she should have joined the police. Not that she'd have fitted in. She never did things by the book. She just loved the thrill of the chase. She said it was what she lived for. The buzz, she called it.'

'Did she say anything about the story she was working on?' Wesley held his breath, telling himself that it was probably too much to hope that her mother might hold the key to the whole thing. But hoping all the same. He glanced at Gerry and saw that he was leaning forward, breath held, awaiting a revelation.

'I remember she said something about a Mr Big. I

presumed it was some criminal so I told her to be careful. She just laughed. But that's what she was like. Fearless. Always was, even as a child.'

'Is this connected to what she was doing down here?'

She sighed. 'To be honest, I don't know. She talked about so many things, I found it hard to keep up.'

'Did she mention Rupert Raybourn?' Gerry asked.

'She did say something about Raybourn and a rent boy but then she said she'd moved on to something else. Said Raybourn was yesterday's news.'

'Anything else you can tell us?'

She shook her head. 'I'm sorry. Can I see her?'

'Of course,' said Rachel, touching the woman's arm gently. 'I'll take you there when you're ready.'

Mrs Flecker nodded her thanks.

'Want anything to eat, love?' Gerry said. 'You should keep your strength up, you know.'

Wesley had half expected her to refuse but instead she nodded. 'That'd be nice. I'll have a sandwich. It's strange, I almost forgot I was hungry.'

'That's perfectly understandable,' said Wesley. Rachel took the orders and went to the bar, leaving the three of them sitting in silence for a few moments. Then Wesley spoke again. 'Did Boo ever mention a woman called Lilith Benley? She was convicted of killing two teenage girls eighteen years ago and she's recently been released from prison. Boo had cuttings about the case in her room at the B and B where she was staying.'

'I don't recall her saying anything about it.'

Wesley thought for a moment. 'Did she mention Zac James at all?'

'Isn't he a pop singer?'

'That's right,' said Gerry. 'Only he's getting a bit past his sell-by date now. He was taking part in the reality TV show with Rupert Raybourn. It was being filmed on the farm where your daughter was found. I just wondered if ...'

'If either of them had a secret they didn't want her to uncover? Surely people don't kill just because some journalist threatens to wash their dirty linen in public.'

'Depends how dirty that linen is,' said Gerry.

'Did she mention anyone else she'd met down here?' Wesley asked gently.

She thought for a moment. 'I'm sorry. She did chatter on and I suppose I was only half listening because I had a lot on my mind. I'm sorry. If I'd known it was important ...'

'Don't worry.'

'I'm annoyed with myself. I should have paid more attention. But over the years I got used to her being excited about her work.' She hesitated. 'Actually she texted me on Monday evening. She sometimes did, you know, when she was onto a new story.'

Wesley leaned forward. 'What did she say?'

Mrs Flecker took a small pink mobile phone out of her handbag, selected a message and passed it to him. He read the message.

Three words. *BIG story. Explosive.*

Chapter 12

Written by Alison Hadness, September 21st 1643

*William drank my infusion this morning and he has taken to his bed
with a fever. I must watch him well. Perhaps he will require more
physic.*

*I went into the town with Dorcas and tried to purchase food but
there was little to be had. The miller is charging heavily for bad flour.
How some delight in profiting from misfortune.*

*They say Mistress Goodley is taken with wild babbling and visions
and there is talk of witchcraft.*

*Last night Elizabeth threatened to tell her father that the evil doll
was mine rather than confess her wickedness. She spoke wildly that I
did bewitch her father and how she hates me more than any other creature on God's earth. Jennet Rudd was taken with spasms, her body
jerking and cold as ice. She has been much with Elizabeth so it may be
that I am not the only object of her spells.*

*While I walked back from the town with Dorcas I saw a young
man who looked most like Thomas. But I know I was mistaken.*

Perhaps my present troubles with Elizabeth have brought him to my mind again.

William is too sick to make demands on me for which I am thankful.

As soon as they left the hotel, Gerry headed for the police station to bring Chief Superintendent Nutter up to date with developments while Wesley made for the hospital to spread a bit of cheer in Neil's direction. Not that he felt particularly cheerful after his meeting with Mrs Flecker. The woman's dignity impressed him but he was still glad it was Rachel rather than him who was taking her to the mortuary.

He found Neil sitting up in bed fidgeting with the bedclothes. There was a thin hardback book lying in front of him on the blue hospital cover, his place marked with a scrap of paper. It was a study of Civil War defences. He didn't intend to lose touch with his excavation during his period of enforced leisure.

'If I stay in this place much longer I'll go berserk,' he said. 'You sure it's okay for me to stay at your place when they let me out?'

'Of course. It's the least we can do.'

'I'll be able to walk on crutches and Dave's promised to pick me up to take me up to the dig every day.' He grinned. 'I'll be there in a purely supervisory capacity before you ask, lording it over everyone in my chair and issuing my orders. Any idea who cut my brake pipes yet?'

'Neston are handling the case but they haven't made much progress. They took statements from the Mumfords and the builders but now it turns out it could have been done earlier that day . . . maybe even in Exeter.'

Neil hauled himself further up on his pillows. 'Evan Mumford drives a Mini. New yellow Cooper S with a black roof. What if someone had it in for him and got mine by mistake?'

Wesley was tempted to laugh, to point out that nobody could mistake the two vehicles, one brand new and flashy, the other old and disreputable. But he said nothing.

'I take it you've given them a statement?'

'Some twelve-year-old plod came and wrote it all down. She was rather sweet,' he added wistfully. 'I've got to find out about those creepy wax dolls. Is yours still safe, by the way?'

'Pam wouldn't have it in the house so I put it in the garden shed.'

Neil looked mildly alarmed. 'You sure it's OK in there? It won't get damaged?'

'It's been stuffed behind panelling in a semi-derelict house for the best part of four hundred years so I don't think a week in my shed will do it any harm.'

'Harriet reckons it's cursed.'

'You seem to be getting very cosy with Harriet.'

'Are you going to question her husband about my accident?'

Wesley raised his eyebrows. 'Just how close have you two been getting?'

'Don't be disgusting,' Neil said with a sly grin.

Wesley knew his instincts were right . . . and his old friend had form for short-term and ill-thought-out dalliances.

Before Wesley left, Neil extracted a promise that he would bring the little coffin and its dreadful contents into the hospital the next day so that Neil could examine it. Wesley didn't know how the staff would react if they saw it but, as it would be Sunday, the hospital would be quiet and, hopefully, nobody would notice.

He walked back to the police station and as soon as he reached the CID office his phone began to ring. The caller display told him it was Mark and a sudden feeling of dread clutched at his stomach. What if it was Maritia? What if something bad had happened and the baby had come too early?

But as soon as he heard Mark's voice his mind was put at rest. He sounded his usual self, calmly enthusiastic. 'I've been asking around. One of my churchwardens has a cousin who knew Lilith Benley and her mother quite well. Her name's Selina Chester and she owns a shop in Neston. She might be able to help you with the witchcraft angle too. She's a Wicca priestess.'

This new lead sounded promising. It would also be useful to talk to someone who actually knew the Benleys, someone who could separate the reality from the legend. And, it was always possible that Lilith had taken refuge with an old friend.

Mark went on to recite Selina's address. A shop down a little passage that branched off Neston's main shopping street, not far from the concrete and glass Municipal offices that looked so out of place in the small, Elizabethan town. If he drove over to Neston now, he could have a chat with Selina, pop into the police station to learn how the investigation into Neil's accident was progressing and maybe even have another word with DS Geoff Gaulter while he was at it. Nobody could accuse him of not making efficient use of police time.

He was about to leave when he saw Tom from Scientific Support bearing down on him, a sheaf of papers clutched in his hand.

'I've been examining Boo Flecker's laptop,' Tom began. 'The only recent e-mails that stand out as unusual are to various schools asking if a Giles Parsons had been a pupil. One of them replied in the affirmative. Welson Hall. It's a minor public school in Buckinghamshire. It's got a website,' he added enthusiastically. 'The school replied, confirming that Parsons had been a pupil but they said they were unable to give out any more information.'

'Anything else?'

'She'd been trawling through the Internet for information on that comedian, Rupert Raybourn, and a man called Carl Cramer who was also some sort of entertainer. And the day before she died she'd been looking up lots of stuff on the Benley case.'

Tom left Wesley with the information and took his leave. Wesley brought up Welson Hall School's website on his own computer but it wasn't much help. All smiling, shiny-faced youth and modern sports facilities. Not the sort of thing he'd imagined would interest Boo Flecker.

He knew Gerry would be closeted with the Chief Superintendent for quite some time so he didn't bother leaving a message. Instead he retrieved the damaged book found at Lilith Benley's cottage from the exhibits store, collected his car and set off for Neston, taking the corner where Neil had had his accident with exaggerated care. When he reached the town the sun had started to peep through the clouds, sending a beam of light streaming down on the half-ruined castle which guarded the end of the high street. After negotiating the byzantine one-way system round the back streets he found a space in a small car park near his destination and walked into the centre of town. As well as the usual high street shops, Neston had an array of New Age outlets on its steep main shopping street selling everything from crystals to alternative remedies to handmade organic clothing, and as he walked he caught a whiff of incense on the air.

Mysterioso was tucked away down a little back alley next door to an organic sandwich shop and its window display featured a variety of robes, athames and books on the occult. There were cloaks too, presumably similar to the one Lilith claimed had gone missing after her break-in. Wesley pushed the door open and a bell jangled somewhere above him, bringing a woman rushing from the back of the shop. The first thing that struck Wesley was how ordinary she looked. Wesley estimated she was in her late sixties and she wore her long, steel-grey hair in a pony tail tied with a bright pink scrunchy. Her only concession to the witch stereotype was a long black skirt but apart from that she looked like your average benevolent granny. Even her smile of greeting was decidedly benign.

She introduced herself as Selina and as soon as Wesley mentioned Mark's name and explained the reason for his visit, she turned the shop sign to closed and led him through into the back.

The little room behind the counter was comfortable with well-worn chintz armchairs and a collection of table lamps that gave the place a cosy glow. As he sat down he began to relax, as though he was having tea with an elderly aunt, only the tea he was offered was herbal and tasted foul.

'I presume you want to know all about the Benleys,' she said as Wesley sipped at his drink politely, trying not to gag on the musty taste.

He was glad she'd come straight to the point.

'I've heard that Lilith's missing. And before you ask, I

haven't seen her or heard from her since her release from prison. I have absolutely no idea where she is but I'm happy to tell you everything I know about her and her mother.'

'Were you surprised when they killed those two young girls?'

'Allegedly killed those two young girls.' She pressed her lips together. 'I was one of the few people who believed they were innocent. I knew them quite well, you see. Especially Lilith. She used to come here quite often.'

'You were friends?'

She considered the question for a second and nodded. 'Yes. I'd say we were friends but I haven't seen her for eighteen years. I did wonder whether to write to her in prison but . . . I suppose I was a coward.'

'So you did have doubts about her innocence?'

She wagged a finger at him. 'You're very perceptive, Detective Inspector. I feel awful about it now but the old saying about there being no smoke without fire always pops into your head at a time like that, doesn't it? But it was just so out of character. Besides, she was a Wiccan like me and the main tenet of our belief is "harm none". Lilith was no Satanist, Inspector. She wouldn't have had anything to do with that sort of thing. Harm none, that's what she believed. Harm none.'

'The authorities judged that her mother was insane. Maybe she killed the girls and Lilith panicked and felt she had to dispose of the bodies to defend the old woman.'

When Selina shook her head a few strands of grey hair escaped the confines of her pony tail and flopped over her face. She pushed them behind her ears with a hand laden with large jewelled rings.

'Her mother suffered from dementia, Inspector. She

wasn't capable of killing those girls any more than Lilith was. What happened to those women was a tragedy. I only heard last night on the news that Lilith had come home and that the police were looking for her. If I'd known she was back I would have called round to offer her my support.' She spoke bravely. But brave talk is easy after the event.

'Did you have, er ... meetings?'

'You mean the coven?'

Wesley nodded. He hadn't really liked to use the word as, in his mind, it conjured pictures of naked prancing in the woods.

'Traditionally there are thirteen in a coven but at that time we only had eleven, nine when Dorothy and Lilith left us. Wicca isn't an organised religion, Inspector, there's no hierarchy. There are lone witches and even online covens. And yes, we met regularly for ceremonies and worship when they were with us. We still do and we now have the requisite thirteen.' She looked down modestly. 'I have the honour of being the priestess. We have a priest too. Our coven is thriving, I'm pleased to say.'

'Lilith and Dorothy were equally committed?'

'If anything, Dorothy was the keenest. I sensed Lilith's enthusiasm didn't match her mother's. I think she had other things in her life.'

'Such as?'

'There were things Lilith kept to herself and before you ask, I've no idea what they were.'

'The woman who was murdered near Lilith's cottage was killed with an athame ... a ceremonial knife. You stock a lot here in the shop.'

'I've already had a couple of your officers round. Mine are all accounted for. I gave them a list of customers who'd

248

purchased them, of course, but I know most of them and I feel I can vouch for them.'

'Who's your supplier?'

'A man called Evan Mumford. He lives locally and imports them from China. He distributes them all over the country.'

'I've met Mr Mumford.'

'Did you like him?'

The question was unexpected and Wesley was about to say that he hadn't particularly taken to the man. But he thought the reply sounded a little unprofessional so instead he turned the question back on Selina. 'Don't you?'

'I can't really say I do. But his wife's a nice woman. She's one of our number.'

'A witch?'

'A follower of Wicca, yes. I'm sure she won't mind me telling you. She's a very talented sculptor, you know. Far too good for that husband of hers in my opinion.'

'Is he in your coven?'

Selina shook her head. 'Evan Mumford worships a very different sort of god and goddess, Inspector. Money.' Selina shut her lips tightly in disapproval.

'There's a lot of it about,' Wesley said with a smile before taking the damaged book from Lilith's cottage out of its protective bag and handing it to her. 'Do you recognise this?'

She opened the book and frowned. 'Who did this?'

'We don't know. Is it a Book of Shadows?'

'It certainly looks like one.'

'It was found in Lilith Benley's cottage.'

Selina said nothing while she flicked through what was left of the pages. 'If someone did this, it's an act of hatred.

A Book of Shadows is a record of a witch's spiritual journey. This is almost like an attack on the witch herself.'

'Lilith told the police it had been stolen.'

'Then somebody took it to destroy it. It's a violation.' She shuddered.

'Is it possible this isn't hers? Maybe her mother had one and . . .'

'Oh no, Inspector. Witches only have one and it's considered so important that it's burned on their death. She would have burned her mother's at the first opportunity.'

Wesley took the book from her gently and replaced it in the bag. She looked glad to be relieved of the burden.

'Why don't you tell me more about Lilith,' he said. 'What brought her to West Fretham?'

'She gave up a good job in London to buy that small-holding. She was a strong-minded woman and she was devoted to her mother. When Dorothy was diagnosed with dementia Lilith refused to put her in an institution, which I think is to her credit.'

'Was there a man in Lilith's life?'

'I believe there had been someone when she was down in London. I sensed a great deal of sadness there. I think it was something she found too painful to discuss.'

'Did she tell you she was being persecuted by local teenagers?'

'She said some stupid girls had been calling her and her mother names. It upset her, of course, but she thought they'd eventually give up if she didn't react. Lilith was a good person and I'll never believe she was capable of what she was accused of. As I said before, harm none, that's what she believed in. Harm none.'

Wesley looked her in the eye. 'You're sure you haven't seen her recently?'

'If I had I would have told you.'

'If you remember anything else, will you let me know?' He handed her his card which she examined carefully before placing it in her skirt pocket.

'If you know anything that might be relevant you're not helping Lilith by keeping quiet. If you've any idea where she might have gone, you have to tell us . . . for Lilith's sake. She could be in danger.'

She stared at him for a few moments and he had the impression she was about to say something, but instead she slipped into pleasantries about next Spring's Arts Festival. Even if there was something more to learn, she wasn't going to reveal it that day. It could be that she just needed time.

He took a token sip of the terrible herbal tea and stood up. He'd just been presented with a very different picture of Lilith Benley. Saint or sinner? He wished he knew the truth.

Unfinished business made Zac James uncomfortable. Not that the sort of people he'd mixed with since his entry into the world of stardom would have suspected this hidden part of his character, the desire to dot the i's and cross the t's was at odds with the image he'd been careful to cultivate. He once wondered whether he was suffering from obsessive compulsive disorder. Maybe he'd mention it to the doctors next time he took a trip to rehab.

He'd heard that the journalist woman who'd been murdered had spoken to his old teacher, Mr Roley. He remembered old Larry Roley fondly. And Larry had sounded so keen to meet when he'd called him, saying he'd love to catch up and hear how he was getting on. He'd known John, as he called him, worked in the music industry but he seemed unaware of his fame. The conversation had been refreshing, untainted by the usual fawning which set a distance between him and the rest of the human race.

Zac was starting to feel nervous about meeting his old teacher again – anxious about what he'd reveal about Boo Flecker's enquiries. And yet he needed Larry's advice ... and his reassurance that what he thought he'd seen was merely a delusion, a terrible vision conjured by those inner demons he'd lived with for so long. There were times when Zac thought he was going mad and he wondered whether the chemicals he'd ingested over the years were responsible. Or was it the memory of what had happened all that time ago – in his other life?

Roley had suggested that they meet at the pub where he'd met Boo Flecker and Zac had agreed. He drove from his hotel in Morbay to West Fretham in the blue Porsche, top down even though the sky was full of threatening clouds, enjoying the freedom of the country roads by driving too fast. When he came to a halt in the car park in front of the Ploughman's Rest he saw there was a CCTV camera trained on the cars so he knew it would be safe to leave his precious Porsche unattended. Things like that bothered him these days.

He sat for a while, his fingers drumming nervously on the steering wheel. A glance at his watch told him he was early so he climbed out of the car, locked it and strolled over to the pub door.

It was Saturday and the place was busy so Zac put on the dark glasses he always wore when he didn't want to be recognised. When he entered the cosily lit pub it took on

252

the appearance of a gloomy cavern so he took them off again and pulled his baseball cap down to shade his face, unaware that his attempt to look inconspicuous was failing miserably.

Roley hadn't arrived and Zac resisted the temptation to order something strong at the bar. He'd been done for drink driving twice before and if it happened again, he knew they'd come down hard on an unrepentant repeat offender. Instead he made his way outside again and waited, leaning against his car, arms folded.

Then he heard someone calling his name. 'Zac. Over here.'

The voice seemed to be coming from the direction of the little wooden signpost at the corner of the car park, next to the public footpath.

Curiosity got the better of him and he began to walk towards the sign. He felt the pulse in his neck throbbing. He needed something to make him think more clearly. But what little white powder he had left was back in the safe in his hotel room.

He was at the entrance to the footpath now and he heard the voice again. 'Please . . . I just want to talk to you, that's all.'

His heart was pounding but he tried to look casual. His feeble attempt at disguise had been in vain; he'd been recognised but it was best to get it over with. He could see a dark figure standing some way away down the footpath in the shadow of the tall hedgerow growing between the path and the field beyond. It began to walk away down the path, glancing back every now and then to make sure he was following.

And when he'd walked a few yards, just far enough to be

hidden by the foliage, the figure turned and bore down on him like a fury. Then, too shocked to move, he saw a flash of polished metal.

While Wesley was at Neston police station he'd asked how the investigation into Neil's accident was progressing. The answer had been disappointing. The enquiries were ongoing. Police speak for they'd drawn a blank.

He'd also had another word with DS Gaulter. Simon Frith's prosecution was going ahead but Wesley suspected Gaulter wasn't altogether happy about it. When he'd asked him if something was bothering him, he'd shrugged his shoulders and said nothing.

As soon as he'd finished in Neston, Wesley returned to the incident room to re-examine some of the witness statements and think things over. But thinking proved difficult in the hubbub of conversation as the team made phone calls and compared notes. Then there was Gerry. He meant well but he had a habit of emerging from behind his desk every so often to chivvy the troops along and to enquire whether there were any new developments.

Wesley was sitting at his desk staring at a blank sheet of paper, trying to concentrate, when Gerry spoke again, his voice booming across the echoing hall.

'Anyone turned up anything on Joanne Trelisip's father yet?'

Wesley looked up and saw that one of the young DCs, a handsome, dark-haired lad who looked as if he might be of Indian descent, had his hand up like a child keen to answer a question in class.

'I've been searching but I can't find any trace of him.'

'Well keep on looking.'

There was another lead Wesley wanted to follow. When Gabby and Joanne vanished, it was immediately assumed that the abductor later identified as Satan Death had been responsible. However, a week after their disappearance the police received the anonymous phone call telling them to look for them at Devil's Tree Cottage and the whole enquiry changed course.

The routine visit to Devil's Tree Cottage to check the place out triggered a full-scale murder enquiry when evidence of the girls' brutal murder was found there. But, in spite of the police's best efforts, the anonymous caller who had put them onto it had never been traced. The call had been made from a public phone box at Morbay Station but there had been no useful evidence among the hundreds of smudged fingerprints and, eighteen years back, there was no helpful working CCTV to record the caller's identity.

The caller was a man – he knew that much but little else. The call had been recorded as a matter of routine and at last the recording Wesley had requested had arrived on his desk: a cassette tape, a relic from the pre-digital age. He'd asked Nick Tarnaby to find a machine to play it on and now a dusty combined radio and tape player that had probably spent years at the back of some store cupboard sat on his desk ready.

Wesley put the tape in and pressed the appropriate button, hoping the tape wouldn't snag. But he was in luck. First he heard the operator's voice, calm and reassuring. 'Emergency. Which service do you require?' Then a few moments of silent hesitation before a muffled voice spoke. 'Those two girls in West Fretham. They went into Devil's Tree Cottage and never came out. I'd look there if I was you.'

Before the operator could ask for details, the call ended abruptly and Wesley sat listening to the dialling tone. He played the tape again. Then again. The voice sounded local and it was muffled, as though the caller was speaking through some sort of cloth. And it was probably disguised as well, unnaturally deep as though a woman was trying to sound like a man. The theory at the time was that it was someone from the village who hadn't wanted to be identified. But Wesley suspected this was because the caller was connected with the case in some way. He rewound the tape and listened to it again. But he was none the wiser.

The Ploughman's Rest had a good reputation for food and Mr and Mrs Fulerton who'd come to Devon for a late break considered it was well deserved. Pleasingly full from their lunch of home-made lasagne with a healthy side salad, Mrs Fulerton – a retired teacher who'd recently developed a taste for long hikes across muddy fields – nodded to her husband who was gazing longingly at the hand pumps on the bar, craving another pint. It was time to go. They had eight miles to cover before returning to their rented cottage in Bereton.

They left the pub, Nordic walking poles at the ready. Mrs Fulerton strode ahead, making for the wooden fingerpost at the far side of the car park which bore the words 'public footpath'. Mr Fulerton followed, holding back a little, yearning for the comfort of the pub. But, yielding to the inevitable, he quickened his pace to catch up with his wife.

As he walked his attention was caught by a blue Porsche parked untidily in the car park. It was new and shiny and he slowed down to admire it. But when he heard a scream he stopped, almost tripping over his poles.

He saw his wife emerging from the entrance to the footpath, her hands reaching out towards him, red and glistening. Her eyes were wild with terror and he saw her open and shut her mouth as though she was trying to speak but had been struck dumb by some terrible curse.

At first Mr Fulerton thought the red fluid dripping from her outstretched hands was paint. And it took him a few seconds to realise it was fresh blood.

Chapter 13

Journal of Thomas Whitcombe, Captain in the King's army, September 21st 1643

I saw Alison walking with a servant and, forgetting for the moment my mission of discovery, I followed her, my clothes soaked with rain and my boots caked in the thick mud from the town streets.

She walked up the steep hill leading to St Leonard's Church. I stayed some way behind and I saw her enter a handsome house set upon the hillside on the edge of the town. From there it was but a short walk beyond the barricades to Hilton Farm. I had not realised my duties as a soldier of the King had brought me so close to her.

The house is set behind a tall gate which gives onto a fine formal garden and I loitered outside as long as I dared. When I saw a servant approaching the gate I feared I had been seen so I hurried away. I would return to Prince Maurice and report what I had learned that day. But I would make no mention of Alison.

I hear more talk of sickness in the town and it is said some are possessed by demons. Today I heard of an old woman who has been seized for cursing Master Cromwell and casting spells against her neighbour, causing her to fall downstairs when she was with child. The child was born early and died. It is said the old woman will hang.

Written by Alison Hadness, September 21st 1643

I ventured out again into the town and this time I know it was indeed Thomas I saw for I espied him again near to Mercy Hall. How my heart leapt at the sight of that dear face for I thought I should never see him again. How I long to speak with him but I cannot request it in prayer for my desire is a grave sin. William's health worsens and Dorcas gives him my physic as instructed. I will not permit Elizabeth to see him and her ill will towards me increases by the day.

Dorcas had no wish to destroy the doll for fear that I should suffer by its burning. I too am afraid and so I keep the thing hidden well in my linen press. Since I, with Dorcas's aid, removed the nails from the wax, my pains are much relieved. It is said that such magic is strong. Dorcas would denounce Elizabeth for sorcery but I fear to bring attention upon our household at this time.

Elizabeth keeps to her chamber and will say nought to me. Before William's sickness he did say there is a gentleman in Neston who has want of a young wife so my dilemma may yet be solved when this siege of our town is ended and Parliament prevails. There is such a lack of grain now at the town mill while Prince Maurice keeps the best produce for himself and hopes to starve us into surrender. I like not foul rye bread so I will not eat it.

There was a look of utter astonishment on the dead man's face. Wesley had an urge to close the wide, horrified eyes but it wasn't his place to touch the dead.

'Where are the people who found him?' Gerry asked.

'Inside the pub. They looked as though they needed a drink. They're a retired couple here on a walking holiday. I don't think they'll be able to tell us much. Wrong place, wrong time.'

'A holiday they won't forget, eh,' said Gerry grimly. 'Get someone to take a statement and tell them they can go home.'

'Already done. They're staying in a rented cottage in Bereton.' He nodded towards the body. 'All hell's going to break loose once the press get hold of this.'

'Do you think I don't know that, Wes? The longer we can keep it under wraps, the better.'

'We should see if Laurence Roley's up to talking. He turned up just after Mrs Fulerton found the body. Says Zac had arranged to meet him here. Wouldn't have thought he was the type to look up an old teacher.'

'Last I heard the landlord took him into the pub for a stiff drink. Any chance he was responsible?'

Wesley didn't reply. Roley's shock had seemed absolutely genuine. But, in his experience, the guilty have been known to produce Oscar-winning performances when the police are around.

'I hear you've been at it again.'

They looked round and saw Jane Partridge standing there, arms folded like the seaside landladies of distant legend.

'Are you trying to make work for me or what?'

'Not our fault, love. We didn't kill 'em,' said Gerry with a hint of defiance.

'Isn't it about time you found who did? And less of the "love" if you don't mind. Any ID on this one?'

'It's Zac James ... the singer,' said Wesley as Gerry

stepped away from the body, subdued, whether by the rebuke for his lack of gender awareness or the implied criticism of his skill as a detective, Wesley couldn't tell. But he guessed it was probably the latter.

'Well he won't be singing any more,' said Jane bluntly, squatting down by the corpse.

Wesley caught Gerry's eye. The woman was developing a sense of humour . . . even if it was of the gallows variety. They watched as she made her initial examination.

'There's a knife wound to his abdomen. Seems identical to that woman's at Jessop's Farm. I'd say the same weapon was used. I thought you'd found it.'

'We did. But the search team's just found another one thrown into that hedge behind you.' Gerry held up an evidence bag. 'An athame again. Identical. The killer's using a new one for each murder. Obviously not a believer in recycling.'

Jane raised her eyebrows. 'Which means he has a supply of the things,' she said.

Wesley nodded. They'd worked that one out for themselves. And Lilith Benley had ordered three from Evan Mumford, the only person locally with an endless supply of ceremonial knives, imported all the way from China in cardboard boxes. Lilith's three knives hadn't been found at the cottage so presumably she'd taken them with her when she disappeared. Boo Flecker had been killed with one and now a second had ended Zac James's life. Which meant she still had one left.

'I can pronounce life extinct and I'll do the postmortem tomorrow,' Jane announced as she stood up. She stared down at the body as if she was racking her brains to think where she'd seen him before. 'Famous, is he?'

'He used to be in a boy band called Ladbeat back in the 1990s. A few years ago he was the subject of every teenage girl's dreams.'

Jane sighed. 'The press don't like dead celebrities so you'll be under some pressure to find whoever did this. On the other hand, they do say an untimely death can revive a flagging career.'

Wesley looked away. In his opinion Jane Partridge lacked Colin Bowman's innate compassion. Or maybe it was just a defensive shell. An act to conceal her true feelings. Sometimes such things are necessary if horror isn't going to get to you. He knew that as much as anyone.

Laurence Roley had been taken home by his partner, Ian, seemingly too shocked to face a police interview for the time being. Gerry was impatient to know why Roley had arranged to meet Zac James at the pub where he'd met Boo Flecker. It seemed a strange coincidence and he wanted to know if Roley should be moved up their suspect list. Wesley thought it unlikely but he wouldn't have wanted to stake his life savings on it.

In the meantime there was somebody else they wanted to see. It was Saturday afternoon and when they arrived at the Mumfords' house, Wesley saw that the builders' pick-up truck was parked in front of the house beside a Mercedes and Harriet's small four-by-four. Mumford's glossy yellow Mini, his plaything, was parked some way away in front of a dilapidated wooden garage. The sight of it reminded Wesley of Neil.

He still had no idea who could have sabotaged his friend's brakes. One of the officers he'd spoken to at Neston had reckoned it was probably nothing personal. Somehow this made it worse. If Neil, a harmless archaeologist, could be the target of a random attempted murder, anybody might be at risk.

Harriet Mumford answered the door. She wore a short denim skirt and a pink T-shirt with a low scooped neck and at first she looked almost pleased to see them. But she swiftly assumed a worried frown, as if she'd suddenly remembered they were police officers.

'Is it about Neil? Is he okay?'

'He's on the mend. They're letting him out of hospital on Monday,' said Wesley.

'We still don't know who cut his brake pipes though,' Gerry chipped in. 'I take it you've no ideas?'

When Harriet shook her head her fine veil of blonde hair flopped over her face. She pushed it back behind her ears.

Wesley had the latest murder weapon in a plastic evidence bag. It was stained with blood, now dried to a russet crust. He held it out for Harriet to see.

'There's been another murder. This appears to be the weapon used.'

'It's the one that you showed me before,' she said, accusingly, as if she thought they were wasting her time.

'It's identical but it's not the same one. That's safely in the exhibits store at the police station.'

'That woman who killed those kids bought three by mail order. I've heard she's gone missing.'

'That's right.'

'Have you found the athames she ordered?'

'Not yet,' said Wesley.

'There you are then. I blame myself for not recognising the name. It should have started alarm bells ringing.'

'Hardly your fault. But we will need to speak to everyone who has a supply of the things. Just routine. Do you know a man called Zac James? He used to be in a boy band called Ladbeat.'

'I think I've heard the name but . . . '

'His real name's John Grimes. You've never met him?'

'Not that I can remember.'

'Where were you this lunchtime, love?' said Gerry sharply.

Wesley noticed a flicker of alarm in Harriet's eyes, there for a moment then swiftly concealed. 'I was here. The builders can vouch for me. Some of them have been coming and going but I think Lee's been here all morning.'

'You haven't been over to your studio in West Fretham?'

'Not today, no.'

'What about your husband?' Wesley asked.

Harriet suddenly didn't look so sure of herself. 'He's been here most of the morning but . . . '

Wesley held his breath, hoping she was about to make a revelation.

'He popped down into Tradmouth around midday. He met a business associate for lunch.'

'Really?' said Gerry. 'Does he usually do business on a Saturday?'

'This customer's only in Devon for a few days so it was the only time he could make it. He's back now so why don't you ask him?'

'We will.'

Harriet hesitated, head bowed. 'Come through to the drawing room. I'll get him.'

As she led the way past the door to the derelict wing Wesley could hear the sound of hammering. According to

264

Dave the mysterious cellar had now been fully excavated and he would have liked to see it. But murder was more urgent.

Harriet left them in the drawing room which was low-beamed and cosy with a huge inglenook fireplace at one end. A large Turkish rug covered the flagstone floor and the dark oak furniture was polished to a shine. Everything was in keeping with the house and shouted prosperity and good taste.

He walked over to the fireplace, a tall oak edifice, intricately carved with figures and foliage. In the centre, in the place usually reserved for a family motto or coat of arms, were three words. Mors Vincit Omnia. Death conquers all. The words made Wesley shudder. This had never been a happy home, he felt. Death had ruled here and someone had carved it there for posterity.

When he spotted a number of photographs in silver frames standing on a Jacobean court cupboard in the corner, he strolled over and began to examine them, suddenly curious to know more about the couple's life. Gerry followed him and looked over his shoulder.

There was a picture of a dashing Evan in morning dress with a red carnation in his buttonhole. It had clearly been taken at a wedding but there was no bride, no smiling Harriet in a white gown and veil. Wesley thought this was unusual: it was a rare bride who didn't want to recall how she looked on her big day. To the right of the solitary bridegroom, in pride of place and in a slightly larger and fancier frame, there was one of Evan Mumford shaking hands with the Mayor.

'There's a familiar face,' said Gerry. He was pointing to a posed photograph obviously taken at a social gathering.

Evan was with a man Wesley recognised as Shane Gulliver, the author. The two men were holding champagne glasses and had their arms around each other's shoulders in a manly, matey manner. The best of friends.

When Harriet returned, saying her husband would join them in a minute or so, Wesley pointed to the photograph.

'You know Shane Gulliver?'

'Yes. That was taken at a party we gave a few weeks ago.'

'Gulliver's done well for himself.'

'Deservedly. Have you read any of his books?'

'No but my wife has. She's reading one at the moment.'

'Shane's a remarkable man. To overcome a background like that and establish yourself as a bestselling author takes some guts.' Harriet Mumford was obviously a member of the Shane Gulliver fan club and Wesley felt it would be churlish not to nod in agreement.

'Well he's made it to the big time now,' said Gerry. 'You know he lives next door to the farm where that journalist's body was found?'

'That's right. It was a terrible shock for him and Gwen.'

'So you know his wife?' Wesley asked.

'Yes, I know her quite well.'

'I've met her son.'

'Alex?' She gave an indulgent smile. 'Gwen says he's going through the teenage years at the moment. Dresses in black and goes round looking as if the end of the world's come. Makes me glad I never had kids.'

'There aren't any pictures of you here.'

She looked at him as though he'd said something distasteful. 'I can't stand having my photograph taken. It's not that unusual. I've got several friends who feel the same ... Gwen included. I don't know why it is but ... Some cultures believe that if someone photographs you they capture your soul, don't they?'

'I was talking to Selina Chester who runs Mysterioso in Neston. She says you're a member of her coven.'

She looked him in the eye. 'That's right, Inspector. I'm a Wiccan. It's no secret.'

'Are Shane and Gwen Gulliver members too?'

She shook her head. 'I don't really think it's their scene. I'll just go and see where Evan's got to.'

She began to make for the door with an eagerness that told Wesley she was finding his questions uncomfortable.

'Just one more thing, Mrs Mumford,' Wesley said to her disappearing back. She turned round. 'How many people have access to your supply of athames?'

Harriet thought for a few seconds before she answered. 'There's myself and Evan, of course. We've never really felt the need for security so anyone who visits the house could help themselves I suppose.'

'Any of the guests at your party?'

She looked doubtful. 'In theory, I suppose. But I can't honestly imagine any of our friends . . . '

'Can you remember anyone asking questions about the knives?'

'Absolutely not.'

'Do you keep a record of how many you have in stock?'

'Of course we do on the computer but we only do an actual stocktake about once a year.'

'Could you do one now, love?' said Gerry. 'Match the ones you have in stock with your records so we can check whether any are missing; just the design Lilith Benley ordered.'

She hesitated for a second. 'No problem.'

They had been alone in the drawing room for a few minutes when Evan Mumford joined them, all innocent concern. His wife, he said, was reconciling the stock with their records and he was anxious to help in any way he could.

Evan's answers matched Harriet's exactly, almost as if they'd agreed on their tactics beforehand. But Wesley told himself that his years in the police had probably given him a suspicious mind.

It was twenty minutes before Harriet burst into the room, a worried frown clouding her face. 'One of the cartons in the storeroom has been opened and six athames are missing.'

'We'll need the names and addresses of everyone who's visited this house in the past few weeks,' said Gerry.

Harriet opened the drawer, took out a note pad and began the list, saying that she wasn't sure of everyone's address. A subdued Evan supplied more details with barely concealed reluctance and when Harriet had finished her list, Wesley took it from her and examined it. Apart from the people he already knew about, the Gullivers and the builders, Selina Chester's name was also there. When he asked Evan about her he said she was a good customer, which made sense. But he'd found another link, however tenuous, between the Mumfords and Lilith Benley so he couldn't help experiencing a small thrill of discovery.

Then he spotted another familiar name on the list. Vera Bourne, Rupert Raybourn's aunt. Harriet described her as her cleaning lady who came in two days a week and spent most of that time complaining about the building work. She lived near Harriet's studio in West Fretham and she used to clean for a lot of people in what she called 'the old days'. Harriet had persuaded her to come out of retirement and paid well for her services because cleaners are hard to find.

Gerry pocketed the list. It was time to go, to take it back to the incident room and give it to some hapless DC to check out.

'How's the cellar coming along?' Wesley asked as Harriet showed them out.

'They've finished digging it out.' She seemed glad of the change of subject. 'And Dave, the archaeologist has had a look at it. He's taken some things away with him to be examined. He said those ... ' She hesitated. 'Those things hidden behind the panelling will probably end up in a museum. I told him I just wanted them out of the house.'

'Before his accident Neil was intending to find out more about a woman who lived here who was hanged for witchcraft. Her name was Alison Hadness.'

'All I've managed to find in the local library was an account of her trial. A lot of her neighbours gave evidence against her.' She hesitated for a moment. 'Actually there is something down in the cellar if you're interested.'

'What's that?'

'I'll show you.'

He allowed her to lead him into the disused wing, Gerry trailing behind. In the room where the panelling had been removed they found the builder, Lee, sitting on a wooden folding chair, drinking tea from a large mug. He watched as they followed Harriet to the open trapdoor leading down to the cellar, and Wesley noticed that his eyes were focused on Harriet's legs.

269

'Is it safe to go down there now?' she said to Lee.

As soon as Wesley saw him nod the two policemen negotiated the stone staircase leading down into the earth. The chamber was clear of soil and debris now and Wesley could see that it was around seven feet high and at least as large as the room above. Whatever it had been used for in times gone by it was now an empty space with stone walls and a dirty flagstone floor. But when Wesley studied the floor more carefully he could make out some marks, as though at one time somebody had drawn on the grey stones. He could just make out the faded outline of a pentagram, a five-pointed star enclosed in a circle, and he knew that its presence there probably meant the accusations against Alison Hadness back in the seventeenth century had contained the seeds of truth: she had indeed dabbled in witchcraft. No wonder they'd hanged her.

He climbed the steps back to the twenty-first century followed by Gerry, panting behind.

'It's a pentagram,' said Harriet who was waiting for them at the top. 'It's an ancient and powerful symbol of magic. We use it in our Wiccan rites too.'

He saw Gerry glance at his watch. He was anxious to go.

They thanked Harriet for her co-operation and Wesley told her that somebody would be along to take a statement and a proper list of everyone who might have had access to the missing knives.

'We'll see ourselves out,' Gerry said as he started towards the front door. Harriet made no attempt to play the perfect hostess and see them off the premises. Instead she stayed in the kitchen with Lee.

When he reached the threshold of the kitchen Wesley

glanced back. Harriet was standing close to Lee. His hand was placed firmly on her backside and she didn't seem to be objecting. But as soon as she saw that Wesley was watching the colour drained from her face and she stepped away quickly.

He followed Gerry along the hall to the front door. At least this snippet of gossip would take the DCI's mind off murder on their journey back to the incident room.

Shane Gulliver paused on the landing and gazed down into the hall. Even though it was Saturday he'd been working because he had a deadline. And besides, it kept him away from Alex. Playing happy families was all very well in small doses but a sulky adolescent Goth obsessed with metal detecting was hardly his idea of stimulating company. Gwen doted on the boy, spoiled him. But Shane preferred to keep his distance. He had wanted Gwen . . . not her baggage from the past, however fondly he might speak of the lad in media interviews.

He saw Gwen emerge from the drawing room, carrying a vase of half-dead flowers carefully in both hands. When he began to walk down the stairs she looked up.

'Alex in?' he asked.

'He's gone into Dukesbridge to meet some friends.' She watched him anxiously. She'd known him long enough to know something was wrong. 'What's up?'

Shane didn't answer. Instead he sunk down onto a thickly carpeted stair, sitting there like a small child refusing to go to bed.

Gwen put the vase down on the hall table, giving him her full attention. There was no point in lying now. Besides, he'd feel better if he shared it with somebody.

'I spoke to my agent yesterday – she's just got back from holiday.'

'And?'

He felt tears pricking his eyes, something he hadn't experienced since boyhood. 'It's all starting to unravel, Gwen. It's all going wrong.'

Chapter 14

Written by Alison Hadness, September 23rd 1643

William rose from his bed this day and drank much to relieve his great thirst. I gave him more of my infusion saying it was good for the headaches that plague him.

He feels most unwell and complains that he cannot see clearly. Dorcas is sick with headaches and issues forth vomit. So it was that I went into the town alone and my heart pounded so heavily I feared it would break from my breast when I saw Thomas in the market drinking ale with some merchants. He wore the homespun cloak of a farmer and yet when last I saw him he was going for a soldier of the King. I was sore tempted to greet him but my fear prevented it.

When I knew him he was a wild young man, a younger son with nought to commend him to my father. And yet I had loved him. I turned my head and saw he had left his companions and was waiting some way off in the street. I approached, my heart pounding in my breast, and when we were close enough to touch he said nothing but took my hand then, looking about him, he led me into an alley that ran between two tall houses. I allowed myself to be led, praying that no neighbour would see. For my mind was filled with sin.

He told me he was now a farmer, having bought land in Bovey Tracey. But I knew this to be a lie as the jewelled dagger he wore beneath his cloak was no farmer's weapon.

In my folly, I agreed to meet him at a barn which lies on my husband's land, my desire for him conquering all right thoughts.

When I arrived home Dorcas was worse and complains that her toes and fingers are cold. Maybe the magic in Elizabeth's doll has turned against an innocent victim.

Laurence Roley had recovered from his shock by the time his statement was taken.

It was a statement that raised more questions than answers. Zac James had called his old teacher out of the blue, saying he wanted to meet. Roley had suggested the Ploughman's Rest because it was a place where you could hold a decent conversation without your words being drowned out by piped music and intrusive fruit machines.

When he'd arrived at the pub he was greeting by the sight of a woman staggering from the entrance to the public footpath, clearly in shock with outstretched, blood-stained hands. She'd walked a few yards then she'd collapsed, sobbing to the ground and a man had run over to help her. Roley had asked the couple what was wrong but the woman had been too upset to answer so he'd made for the footpath and seen the body lying there, just out of sight of the car park and the road. It had taken him a few moments to realise that it was Zac – or John as he kept calling him – and he'd used his mobile phone to summon an ambulance.

Even though Roley seemed genuinely distressed he still

had the presence of mind to make a coherent statement. When Zac had called him he'd said he wanted to talk about something he thought he'd seen. He needed his advice. Roley couldn't be absolutely sure because the call had been a little vague. In fact he thought his former pupil might have been high on drugs. He'd read about his problems in the newspapers. Such a shame. The lad had had so much promise.

If Zac had been clearer about the purpose of the meeting, it would have made the investigation into his death a lot easier. It was frustrating. But, in Wesley's experience, life often was.

At seven Gerry announced they'd have to make an early start in the morning because the press had already got hold of the story and soon all hell would break loose. Laurence Roley had been willing to identify the body and the dead man's parents and sister had been contacted. They were coming down to Devon, the county that had been their home until Zac hit the big time and moved the whole family to the South East.

There was a visit Wesley wanted to make before he went home that evening. Vera Bourne's name had come up already and the fact that she cleaned for Harriet Mumford and had access to the athames was playing on his mind.

Gerry volunteered to go with him, saying that he hoped Vera made a decent cup of tea. Her house turned out to be just round the corner from Harriet's studio, which was now locked up with a closed sign on the door. Gerry stopped and stared into the window of the converted shop. There were clay models in various stages of production; hares, boxing and solitary; cats and dogs of various breeds. A whole menagerie in clay as well as figures of children and dancers. Harriet had stuck with the popular rather than anything too avant-garde.

Vera Bourne answered her door virtually as soon as they rang the bell, as if she'd been expecting them.

'We haven't met before,' said Gerry after introductions had been made.

'I've had a couple of detectives round already. I told them everything I know.' Her words sounded defensive, as though she was guarding some precious secret.

'You're Rupert Raybourn's aunt.'

'That's right,' she said. At the mention of her nephew, her manner changed and they listened for a while as she sang his praises, bristling with pride. He always remembered to visit her whenever he was in the area. Such a good boy. And so talented.

Wesley watched Gerry smile indulgently and, once the eulogy was over, they were offered tea, almost as if they'd just passed some test.

However, when they asked her about Lilith Benley she became quite agitated, expressing the hope that she was dead after what she'd done to 'those poor lambs', not to mention the people she'd killed more recently. Yes, she'd heard about the pop singer. And if she spotted Lilith Benley she assured them she'd dial 999 right away.

'You knew Lilith and her mother before the murders?'

'Certainly not.'

'What about the girls they killed?'

'I used to see them around but I didn't know them well. I knew Gabrielle's mother to say hello to but . . .'

'What about Joanne Trelisip?'

'That poor mother of hers. Never got over her husband running off.'

'Have you seen her recently?'

Vera shook her head.

'I understand you clean for Harriet Mumford,' Wesley said after taking a sip of tea.

'Yes. Why?' The question was guarded as though she suspected it was some sort of trap.

'Evan Mumford imports knives – for ceremonies.' Wesley caught Gerry's eye.

'I don't know anything about that. I just clean.'

'So you've no idea who might have taken six knives from a box in their storeroom?'

'Well it wasn't me,' she said, affronted.

'We never said it was, love,' said Gerry. 'We just wondered whether you'd seen anything, that's all.'

'No. But those Mumfords have got some very odd friends. Harriet's nice enough. She's got that little studio round the corner. Used to be a butcher's in the old days.'

'What about Evan?'

She leaned forward. 'He's not a nice man.'

'What do you mean?'

She ignored the question.

'They're friendly with that writer who lives at the Rectory, you know. I've not seen much of him, mind. And I don't think I've ever set eyes on his wife. But I'll tell you one thing for free.' She lowered her voice. 'You know that woman who was murdered, the reporter?'

'What about her?'

'I was driving through the village and I saw that writer talking to a woman – could have been the one that got killed. I drove past him and I've never seen anyone look so cross.'

'You think he was talking to Boo Flecker?'

277

'She was wearing a bright red coat but I couldn't see her face.'

'When was this?'

'It was Monday . . . the day before she was found dead. I know because I clean for the Mumfords on Mondays and I was on my way to Tradmouth.' She hesitated. 'I'll tell you something else about Evan Mumford. I saw him hit her once. Right crack he gave her.'

'Who?'

'His wife, of course. Evan Mumford is a nasty piece of work.'

Wesley suggested they pay Shane Gulliver a visit but when they called at the house there was no answer so Gerry said it would have to wait till the next morning. Besides, it was time they went home and got some rest.

When Wesley arrived home Pam met him at the door and he kissed her absentmindedly. After he'd greeted the children, receiving a hug from Amelia and little more than a grunt from Michael, Pam led him to the kitchen.

'My mother called,' she said, sitting down at the table where the remnants of a meal still lay, cold and congealing. 'She was on about Simon Frith again.'

'There's nothing more I can do. And even if there was, I'm not sure I'd want to.'

Even though he hadn't been convicted in a court of law, to Wesley, Frith was still a man who'd assaulted an under-age girl – the very accusation had stained him. Wesley had been the victim of prejudice from time to time in the past and he hated it. But he found he couldn't help how he felt. And it disturbed him.

Pam sat in silence for a few moments, watching him

intently as though she could read his thoughts. Then she spoke. 'You know you said this case you're involved in might be linked to the murders of those two girls at West Fretham eighteen years ago.'

'That's right.'

'My mother said Simon used to teach at their school.'

Wesley stared at her. This was something new. Something he didn't feel inclined to ignore.

'He taught History at Dukesbridge Comp for a while. He must have been quite young ... just starting out on the glittering career that is the modern teaching profession.'

'So he knew the dead girls?'

'I don't know about that – it's a big school with a huge staff.'

Wesley nodded. For the moment he couldn't really see how the connection was relevant to his investigation but he'd bear it in mind. Sometimes leads can come from the most unexpected sources.

Pam was shocked when he told her about Zac James. 'I remember him in Ladbeat,' she said. 'He was very good looking. You think his death's connected with the murder of that journalist?'

'It's exactly the same MO.'

'Has that Benley woman been found yet?'

'We're still looking.' He suddenly felt like changing the subject. 'You sure you're OK with Neil stopping here for a while?'

She looked at him sideways, a hint of calculation in her eyes. 'He's always got on well with Michael, hasn't he? I think there might even be a bit of hero worship there. The Indiana Jones figure and all that. Maybe he'll be able to persuade him that academic study isn't just for wimps.'

'Good thinking.' Wesley reached across the table and took her hand. 'If your mother wants to make herself useful why don't you get her over to babysit while we go out?' He felt tired but he thought he'd better make the effort.

He was almost relieved when she told him that Della already had plans for the evening. A new man on the horizon. Somehow Wesley wasn't surprised. He just hoped this one would be an improvement on her catalogue of past disasters.

He noticed a paperback book lying next to Pam on the kitchen table; Shane Gulliver's *Rejected*. 'Still not finished it?'

Pam picked up the book and flicked through the pages. 'I'm finding it a bit heavy going, to be honest.' She studied the back cover for a while, as if she was reminding herself of the narrative. 'You've met Gulliver – what's he like?'

'I'm not sure what to make of him. If his hype has any truth in it, he's certainly come up in the world.' Before he could say any more his mobile phone began to ring and Wesley cursed under his breath. He'd been hoping for an undisturbed evening before the inevitable pressure of the following day. Sunday would be no day of rest . . . quite the reverse.

He'd half expected it to be Gerry or someone from the incident room, but the unfamiliar caller's number on the tiny display aroused his curiosity. He answered with a cautious hello.

Even when the caller said his name, it took Wesley a few seconds to place him. Richard Twigg, also known as Richard the Pillock, spoke in an urgent whisper. 'I heard about John Grimes on the news.' He sounded worried. 'Look, I've been thinking things over and . . . '

Wesley saw Pam watching him, straining to hear. When he covered the mouthpiece and mouthed the word 'work' he saw her roll her eyes.

'What is it?' he asked. Richard had sounded as if he was afraid someone might be listening. Maybe Zac James's death had made him nervous and he couldn't help wondering if the reaction was justified. Probably not. But people like to feel important.

'They said on the news that you're linking it with that other one. Sorry for calling so late but I figured that the sooner I told you everything I knew, the safer I'd be.'

Wesley suspected that Richard was enjoying a bit of vicarious drama but he'd wait to hear what he had to say before passing final judgement.

'So what do you want to tell me?'

There was a pause. 'I don't know whether it's important but a couple of weeks before Jo and Gabby were murdered I was in the cloakroom at school and they were there. I was behind some lockers and they didn't know I could hear . . .'

Wesley murmured some words of encouragement, wishing he'd get on with it.

'Anyway they were arguing. Jo said she'd met some posh bloke from London who was staying over at Millicombe. Gabby asked her what she was going to do about John but Jo just laughed at her. Then a few days later John started going round with Gabby.'

Wesley felt disappointed. He'd expected more than an account of some teenage falling out over boys. 'Anything else?' he asked, hoping the best was still to come.

'Jo called Gabby chicken. Said she was a coward. Then she said something about a witch – or it could have been a

281

bitch – and something like "He's dead and she killed him."
At least that's what it sounded like.'

'This was a couple of weeks before they were killed?'

'Yeah, about that.'

'You didn't tell the police at the time?'

'I was off school with tonsillitis so they never spoke to
me. Anyway, I didn't think it was important at the time. You
did say if I remembered anything at all . . . '

Wesley was about to say that it was hardly urgent, that it
could have waited till tomorrow, but Richard sounded so
eager that he hadn't the heart. He said he'd check to see if
anyone connected to Joanne had died in the period before
her murder and ended the call as politely as he could. Then
he returned to the kitchen where he found Pam with Shane
Gulliver's book open in front of her. But her eyes were
closed.

Wesley told Gerry about Richard's call as soon as he arrived
at the incident room on Sunday morning 'Think it's relevant?' he asked. He wasn't sure of the answer and wanted
a second opinion.

'Not unless this mystery man followed Joanne here and
murdered her and her mate. But that's hardly likely. The
evidence against the Benleys was overwhelming.'

'What about the "he's dead" bit?'

Gerry shrugged. 'Who knows? It's all a bit vague.'

Wesley saw that Gerry had been looking though all the
information they had on Evan Mumford. And at that
moment it seemed more relevant than some half-remembered conversation from the dead girls' school days.

'I want to know more about Mumford. He supplied the
murder weapons and his wife supplied his alibis,' said Gerry.

'Vera Bourne certainly doesn't like him. Accused him of domestic violence.'

'And don't forget Neil was nearly killed while he was working at his house. What if Mumford was afraid of him stumbling on something he wanted to keep hidden so he thought he'd get rid of him by arranging a convenient accident?'

This wasn't something Wesley had considered before. But now it didn't sound so far-fetched.

'What about Boo Flecker.'

'Maybe he thought she had something on him.'

'And Zac James?'

'Perhaps he's a music lover,' said Gerry quickly. 'I don't know. Maybe if we dig deeper we'll find out. But Lilith Benley's still top of our list.'

Gerry shuffled some papers on his desk. 'Boo Flecker's phone records have turned up at last but there's nothing of much interest that we don't already know about. There's only one – a London number that turns out to be a literary agent. Imogen Barnes and Associates. It's the weekend so the office is closed but I got someone to look this agent up on the Internet and it turns out that one of her clients is Shane Gulliver. Now if Vera Bourne really did see him talking to Boo ... '

'She says she only saw him from a distance. He could have been talking to anyone in a red coat, even his wife.' Wesley hesitated. 'Mind you, didn't Boo Flecker tell her mum she was onto a "Mr Big". Her mum assumed it was some criminal mastermind but what if she meant Gulliver?'

Gerry frowned.

'Mr Big. Gulliver's Travels. Lilliput. Jonathan Swift.'

Gerry suddenly twigged. 'I think we should pay Mr Gulliver a call.' He looked at his watch. 'No time like the present.'

It was Alex Gulliver who opened the door. He even greeted Wesley with a half-hearted smile, until he noticed Gerry Heffernan standing behind him and the smile turned into an uncertain frown.

'Your dad in?' Gerry said.

'If you mean Shane, yes. He's not my dad,' the boy added as though it was important to make this plain. He stood aside to let them in. 'I'll tell mum you're here. Shane's working and he doesn't want to be disturbed.'

Wesley was about to say that he wouldn't have any choice in the matter but, not wanting to put the boy on the receiving end of Gulliver's wrath, he agreed to speak to Gwen instead. She could do the dirty deed and prise the author away from his laptop. She showed them into the drawing room and asked them to wait before hurrying away.

When Gulliver finally appeared his face was red. Wesley half expected him to deliver an impassioned speech about living in a police state but instead he feigned civility.

'I see we're not the only ones who have to work on Sunday,' Wesley began.

'I have a deadline to meet. How can I help you?'

'We believe the woman who was murdered at the farm next door tried to contact your agent.'

'Really?' The word was casual. 'Perhaps she was writing a book. A lot of journalists seem to these days.'

'We've also had information that you were seen talking to her the day before she died,' Wesley added, taking the risk that Vera Bourne's vague testimony was true. He watched

Gulliver's face carefully for a reaction. His expression gave nothing away but Wesley could see the man's fingers pulling nervously at his shirt sleeve.

He waited, hoping the author would feel the urge to fill the silence. Eventually the tactic paid off.

Gulliver took a deep breath. 'OK. She called at the house but I refused to speak to her. Then she stopped me in the village.'

'Did she threaten you?'

There was a long silence before he answered. 'She threatened to make things public that I'd rather keep private.'

'Such as? You might as well tell us, Mr Gulliver. We've got a team of experienced detectives back at the incident room who'll trawl through every record they can lay their hands on.'

'They won't get very far.' He looked away.

'Why's that?' said Gerry.

Another silence. Then Gulliver spoke quietly, as if he didn't want to be overheard. 'Look, if this comes out it could finish me. Make me a laughing stock. I need your absolute assurance that anything I tell you will be treated as confidential.'

'If it has no connection with the murder, you have our word that anything you tell us in this room will go no further.' Wesley looked at Gerry who nodded earnestly in agreement.

Gulliver sank down on the sofa opposite the two policemen and put his head in his hands. After a few moments he looked up. 'When I began writing I couldn't get anything published.' The man had suddenly lost his East End accent. 'I'd written four literary novels which, for some inexplicable reason, all the major publishing houses rejected. I'd acquired an agent by then – a clever woman who knew the market – and she suggested that I begin again. A rebirth, she called it. This was the period when memoires of the more lurid variety were starting to dominate the bestseller list and the worse the catalogue of misery and abuse, the more the public seemed to lap it up. She suggested I change my name, assume the persona of a boy from the East End who'd survived a horrific childhood – dead prostitute mother, violent alcoholic father, sexually abusive uncles and all that – and progressed to a feral life among drug addicts and criminal gangs. I was, er …"discovered" by my agent through a prison creative writing class. Only I wasn't. I'd never seen the inside of a prison until I went to Wandsworth to do a talk. I had an extremely comfortable upbringing and went to a minor public school.'

'Welson Hall?'

Gulliver looked at Wesley, astonished. 'How did you know?'

'Boo Flecker contacted the school. I presume your real name is Giles Parsons?'

The answer was a meek nod. 'My father was in the army so I boarded at school and never settled anywhere long enough to make roots and contacts. My agent said that was to my advantage if I was to assume a new identity. So was the fact that I was an only child and my parents were both dead.'

When he looked up, Wesley could see pain in his eyes. This man had denied who he really was … and it had come at a price.

'I presume your wife knows your real identity.'

'Of course. Although I didn't come clean till a week

before the wedding. Shane Gulliver's my real name now, incidentally. I changed it by deed poll.'

'How did your wife react when you told her?' Wesley asked, full of curiosity.

'I was afraid she'd call it off at first. After all, she chose Shane Gulliver, the successful author . . . not Giles Parsons, the failed literary novelist from a boring middle-class background. She was shocked, of course, but she came to terms with it. I suppose I should have confessed earlier but I was reluctant to rock the boat. She'd had enough problems of her own . . . what with Alex's father and . . . '

'Who is Alex's father?' It was Gerry who asked the question, unable to contain his curiosity.

'She met him when she was young and he's long gone. But there was a time she was scared he'd find them.'

'Is that why she doesn't like having her photo taken?'

Gulliver raised his eyebrows. 'How did you know that?'

'Harriet Mumford told us. I suppose in Gwen's case it's understandable . . . if there's an ex in the background she wants to avoid.'

'The trouble with photographs these days is you don't know who gets hold of them, what with the Internet and social networks. The last thing Gwen wants is the ex tracking her and Alex down. He was bad news.'

'What's his name?'

'She always said it was better I never knew. That was in the past.'

'And he's never tried to make contact with Alex?'

'Gwen broke up with him when Alex was a baby. Alex has no memory of him and Gwen wants it to stay that way.' He sighed. 'Well, gentlemen, you've got the truth out of me but I'd be grateful if you didn't spread it around. I'm sure you'll appreciate that I'd like my ... ' He searched for the word. 'Deception kept quiet. If it came out it could ruin everything.'

'And if Boo Flecker had lived the story would have been spread all over the papers,' said Wesley. 'You had every reason to kill her, Mr Gulliver.'

The author bowed his head. Wesley could see a pale patch of scalp amongst the dark curls; he was beginning to lose his hair. 'I can see it might look that way but I swear I've never killed anybody. I couldn't.'

'She threatened your livelihood and your reputation.'

'If the worst came to the worst I would have trusted my agent to deal with it. She'd have sorted everything out.' He smiled bravely. 'And, who knows, if the truth came out and it was handled right it might even be good publicity at this stage in my career; that's what my agent said anyway.'

Wesley suspected that the man's agent had taken the place of his long-dead mother, the protector, the one he could rely on. And somehow he believed his claims of innocence.

'Anyway, I was in London when that woman died. I saw my editor first thing then I had lunch with a friend.'

'Have you heard about the murder yesterday? Zac James. One of the celebrities who took part in the filming next door.'

'I did hear something about it on the news and I've seen a lot of police cars speeding past.'

Gerry had been listening carefully and now he spoke. 'Where were you yesterday, around lunchtime?'

'I was here.'

'Any witnesses?'

'My wife was at work – she works part time at an art

gallery in Neston – and Alex was in his room doing God knows what. I wasn't aware I needed an alibi so I didn't arrange one.'

Wesley stood up. 'We might need to talk to you again.'

They left the house and as they walked back to the incident room Gerry caught Wesley's arm. 'He's got a whacking great motive, Wes. We need to check times with the friend he had lunch with. He could have caught an earlier train.'

'I believed him.'

'That's because he's been living a lie for years and it's second nature to him. He's no alibi for the time Zac James was killed.'

'We can check whether anyone saw him walking to the village at the appropriate time.'

'You get someone onto it, Wes. And if you get the wrong answer, Shane Gulliver comes straight in.'

Gulliver had indeed met his editor on the morning of Boo Flecker's murder. However, the friend he claimed to have met for lunch wasn't answering his phone so he could still have caught an early train back and reached West Fretham in time to kill. As for the time of Zac James's murder, he'd claimed that he was in the house alone with Alex, Gwen having gone to work. Only Alex was denying he was there. Although Wesley wouldn't have put it past him to lie to get his stepfather into trouble.

Wesley sat for a while thinking. They had no idea where Lilith Benley was, or even whether she was still alive. But he had an uncomfortable feeling that she was in danger. He recalled the doll they'd found at Devil's Tree Cottage with the rusty nail thrust into its roughly shaped wax flesh. Its message was that somebody wished Lilith dead. But had that wish been acted on?

When he'd first met Lilith she'd seemed so determined to defy public opinion and resume her life in Devon. If she was still alive, something terrible must have happened that night to make her flee her home and go into hiding – and he felt it was up to him to find out what had become of her. But each new discovery only seemed to confuse things, like another pebble thrown into a pool, churning up the dark mud at the bottom, turning the water into an opaque soup.

He felt he needed a diversion, time to get things straight in his head. And he had a promise to keep. He'd promised to take the wax doll from Mercy Hall to Neil in hospital.

Before setting off that morning he'd put the thing in the boot of his car. He hadn't told Pam what he was doing because he knew the very sight of it disturbed her. All the time he'd been driving to West Fretham he'd been aware of its malevolent presence, however much he tried to persuade himself that it was just his imagination. It was an object – a mass of wax, wood, hair and nails. Nothing more. It had no power to hurt.

When he said he was going out, Gerry told him not to be long. It was Sunday so there wasn't much traffic and as he was driving past Bereton sands, heading for Tradmouth, his phone began to ring so he brought the car to a halt in the deserted car park.

When he answered the call he heard Pam's voice. 'Simon Frith tried to kill himself last night. He took an overdose of antidepressants. Della found him. Luckily she was in time.'

Wesley said nothing for a few moments, taking in the news. 'This implies he's guilty as charged, don't you think?'

'Not necessarily. What if the accusation has made his life

unbearable? He could lose everything, Wes. His job; his freedom; his reputation; his family. How would you cope with something like that?'

Wesley was about to utter something trite, like 'if you can't do the time, don't do the crime'. But something stopped him. Instead he asked where the man had been taken and the answer was Tradmouth Hospital, where he was heading to brighten Neil's day. He ended the call and drove on.

He found Neil sitting up in bed looking bored. The wounds on his face bristled with spiky black stitches and the flesh around them was bruised and discoloured. He still looked awful but Wesley could tell he was feeling better. There was a new restlessness about him that suggested he was anxious to be out of there.

'Have you got it?' were his first words.

Wesley had the coffin safe in a large Marks & Spencer carrier bag and he placed it on the bedclothes. Neil leaned forward stiffly and delved into the bag but when he tried to lift the thing, he gave a yelp of agony and sank back on his pillows. Wesley had no choice but to help him out.

The wood felt cold and rough as he eased it from its protective covering, careful to keep the plastic between the unhygienic artefact and the bed cover.

Neil shuffled forward and watched Wesley prise off the wooden top, revealing the wax doll beneath.

'Ugly looking bugger, isn't he?'

'It's got a skirt. Must be a she.'

Neil stared down into the box. 'Someone didn't like her, whoever she was.' Cautiously he leaned further forward. 'I noticed there was a layer of paper in the bottom . . . underneath the doll.'

Wesley peered into the box. And as he looked at the thing he felt a cold tingle pass through his body. He'd heard inanimate objects described as evil but he'd never really believed it, until now.

'Found the bastard who cut my brake pipes yet?'

'Sorry.' Wesley hesitated. 'Has Evan Mumford ever threatened you?'

Neil's expression was a blend of shock and amusement. 'How do you mean?'

'If he thought you and Harriet . . . '

'Oh come on, Wes. She's a bit of a tease but . . . '

Neil sat quietly for a few seconds, fidgeting with the bed-clothes. Then the smile vanished from his face. 'Actually Harriet has been coming on to me. Not that I've had the opportunity to do much about it. As for the inclination . . . well, she's an attractive woman. However, unlike some people, I've never found danger much of an aphrodisiac if you know what I mean. You don't think Evan might have got the wrong idea and . . . ?'

'It's not my case but I can always arrange for a few questions to be asked. Never underestimate a jealous husband.'

Neil shrugged. 'I can't see it myself. Besides, Harriet's like that with everyone. She's always flirting with those builders.'

He returned his attention to the strange object on the bed, taking the doll out carefully and laying it beside the box. It had been lying on several sheets of ancient paper or parchment, folded, yellowed and fragile, and as Wesley stared at it, he saw that it was covered with faded writing.

Neil's eyes met his. 'This should go straight to the conservation lab but if we're very careful it won't do any harm to have a quick look.' He unfolded the delicate paper with

292

great care and began to read the faint letters. But after a few seconds he gave up. 'I think it's in some sort of code.'

He pushed it towards Wesley who studied it for a few moments. 'I think it's a simple substitution code. If you move one letter back it makes sense. B for A, F for E and so on.'

Neil gave him a rueful grin as he took it from him. 'Should have realised. Must be the concussion.'

'I'll leave you to wrestle with it. Give your brain a bit of exercise.' Wesley looked at his watch. 'I told Gerry I wouldn't be long.' He nodded towards the doll. 'Shall I leave that with you?'

'It might be an interesting conversation piece. There's one nurse in particular who might appreciate it.' He yawned. The effort of talking had tired him. 'With any luck I'll be out tomorrow morning,' he said. 'Dave's promised to pick me up.' He looked at the doll. 'And my friend here.'

When Wesley left the ward he made his way to Reception and enquired about Simon Frith. He was directed to one of the medical wards where he found Simon lying on his back staring at the ceiling, a drip in his arm. At the nurses' station he showed his ID and asked whether it was okay to have a quick word. The dismissive way the nurse waved him towards the bed told him she hadn't much sympathy for attempted suicides. Wesley couldn't agree with her. Pain comes in all varieties, not just the physical.

He pulled up a chair and sat by Simon's bed but the man didn't seem to register his presence.

He asked how the patient was feeling but received no reply. Then Simon closed his eyes, as though he was asleep. But Wesley knew otherwise. He pushed his chair back quietly and hurried out of the ward. If Simon Frith didn't want to talk, that suited him fine.

Pauline Parry – formerly Pauline Trelisip in those far off, well-remembered days when she'd been lovable and loved – hoped that social worker wouldn't come again. She'd asked too many questions ... and none of those questions had been about her Joanne.

It was time to go out again. If she spent enough time wandering the streets she might see her. And if she did, she wouldn't stare in dumb amazement like she had last time. She'd rush to her and enfold her in her arms and never let go. They'd be reunited. The living and the dead.

She made her way slowly and breathlessly down the steep hill into the town, her legs aching with the effort and the gradient. But hope buoyed her up, killing the pain, making time irrelevant.

It took her half an hour to reach the waterfront and once there she sat down on a damp bench, hugging her coat around her for protection. A chill breeze was whipping in over the choppy water but she didn't notice the cold gnawing at her hands. She shut her eyes tight and muttered half-formed, incoherent prayers. Last time it had happened here on the quayside and now she was yearning for a second miracle. That her long-dead daughter would return to life.

After a while she opened her eyes, stood up and moved closer to the unguarded edge, staring into the dark, shifting river, longing to see Joanne's face gazing back at her from the water, expressionless and pale. She took another unsteady step forward. Then another. Then somebody shouted and she heard running feet, pounding like a heartbeat on the cobbled embankment.

When her body hit the river she gasped with the sudden shock of the chill water, swallowing salty liquid through her gaping mouth, flailing round, half aware that Joanne was there beside her, whispering in her ear. Stop fighting. Let the water take you. Embrace death as I did.

And when she was hauled out by a couple of fishermen who'd been nearby, preparing their boat for a night at sea, the only thing she could tell them was that the dead walk.

Chapter 15

Written by Alison Hadness, September 24th 1643

I met Thomas in the barn and, forgetting my marriage vows, I lay with him there.

How sweetly we lay in each other's arms, his flesh joined with mine once more. He said I had an appetite for sin that matches his own. And yet it did not feel like sin.

He talked as we lay, saying how Prince Maurice plans to attack this town and bring it under the King's rule once more. He says his men grow restless with this constant rain that turns all to mire. They complain of aching joints and it is only the good supply of food and ale hereabouts that keeps them from mutiny. I told him that, despite the people's hunger, Tradmouth continues defiant.

He said there is talk of witchcraft amongst the men. Some say spells have been cast that makes the prince unwell and some say the Devil is feeding the townsfolk with huge catches of fish from the river. I told him the tale of the fish was a lie. If Satan feeds us, why are there so many empty bellies?

When I returned to the house Elizabeth met me with a look of such hatred it was like a dagger to my heart. I found Dorcas in great pain. Her body stiffens and she cries with agony and vomits forth all she consumes. She says Elizabeth hath bewitched her because she knows I hold her in great affection. Many of our neighbours are similarly afflicted and there is talk that demons stalk the town, entering folk and making them mad, their bodies twitching and jerking with visions of Satan and hell itself.

Thomas has promised to bring good bread when we next meet for I will not share the foul bread the townsfolk must endure.

Neil was grateful to Pam and Wesley for providing him with a temporary refuge until he was fit to return to his Exeter flat.

After the doctor had told him he was free to leave hospital, provided he was careful, Dave picked him up and took him straight to Wesley's house. He sat in the passenger seat of Dave's rickety Land Rover, wishing it had been blessed with better suspension because every jolt shot pain through his body as though some sadistic torturer was applying electrodes to his flesh. Eventually they arrived in the small, modern cul-de-sac at the top of the town and Dave sought out the key which Pam had promised to leave underneath a plant pot by the front door. For a policeman, Wesley was remarkably cavalier with his security arrangements, Neil thought. But as both he and Pam were at work, he supposed there was little choice.

Dave had put the bag containing the little coffin in the back of the Land Rover, paying more attention to its comfort and safety than he had to Neil's. Now he carried it carefully into the house and, once Neil was settled on the sofa, he placed it on the Petersons' coffee table where it shed dirt and splinters over the clean wooden top.

'I managed to transcribe that manuscript last night,' said Neil. 'The nurses weren't too pleased with the dirt on the bedclothes but . . . '

'Did they see the doll?' Dave asked.

Neil shook his head. The delicate manuscript was inside a plastic bag that was designed to hold patients' dirty laundry. He took it out with exaggerated care and handed it to Dave along with a few sheets of lined paper. 'This is only part of the story. Did they find more of it in the other boxes?'

'I believe so. They're at the lab in Exeter. I'll get copies for you as soon as I can – translating it'll give you something to do. What does it say?'

'It's a journal written by a woman called Alison Hadness – and, from the dates, it must be the same Alison Hadness who was hanged for witchcraft in 1643.' He touched the lined paper Dave was holding. 'She was married to an older man who already had a teenage daughter called Elizabeth who sounds like the classic stroppy adolescent. During the siege of Tradmouth everyone was starving and having to make bread out of rotten grain because the Royalists were commandeering all the food and drink from the countryside round about and blockading the town. And while all this was going on Alison met an old boyfriend.'

'What's his name?'

Neil consulted his notes. 'Thomas Whitcombe.'

Dave's eyes lit up. 'I've come across that name. He was one of the officers with the besieging Royalist army – Prince Maurice's lot stationed at Hilton Farm. Thomas's journal's in the library in Exeter. It was one of the contemporary accounts I looked at before the dig began.'

'Great. See what else you can find out. Harriet Mumford said she was looking up Alison's trial in Tradmouth Library. Any chance you can ask her how far she's got?'

'I can try.'

Neil hesitated for a moment. 'Do you think Harriet's scared of her husband?'

Dave gave Neil an enquiring look. 'Now you come to mention it she does seem a bit tense when he's around.'

'I think he's a bully.'

There was a long pause. Then eventually Dave spoke. 'It's not often I take a dislike to someone but I must admit that whenever I visit Mercy Hall I find myself hoping Evan Mumford won't put in an appearance. Are you feeling up to coming out to the dig? We're still turning up loads of arte-facts from the Royalist army in that new trench.'

'The doc said I should take it easy today. But I'll be there tomorrow. Pick me up first thing. And if you can get hold of the rest of that manuscript . . . '

'I'm going up to Exeter later. I'll pop into the lab and get you a copy.'

'Great.' Neil gave Dave a wide grin. 'Don't suppose there's any chance of a coffee? They keep it in the top left-hand cupboard.'

Pauline Parry's encounter with the river was treated as a routine matter; an accident. But as Pauline had a connec-tion with the Lilith Benley case, somebody at Tradmouth Police Station had used their initiative and decided to inform the Major Incident Team.

Rachel had been sent down to Tradmouth Hospital to have a word with the woman who had been kept in overnight as a precaution after swallowing a stomachful of river water. She'd been lucky, the staff told her. Local legend had it that every year the River Trad claimed a life, but it seemed that Pauline Parry had been rejected as the annual sacrifice.

When Rachel returned to the incident room Wesley watched as she greeted her housemate, Trish, with only the faintest of smiles. He called to her, asking if he could have a word, and she walked over to his desk, still in her coat, hands in pockets and a faraway look in her eyes.

'How's Pauline Parry?'

Rachel slumped down on the chair beside his desk. He could see sadness in her eyes. 'She's saying she saw her daughter in the water, beckoning to her. She believes it, Wes. She really believes she saw Joanne. Maybe after this she'll get some proper help.'

Wesley gave her a weak smile.

His mobile phone rang and he looked at the caller display but didn't recognise the number. When he answered he heard a breathless female voice which it took him a while to place. It was Selina Chester and she wanted to see him.

Wesley was only too eager to leave behind the intense atmosphere of the incident room and head for Neston. West Fretham was a pleasant village, pretty even, but he would always associate the place with violent death. Perhaps it had been cursed ever since Dorothy and Lilith Benley had ended the lives of two schoolgirls there. Some locations never recover from something like that. As he climbed into the car he told himself he was being fanciful. People made evil things happen, not places.

When he reached Neston it was teeming with life. It was market day and on the square in front of the municipal offices, New Age enthusiasts in colourful clothes brushed shoulders with farming families and elderly locals browsing the stalls. A busker with a guitar and faithful dog was doing a roaring trade going through the collected works of Bob Dylan and as Wesley strolled towards Selina's shop, he felt optimistic for the first time that day.

As soon as he entered the shop Selina greeted him as if she was anxious to share a secret ... or get something off her conscience. She hurried out from behind the counter and locked the shop door before leading Wesley into the back. He was relieved when she didn't offer herbal tea.

She sat for a while, her eyes closed as though she was meditating. Then she opened them and looked straight at Wesley. 'I take it you still haven't found Lilith?'

He shook his head.

'You said it wouldn't help Lilith if I didn't tell you everything I knew.' She hesitated. 'I've been thinking it over and there is something she told me in confidence. And if somebody confides in you, trusts you with their secrets, it seems wrong to break that trust, doesn't it?'

'Sometimes,' said Wesley. 'But if it helps us find out what's happened to her ... '

'That's just it. I don't know whether it will. It might be totally irrelevant.'

'Let me be the judge of that.'

She sat back in the chair and arched her thin fingers. Her nails, he noticed, were painted scarlet today; a small vanity. It was a while before she spoke.

'When Lilith first came here we met through our mutual interest in Wicca and we became friends. She was looking after her mother and running the smallholding and I think she was quite lonely. I could never quite work out why she'd left a good job in London and thrown everything up to move to Devon. Then one day I asked her.'

'What did she say?'

'Up till then I never knew whether she was so devoted to her mother that she was willing to sacrifice everything for her, or whether she was trying to escape from something. It turned out it was neither of those things and I was surprised when I found out the truth.'

Wesley held his breath, hoping that he was about the learn something important.

'I mentioned that there was a man in London. Well, she'd come down to Morbay on holiday in the late 1980s and she'd met him at the theatre. He was some sort of performer and he left his wife and daughter. He moved to London to be with her.'

'What happened to him?'

'She told me he'd died.'

'How?'

'Heart attack I think. After it happened she moved back in with her mother and then she decided to throw up everything and move to a smallholding in Devon. I suppose lots of city dwellers find the rural dream irresistible.' Selina thought for a few moments. 'I don't think she had many close friends in London and she certainly didn't have any here. I suppose I felt quite honoured that she chose to confide in me. That's why I've felt reluctant to tell you. It almost seems like a betrayal.'

'You've done the right thing, Selina. But it would help if I knew who this man in Lilith's life was. Did she mention his name at all?'

'I think it was Cramer and his first name began with C as well. Sorry, I can't remember.'

'What sort of entertainer was he?'

'He was a comedian ... or was it a magician? I'm not really sure.'

Wesley thanked her. Boo Flecker had been looking up someone called Carl Cramer on her laptop but they'd been so busy concentrating on Shane Gulliver that they hadn't given it much attention.

'Are you sure you don't know where Lilith is?' He asked the question gently.

Selina pressed her lips together. Maybe this was a betrayal too far. Then she spoke. 'I don't believe she murdered those girls. But even if she did, she's served her sentence.'

'Two people have died in West Fretham, Selina, and either Lilith killed them or she's in danger herself. She might even be dead already.' He was about to add that he could arrest her for obstructing the police but he was loath to go that far ... unless there was no alternative.

'I don't know where she is,' she said. 'If I knew, I'd tell you.'

But he didn't believe her for one moment.

'Frith tried to top himself.'

'How do you mean?' Alex stared at Jessica who was perched on the office chair he usually kept by his desk. It was on castors and she'd wheeled it over to the bed where he was sitting propped up against the headboard, steering it with her long, slim legs.

She'd arrived at the front door, all anxiety, and his mother had shown her up to his room. She'd thought the company would cheer him up. But it was all he needed.

'He took an overdose. I heard my dad on the phone

talking to the police.' She swallowed hard, fighting back tears. 'He said the police thought it meant he was guilty.'

Alex turned his head away. 'I wouldn't worry about it.'

'It was meant to be a laugh but now I feel like a murderer.'

'You didn't make him do it.'

'But I did. Why did you tell me to say it?'

''Cause he was a pervert and perverts deserve all they fucking get.'

'But he never did anything. I lied to the police and if they found out I could get into trouble.'

'Then don't tell them.'

'But . . . '

'Look, from what I heard, it was only a matter of time before he started touching you up . . . or worse.' He leaned forward and grabbed her wrist, so tightly that she squeaked with pain. 'Don't go soft on me now, Jess. Remember what we agreed.'

Jessica broke free and pushed the chair across the room. Then, slinging her bag onto her shoulder she marched out, not even bothering to say goodbye. And Alex feared he'd lost control.

As soon as Wesley returned to the incident room the phone on his desk began to ring. It was DS Geoff Gaulter from Neston. And he had news.

'Jessica Gaunt's just been in to see me with her dad. She's withdrawn her accusation against Simon Frith. Said it was a joke that had got out of hand. Just thought you'd like to know, seeing as you were taking an interest.' He paused. 'Frith's off the hook on this one. But the trouble is, the damage may have already been done. You can produce evidence of innocence till you're blue in the face but an accusation like that never really goes away.'

'What'll happen to the girl?'

'I'd like to charge her with wasting police time but I don't think I'll get the CPS to buy it. It was her dad who dragged her in so I reckon her parents are going to give her a tough time if that's any consolation.'

Wesley's mind was working overtime. 'Think someone put her up to it?'

'Your guess is as good as mine.' There was another long pause. 'You know Frith tried to kill himself?'

'Yeah. Bad business.'

'And that little madam'll probably get away with it.' There was bitterness in Gaulter's voice.

'Heard any more about my friend Neil's car?'

There was a moment of silence while Gaulter retrieved the case from the back of his memory. 'Afraid not. He told us he left it parked on the street in Exeter so it was probably kids messing about.'

Wesley didn't answer. It was all too trite, the fictitious kids who went around reaching under cars and cutting strangers' brake pipes in the hope of causing a serious accident they probably wouldn't be around to witness. He couldn't believe it.

And things didn't start to become clearer until the call came to say that Evan Mumford was dead.

Pam left work early, sneaking out before the headmistress could collar her. Sometimes she felt like a naughty child herself, always guilty at abandoning her post even though she was taking home several hours' worth of marking. But her instincts told her that Michael needed her.

Amelia was waiting for her in her classroom as usual, reading in the library corner. She jumped up when she saw her mother and grabbed hold of her hand but Michael was nowhere to be seen. He'd said he was walking back with his mates. The mates she couldn't quite bring herself to approve of. Hopefully, having asserted his independence, he'd be waiting for her back at the house and she chatted to Amelia as she drove home, trying not to show her nagging anxiety.

When she reached the house she saw a light in the front room and she hoped Neil was in there entertaining Michael, maybe even helping with his homework. But when she opened the front door she found Neil alone, reading through what looked like some old documents. There was a layer of dirt on the coffee table but she had more important things on her mind than housekeeping.

'Is Michael back?'

'Not yet.' Neil looked up, suddenly picking up on her concern. 'Should he be?'

'He insisted on walking back. I told him to come straight home. I said you'd be here.'

'He'll have gone to a mate's or something. He'll be fine.'

Pam didn't answer. She went into the kitchen and busied herself with trivia, and half an hour later when the doorbell rang, she ran to the front door.

When she opened it she saw Michael standing there, head bowed. And behind him was a well-built police constable in a high-vis jacket. She could see a patrol car parked across the drive.

She reached out to Michael but his eyes didn't meet hers.

'Mrs Peterson?'

'Yes. What is it? What's happened?'

'I take it this is your son?'

She nodded, wondering why Michael had made no attempt to move.

'He was with a group of lads who were nicking sweets from a shop in George Road.'

Pam felt numb, strangely detached from the situation as if it was happening to somebody else.

The policeman was speaking again. 'The shopkeeper is insisting on taking it further with the other boys but your lad was just hanging round by the door waiting for them so it's unlikely charges will be brought.' The policeman's eyes met hers and she could see a trace of sympathy there. 'I'm surprised he didn't leg it.'

It seemed he had the measure of the situation. The impressionable kid taken along for the ride, paralysed by fear when things went pear-shaped. She reached out again and this time Michael stepped forward, allowing her to put a protective arm around his shoulders. 'I'm sorry for any trouble he's caused.' It was the only thing she could think of to say. 'We'll have a word ... make sure it doesn't happen again.'

The constable's face suddenly lit up with recognition, and something else. Calculation maybe. 'Peterson. You're not Inspector Peterson's missus?'

Pam resisted the temptation to lie so that the incident wouldn't be the subject of police station gossip. But she knew lies would only make the situation worse.

'Hopefully this will have taught him a lesson,' she heard herself saying in a surprisingly steady voice. She looked down at Michael but he was still refusing to meet her eyes. 'I'll let my husband know.'

The constable left, a slight grin on his lips, no doubt keen to get back and spread the news to his colleagues. An inspector's son in hot water.

Michael shuffled into the house and discarded his coat on the hall floor. And when he turned to face her she saw he was crying.

Pauline Parry sat on the back seat of the bus in a trance, staring out over the fields and the wide expanse of sea as the vehicle trundled along at its unhurried pace, stopping every now and then to pick up passengers in the outlying villages.

It was a long time since she'd set foot in West Fretham, the village which held such horrific memories. The village where those women – those witches – had murdered her precious daughter. She alighted at the little bus stop in the village centre, a tiny roofed structure like a shrunken cottage open to the elements on the side nearest the road, its interior decorated with posters announcing local events from yoga classes to playgroup cake sales.

For a while she stood at the side of the road, getting her bearings. She'd once lived a hundred yards down the hill, in the small enclave of pebbledashed council houses at the edge of the village; a post-war afterthought. She began to walk in that direction. Joanne might have come home and if she went back to her old house she might find her. The light was fading now, turning everything to grey, and some of the houses she passed had lights in their windows, giving her a glimpse of the scene within. Cosy rooms; happy families. Many years ago she'd lived like that. Until Joanne's father had left and her world had been ripped apart.

Eventually she found the house. It had new plastic windows with garish white frames and a white plastic front door but she still recognised it. The front room curtains were open and the light was on and she could see unfamiliar wallpaper on the fireplace wall – huge blue flowers. And there was a car in the drive. A small black VW. She stood there staring, unsure what to do. Somehow she'd imagined everything would be the same as the day she'd left.

She stumbled away, hot tears burning her eyes. Her mind, so long confused and numbed with chemicals, seemed strangely clear now. Coming back had been a mistake. But she had to know whether her sighting of Joanne was a hallucination as they'd said . . . or if, by some miracle she hardly dared to believe in, she had survived the witches' slaughterhouse. In her heart she knew the answer. But if she didn't have hope, she knew how it would end. The river had rejected her once. Next time would be different.

She walked away from the house, back to the centre of the village, and stopped at the butcher's. Only it wasn't the butcher's any more. Models of people and animals had replaced the sausages and cuts of meat in the shop window but the lights weren't on so she couldn't see clearly. Her Joanne had been good at making things. Her teachers had always said she was good with her hands.

She staggered along the road towards the bus stop. Unlike in Tradmouth, there was no pavement here and cars whizzed by, dangerously close, sending cold splashes up her bare legs from the puddles left by last night's rain.

'Pauline.'

The sound of her name made her turn round, half fearful, half hopeful. But Joanne would have called her mum, not Pauline.

'I thought it was you.' An elderly woman hobbled towards her and took hold of her arm gently. 'I heard you'd moved to Tradmouth but I didn't know your address or I would have kept in touch. Have you got time for a cup of tea? I'm in the same place ... just down the road. My nephew came to see me the other day. You know, Eric ... he's on the telly. He's been doing that show at Jessop's Farm. He reached the final two.'

Even in the circumstances Vera Bourne couldn't resist the chance to boast to anyone who cared to listen about her famous nephew. But Pauline couldn't give a damn about Eric Bourne ... or Rupert whatever he was calling himself these days. He couldn't hold a candle to her Arnold. He'd been an entertainer too. And a better one than Eric Bourne. He just hadn't had the lucky breaks.

She stared at Vera, thinking that she had aged almost beyond recognition in the past eighteen years. Her pale grey hair was thin, giving glimpses of the scalp beneath, and she walked slowly and painfully with a metal crutch.

'I'm looking for Joanne,' she said.

Vera's expression changed from sympathy to shock then back to sympathy. 'I know, love. It's terrible when you haven't got a body to bury, isn't it? People need closure.' She gave Pauline's arm a gentle squeeze as if to emphasise her understanding. 'Why don't you come back and have that cup of tea?'

'I heard that woman's come back.'

Vera dropped her hand to her side. 'She was back but now she's gone again. Killed two more people, she has; some reporter and that singer your Joanne was at school with.' She looked around the deserted lane, suddenly nervous. 'She's still out there somewhere so no one's safe. I only came out 'cause I needed a pint of milk from Spar.' She nodded at the canvas bag hooked over her elbow, weighed down by a single carton. 'You really shouldn't be out here on your own, you know. Come on home with me.'

Pauline walked slightly behind Vera, shuffling up the hill towards the small crescent of bungalows.

'They should have hanged that Benley woman for what she did,' Vera Bourne said when they reached her front door. 'And I'd have tied the noose myself.'

Chapter 16

Written by Alison Hadness, September 25th 1643

William being abed there is no restraint upon Elizabeth now and I despaired when she told me that she had followed me to the barn and spied upon me. Then she put her face close to mine and whispered that she had seen me conjure demons and have carnal knowledge of the Devil. Then she pointed at me and uttered one word which struck dread into my heart. Witch.

William is close to death, hardly able to open his eyes and look upon those around him. Elizabeth weeps at his bedside. Dorcas too is most grievously sick, as are many of our neighbours, screaming that demons torment them and burn their flesh, their bodies shuddering and shaking in agony. It is said that there is witchcraft abroad and I fear Elizabeth's tales of my wickedness will be given credence. Her spite against me knows no bounds and some folk hang upon her words as she whispers her venom into any ear willing to hear.

Today I found within my linen chest another most hideous image of a woman stabbed with nails. It is no work of mine and I fear it represents Dorcas. I have hidden it with the other within rough wooden boxes I found in the outhouse for I cannot destroy them for fear of magic.

Elizabeth grows thinner by the day and will take no nourishment. Her eyes are wild with loathing. I fear her.

Evan Mumford had been on his way to Dukesbridge for a meeting with his accountant. Business had been flagging. The situation was getting serious and they needed to talk.

Evan had anticipated trouble as he set off in his Mini. And trouble had followed him onto the lonely single-track lane that snaked down from the crossroads at Hugford to Whitepool Sands. The Mini had ended up mangled beneath the wheels of a tractor moving slowly in the other direction. Evan Mumford, according to the emergency services attending the scene, had probably been aware of very little after the first terrible realisation that his life was about to be brought to an abrupt close. The farmer driving the tractor was treated for shock. Mumford was pronounced dead at the scene.

It was Uniform's job to inform the next of kin but when Gerry heard about the accident, he decided to visit Harriet Mumford himself. Wesley wasn't sure what had brought on this decision. Perhaps it was the fact that Evan's crash mirrored Neil's. Or maybe it was the Mumfords' connection with the West Fretham case.

Pam had just called to tell him about Michael's latest exploit. When she'd asked what time he'd be home he could hear the anxiety in her voice. He promised to get back as soon as possible and when the call was over he sat there for a while, stunned by the news. When Gerry asked him what was wrong he decided to share his troubles and he was surprised by the DCI's casual reaction. It was all part of growing up, he claimed. He himself had nicked sweets from Woolworths in Liverpool with his mates when he was a nipper. Only he'd never got caught. Fine example Uncle Gerry was, he added with a chuckle. But he'd ended up a DCI so there was still hope. Wesley didn't answer. Things had changed since Gerry's misspent youth and childish folly could dog you for the rest of your life.

But Michael's misdemeanour wasn't all that was bothering Wesley. He couldn't get Selina's revelation about Lilith's lover out of his mind. He'd just learned that the photographer, Dan Sericold, had decided not to press charges against Raybourn after all. No real harm had been done and Sericold claimed he couldn't be bothered with the fuss and the paperwork. But even though Raybourn was off that particular hook, Wesley still wanted to speak to him again and ask the question that had been niggling in his mind.

Raybourn was still staying at the Marina Hotel, waiting for the filming to resume in a couple of days. The disgraced MP, the last to be voted off, was returning to take Zac James's place. The producer had promised a tasteful tribute to Zac in the closing credits, although Wesley suspected that hard cash rather than good taste was driving the project forward.

When he told Gerry where he was going, the DCI was keen to be in on the action. They could see Raybourn in Tradmouth then pay Mumford's widow a visit.

Wesley's route took him past the entrance to the lane where Evan Mumford had met his death; a sharp corner flanked by a pair of bright pink thatched cottages overlooking the tree-fringed beach on the other side of the coast road. Police tape sealed off the corner and he could visualise the investigation team going about their business further up the lane, out of sight of passers-by.

He had called ahead and Raybourn was waiting for them in the hotel lounge, a large whisky on the table in front of him. He was looking tired and Wesley noticed a small stain on his pale blue cashmere sweater. He rose to shake hands as soon as he saw them, as if he was anxious to keep on the right side of the law.

'I believe the charges against you have been dropped,' Wesley began.

'Yes, I'm rather relieved about that. That man pushed and pushed till I lost my temper. When you're in the public eye people think you're fair game ... that you don't have any feelings.' Raybourn looked from Wesley to Gerry as if he was anxious that they should understand.

'But the story about the rent boy was true ... and the racist remarks?' Gerry asked.

There was a look of concentration on the man's face, as though he was searching for the least damaging answer. 'No to the second but yes to the first.' He paused and lowered his eyes. 'We all do stupid things we regret. Use foolish ways to fill the emptiness.'

Wesley knew he was playing for sympathy but he was finding it hard to conjure any. He still hadn't made up his mind about the man. Perhaps he never would. He saw Gerry was watching him, waiting for him to continue.

'Have you ever come across anyone called Carl Cramer? Might be a fellow comedian. Or maybe a magician.'

When Raybourn looked up Wesley saw a spark of recognition in his eyes and he knew his visit wasn't in vain.

'Carl Cramer. Now there's a blast from the past.' He spoke with a false bonhomie that Wesley had heard before.

'We've heard he was involved with Lilith Benley.'

Raybourn fell silent for a while. Then he cleared his throat. 'Who told you that?'

'Never mind who told us,' Gerry growled. 'What do you know about him?'

Raybourn took a sip of whisky, smacking his lips as though he was trying to delay the moment of revelation. When he finally spoke, he focused his eyes on the glass.

'OK. Carl and I were on the same bill at the Pavilion Gardens in the late 1980s. I was top of the bill back then but Carl hadn't made the breakthrough. Not that his act wasn't good, he just hadn't had the lucky breaks. He was married with a kid but he was always one for the ladies and one night we went for a drink after the show and met this striking bird. Anyway, to cut a long story short, she was down here from London, taking her old mum to the seaside for a break. Her and Carl hit it off and he ended up leaving his missus and moving to London to be with this Lilith. I remember her name because it was unusual. After that I never heard of him again.'

'But you heard of Lilith,' said Wesley.

'When she was charged with killing those two girls I recognised her picture in the papers and I couldn't believe it. And I couldn't believe she'd been living in West Fretham 'cause that's where Carl came from. After it happened my aunty said Lilith and her mum had been living alone in that cottage so I don't know what had become of Carl. I thought he might have gone back to his missus and Lilith had followed him there but Aunty Vera said there was no sign of him. She knew his wife, you see.'

Wesley and Gerry looked at each other.

'Have you any idea where Lilith is now?' Gerry asked.

Raybourn shook his head. 'Of course not. Why should I?'

'Did you see her while you were at Jessop's Farm?'

Raybourn shook his head. Then he looked up and Wesley sensed that some sort of confession was coming. 'OK, I admit I went up to her cottage once … after that woman was murdered. I wanted to ask her what was going on … and what had become of Carl. But she didn't answer the door.'

'You didn't break in?'

'No way.'

Wesley sat forward. 'Do you know where we can find Carl Cramer's wife?'

'No idea. But I know what his real name is if that's any help. It's Trelisip. Arnold Trelisip.' There was a pause. 'Lilith Benley murdered his daughter.'

They were in the car heading out of Tradmouth when Gerry took the call. Rachel and Trish had gone straight to Pauline Parry's maisonette as requested but the woman wasn't answering her door. Wesley couldn't help feeling uneasy: Lilith Benley was still at large and if she found Pauline, unbalanced and vulnerable … He said as much to Gerry but he didn't reply.

Wesley was turning over all the possibilities in his mind as he took the main road out of town, putting the car into third gear to climb the hill. The news that Lilith Benley had killed her lover's daughter had come as a shock. And the more he thought about it, the more this new discovery seemed to confirm her guilt. And yet he felt there was more to learn. More shadows to be dragged into the light.

In the meantime they had a visit to make and as soon as they reached Mercy Hall he felt apprehensive, unsure what he was going to say to Harriet Mumford who was, after all, a recently bereaved widow.

When they reached their destination it was Gerry who hurried to the front door and rang the doorbell. Wesley stood behind him and looked round. He could see Harriet's car parked beside the builder's pick-up. There was no sign of Dave's vehicle; he was probably back at Princes Bower, digging up relics of the Civil War.

There was no reply and when Gerry rang again, impatient, Wesley noticed that the door was slightly ajar, as if someone had closed it but the lock hadn't caught. He put out his hand and gave it a push. It swung open smoothly.

He was expecting to find a weeping woman being comforted by friends or relatives, sitting on the edge of a sofa, twisting a damp handkerchief in shaking fingers. He had encountered the scene so often in the course of his career. But instead he saw Harriet Mumford standing at the top of the oak staircase, clutching a sheet around her naked body. Her blonde hair hung around her shoulders and from a distance she looked more like a model on a photo shoot than a woman who'd just received news of her husband's death.

'How the hell did you get in?'

'Your front door was open, love,' said Gerry. 'Sorry to hear about your husband.'

'Thanks. Look, I was just . . . having a shower. Can this keep for another time?'

'Sure,' said Wesley, preparing to leave. 'Sorry to have bothered you.'

But Gerry stood his ground, staring up at the woman. Wesley nudged his arm but he didn't move.

'Is someone up there with you, love?'

'No.' The word was defensive.

'I heard a voice.'

Wesley watched Gerry stride forward, annoyed with himself that he hadn't been paying attention. But the problem of Michael and his recent discovery about Lilith Benley hovered there at the back of his mind, distracting him.

As Gerry put a foot on the bottom stair Harriet began to retreat, the sheet still clutched to her body. 'We need to have a word, Mrs Mumford,' he shouted. 'It won't take long then you can get back to whatever it is you were doing.' His words were full of innuendo.

Harriet was heading for the bedroom at the end of the landing, moving fast, almost tripping over the trailing sheet. Wesley had followed Gerry up the stairs and he arrived on the landing just in time to see a bedroom door open to reveal a chubby man in washed-out boxer shorts. The man stood quite still for a few seconds, his mouth hanging open in astonishment. Then he swore loudly and slammed the door shut, leaving Harriet stranded on the landing, grasping the sheet so tightly around her that her knuckles matched the fabric.

'Seeking comfort in our grief, are we, Mrs Mumford?' said Gerry. 'That's nice.'

Wesley stood there, lost for words. He wasn't particularly surprised by the Lady Chatterley scenario, but her choice of lover was rather unexpected. It was the unappealing builder, Lee, who'd been invited to take the dead husband's place in Harriet's bed – which showed that there was no accounting for the vagaries of the human desire.

All of a sudden Lee burst out onto the landing again, this time fully dressed. Eyes wild, he stared at them for a moment before dodging forward like an advancing rugby player, barging past Gerry and almost knocking him to the floor. Without thinking, Wesley hurtled downstairs after him and grabbed at his grey hooded sweatshirt. He felt the cloth stretching in his fingers, pulling him off balance. And as he stumbled and fell the man in front of him landed on the floor with a thud. With nothing hurt but his pride, Wesley struggled to his feet, looming over the man who was lying there, staring up at him in terror.

'It wasn't my idea,' Lee said in a self-righteous whine. 'And I never meant that Neil to get hurt. It was all a mistake.'

And it was the builder rather than the widow who began to cry.

Fully dressed now, Harriet sprang down the stairs past them, taking them by surprise. And before Wesley could stop her she'd dashed out to her car and started the engine.

One of the ewes up in the top field had shown signs of lameness that morning and Joe Jessop couldn't relax until he'd checked her out. If she was no better he'd call the vet. It would be more expense but the livestock came first. Always had.

Once he'd trudged up to the field, he ordered Fin to separate the ewe from the rest of the flock and made a quick examination of her legs, before letting her run back to her companions. Joe hadn't been able to see anything wrong but he would keep an eye on her, just in case. Creatures in distress needed to be cared for.

He walked to the locked gate set into the hedge and stood there, gazing over the undulating landscape, idly stroking Fin's head. The light had almost gone now but he could make out the shape of Devil's Tree Cottage in the distance surrounded by skeletal trees. There was a light in the cottage window. Which meant Lilith Benley was home. Either that or there was an intruder.

He turned and began to walk down the hill back towards his farmhouse with Fin trotting by his side, awaiting further instructions.

It had taken Lilith a while to summon the courage to sneak back to Devil's Tree Cottage after that night of fear, the night the intruder had invaded her home. But she had returned and now she sat staring at her mother's rocking chair. When she closed her eyes she could see the old woman rocking gently to and fro, her face covered by a handkerchief to keep out the light. She'd looked like a corpse with her face covered like that. Lilith had loathed the sight of that white square of linen draped over the wrinkled face like a shroud.

All those years ago Lilith had tried to control her fate through spells and ancient wisdom. At that dark time before her arrest her Book of Shadows had been filled with pleas to the Mother Goddess to put everything right. But now that book had been violated and torn. Once she'd believed that her own actions harmed none. But that hadn't been true. There were people she'd injured. Lives she'd destroyed.

She should have realised that it had been naïve to return to West Fretham and expect the past to be forgotten.

When she'd heard the intruder enter Devil's Tree Cottage she'd squeezed herself into the pantry where she'd hidden those knives that had arrived in the post unbidden – the parcel she'd taken for some sick joke. As soon as she was sure the visitor had gone she'd returned to the parlour and there she'd found the doll on the floor. The cursed thing made in her image. And when she'd found her Book of Shadows had been returned defiled, she'd understood the message. That's why she'd fled. Fear had made her run, unaware of anything but the need to get away.

There was only one person in that village who'd ever shown her kindness; and that was another lonely soul desperate for company. Joe Jessop had found her in the lane and he'd taken her back to his cottage and given her tea, hardly talking as if he was unused to words. He'd allowed her to stay in a run-down cottage on the far side of his land where his family had once housed their farm workers. He had taken pity on her and kept her from prying eyes, bringing her provisions and making monosyllabic conversation. But most importantly of all, he'd muttered that he hadn't believed in her guilt all those years ago. She'd been grateful for his clumsy kindness and the fact that he hadn't betrayed her to the police. She knew she didn't deserve his generosity.

She hadn't told him she was going back to Devil's Tree Cottage. If she had, she knew he'd have tried to dissuade her. Now, as she sat there, she heard a sound from the back room, the shuffling of furtive footsteps, and she waited, hoping Joe had guessed her plans and followed her.

She held her breath and listened, as the slow realisation dawned that those furtive footsteps didn't belong to Joe. She switched off the old lamp on the table next to the chair and waited, paralysed by fear.

The hinges creaked a loud warning as the door swung open. It was too late to escape this time. She was trapped. In the moonlight she saw a cloaked figure standing in the shadows like a witch in a fairy tale. It was the cloak that had been stolen from her, the one she'd chosen all those years ago, black and glossy like crow's wings. The hood was pulled down to hide the wearer's face but Lilith knew who it was and suddenly everything fitted together. The truth and the lies. The living and the dead.

Summoning all her courage, she stood up. 'What do you want?'

There was no answer. Then the hood was pushed back and Lilith saw the instrument of execution.

'I don't think Lee's one of nature's murderers,' said Gerry. 'I think he was grateful to get everything off his chest.'

'But he did cut Evan Mumford's brake pipes. According to him, Harriet asked him to cut the pipes on the yellow Mini. Only the first time he got the wrong yellow Mini. Evan's was a flash brand-new Mini Cooper and Neil's had been around since the Neolithic period so I don't see how he could have made the mistake.'

'He wasn't at the front of the queue when the brains were being handed out, Wes. If what he's alleging is true, Harriet Mumford should have picked someone brighter to do her dirty work. But then anyone brighter wouldn't have gone along with it. Or if they had they would have expected a lot more than the occasional bout of rumpy pumpy.' Gerry sighed. 'She'll deny everything of course. All patrols are on the lookout for her car but what's the betting that when we pick her up she'll plead ignorance and say Lee did it out of jealousy. She could lead that poor bloke by the prick, no questions about that. But it's a matter of proving it.'

'Easier said than done,' Wesley said. He knew that when

it came down to it, it would be Lee's word against Harriet Mumford's unless they could get her to confess, which was unlikely. But he had other things on his mind.

He'd just rung home. Pam had promised Michael a good telling off from his father. And Wesley found the role of the stern disciplinarian an uncomfortable one. Neil, in the meantime, reckoned the lad was contrite and he'd promised to take him to a community dig planned for the spring. An interest would do him good, he said. But Wesley wasn't so sure. Perhaps the dig would seem like a reward for bad behaviour. The matter would need some thought.

Gerry told him to get off home and see his son. They'd make an early start in the morning.

Wesley put his coat on, unable to get the West Fretham case out of his mind. Pauline Parry still hadn't turned up at her address and they really needed to speak to her about Raybourn's statement. They needed to ask her about her estranged husband and his connection with Lilith Benley. Although he wasn't hopeful that they'd get much sense out of her.

There was no sign of Lilith either and he couldn't help thinking the worst. In his mind's eye he saw her dead in one of the copses that littered the landscape, hanging from a tree or, more likely, snuggled in the undergrowth after taking some pills and lying down to die in peace. Gerry was still convinced that she'd killed Boo Flecker and Zac James. But he had nagging doubts. And in spite of the fact that she was a convicted murderer, he felt an unexpected twinge of pity whenever he thought of her.

The phone on his desk rang and when he heard Rachel's voice he sat down again, hoping she had news of some new development. Then he remembered Pam and experienced a pang of guilt that he suddenly felt so keen to delay going home.

'I've had a call from Vera Bourne,' Rachel said. 'She found Pauline Parry wandering round West Fretham saying she was looking for Joanne. Vera took her home for a cup of tea.' She sighed. 'I offered to go over and give Pauline a lift back home to Tradmouth but she did a runner while Vera was making the call. She's vulnerable so I've asked all patrols to be on the lookout.'

'Nothing else you could do, Rach. Keep me posted, won't you?'

As soon as he'd replaced the receiver the phone rang again. It took him a few moments to recognise Geoff Gaulter's voice.

'I've just had an interesting visit from Jessica Gaunt's father,' Gaulter began. 'I thought you might like to know because I believe the lad's name's cropped up in your murder case. Alexander Gulliver.'

'What about him?'

'Jessica Gaunt visited Alex Gulliver and when she arrived home in tears her parents assumed there'd been a falling out ... the usual teenage stuff. Then Jessica told us she wanted to drop the charges – that it had been a joke that got out of hand.'

'I know. Has something else happened?'

'Yes. She's just told her mum that it was Alex who put her up to accusing Frith. It seems she's feeling really bad about his suicide attempt.'

'Have you heard how Frith is?'

'He'll live,' said Gaulter. 'Jessica's father's worried that we'll bring charges.'

'Will you?'

325

'I want to get the whole story before I make any decisions. I'm going to have a word with this Alex Gulliver. It could be some sort of vendetta against Frith him and Jessica cooked up between them.'

'But Alex doesn't know Frith, does he? Frith teaches at the FE college, not at Alex's school.'

'That's what's puzzling me. Anyway, I'll make more enquiries and keep you posted.'

Wesley thanked him and put the phone down.

Neil's body was mending rapidly and although Pam and Wesley assured him they were in no rush to have the house to themselves again, he felt it would soon be time to move on. He'd resumed work at the dig in a purely supervisory capacity and he was making plans to buy himself a second-hand Mini, younger and sturdier than the last one. He'd promised Pam he'd get it properly serviced and check the brakes regularly but he knew he'd probably lapse into his old ways once the memory of his trauma had faded.

Wesley had rung to tell him that Harriet Mumford had been discovered in bed with Lee the builder and that the police wanted to interview her regarding conspiracy to murder. Neil's response was to say he found it hard to believe because Harriet had seemed so ... He'd searched for a suitable word but all he could come up with was 'nice'.

But all this made no difference to Neil's desire to find out the truth about Alison Hadness. Ever since he'd seen the carving of the hanged woman in the garden, the history of Mercy Hall had haunted him. True to his word, Dave had brought him copies of the rest of the journal, found folded beneath the wax dolls in the little coffins that were now at the conservation lab in Exeter, and as he'd read Alison's inmost thought and secrets he was beginning to feel he knew her.

Dave had also been researching the story of the Royalist army that had besieged the town, told in various journals, including that of Thomas Whitcombe. And then there was the story of the people trapped in Tradmouth with Prince Maurice's troops camped outside, taking supplies of food from the fertile countryside round about and leaving the townsfolk to their fate.

Neil occupied his convalescent hours reading Alison's account of the siege, written in a simple code that her husband might find hard to decipher if he found it. Alison's journal told of a household fraught with hatred, sickness, betrayal and witchcraft. Mercy Hall had a disturbing past to match its tragic present.

He'd also studied an account of Alison's trial and the statements of the neighbours who'd blamed her for the sickness that plagued the town during the siege, those same neighbours who'd seen her with a good-looking young man they'd taken for the devil himself.

As he re-read the accounts of the events of 1643 something bothered him. He'd come across something similar before. He switched on his laptop. There was something he wanted to check.

Even though Joe had seen the light in Devil's Tree Cottage, he hadn't liked to intrude. Sometimes people wanted to be left alone. However, when Lilith hadn't returned to the farm cottage by eight he began to feel uneasy. Lilith needed shelter and protection and he wondered what had made her go out again into a world that had treated her so cruelly.

He ate his evening meal of sausage and beans in

brooding silence as Fin gazed up at him adoringly. 'Where is she, lad?' he muttered to the dog as he stroked his head. 'I thought she'd be back by now.'

As soon as he'd finished eating, Joe pulled on his boots and found a torch. He would walk over to Devil's Tree Cottage to make sure she'd come to no harm. Then he'd bring her back. It was the least he could do.

With Fin by his side he left the farmhouse and headed up the fields. Stars dotted the clear sky and the full moon cast a silvery glow over the landscape. When he reached the gate that separated his land from Lilith's he hesitated for a moment before climbing over.

The land sloped away gently beyond the gate, rising again just behind where the cottage stood. Although he'd lived next door since boyhood, he'd never ventured onto Devil's Tree Cottage land before. He had never been on visiting terms with either the Benleys or their predecessors and when the house had lain empty all those years during Lilith's incarceration, some almost superstitious misgiving meant that he hadn't cared to trespass.

He could see Devil's Tree Cottage but there was no light in the window now. If Lilith had gone back, she wasn't there any more. But he had to make sure so he walked down the hill passing a copse of trees to his right, the half-naked branches dotted with crows' nests outlined against the moonlit sky like musical notes on a stave.

Suddenly he was aware of Fin bounding off towards the trees. Joe knew there must be something in there to attract him. Even the most obedient dog could have his head turned by the scent of something irresistible. He called the dog's name. Once. Twice. And an answering bark told him that Fin had found something in the trees.

A feeling of dread clutched at his stomach and in his mind's eye he saw Lilith lying dead in the undergrowth. But as he steeled himself to enter the copse the dog burst out of the trees, bounding towards him with something in his mouth. Tail wagging, proud of the thing he placed at his master's feet.

Joe squatted down to view the trophy, taking his torch from his pocket and shining it at the ground. The bone lying there might have belonged to an animal. But on the other hand, it was about the right size to be human.

Inside the cottage Lilith sat perfectly still in the rocking chair, her feet planted on the floor, preparing for escape.

'What do you want?' she said softly, unwilling to raise her voice in case it goaded her tormentor into further cruelty.

'It's not fair that you only got eighteen miserable years for what you did.'

'I was innocent.'

'What about the reporter and that singer?'

'I never even met them.'

'But you're responsible for their deaths.'

Lilith shifted in her seat, her short nails digging into the worn fabric of the chair arm. She wished she could see her tormentor's face and she was tempted to reach for the lamp and switch it on. But she knew the blade was there, half hidden by the cloak.

'I never killed anyone,' she said, summoning what little courage she had left. 'Neither did my mother.'

'She confessed.'

'Her mind was so twisted by stories of witchcraft that she'd have admitted to any far-fetched tale the police put into her head. I always told the truth.

The stranger raised a hand to push the hood back and as it fell Lilith caught her breath. That face had been etched on her memory since that night. That pretty cat face twisted in hatred as the lips had formed the words. Witch, witch, witch.

She looked different now. Older. The features coarsened with the years. The hair was a different style and colour but those eyes, glinting with hatred, hadn't changed. Suddenly Lilith began to see how the conjuring trick had been done. And she knew that people had died to maintain this particular illusion.

'What do you want?' Lilith asked softly.

'It's what *you* want. You're can't stand living with the guilt any more so you've decided to kill yourself.' The determination in her voice chilled Lilith's blood.

'If I'm going to die I might as well know what really happened. I've spent eighteen years wondering about it.' If she played for time there might be some way out.

There was a long silence, as though the visitor was deciding where to begin. 'Our lives fell apart when you took my dad away. Mum had a breakdown and never got over it. You destroyed us. Then you destroyed him.'

'I never meant to hurt anyone. Your father and I were in love.'

'Shut up.' The words were barked like an order. 'Why did you have to come and live here? You wanted to gloat, didn't you?'

Lilith felt a sudden impulse to justify her actions. 'Honestly I didn't think you'd still be here. I needed to get away from London after your father died and when I saw this place was for sale I thought . . . It was in Arnold's village so it seemed it was . . . meant. Mother started with dementia and I thought that if I could run a smallholding . . . if I didn't have to go out to work, then I could look after her. And I'd heard you'd moved away so . . . '

'Well you heard wrong. When you came to live here it drove my mum over the edge.'

'I'm sorry.'

'I wasn't going to have the smug, gloating bitch who ruined our lives and killed my dad living here in my village.'

'I didn't kill . . . '

'Liar. I was going to kill you then I had a better idea. If you were put away for murder then everybody would know what you were. I told Gabby we were going to torment a couple of old witches and . . . '

'What happened to her? Is she still alive?'

There was a long silence. 'Remember you saw us running away that night?'

Lilith nodded.

'I'd brought a knife with me and as soon as we reached the woods I stuck it in her. I didn't know it'd take her so long to die.' She smirked, as though she found the memory exciting.

'Why did you kill her? I don't understand.'

'Because I needed evidence to put you away. And she was a snide little bitch who'd just pinched my boyfriend so she deserved all she got.'

There was petulance in her voice, the petulance of the disturbed adolescent she'd once been, and Lilith felt a wave of cold panic. Her tormentor was starting to lose control.

'What did you do with her body?' Keep her talking. Play for time.

'I waited till I knew John would be home then I ran to the village and called him from the phone box. It was dark so nobody saw me.'

'John?'

'The boyfriend she took from me. Ironic, isn't it? I told him she'd fallen on the knife by accident and I needed him to help me bury her. It was only a shallow grave but it didn't matter because nobody ever went there.'

'Why didn't John tell anyone?'

'Because I threatened to tell the police he killed her unless he did what I said and I made sure her blood got on his sweatshirt. He freaked out but he went along with it. He knew I could be very convincing, you see. I've been convincing everyone I was dead for eighteen years.'

'Didn't the police search the woods?'

'They found everything they needed to put you away here in this cottage so they never bothered searching further afield. I created an illusion. Shadows and mirrors. Misdirection, they call it,' she said, pleased with her own brilliance.

'How did you get away?'

Joanne – Arnold's daughter back from the grave – leaned against the table and folded her arms. Lilith knew how powerful the desire to explain can be; the need to justify your basest actions. She saw the knife clutched tightly in her hand, shining and lethal.

'I lay low in a disused barn on Jessop's land and I got John to bring me what I needed.' She paused. 'He became famous, you know. He changed his name to Zac James and moved his whole family away from here but I bet he was always terrified that his secret would come out one day. Maybe that's why he went on that farm show – he needed to convince himself he'd got away with it. Facing your demons they call it. He was in and out of rehab so he knew all about demons. He saw me one day.' She laughed. 'He

332

must have been shitting himself. I'd photographed him burying Gabby, you see. I've still got the pictures but they're well hidden where nobody'll ever find them. I kept them as my insurance policy, just to make sure he didn't have a fit of conscience. But in the end I knew he couldn't be trusted.'

'So you killed him?'

'I didn't have a chance to get to him while he was on the farm show but one day I saw him drive past in that blue Porsche of his and park at the Ploughman's Rest. After that it was easy.'

Her words were cold. Unemotional. As though killing meant nothing to her. Her friend, Gabby, and her former boyfriend, John, had been disposable – she'd used them for her own twisted purpose then discarded them. Hatred had blinded her to any human compassion. And now that hatred was focused on Lilith.

'So you planned the whole thing to get me arrested?'

'Got it in one. Before John arrived to help me bury Gabby I came back here and smeared your pigsty with her blood and I cut myself so that if they did tests they'd find mine there as well. I'd read about some gangsters feeding bodies to pigs and I thought it was a nice touch. I hid Gabby's bloodstained clothes and some with my blood on in your outhouse along with a few other things I'd collected. Black magic things so the police would know what they were dealing with. Then I lay low and waited and a week later I told John to call the cops from a phone box at Morbay station. John gave me some cash and I went to London. I'd met this bloke in Millicombe – rich guy from London who was down here on holiday. He let me stay with him for a while. I'd already told him I was nineteen and given him a false name – I'd chosen it off one of the gravestones in West Fretham churchyard. It wasn't hard to change my identity.'

She was talking quickly now, delighting in her own cleverness. 'I lied about my age and worked in a pub. Then I met another bloke who was married and he set me up in a nice little flat. I changed my appearance, shed my pathetic past and ended up working in PR while you rotted in jail.'

'But you came back to the village. Why was that?'

'I managed to brazen it out for a while. My mum wasn't here any more and I was careful to keep myself to myself. It all worked fine till you came back then everything started to go wrong.' The words sounded peevish. 'First John came back here for that stupid programme. Then that bitch of a journalist began watching the house and I knew she was onto me.'

'So you killed two people ... '

The woman who had once been Joanne Trelisip stepped forward, looming over her. 'No, like I said before, you killed them. If it wasn't for you, none of this would have happened. You're a jinx. You're cursed.'

'You sent me those athames, didn't you? You wanted to make sure I'd get the blame again.'

'It's what you deserve.'

Lilith felt a stinging blow across her face. Then a sharp pain as the knife pierced her flesh.

Joe stood by the gate watching with Fin at his side, his eyes fixed on the distant cottage. The dog had found more bones but now seemed to be satisfied with his hoard. Joe had piled them up next to the hedge. Rib bones, thigh bones, a pelvis. He would alert the police in the morning. Or would he? If they were on Lilith's land, they were probably connected with her in some way. Maybe he'd think about it.

Suddenly he saw something flit out of the cottage and disappear down the drive like a wraith. It didn't look like Lilith. It was smaller and lighter and moved like a creature of the night, a thing of shadows.

Fin began to bark as if he sensed something was wrong. Then without warning he left Joe's side and hared down the slope towards Devil's Tree Cottage, stopping every so often to make sure his master was following. Long experience had taught Joe to heed his dog's instincts so he headed after him.

The cottage was in darkness but when he pushed the front door it swung open. Fin entered first while Joe hesitated on the threshold. Then Joe heard barking, loud and urgent, and followed the noise.

At the entrance to the parlour he almost stumbled over a dark shape lying on the ground. And when he lowered his torch he saw that it was Lilith.

Chapter 17

Journal of Alison Hadness, September 28th 1643

Elizabeth hath denounced me and such is the fear in the town that men came to seize me and drag me before the Magistrate. Dorcas was near death when I was taken and her feet have turned black and foul smelling. Many in the town have fallen ill with the same malady and I am blamed. William too is become weak and blind. I pray to God that the truth will be found and yet I am a sinner, an adulteress, so this may be my punishment.

The dolls Elizabeth made were discovered and held up for all to see that I was a curser of innocent Christian souls. My attempts to explain that one of the images was myself and that Elizabeth was responsible for the abomination fell on the stoniest of grounds. It is well known that a witch can never speak the truth.

On the instructions of Elizabeth the Magistrate's men made a thorough search of the house and came upon divers and terrible things in the cellar beneath the chamber where Elizabeth sleeps. A coffin with a wax doll stuck with pins in the form of a man which was terrible to behold.

And on the floor was painted a star which they said was a witch's sign. Elizabeth lied, saying it was my private chamber where I conjure demons. Yet I know now it is she who conjures the devil in her quest for vengeance. I told this to the Magistrate and denied all but I was not believed.

When I was taken to the house of the Magistrate I was stripped and examined by two women of the town. They dealt with me roughly and I could see the hatred and fear in their eyes. I was a witch and I bore the mark of Satan, a teat from which I suckled my master. They were deaf to my pleas and I knew that there would be no mercy.

My neighbours were brought in to denounce me, to say they saw me with the devil and that I cursed them with spells and many have died or writhe in agony of my making. They cannot take me to Exeter to stand trial for the town is besieged so I am thrown into a cellar in the Magistrate's house where I starve.

Wesley watched as the crime scene people went about their business under the floodlights that had been brought to Devil's Tree Cottage for the occasion. He had only been home an hour and a half, just time to have a quick word with Michael and shovel down his dinner, before he'd received the news that Joe Jessop had found Lilith Benley stabbed in her cottage. When Joe was asked whether he knew where Lilith had been since her disappearance, he'd said nothing. Wesley would have another word with him later. The concerned neighbour story didn't wash somehow.

Gerry had been chatting to some CSIs and now he came to join him. 'She's lost a lot of blood,' he said. 'They're taking her to Tradmouth.'

'Think it's a suicide attempt?'

'Jessop thinks he saw someone running away. And there was no weapon near her.'

'Attempted murder then.'

'There are clear signs of a struggle. She put up a fight.'

Wesley's mobile rang. To his surprise when he answered he heard Geoff Gaulter's voice. Like them, he was working late.

'Sorry if I've disturbed anything but I just thought I'd let you know. There's been another development in the Simon Frith case . . . if you can still call it a case now all the charges have been dropped.'

As far as Wesley was concerned the affair of Simon Frith was over. Egged on by her boyfriend, a silly teenage girl had lied to get her tutor in hot water and now she'd confessed. But Gaulter's next words grabbed his attention.

'You know Jessica Gaunt said it was all Alex Gulliver's idea? Well, I've had a word with Master Gulliver and he told me something rather interesting.'

Wesley waited for him to continue, his eyes focused on the patch of drying blood on Lilith Benley's carpet.

'Alex's stepfather – the author – asked Frith to give Alex some tuition for his GCSEs because Jessica's parents recommended him. But when Alex's mum found out she went crazy and told Alex she'd heard Frith had a conviction for abusing a couple of his pupils so there was no way she wanted him teaching Alex. She said Gulliver was stubborn and he'd take no notice if she told him.'

'Even after being told his kid's tutor was a child abuser?'

'It doesn't make sense, does it? Anyway, she suggested that Alex persuade Jessica to accuse Frith of assaulting her so Shane would be forced to back down. Now, we know for certain that Frith has no such conviction – there wasn't a whiff of anything like that before Jessica made her accusation. So it begs the question, what on earth was the Gulliver woman up to?'

Wesley thanked him and stood for a while, thinking. Gerry nudged his arm. 'What is it?'

'I'm going to call Simon Frith. There's something I just need to check.'

Wesley made the call. And when he'd finished he walked to the door and discarded his crime scene suit. Gerry followed, full of curiosity. 'What did Frith say?'

When Wesley told him, both men hurried out of the cottage. They took the car and when they pulled up in front of the Old Rectory a few minutes later, Wesley saw the lights were on.

They were approaching the front door when it suddenly burst open. Shane Gulliver was standing there, framed in the brightly lit doorway, his arms outstretched. As soon as he saw them he roared, a primal, desperate sound, and fell to his knees, sobbing.

Gerry rushed over and squatted down beside him while Wesley dashed past him into the hall.

'I need a drink,' said Gerry.

Wesley knew they should have gone straight to the incident room after the ambulance had taken Gwen away and the statements had been taken. But instead Gerry had headed for the Ploughman's Rest and ordered himself a large scotch. Not his usual tipple. Wesley was driving so he made do with a shandy.

Gerry downed his scotch and ordered another. 'How did we get it so wrong eighteen years ago?' he asked, staring at the optics behind the bar. 'I was never particularly happy with the way the investigation went. Seemed too neat somehow.'

Wesley said nothing. Hindsight was a wonderful thing.

'How did you know it was her?'

'I didn't know for certain till I talked to Simon Frith. Della said he'd taught History at Dukesbridge Comp when Joanne and Gabby were there. I had to ask him whether he'd actually taught them and it turns out he did. He'd taught Joanne all those years ago and she couldn't risk being recognised if he came to the house so she dealt with the situation by screwing up his career.'

'I just can't understand why the hell she came back here, Wes. Surely there was always a risk someone would recognise her.'

'I don't think she wanted to come back but Gulliver presented her with a fait accompli when he bought the place. Can you imagine the scene? "I've just bought a lovely house in the Devon countryside. Perfect . . . except for the fact that it's the one place you don't want to see again in your life . . . ever." No wonder she wouldn't have her picture taken . . . or venture into the village. OK, she'd changed her appearance over the years but . . . '

'She couldn't resist seeing her mother though.'

'The dead walk. Everyone thought Pauline Parry was deluded but she was telling the truth. She had seen her dead daughter.'

'Joanne must have got the shock of her life when Lilith was released from prison,' said Gerry, taking another sip from his glass.

'That's probably when she decided to arm herself with those knives . . . like an insurance policy. I reckon she pinched them from the Mumfords' place when she was at their last party. Easy to conceal in a large handbag. Three unused ones with the labels still intact were found hidden at the Gullivers' place, you know. And she took the precaution of ordering some in Lilith's name to incriminate her.'

'So she had it all planned?'

'When Boo Flecker was stalking Gulliver intending to expose his lies about his background, Gwen must have thought she was onto her. She probably wasn't. It wouldn't have occurred to her that one of the girls had survived. But once she found out that Lilith was back in residence Boo did start researching that story again too in case she could come up with a new angle ... or get an exclusive interview with the notorious murderess.'

'The big story?'

'Probably Shane Gulliver being a public schoolboy. Mr Big. Of course it's always possible that Boo might have looked at those press cuttings, seen Gwen and put two and two together. I don't suppose we'll ever know. But it's no wonder Gwen panicked when she saw her hanging round and decided to use one of the knives on her. And Zac James was playing a dangerous game too. Once she knew he was back in the village she couldn't take the risk of him seeing her and giving her away. She must have bided her time waiting for a chance to get him alone.'

'And did he see her?'

'I think so but he wasn't sure. That's probably why he wanted to talk to Laurence Roley. But she wasn't taking any chances. Will Lilith live?'

'She's in a bad way so it's too early to say.' Gerry bowed his head.

'It must have been a hell of a strain for Joanne to keep up the deception. Shane Gulliver had no idea that he wasn't the only one living a lie.'

'You're right, Wes. Joanne blamed Lilith for everything

bad that happened to her including her mother's breakdown. When Lilith and her mother moved here she
tormented them until she hit on the idea of taking the ultimate revenge. That sort of bitterness can only end one
way.'

'I'm worried about Alex ... for him to witness his
mother ...'

'It looks as if she was injured when Lilith tried to defend
herself. Tripped on her own knife, managed to get back
home but didn't make it up the stairs.'

'Could her injury be self-inflicted?'

'It's always possible, Wes. We won't know till we have a
chance to interview her. She's been taken to Morbay and
she's undergoing surgery. Good job they took Lilith to
Tradmouth.'

They fell silent, staring into their drinks. And when
they'd finished they returned to the incident room. But neither of them felt much like celebrating.

Wesley didn't get back home till just after midnight and
when he crept into the house he found Pam waiting up for
him, curled up on the sofa in her towelling dressing gown,
a glass of wine in one hand and a book in the other. Shane
Gulliver's latest offering. The thought that Gulliver would
be able to write about misery and tragedy from first-hand
experience from now on flashed through his head.

'Where's Neil?'

'In bed. He was tired. All that fresh air up at Princes
Bower. That and a bottle of Merlot. He wants to know
what's going to happen to Harriet Mumford, by the way.
Says those horrible doll things officially belong to her so
he'll need her permission to display them in a museum.'

'They've brought her in and she'll be questioned in the

342

morning. I'd say those dolls are the least of her worries with a charge of conspiracy to murder hanging over her. Although she's claiming that it was self-defence – said she'd suffered physical and mental cruelty from her husband for years. It wouldn't surprise me if she got off. She's a very persuasive lady. How's Michael?'

'Did his homework without a murmur. It probably won't last.'

Wesley slumped down by her side and kissed her. And when she handed him her glass, he took it gratefully.

Three days later Wesley received a message that Lilith Benley was asking to see him. She was still extremely weak but the doctors were optimistic. Likewise her tormentor, Joanne Trelisip alias Gwen Gulliver, was still in hospital following surgery, under police guard and under arrest.

According to reports from the officers on duty outside her private room in Morbay Hospital, her son, Alex, had been spending a lot of time at his mother's bedside, talking in whispers, holding her hand. If she hadn't been a ruthless murderer, the officer said, it would have been rather touching. Shane Gulliver, on the other hand, hadn't visited at all.

The previous day Joe Jessop had showed up at the incident room to tell them about the bones from the copse. The bones were piled up by the hedge if the police wanted to see them, he'd said matter of factly. His statement had sent the crime scene team hurrying down there and now the place was festooned with police tape. A skull was recovered from the woodland. And from what Lilith had already told them about Joanne's confession it was probable the bones belonged to Gabby Soames. Like Lilith, the pigs had been blameless. And for the Soameses, living their new lives up in

Durham, the pain of the past would come flooding back once more.

Wesley found Lilith propped up in bed, tubes sprouting from her arms and a bleeping machine recording her every heartbeat.

Struggling to speak, she managed to thank him and ask about Joanne. Wesley had to tell her that so far she'd refused to make a statement to the police. For the moment they were relying on Lilith's account of the confession she'd made, the confession she'd thought would never be repeated.

Then Lilith asked about Alex. Strange that she should be so concerned about the boy, Wesley thought, when his mother had caused her to spend eighteen years in jail for something she hadn't done before trying her best to kill her.

'I haven't seen him,' Wesley answered. 'But I believe he's being looked after by his stepfather.'

'I hope he's all right. It's not his fault, you know.' Her voice was weak and he knew every word was an effort. 'It's always the children who suffer. I've come to see that now.'

Wesley touched her arm gently, a gesture of reassurance he couldn't have imagined making just a few days earlier when, like everyone else, he'd believed in her guilt. 'What will you do when you get out of here?'

'Sell Devil's Tree Cottage. If anyone will buy it after . . .'

'It might be best to change the name.'

'Like Joanne did. You can change a name but you can't change what's inside. It's an unlucky place, Inspector. Mother and I were never really happy there.' She closed her eyes and the ghost of a smile played on her dry, bloodless lips. 'Joe says I can stay at the cottage where I've been . . .' She searched for the word. 'Hiding, for as long as

344

I like. I think he's lonely in that farmhouse on his own, you know. I think he likes having someone nearby. I suppose I'll have to do something with Devil's Tree Cottage if I want to sell. It's in a terrible state.'

Wesley didn't answer.

The smile vanished. 'I blame myself for what she did, you know.' He saw tears forming in her eyes. 'I was responsible. I didn't mean to but . . . '

'What do you mean?'

But before she could answer a nurse bustled up and told him that was enough. If he wanted to question her any further he'd have to come back.

When he returned to the incident room, now in the process of being packed up, he requested an inquest report and made a call to the Met. There was something he hadn't checked and he felt uneasy about the omission.

He had an uneasy feeling that a secret still lay hidden. Something that held the key to the whole affair.

Chapter 18

Statement of Joan Booker, aged nine years, October 1st 1643

On a Monday while the King's soldiers were at Hilton Farm I did see Mistress Hadness in the lane near my house. Knowing she was a lady of some wealth I asked her for a penny but she said children like me should not beg and then she cursed me and my kin. The next day my mother fell ill with a fever and died, twisting in pain and crying out as the devil possessed her body. A week later I saw Mistress Hadness with a black cat that was her familiar. It turned into the Devil and chased me down the lane but it did not catch me.

Statement of Alice Buddiford, October 1st 1643

One day in September my son, John, came to me and said that he'd seen Mistress Hadness in the churchyard gathering flowers that were yellow and purple. She had a black dog with her and when the dog saw my son it ran toward him and barked with the voice of a man. My son swore it was the voice of Satan. Mistress Hadness turned and told my son to be away and that the churchyard was no place for a boy of such tender years. He ran home frightened and three days later he died of a fever, uttering such strange words that they could only have come from sorcery.

That same week three of my cattle sickened and died. Mistress Hadness had walked across the field where they grazed and it was only after she had looked upon them that they sickened.

Statement of Elizabeth Hadness, October 1st 1643

I saw my stepmother in the trees beside our house and she was cavorting with the Devil. He was in the guise of a man with black hair and blue eyes and he had a pleasing countenance. She was kissing him and he was touching her private parts. When I called out to her he assumed the form of a cat and ran off.

Statement of Alison Hadness, October 3rd 1643

This day I shall meet my death and so I make my peace with God. My husband is dead, as are many in the town who are possessed by demons that rack their bodies with agony and rot their living flesh.

I have denied all to the Magistrate for the accusations against me are false. They say that, being blind with lust and not having the fear of God before my eyes I did create dolls of wax in the form of my husband, his daughter Elizabeth, and my maidservant Dorcas. They say I took them to the cellar to cast spells which brought about the deaths of those they represent. It is said that I consorted with the Devil and I intended evil to my neighbours and that I am the most wicked of women who deserves death.

I have no knowledge of this evil yet I know that it is Elizabeth who fashioned the dolls and the cellar is beneath her chamber and not mine, but with Dorcas and William dead there is no person to bear witness to this.

Who will believe my innocence in this matter? Even our vicar says I am lost to Heaven. Now he sickens but I wished him no ill. May the Lord have mercy on my soul.

Journal of Thomas Whitcombe, Captain in the King's army, October 5th 1643

The town of Tradmouth has been under siege a month now and today, in the endless rain, we attacked from Battlefleet Creek, taking the road block at the mill and seizing the fort there. The defenders fought valiantly with the loss of many men yet we prevailed and Tradmouth is now for the King with a garrison of our men to ensure the loyalty of the townsfolk.

I enquired for Alison but word had it she was held for sorcery because evil tongues had spoken against her and two days before we took the town she was dragged to the crossroads on the edge of the town and hanged in full view of the townsfolk. I pray the Lord to have mercy on her soul.

Neil was disappointed when Wesley told him Colin Bowman was still on holiday enjoying a cruise, well away from his usual complement of corpses. But this didn't stop him contacting Colin's replacement, a formidable lady called Jane Partridge who agreed to meet him at Morbay Hospital. He persuaded Dave to give him a lift there, saying it was relevant to the dig up at Princes Bower. The final piece of the jigsaw, he'd said, and Dave had believed him.

He had never visited the mortuary at Morbay Hospital before and he felt a little apprehensive as he pushed open the swing doors. Luckily Dr Partridge's office was near the entrance so he didn't have to venture far into the mysterious realm of death.

When he knocked on her door he heard a curt 'come'. Wesley had already briefed him so he knew what to expect. She was sitting by her desk reading a file and she peered at him over her glasses.

'Dr Watson, I presume.' She stood up and offered her hand. Neil took it, surprised at her hearty grip. 'How can I help you?'

Neil explained. He'd brought copies of various documents and a translation of Alison's coded diary. He laid them in front of her and waited while she read.

'I see what you mean,' she said after a long period of silence.

'The Salem witch trials gave me the idea. There's a theory that . . . '

'Ergot. Otherwise known as St Anthony's fire. These accounts mention the classic symptoms of ergot poisoning; vomiting, convulsions, hallucinations and eventual gangrene. The hallucinations account for the victims' claims of seeing the Devil and experiencing flying and all that sort of thing. And it's a fungus that affects cereal grain, especially rye. These accounts say that during the siege they were making bread from old rye flour so it seems to fit.'

'It certainly does,' Neil agreed.

He had kept one paper back and now he gave it to Jane with a hint of triumph. 'Apart from this account of William Hadness's illness. That seems different.'

He waited while Jane studied the document and after a minute or so she looked up.

'Alison mentions gathering henbane to cure a swelling of her husband's privates. Only she says she prepared an fusion when it should only have been used externally. The symptoms described are classic hyosine poisoning; blindness, drowsiness, vertigo and extreme thirst. Dr Crippen used it to murder his wife. I think Alison poisoned her husband.'

'Deliberately?'

'I don't doubt it. If she was used to preparing herbal remedies, as many women were in those days, she would have known only too well which plants should be ingested and which should only be used externally.' There was a moment's pause. 'Did you find out what became of the ghastly Elizabeth, by the way?'

'Yes. She inherited Mercy Hall, married a wealthy man and lived to a ripe old age.'

'No justice in the world, is there?'

Neil thanked her and gathered up his papers and as he was about to leave Jane spoke again.

'From what I've just read of William Hadness, he sounded like a dreadful bore. Can't really blame Alison, can you?'

And for the first time he saw her smile.

Wesley hadn't visited Lilith again. But he rang the hospital each day to check on her progress. Her condition was improving slowly.

Joanne Trelisip, alias Gwen Gulliver, had now recovered sufficiently to be remanded in custody to a prison hospital. She would stand trial. But she was still saying nothing. 'No comment' were the only words she'd uttered when she'd been interviewed.

A couple of days after the investigation team abandoned the village hall at West Fretham and returned to

Tradmouth Police Station, Wesley came out of a long meeting with the Crown Prosecution Service regarding charges against Harriet Mumford and found a message in Trish Walton's neat handwriting waiting in the middle of his desk.

'Enquiry into the death of Arnold Trelisip. Please call this number.'

It was a London number. The direct line to the Met officer's desk. Wesley dialled it and, after a lengthy conversation, he told Gerry he was going out. There was something he needed to clear up.

When he arrived at the hospital he found Lilith looking a lot better. The tubes had been removed along with the bleeping monitoring equipment. She was still in a ward on her own. Perhaps, in view of her notoriety, the Sister in charge had decided it was for the best.

He sat down on the plastic chair by the bed and asked her how she was feeling.

'Better, thank you.' She didn't meet his eyes and the words sounded formal.

Wesley thought it would be best to come straight to the point. 'I've been talking to an officer from the Met about the death of Arnold Trelisip. They didn't have enough evidence to bring charges, did they?'

She bowed her head but there was no answer.

'The pathologist was never really satisfied with your claim that he suffered a heart attack and fell downstairs, was he? He said it could easily have been the other way round. Someone gave him a push and he had the heart attack as a result. It's my guess that his daughter, Joanne, found out about it somehow when she was living in London. Perhaps she made enquiries of her own. She'd

351

already taken her revenge on you for taking her father away when you were convicted of double murder. But then she discovered there were question marks over her father's death.'

'There was no evidence against me.'

'Only the neighbours' statement that they heard you and Trelisip arguing. They said you had a volatile relationship.'

The defiance he'd seen in her eyes the first time they'd met had returned. 'That's hardly evidence. Yes, our relationship was passionate. We loved each other. Everybody quarrels, don't they?'

'Last time we spoke you said you blamed yourself for what Joanne did.'

She bowed her head and said nothing.

Wesley sat there watching her. He would have liked to tell her that he'd get proof and bring her to justice for the one crime she did commit. But he knew it was unlikely after all this time. And besides, she'd already received her punishment. Eighteen years locked away from society.

He glanced at his watch as he left the hospital. Simon Frith was taking him and Pam out for a meal that evening as a thank you for clearing his name. It was a nice gesture but Wesley wasn't sure whether it was necessary . . . or that he was in the mood for a cosy dinner. There was still too much on his mind.

Neil, who was feeling a lot better, was still ensconced in their spare bedroom and had offered to babysit and help Michael with his work. Why was it Michael never argued with Neil when it came to homework? Maybe he and Pam were just ineffective parents. Or maybe all kids were like that.

The case was over but unfinished business always made

him feel a little uneasy, like a minor nagging ache that comes and goes.

On his way back to the station he passed a shop window filled with pumpkins, spiders' webs and Halloween masks. There was only one way to deal with Lilith Benley. And that was to forget her.

Two weeks later

There seemed to be no reason to stay in Devon. Not after what had happened. Shane Gulliver's publicist reckoned that his personal tragedy would only increase sales. When she'd said it, Shane had slammed the phone down on the flint-hearted bitch.

He still had the apartment in London and Alex seemed keen on moving there. Alex's maternal grandmother was in no fit state to care for him, having been admitted to a psychiatric hospital following Gwen's injury and subsequent arrest. Gwen would stand trial and if she was convicted, she'd be put away for a long time. Alex's natural father, the married man who'd set Gwen up in a flat and abandoned her shortly after the boy's birth, was hardly likely to assume any responsibility even if he could be traced, so as Alex was far too young to fend for himself, Shane knew he was stuck with him.

At times he resented the responsibility and at others he knew he'd need someone to share his life in the dark days to come, even if that someone was a damaged adolescent who spent half his days staring into space, lost in his own bitter thoughts. Even the metal detecting was a thing of the past and Alex's dyed black hair now showed brown at the roots.

The boy hadn't said much since that terrible night. And when Shane asked him what his mother had said during his visits to the hospital, he'd refused to answer, carrying her words like some precious burden she'd entrusted to his care. Shane hoped they'd been words of love ... not the poisoned words of a twisted, vengeful mind. But until Alex decided to confide in him there was no way of knowing.

The removal van had already squeezed itself down the narrow lane, its tall sides scratched by a thousand twigs and brambles in the leafless hedgerows. Now it was time to follow in the Range Rover. But Alex was nowhere to be found.

Shane checked the house before walking round to the entrance to Jessop's Farm. The TV people were back with their vans and equipment. Shane had heard that a previous runner-up, a disgraced MP, had taken Zac James's place in the contest, up against Rupert Raybourn. He should have learned long ago that nothing halts the progress of commerce. The show goes on.

He retraced his steps and as he climbed into the Range Rover, he suddenly sensed that something was wrong, a dreadful feeling of foreboding like a heavy weight on his heart. He had never been to Devil's Tree Cottage but he knew he had to go there now.

He drove the short distance and parked halfway up the overgrown drive. He'd thought the Benley woman would leave the area after everything that had happened but he knew she had returned there on her release from hospital. He imagined her squatting in the crumbling cottage like a malevolent toad, cursing all she came into contact with.

He started the car engine again and drove slowly up to the house. The place looked unoccupied – the windows cloudy with dirt and the paintwork flaking. But the front door was open. And Alex was standing in the doorway.

Shane undid his seat belt and as he leapt from the car the boy didn't move. He stood perfectly still, staring wide-eyed at his stepfather as if he'd seen a vision of hell. Shane began to run towards him, his legs slowed by some unseen force. When he reached Alex he grabbed his arm and dragged him to the car. Alex put up no resistance and once he was safely installed in the passenger seat, Shane flicked the key fob to lock the car doors and rushed back to the cottage.

When he reached the open front door he called out a nervous hello. But there was no sound of movement so he stepped into the small, shadowy hallway. He stood for a moment and listened but all he could hear was the faint cawing of the crows in the nearby trees.

He called out again. 'Hello. Anybody there?' And when there was no reply he pushed open the door to the parlour and held his breath.

Lilith Benley lay sprawled across the old sofa, her eyes bulging, staring at him accusingly. He could see the red marks on her neck. Alex had big hands for his age. Strong.

He bent over her and closed her eyes with shaking fingers before wiping all the surrounding surfaces with a duster he found lying on a side table and tiptoeing out.

It was time to leave the poison behind. It was time to go to London and make a new beginning.

Historical Note

Although the Hadness family and Mercy Hall are figments of my imagination, the story of the siege of Tradmouth is based on historical fact.

Few places in Devon would have escaped the effects of the English Civil War as there was continuous destructive campaigning in the county from 1642 to 1646. In September 1643, King Charles I's nephew, Prince Maurice (brother of the more famous Prince Rupert), decided to attack the port of Dartmouth while he was en route from defeated Exeter to Plymouth. Like many sea ports heavily burdened with the King's taxes and duties, Dartmouth espoused the cause of Parliament. The town offered spirited resistance to Maurice's army, even fortifying the church towers, and the siege lasted a full month (in appalling weather). When Prince Maurice fell ill the King sent his physician, William Harvey (later famed for his discovery of the circulation of blood), to attend him. In early October the Royalist troops finally attacked and took the town but the defenders fought hard with the loss of seventeen men.

The fortifications built by the Royalist garrison to defend the defeated town can still be seen at Gallants Bower above Dartmouth Castle. Gallants Bower is a well-preserved earthwork and a fine example of Civil War military engineering on land owned by the National Trust.

The 1643 siege must have been a time of great strain for the people of Dartmouth but the seventeenth century in general was a period of paranoia when accusations of witchcraft were rife throughout the country (although there is no evidence to suggest that Dartmouth suffered in this way at that particular time). This was the century of the Pendle witch trials when ten alleged witches were hanged up in Lancashire in 1612. Bideford in Devon saw its own witch trials in 1682, resulting in the last hangings for witchcraft in England.

Some of the world's most famous witch trials were held in Salem, Massachusetts in 1692. In late December 1691 about eight girls were afflicted by convulsions and strange delusions. This may have been a result of mass hysteria but one theory put forward was that the girls were the victims of ergot poisoning, caused by consuming bread made of affected rye. Of course, this will never be known for certain but it does seem a likely explanation for the strange phenomenon and it is one I have used in this book.

Returning to the Civil War, the forces of Parliament, under Oliver Cromwell, defeated the Royalists and King Charles I was executed in London in 1649. England was then ruled by Parliament for the next eleven years, during which time Puritanism was in the ascendant (and even the celebration of Christmas was banned).

However, in 1660, the country having tired of years of Puritan rule, Charles I's son, Charles II was invited to return to England to take the throne. Charles II, unlike his father, turned out to be a popular king (whose lifestyle was far from puritanical) and he was known by the affectionate title of 'The Merry Monarch'.

Do you love crime fiction?

Want the chance to hear news about your favourite
authors (and the chance to win free books)?

Kate Brady
Frances Brody
Nick Brownlee
Kate Ellis
Shamini Flint
Linda Howard
Julie Kramer
Kathleen McCaul
J. D. Robb
Jeffrey Siger

Then visit the Piatkus website and blog
www.piatkus.co.uk | www.piatkusbooks.net

And follow us on Facebook and Twitter
www.facebook.com/piatkusfiction | www.twitter.com/piatkusbooks

piatkus